Dawn of Hope

DAWN OF HOPE

AMANDA BRIAR

Dawn of Hope
Text Copyright © 2024 by Amanda Briar
Cover Copyright © 2024 by Amanda Briar
Map Copyright © 2024 by Amanda Briar

Fun Size Publishing is an imprint of Fun Size Media LLC.

Fun Size Media LLC
Antioch, CA 94509
business@funsizemedia.com

Editing by K. Morton Editing Services

Formatting by Fun Size Publishing

Cover Art by Fun Size Publishing

Map Design by Fun Size Publishing
Original Illustrations from Map Effects Fantasy Map Builder

Library of Congress Control Number: 2024917672

Paperback
ISBN 978-1-964819-01-3

Hardcover
ISBN 978-1-964819-02-0

Special Edition Paperback
ISBN 978-1-964819-03-7

Special Edition Hardcover
ISBN 978-1-964819-04-4

Ebook
ISBN 978-1-964819-00-6

Audiobook
ISBN 978-1-964819-05-1

Published in September 2024

www.amandabriar.com

*For my babies, I love you more than
anything in this world.*

*And for Walt, thank you for teaching me it is
possible to make your dreams come true.*

AUTHOR'S NOTE

Dawn of Hope is a New Adult Fantasy Romance novel filled with adventure and high stakes. The story includes mention of loss of family members, death/illness of a parent, adult language, some explicit sexual content, isolation, violence, and life or death situations. Readers who are sensitive to these themes please take note.

Dawnlin

PROLOGUE

Silence enveloped the throne room, the chaos of the night left behind. Shadows fell across the floor, casting the once lively room in a blanket of despair. It was as if the room knew what had happened just a short time ago and was already in mourning for the kingdom's loss.

The king entered the room, his feet shuffling and scraping along the stone floor. He walked past the first chair and averted his eyes to the floor. It was too soon. It was too painful. He couldn't deal with the pain yet.

He had other things to focus on.

The king dropped his body onto his throne, sinking into the familiar cushions and soft fabric. He'd been intimate with it for far too long, longer than most kings, especially at his age.

His shoulders slumped as he looked down at the small body he cradled in his arms. The soiled blankets had been replaced with clean and soft ones, enough to keep the baby warm in the absence of her mother.

He gazed into her face. He had been consumed with joy the day he found out he would have this face to look upon, but now it brought a mixture of emotions.

Mostly pain.

Loss.

But also gain.

This moment was supposed to be the happiest of his life, gazing into the face of his beautiful baby girl, the princess that he would raise to take his place. He hoped he would have more time with her than he had with his own father, enough to prepare her for what was to come in her life and give her far more preparation than he had.

That moment was stolen from him.

A single tear slid down his cheek, but he refused to wipe it away.

Quiet footsteps approached from the doorway and stopped in front of him.

"The baby?" The words were soft and full of concern. The king did not startle at the voice. He was too familiar with it. He'd known it since he was a boy.

"Lives," he answered solemnly, without pulling his eyes away from her. Her face scrunched in a quick look of discontent before softening and slumbering again.

The man took a few steps closer. "A girl or a boy?"

"A girl." The king knew he did not have to be long winded with the man. He knew him well enough to hear the meaning behind words. "Lennox."

"Like her mother wanted," the man whispered.

The king nodded, another silent tear falling down his cheek. He was not afraid of the man seeing the tear or seeing him weak. The king hid nothing from him.

"And the queen?"

The king did not answer. He sat staring at his daughter, trying to find the words.

"The healers say she is alive. Her body lives, but her mind…" He trailed off, feeling the same stabbing pain in his chest from before, when he heard he had lost her. He continued. "They do not know what will come of her mind, or if she will ever wake. Yet her body lives. For how long is unknown."

The man closed the distance between the king and the throne and placed his hand on the king's shoulder.

"I'm sorry," he murmured.

The king turned toward the touch, acknowledging the sincerity in it.

"Has he been found?" The king asked.

"Not yet, but he will be," the man said as he removed his hand from the king. "The castle is being searched, and patrols are headed out into the city as we speak."

"Good."

The man stepped forward in front of the king and looked down into the face of the baby. "She will need to be protected."

The king nodded. "They both will need to be."

"And what of the kingdom? What are you going to say happened?"

"Complications of childbirth. That is all they need to know."

The man nodded and took a step back, waiting for a command.

"You may go. I want to be alone with my daughter."

The man bowed his head, not in reverence to his king, but in understanding of a friend. "I will be here if you need me," he said. He turned and walked through the shadows, leaving the room the same way he came.

The baby whined softly, her face crumbling as she started to cry. The king soothed her, rocking her in his arms and stroking her hair through the blanket.

This precious girl, his Lennox, was all he had left of the queen, the woman who made his lonely and painful life worth living. He had hoped to grow old with her and with many of their children.

Fate had other plans for him. It always seemed to have other plans.

He wouldn't let Lennox be taken like her mother. He refused to put her in any danger.

He would protect her, even if she didn't grow to understand it or appreciate it.

Even if she grew to hate him for it.

He would do everything in his power to keep her safe, and anything to find answers for the queen.

He sat in the shadows and felt the palpable silence around him, but as he stared at this tiny face, this person who in a few terrifying moments had become his entire world, he tried to only focus on one thing.

Hope that fate could change.

CHAPTER ONE

I drop my training blade in the damp dirt at Brynne's feet and storm out of the sparring ring. It doesn't matter that I am covered in sweat and dried mud. When the king calls, you answer.

At least I do.

The sound of my footsteps echoes off the stone walls as I make my way down the hall toward the throne room. The slam of a wooden door followed by the familiar clink of armor and surefooted steps stops me in my tracks as Brynne quickly catches up with me.

My father doesn't summon me often, so I know that when he does, there is a reason. When he does, there is no ignoring it. I stop what I am doing and go to him, wondering along the way what new demand or restriction he is going to put in place.

I am already isolated and forbidden from leaving the castle grounds. I have no one close other than Brynne and Edmond, but even they are required to spend time with me. Brynne for protection, and Edmond for education. My days are planned down to the minute, my evenings spent alone in my rooms, reading whatever I can get my hands on.

He can't take much more away from me, which can only mean one thing. He wants something.

"We could have at least finished the fight before you stormed off," Brynne mutters as she steps into stride behind me.

"You know how he is. I can't keep him waiting."

"I'm sure a few minutes wouldn't have mattered."

We slow as we near the ornate gold and black wooden doors. I place my hand on the giant gold handle as I turn back toward Brynne.

"Let's just get this over with. Then I can go back to being ignored."

I push the door open, the throne room extending in front of me, empty except for two men standing on the dais. I stride quickly down the walkway and come to a halt at the foot of the few steps below the two empty thrones. My father stands before his, murmuring to the man in charge of the day-to-day functions of the castle. I catch his eye and he looks up, quickly dismissing the man.

"Father." I drop into a small curtsy that feels awkward and clunky in my training boots and breeches. I wasn't going to change into one of my usual plain dresses just because his summons came during my training session. "You called for me?"

His eyes glance over my attire, catching on the dried mud caked on the fabric. His lack of approval over how I chose to meet with the king is clear.

Too bad.

As always, when his eyes come to my face, they quickly dart away, a look flashing across his before he schools it back into a mask of indifference.

I shift uncomfortably at his disapproval and clasp my hands behind my back. "I came as soon as I could."

"I want to discuss the ceremony with you." He turns to sit on his throne, eyes still falling anywhere but my face.

Brynne's armor clanks as she shifts behind me. She notices his obvious dismissal too.

"The ceremony and ball," I say. I am one of the few people in the castle who dares to correct the king.

He continues without acknowledging my addition. "As I'm sure you know, the celebration stems from Blackwood tradition. There are many elements of the ceremony that are integral for the future queen of this kingdom. I have instructed Edmond to ensure that your lessons over the next few weeks will make you adequately prepared for it. A few weeks is a sufficient amount of time. I expect the ceremony will go smoothly. Understood?"

I nod. "Of course."

He speaks as if this ceremony is news to me, not that I have been dreaming about it for years. As a child, I had little to do after completing my day's lessons than wander the castle and read. I would get lost for hours in books filled with magic and balls, princesses being swept off of their feet and living happily ever after. Finding out about the coming-of-age ceremony for the rulers of Blackwood only fueled my naïve excitement that one day I would get to experience the same thing.

As I grew older, I still looked forward to my twenty-first birthday and the ceremony, but not for the same reasons. I was no longer naïve enough to believe in magic or being swept away by a prince, but I hoped that for just one night I could escape the intense loneliness that followed me around the castle halls, sinking deep into my bones. I wanted a real escape, not one just between the pages of books.

The stories grew as I did and were no longer filled with solely happily ever afters. There was plenty of political scheming, backstabbing, and forbidden romance.

I didn't want to admit it, but I still deep down wondered if the night of my ceremony, the night I would be officially recognized as the future queen of Blackwood and able to rule the kingdom if something were to happen to my father, would actually be the night that my life would change.

Maybe opening our doors to other kingdoms and establishing relationships with other future leaders would help break my father's hold on me, his so-called 'protection' from whatever he was afraid of.

These kinds of events were not just the things of storybooks and actually had political use. Many trade deals were struck, allies formed, and even marriage contracts negotiated. Marriage was not at all on my list of concerns for this event. My father would never allow it, not yet anyway. Not until it was absolutely necessary to further the line of Blackwood. If it was, he wouldn't have hidden me from everyone in the land, including our own people. In twenty years, they have never once laid eyes on their own princess.

He lifts his arm and gestures to the back of the room, beckoning someone forward.

I glance over my shoulder to see Tila striding toward the throne. Her apprentices follow closely behind her, their arms laden with bolts of fabric.

"Are there any topics you'd like us to review regarding the other kingdoms? I want to be prepared in case things such as goods or trade routes come up—"

"I will handle those discussions." He cuts me off, and heat rises on the back of my neck.

I keep my face blank, but my gaze trained on him.

Why doesn't he want me to be prepared for conversations with other kingdoms? The sons and daughters of the current monarchs are to be my peers one day. How does he expect me to be the queen of Blackwood if I have no relationships or history with any of them? I will look like a porcelain princess in their eyes, never involved in anything of substance, just there to sit on the throne and look pretty.

This ceremony, my birthday, is to be my first impression, and I don't want to disappoint. I want to be seen as a strong future queen, and a force to be reckoned with.

In my lifetime, my father has never invited neighboring rulers or allies into the castle. There are stories, whispers amongst the staff, or snippets of Edmond's reminiscing, which told me that this was not how things used to be. As a young king who walked among the people, he heard their struggles and successes, their happiness and sadness. He cared about them, and they cared about him, earning loyalty both ways.

He would hold meetings with other kings, and my mother would host grand balls to welcome everyone. There were picnics and hunts, things that showed off all the kingdom of Blackwood had to offer to the visitors.

Our forests filled with unique sky high black wooded trees are a source of awe, and a thriving trade that brings in a significant amount of money for our people. Keeping up these relationships is important for the success of our kingdom.

All of this stopped as soon as my mother was gone. As soon as I was here.

I never knew this world. Not once was there a party at the castle, or friends to invite from other kingdoms. I never knew the prospect of meeting princes I could marry. I had no hope for a happily ever after, like I read about as a child. What made me actually think I could have a happy ending when I watched my father be so unhappy every day of his life?

Maybe this celebration would finally convince my father that things could be different, and he didn't have to hide me away. I can prove to him I belong amongst the other rulers and could begin to build relationships with them for the future of our kingdom.

If only he didn't keep shutting me down every time I try to show him I am ready for my place in the kingdom.

"Your majesty." The royal seamstress, Tila, dips into a deep curtsy, bowing her head toward my father. She steps in front of me, looking me up and down.

"Tsk, tsk, tsk," she clucks as she glides around, assessing me on all sides. "Be mindful of the mud. I do not want the fabrics ruined." Her assistants scurry around me, one of them placing a small pedestal at my feet.

"Sorry Tila." The stoic face I keep for my father cracks and softens slightly as I mutter my apology and step up on the pedestal. I always feel like a child again when I stand on it in front of everyone, not only because the position brings back memories of Tila dressing me for as long as I can remember, but also because my height makes me feel like a child in comparison. The pedestal does nothing but elevate my short stature, and make it easier for them to move about, sticking me with pins and pulling things tight.

Tila gives me a soft smile. She knows me almost as well as Brynne and Edmond. She hates that I don't love the extravagant gowns and showy clothes she always wants to create, not that I have much occasion to wear them. I'd much rather wear mud covered pants or a simple soft dress than the ball gown, but she doesn't judge me for it. Too much, at least.

Her assistants get to work, wrapping their tape measures around my body and jostling me into different positions.

Tila turns back toward my father and claps her hands. "This is to be the grandest dress we've made for her highness to date. Traditional, of course, but grand. I'm thinking satin, in the kingdom's colors. The gold will complement her hair." Tila gestures at my hair, my normal wavy golden tresses bound into a tight braid that falls over my shoulder, then gives a sound of disgust. "At least it will when she isn't covered in dirt and grime." She looks back toward my father. "Are there any specifics you have in mind, your majesty?"

"No Tila, thank you." A small smile lifts his face, following his quick response.

I feel a pang in my chest at the tiny gesture. Many would not notice it, but I do. How can everyone else in the castle earn such respect and acknowledgement from my father, but for years, he has barely looked at or spoken to me? It has only worsened as I age, and I do not understand it. No matter what I try to do, how well I perform at my lessons, or how skilled I am in training, nothing is ever enough.

The girls jostle me as Tila gives them direction, but I'm not listening.

Instead, I am focused on my father as he turns his attention to Brynne.

"Since you have not yet been present for a ceremony, you may be unaware of a crucial element. The ceremony involves the presentation of the future queen with her own dagger for protection. Have you been including dagger skills in her training?"

"Rarely, your majesty. She is competent with a sword and a bow. I will adjust her training regimen to incorporate dagger work."

My eyes flick down to the dagger at my father's side. I'd always admired it growing up. It is gorgeous, with a red jeweled handle set in gold, and never leaves his side. Every reigning king or queen designs a dagger for their heir's ceremony and presents it to them on their twenty-first birthday. They are never to part with it, even in death, to ensure they are always protected.

The dagger would be useless if I don't know how to use it, so I'm sure our interrupted spar would be forgotten, and instead I'd be working on honing those skills.

"Be sure that you do. It is important." He gives Brynne a terse nod, sealing his command.

Brynne bows in acknowledgement. "Yes, your majesty."

He stands from his throne, still refusing to look me in the eye. "You may go." His words are quiet but firm as he strides toward the doorway off to the right of the dais.

The dismissal is clear, but I cannot move. Tila's assistants have me wrapped in a fabric that is draped behind me, halfway down the aisle.

I make a sound of distaste as I look back at it.

"Don't scoff. Scoffing isn't for princesses." Tila's voice is hard with a mock scolding.

I roll my eyes as I turn back to her. "You know I hate tripping on gowns."

"Well, that should not be a problem, as there will be no need to make a hasty getaway in this one." She smirks and then claps her hands. "I think we are done here. We have enough to get started. We are on a tight schedule, but I will make it work."

"Thank you Tila. I'm sure it will be beautiful." I smile at her as I step off the pedestal.

She returns it warmly. "It will be. Just like the future queen wearing it." She steps around me and quickly makes her way out of the throne room, her assistants trailing behind her. Tila is an older woman, and while we don't interact daily, I've known her my whole life. She is like a protective aunt, in the absence of a real one, since neither of my parents had siblings. Hearing the pride in her voice brings a tickle of a tear to my eye.

I turn on my heel and stride quickly toward the door. Brynne's sure footsteps trail behind me, but she doesn't say a word. She knows how I feel after these meetings with my father and knows that even though we have been training all afternoon, I am going to need to work off some more steam.

Thoughts of the upcoming ceremony flood my mind.

Why is my father so insistent that I leave all political duties to him? I've been preparing for this day for years, and it is finally my time to cement my place as a future ruler of this kingdom.

It seems like he doesn't want me to be.

But why? I race through the possibilities, coming up with nothing except for one glaring reality.

He doesn't think I am capable of being queen.

Is that the reason he doesn't trust me to discuss important topics with the other heirs? Is it why he keeps me locked away, preventing anyone from knowing me, or letting me experience the world outside these walls? He doesn't even want our people to know anything more than my name.

What kind of king completely disregards his heir?

He hasn't even acknowledged that this is to take place on my birthday. He never did. Year after year to him, it is just another day.

Fuck him.

I will prove he is wrong.

There are a few weeks left to prepare to be the best representation of Blackwood that our people and the other kingdoms would *finally* see.

I will prove to him I can be queen, that I can hold my own amongst the other leaders despite years of being hidden away, giving me less of an advantage. I will be the best queen this kingdom doesn't have a choice but to accept.

I am tired of being alone and disregarded. It is my time, a time I've been looking forward to for years, and I will not let him take it away from me.

CHAPTER TWO

"You can stop pretending to be so formal now."

Brynne's words ring through the hall, and bounce right off my tense shoulders. The wooden door slams into the wall as I push my way through it. I step outside the castle and immediately flinch at the bite of the cold on my sweat-soaked clothes.

The mist and fog that covers our kingdom every day hangs in the air and immediately dampens my hair. I can see my breath as I huff my way toward the practice weapons. I just want to get back to the ring and work off this energy. I need to do something, feel something other than anger coursing through my veins.

"I'm not being fucking formal," I call out, refusing to look back at her.

"That's better." She is just behind me now, her longer steps have caught up easily to my short ones.

"I just want to get back to the training from before we were so uselessly interrupted." I stalk over to the rack of weapons and reach for a sword. It isn't one of my strongest weapons, which is why I need to practice it more often. I am much more comfortable with a bow, but Brynne constantly reminds me a bow is useless if someone attacks at close range.

"Not so fast." Brynne grabs my arm and turns me back to her. She reaches behind and pulls a dagger from her belt, extending it out to me. I grasp the hilt and pull it from the sheath, flipping the handle to get a feel for the weight. The blade is dull, just like the practice swords I am accustomed to sparring with, but I've never used a weapon this small before. It feels too light and awkward in my hands.

I groan. "Not today, Brynne, please? Can't we just start those lessons tomorrow?"

"No." She releases an impatient sigh and pulls out a dagger of her own. "We're running out of time. I gave the king my word that I was going to work on these skills, and I'm not going back on it. We only have a few weeks until the ceremony."

"Fine," I grumble. I wrap my fingers around the hilt, pointing the blade down at the ground. I am ready to move into my stance when I feel the slap of metal sting across the top of my hand.

I hiss and snatch my hand back to my body as the dagger I drop hits the hard dirt at my feet. "What the fuck was that for?" My scowl is met by a smirk as she re-sheathes her sword.

"To show you without telling you that you were holding it wrong, and how easily you can be harmed if you don't hone your skills."

I rub the back of my hand and bend to retrieve the dagger. "Fine. Show me."

Brynne proceeds with her lesson, explaining the grip and positioning, and walking me through a few movements that are so vastly different from the loud and exaggerated ones I use with long swords.

"Dagger fights are more intimate than those with a sword." She takes a step toward me and feigns swiping across my body. "You'll be much closer to your attacker in order to strike them, and sometimes the dagger is all you have when they still have a sword. It makes it more difficult for you to strike a blow, and you have to put yourself at risk to make the strike count."

"Why wouldn't I just carry a sword, then? Isn't the whole point of this to protect me from anyone who wants to hurt me, not put me closer to getting hurt when I try to fight them?"

Brynne smirks. "Because when they take your sword," she says as she reaches behind her and pulls a dagger from a hidden sheath in her waistband, "they won't know you're still armed. You'll have the element of surprise. At least for a few seconds." She proceeds to pull out two more daggers hidden in her armor that, despite training together for all these years, I never knew she carried.

"Alright, I get it. Let's practice then."

We weave through clusters of guards standing around and waiting for their turn in a ring. They are used to seeing their princess out amongst the ranks, and while some acknowledge me with a quick bow and a mumbled greeting, others don't react. Our presence amongst them is too normal.

The clang of metal on metal rings through the air, followed by grunts and loud thuds as we make our way to a far ring where a bout is just ending.

"We're next," Brynne calls out as she swings her body under the wooden beams of the fence surrounding the pit.

The victor from the last round nods at her as he reaches down and pulls the other to his feet. They both mutter a quick greeting to us before exiting the ring and standing just outside it with the rest of the group.

While I am used to training with Brynne in the middle of large groups of guards, I don't love it, especially on days I'm already worked up from talking to my father.

"Just ignore them," Brynne directs as we step into the center, facing each other.

Far too many times, Brynne has had to scold other guards for leering and watching us fight. They claim they are supporting their princess, but I think they just like to watch Brynne kick my ass. Most of the time, they are respectful, but every so often, one asshole wants to pick a fight.

I try to push everything out of my mind as I take the stance Brynne showed me a few minutes ago. Brynne looks much more relaxed than I feel as she stands waiting for me to strike.

I step to the right and Brynne follows. We slowly circle each other as I wait for the right moment to make my move.

"Get on with it already." A gruff voice breaks through the clatter of the fighting from the other rings, followed by a few snickers. I watch Brynne's eyes harden as she glares past me to the guards.

I find my opportunity.

Charging forward, I close the space between us and slash at her. Her gaze refocuses on me as soon as I take my first step, and she blocks the movement with her blade. Her feet move quickly as she strikes at me in response. I try to block her jab, but my feet tangle under me and I fall backward on my ass.

"Fuck." I can feel the moisture from the damp ground seeping into my pants.

That is going to hurt tomorrow.

I push myself to stand, ignoring Brynne's outstretched hand. She says nothing, just readies herself again. This time she makes the first move, charging at me swiftly. I sidestep and dodge, swirling around and swiping at her side. She blocks the blow and pushes at my extended arm, knocking me off balance. I stumble forward but quickly right myself, just before I hear the snickering of the guards behind me again.

Anger rises inside me, breaking down the walls I construct to block out my feelings, especially after today's meeting. The walls are crumbling now, and I feel that anger boil up and over into my limbs. I can't control my movements, I just strike out wildly at Brynne.

No control, only emotion.

She blocks my advances easily, knocking my slices out of the way.

I keep charging at her, missing my strikes, all the while she remains cool and collected.

I grit my teeth and put everything I have into this blow. I want this fight to be over. I want the guards to stop mocking me. I want my father to trust me. I want the life that I had been waiting for, the one I thought was coming once I reached this final milestone.

Instead, with just a few words, my father dashed every fantasy I ever had about what life would be once I was of age to rule.

All the emotions reach the surface. The anger, hurt, embarrassment. I channel them into this strike. I spin my body, gripping the hilt of the dagger with both hands, visualizing the blow just as Brynne taught me.

My muscles pull tight as I whip the dagger around toward her. I let out a cry, like the emotions I am holding on to can't stay in any longer as I slice through the air toward Brynne's protective armor.

My battle cry is cut short, and I am suddenly flying through the air, my momentum from the spin carrying me and slamming my body into the ground. I taste the musk of the earthy soil and feel the grit crunch between my teeth as my face hits the floor.

Gasping for the air knocked out of me, I quickly spin onto my back. I know never to give my back to an opponent, even if it is just sparring practice. I find Brynne standing over me, the dull point of her sword held over the pulse in my neck.

"Yield?"

I give a curt nod and before I have even finished, she bends down over me, pulling me off the ground and toward her. She wraps her sword arm around my back and pulls me close.

"Don't let them see you cry," she whispers quickly, her mouth close to my ear to ensure I am the only one who can hear.

It is then that I feel the hot tears running down my face. I don't know what emotion these tears are from, but I know she is right. My soldiers can't see their future leader crying when she gets knocked down. They don't know everything else that is behind them.

I tuck in my chin as I step away from her and spit on the ground. I swat at my face, hoping to look like I am brushing off dirt angrily, not brushing off tears before anyone sees.

"Nice move." I spit again, still trying to rid my mouth of the grit.

"It would have worked if you weren't so in your head. What have I told you?"

I roll my eyes. She tells me never to fight with my emotions, but I can't help it today. There is just too much going on, and I couldn't keep it out of the ring.

To be honest, I don't really agree with Brynne. As the future queen, if I ever find myself in a fight, I can't imagine emotions not being part of it. Otherwise, I have been taught to find a diplomatic solution and avoid stabbing people with swords.

"I'll try not to let it happen again. Today wasn't the day."

"Well, if I have to keep knocking you on your ass to get that lesson through, so be it."

I narrow my eyes at her, a face that she returns, and I know she will hold to that promise.

"We're done," Brynne calls out. "Next spar up. The ring is yours."

The clang of armor sounds through the air as the next guards climb over the wooden barricades into the ring. Before we make it to the other side, a voice from behind catches my attention.

"Piss poor excuse for a future queen, if you ask me. Like I've said for years, the king should have found himself a new woman and made a new heir. At least then we'd have a chance at another king."

I feel the sharp stab of his words in my chest as I fall deeper into my feelings of inadequacy, but it isn't me he has to worry about. I turn and reach out to grab hold of Brynne to keep her from making a scene, but I am not fast enough.

With her long strides, she is already halfway across the ring. The surrounding conversations grow quiet as the focus of the guards shifts once again to the spectacle that is about to take place.

Brynne is tall and her height gives her the same advantage as most of the men that make up the guards. But her stature and strength aren't the only reasons she has authority. Her position as Second Guard protecting the princess is the highest of them all, below only First Guard, who protects the King.

But there is no First Guard. There hasn't been one for as long as I can remember. My father chose never to fill the position, leaving Brynne the highest-ranking guard in the castle. No one knows why the king refuses to choose a First Guard, but it doesn't stop everyone, including Brynne, from coveting the position.

She reaches the man who I assume made the comment, and if I have to guess, was the source of the snickers from earlier. The guards around him take half a step back, leaving him alone at the edge of the ring to receive the wrath of their commanding officer. They are smart. I've seen what Brynne does to guards who step out of line, and I wouldn't want to be associated with that either.

"What did you just say?" Brynne growls at him.

The smug look on his face doesn't waver as he stares her down with a hardened gaze. He remains silent.

"I'm going to give you one more chance to answer, soldier, and you will not be happy with the result if you don't. I said—" She reaches out over the wooden beam, grabbing him by the collar and yanks him forward. He flips over it, landing flat on his back. Pained wheezes break through the air as he gasps for breath.

"What. Did you. Say."

He stares up at her from the ground, flat on his back. His lips seal shut as he stays focused on her, but refuses to speak.

She nods a few times in thought.

"Clearly, you have thoughts about the king and your future queen. I'd say they are borderline traitorous. Do you agree?" She looks around at the guards who stood with the man. All of them remain silent, but continue to watch.

"I think you may be a bit too comfortable here at the castle, and maybe it is time to relocate. A good stint out at the border should do you well. You leave tomorrow."

Despite my position, and despite the years I've spent training alongside the guards, there are still some I need to win over. Most of them treat me with respect inside the castle, and like I am part of their group while we are training, but every so often we run into someone like this man who has a different opinion. Brynne always takes care of them, and I never see them again.

The man glares up at Brynne and rolls over onto his stomach, but Brynne doesn't let him get far.

"Stop. First, you kneel before your future queen and swear loyalty to the kingdom."

The guard looks up at me and scowls. I don't let him see how his words hurt me, and scowl right back. He holds my stare, refusing to back down, but so do I. Brynne towers over him, arms crossed with a look I have seen a million times before. Pure authority.

The man finally pushes up off the ground and stands. He takes a slow, measured step, then another, closing the gap between us. I feel the urge to reach for a weapon before I remember the ones I have are dull. They would not even make him bleed.

He stops and drops to a knee directly in front of me. A ringing echoes as he pulls his sword from the scabbard at his side. He plants the tip of the blade into the ground in front of him and places both hands on the hilt.

"I pledge my service to the kingdom of Blackwood and give my sword to protect the royal family. I swear my loyalty to the king, Remington Holt, and his heir, Princess Lennox. Long live the king. Long live the princess."

His head is bowed, his eyes downcast as he recites the same pledge I've heard countless times from ceremonies past.

It's my part that comes next. "Blackwood honors your service and loyalty. You may rise."

Before he can stand on his own, Brynne grabs his shoulders and hauls him off the ground, pushing him toward the fence.

"Get back to work." Brynne strides back toward me, the air of authority seeping from her as she walks. It was the same walk she had the first time I saw her.

Years ago, when I reached an age where I was no longer a child and could move freely about the castle, my father held a tournament. The winner would be granted the position of Second Guard, the personal guard to the princess. It was intended to be filled by a guard already within our ranks, however, most of them wanted the coveted First Guard position my father refused to fill.

Brynne walked into the castle that day, wearing her own set of armor and claiming no kingdom. She was the only woman who signed up for the tournament and was immediately underestimated. She looked as if she was barely a few years older than me, clearly unable to hold her own against the well-trained soldiers of Blackwood. I was the one who didn't underestimate her. She walked with confidence, and I knew she would fight for the position and fight to protect me.

It inspired me seeing someone so close to my age fight as if she were one of the men, having more experience than they anticipated. I rooted for her silently, because it wasn't proper for the princess to choose sides. She was everything I wasn't: strong, confident, aggressive. She didn't cower at anyone and demanded respect as one of their peers. I wanted to be her, or to at least be around her so that maybe she would rub off on my meticulously controlled and lonely life.

I didn't realize as I placed the Second Guard sword in her hands and congratulated her on winning the tournament that she would grow to become one of my only friends. After that day, Brynne never had to deal with being underestimated by our guards again.

"Your highness." She gestures for me to walk ahead of her, indicating the end of our lesson for the day.

I am glad. We had been out here prior to being summoned by my father. My body is exhausted, but my mind is still reeling.

I walk to the edge of the ring and swing my leg over the bottom rung of the fence, dipping under and exiting so the next match can start. The murmur from the guards has stopped, and the normal ruckus and banter of the men in service has started again, with Brynne and me no longer the center of attention.

I drop my practice dagger and sword into the rack with a clang as Brynne does the same.

"I think I'm going to stay and shoot for a little while." I grab my favorite bow and a full quiver from the rack and slip the strap over my shoulder.

"Do you want to talk about it?"

"No."

She nods and looks up at the darkening overcast sky. "You have a little daylight left. I'll come back and check on you if you're still here by the time I complete my rounds."

I nod, and walk to the shooting lanes that are slowly emptying as the guards make their way to the barracks. I stride toward the farthest lane, not wanting to be bothered. I just needed to be alone with my thoughts and focus on something other than the anger at my father.

Reaching over my shoulder, I pull an arrow from the quiver and nock it quickly before pulling back the string. I feel the tension of the tight bow on my shoulders and move my front arm to line up with the target. My fingers brush my cheek as I narrow my eyes and focus. Inhaling slowly, I focus on nothing but my breath and the target. I let out the breath, releasing the arrow right at the end, and watch it slam into the target.

I completely missed the circles, striking the hay bale in the bottom corner.

"Shit." I curse at myself under my breath.

Shooting has always been a place of solace, where I can focus and completely drown out the world around me. Usually, I can still hit the target, even if I am riled up from an interaction with my father.

I'm really in my head this time. How can I not be? Everything I have been waiting for is in question. The aching loneliness I thought had a fast approaching end date is now in question. The doubt my father's words cast is making my fingers tingle.

I squeeze the bow tighter, willing the sensation away and nock another arrow. I pull it back as far as I can, my shoulders screaming in protest as I focus on the target. I release the arrow, and this time the loud thunk gives me a deep satisfaction knowing my arrow has struck true. Gazing down the lane to confirm, I see it, right in the center, right where I expected it.

If I cannot rely on my father to fulfill his responsibility as king to present me and prepare me to be his heir, at least I can still rely on myself.

This arrow proves it.

Despite the pressure and doubt, I can still accomplish what I set my mind to. I can still be who I want to be and do what a queen should do, no matter how much he refuses to believe in me.

CHAPTER THREE

 continue shooting, focusing on nothing but the target and the pull of the bow until the clouds covering the sky darken and the evening chill sets in. The light from the torches surrounding the training area is no longer enough to keep practicing, so I know it is well past when I should be back inside.

I will be sore tomorrow, but I welcome it. Physical pain is easier to focus on than the pain and disappointment from my meeting with the king.

I place the bow and quiver on the rack and make my way inside. The castle is quiet, and my footsteps echo off the cold, grey stone hallways. My stomach growls, breaking the silence as I ascend the main staircase.

Hopefully Addy saved me some dinner and had it sent to my room. She knows on training days there is a high possibility that I will miss dinner, since it has happened enough in the past.

I take the last step at the top of the staircase and come to an abrupt halt. Goosebumps cover the exposed skin on my neck and my breaths quicken as I try to calm the panic rising inside of me.

The door is open.

Not fully open, but cracked, and the light from the room pours across the stone floor.

My heart beats wildly, and I clench my fists at my sides as my feet move of what seems like their own volition. I can't stop it. Some unknown pull draws me closer to the door, filling me with the need to look inside.

It has been so long since the last time I felt this pull, and then I only snuck a passing glance on the way to my room. Feelings war inside me. My head tells me to stay away, but my body tells me to get closer. Try as I might, I can't stop myself.

I creep toward it, knowing my training boots are not the stealthiest footwear. I try not to make a sound, taking each step on my toes as I inch closer, trying to stay out of sight. I peer around the edge of the doorway and feel my breath catch.

My father sits in a chair, his back to me, facing the large tidy bed in the center of the room. The ornate bedding is so well kept it looks as if the room is unoccupied. He sits silently, leaning forward, resting his hands on the edge of the bed.

I creep closer, leaning slightly to see past the edge of the door. That's when I hear it.

I don't recognize it at first, but the longer I stand watching, the more it becomes clear. Sniffling, followed by tiny movements of his shoulders. His hand reaches up to wipe his face.

Crying.

My father is crying.

I lean in, trying to get a better look, to see if there is some reason he is sitting alone crying in her room, when the sound of a voice mumbling catches me off guard.

I stifle a gasp and pull myself back from the doorway, pressing my body against the wall, making myself as small as possible. I suck in deep, measured breaths, trying to still the heaving of my chest at the thought of being caught.

Who is speaking? Who is my father openly crying in front of?

In nearly twenty-one years, I have never seen my father cry.

My shallow breaths and heartbeat pumping through my ears make it difficult to hear. I strain to hear who is speaking, and make out the words that are affecting my father so strongly.

I inch closer and start the breathing exercises Brynne taught me to keep me from getting winded.

Breathe in, hold, slowly breathe out.

On the hold, I listen harder, and can pick up the low voices.

"Are you sure there has been no change?" My father's voice sounds strained, a small crack of emotion breaks through his words.

"Yes, your majesty. I'm afraid so."

The healer. It makes sense that he is the one speaking to my father. He has monitored my mother for as long as I can remember, giving my father updates regularly over the years that her health remains unchanged.

"If I may, your majesty." He pauses.

I push closer to the wall, as if removing that slight bit of space will help my hearing.

"It has been quite some time. Our healers have no explanation for her majesty's lack of decline, considering her state. However, we feel it is time to contemplate letting her go."

Silence fills the room and I hold my breath, waiting for my father's response. As far as I know, no one has ever suggested this to the king, until now.

But why now?

"I'll consider it," he grumbles, his voice heavy with emotion. I'm not used to hearing him like this, so different from the cold, short way he speaks to me.

"Of course, your majesty. There is no rushing the matter. Please let us know what you decide." I hear rustling as the healer gathers his things and I frantically look around the hall. If I walk past the room now, I'll surely be noticed, and I don't want to be caught eavesdropping on my father.

I eye the large tapestry next to me and slide behind it. Not the most creative space, but it will have to do. It just brushes the ground, so they won't see my feet hiding under it. I flatten my body against the wall behind it and wait for the healer to exit the room. His footsteps shuffle past me and I wait a few moments longer to ensure my father doesn't decide to follow. The quiet sniffling resumes so I'm safe to come out.

He hasn't left.

I contemplate heading straight to my room, but something makes me stop again and listen. The soft sniffles grow into low sobs. I stand in the hallway, listening to my father cry over a woman I never knew, but so desperately wish I did. I brush a rogue tear off my cheek, the emotion coming from the room overwhelming.

To say my father and I aren't close is an understatement. He barely tolerates me. It has been that way my entire childhood. I had more interaction with Edmond and Tila, and even Addy and Brynne, than I had with him. Every time he looks at me, I see pain in his eyes.

Pain I had caused.

This is why I avoid this door, and why every time I walk down the hallway, I am slapped with the reminder of what I had done. Tonight is an even harsher reminder of how I stole my father's happiness, and how I have never been enough to fill that void for him over the past twenty years.

I'd taken my mother away from him, ripped her out of this world and into this state of in-between, where everyone is reminded she is there, but not truly. We have to walk by her chambers every day knowing she lies behind the closed door, unmoving, unable to wake, and unable to live the life she planned with my father.

Because of me.

Not only did I take her away from him, simply by being born, but I took her away from myself. I have never known this woman. All I've known is the dream of what a mother would be like, and how it could never be her as she lies in this room, unable to wake.

And now?

Listening to the healer tell my father it is time to let her go, all hope of ever meeting her, of having a parent who cared for me and wanted me there is gone. My fantasy that one day she would wake, and I would know the unconditional love of a parent, and live out the rest of our days making up for lost time is disintegrating.

Despite our relationship, seeing my father so upset about losing her for good brings me sadness, but there is more to it.

The realization that I am also losing her, the only her I have ever known, feels overwhelming. It is a loss of possibility, not a loss of someone I knew and loved, not like my father is losing.

I swipe at the tears welling inside my eyes, and clear the thickness building in my throat. I don't care if my father hears me. I stride strongly down the hallway toward my rooms, holding my head high. I need to let this fantasy go. I will never know her.

You aren't really losing her, you never had her.

I squash the hope I had down deep into myself, never wanting to feel it ever again.

If only that were possible.

CHAPTER
FOUR

"Good morning, Princess."

I startle at Edmond's words and slam my book shut, tucking it into the large, winged chair cushion next to me. I got to the library for my lessons early this morning, finding that my time spent in the quiet amongst the full shelves is some of my most calm. I have met with Edmond in the castle library every day since childhood. He's taught me everything I know, every lesson on politics, geography, customs. He has made me the future queen I am today.

"Good morning, Edmond." I sit up straighter before letting out a large, very un-princess like yawn, stretching my arms above my head.

"Catching up on some reading?"

"Yes. I was up reading until it was almost light." It is the truth. After leaving my father crying over my mother last night, I could not quiet my mind, so I resorted to distraction.

"Something educational, I hope." His eyebrows rise as he quirks his head.

"Of course." I will the blush out of my cheeks. I don't want to get into *what* I am reading.

I'd discovered Tila's stash of books years ago. I was bored, waiting for her to arrive in her chambers, when I started snooping through her things. A row of neatly lined books caught my eye on the shelf above where she did her sewing, and I decided to ignore boundaries and look. I stood on her stool and pulled one down, expecting to find patterns or instructions for crafting all the clothing she made.

As my eyes scanned the text, I was shocked to find the book had nothing to do with sewing. I pulled down book after book and skimmed random pages. They were stories. *Romances.* And some of them were… naughty. My eyes scanned the covers, but did not find a single detail hinting at what was inside.

I have been sneaking into her rooms and borrowing books from her shelf ever since.

I truly think she knows and pretends not to, because I notice new ones appearing all the time, and she never seems to notice when one is missing.

Ever since, I have loved to read about love, craving the escape, the longing, the happy ending.

The idea of someone loving someone else that much makes my chest squeeze. I've never known that kind of love, never truly seen it either, unless you count the times I've seen my father sitting in with my mother.

I want what I read in Tila's books. It is one reason I am so upset about my father's refusal to involve me in anything for the kingdom and my continued isolation.

Am I doomed to be isolated and unloved for my entire life?

So, I find it in the books, who have been my constant companions for years. I don't lie to Edmond when I say I am reading something educational. The books can be *very* educational, especially when I was younger and didn't have a mother to explain these things to me. Gods know my father never will, and maybe this is why he never discussed any betrothal or marriage agreement with me. He avoids any mention of moving forward in my life at all costs.

Edmond chuckles as he takes a seat. "You and your stories. Just make sure to return them to Tila when you are finished."

My jaw drops as I take in his lighthearted look.

How does he know?

"There isn't anything that happens with books in this castle that I am unaware of." I gape at him as he sits in the chair across from me, as he has done every day for years.

After a few beats of silence, I finally find words. "I read them to escape. It's nice to live in someone else's head for a little while."

Despite the initial discomfort of him knowing what I am reading, it is fairly normal for me to be this open with Edmond. If Tila is like a mother figure, then Edmond is like my grandfather, one I am very close to. Just as Tila has been there my entire childhood, so has Edmond. My father assigned people to look after me as a child, and they have remained unchanged all this time. Brynne is actually the newest, and she has already been around for years.

But Edmond is more than just my tutor. He is a confidant, someone I spend my days with and who knows me better than anyone else, even Brynne. It doesn't bother me he is at least three times my age. I know he loves me and cares for me, as if I am his own family, his own daughter. For all I know, he considers me as such, because he has no family of his own.

"Despite the…vivid imagery I am sure are in the books you and Tila read, we can learn a lot from stories if we pay attention." I chortle at his insinuation, despite knowing he is completely right. "Is that the lesson that you want to have this morning?"

"I thought we had to go over things for the ceremony?"

"That can wait until later." He rests his face on his hand, leaning on the armchair as he often does when he gets ready to lecture, and gazes at me through squinted eyes.

"What?" I squirm in my chair at the intensity. Just like any father figure, he can instantly make me feel like a child who did something wrong, though with Edmond, nothing I do has or will ever make him mad at me. In my younger years, I definitely tried. No matter what I did, instead of resorting to anger or punishment, he instead instantly taught a lesson from my behavior, turning a negative experience into a positive one.

"I'm just trying to remember if I've told you this story before. It's one I used to tell my son. Even so, if you've already heard it, let's just pretend it is the first time. Understood?"

My jaw drops at his words.

Son?

"I'm sorry, your son? You have a son?" His eyes mist at my question and an emotion that I've ever seen crosses his face. Longing? Nostalgia? I can't quite tell.

"Yes, I have a son. He's been gone for quite some time now."

Is this why Edmond never brings up his family? I assume his son died, but how? What happened? It must have been before I was born, or at least a few years after, because I have no recollection of Edmond ever having any family at all.

I can see the sadness and love in his eyes at bringing up his son, and I want to ask more, but I don't want to hurt him. In twenty years, this is the first he's ever trusted me with this information. I want him to know I care, but don't want to make his sharing more difficult than it already is.

I pick at a seam in my simple, deep green wool gown as I contemplate my choice of words before uttering them slowly. "Why have you never mentioned him before?"

He raises a hand to his face, his fingers covering his lips as he thinks before answering. "As I'm sure you know, some things are difficult to think about, let alone talk about. But they still live with us every day. We do not forget."

I shrink back slightly at his words. He's right. People live every day with things that are hard to think about. Edmond is finally giving me a glimpse into his, and we both know I have mine.

I swallow before I speak again. "I'm sorry for whatever happened. Tell me the story? Please?"

I've spent almost every day of my life with Edmond, and he can't remember if he had told me a story he used to tell his son. If he hadn't, it might have been over twenty years since he had told anyone this story. I don't want to rush him, especially since it might bring up more memories, making what was supposed to be a typical morning of lessons a difficult one.

He shifts and lowers his hand to his lap, intertwining his fingers, but staying silent. After a few moments, he clears his throat and begins.

"It is not just the kingdom of Blackwood that exists in this world. As you know from the countless lessons of geography we have covered through the years, as well as the inter kingdom affairs and politics, there are neighboring kingdoms on this continent, and afar. Blackwood, as a whole, is a rich kingdom, filled with skilled craftsmen, and raw goods to trade or sell to other kingdoms. The natural wealth of the land provides us with jobs to support our people, to ensure that our citizens can live comfortably and care for their families. While this is the reality for Blackwood, not all others within our reach are as successful, and as such, are not immune to suffering, disease, and death."

This is not the type of story I was expecting. When he spoke of a story he told his son, I expected more lighthearted words, not something that sounded like it is being quoted directly from the books we study.

I expected something with a plot and hidden meaning, something he would make me pull a lesson from. I do not know where he is heading, and after last night, I don't know if I can handle a story about death and suffering. I shift uncomfortably in the chair and wait for him to continue.

He presses on. "Despite the advances in medicines and healing that many kingdoms, ours included, have benefited from, there are still many ailments or illnesses that cannot be treated. Many of which cannot be explained. Families and friends are forced to watch their loved one suffer with no hope of survival. It is only natural that they yearn for answers, from medicines and healers…or elsewhere."

I swallow the lump in my throat that formed after his words.

Cannot be explained.

This story is hitting too close to my heart after everything I dealt with last night.

Our healers have no explanation for her majesty's lack of decline in her state.

Is this the reason Edmond brings up the story today of all days? He hasn't for almost twenty-one years, but suddenly he deems it so important that we need to push off preparing for the ceremony so I can hear it. How much does Edmond know about my mother's health?

"In short, they need a miracle. A cure. Something to save the life of those they love, healing injury and combating illnesses that plague them. Some, desperate enough to save a loved one, would give up everything they had, or do anything they could to save a child, a spouse, a parent, a sibling, even a friend."

This no longer feels like a coincidence. This lesson is targeted. Edmond must know. He must have talked to my father last night, or the healer, at the least. But what I cannot figure out is the reason.

There is no longer any hope, the healer said so himself. She needs to be let go, and if anyone needs to hear this story about doing anything to save someone they love, maybe it is my father. Maybe he should do something more with his influence and power than hold vigil by her bedside for twenty years.

He continues.

"Many tales have been passed down through the generations, talking of different treatments to cure certain ailments, but alas, nothing is guaranteed. Many people still die or are permanently changed from their injury for the rest of their lives."

He stops, and I remain silent. He seems to be contemplating how to tell the next part of the story, or whether he to tell it at all. He has built it up this far, and I need him to finish, need to know why he is telling it, and how this pertains to me. What lesson is he trying to teach me?

The pause finally ends, as if he is convinced I am listening, and it is worth finishing.

"There is a myth of a land named Dawnlin. The story has been passed down through generations. The myth states that this land contains an element of some sort said to cure any disease or heal any injury, restoring the perfect health to a person. The land itself is shrouded in secrecy. No one truly knows how to find it, and no one truly knows what the element is.

"There have been no confirmed cases of some sort of magical element, only stories of miraculous recoveries in people who were otherwise doomed to die. The accounts of the family members or friends do not shed any light on the recoveries, as they swear they do not know how it happened. No one can confirm that any sort of element or elixir was used, only that the patient, who many times was ready to part from this world, was instead back to their normal ways in the blink of an eye.

"As you can assume, this magical element, if it did exist, would be highly coveted. The number of people who would fight to get their hands on it for personal gains, control, and influence in our kingdoms could be astronomical. Can you imagine the number of people who would do or pay anything to use it? To ensure they or someone they loved wouldn't die? Or those who would hoard that power over others for their own gain?"

"I can imagine that there would be many people who would use it to extort others," I say. The possibilities would be endless. I can only imagine the shift in power or the sheer amount of gold that would be paid to obtain it. Would men or women who hoarded this magic take over and rule the land, deciding who would live and who would die? Would kings give up their kingdoms in order to save someone they loved?

Would my father give up his for my mother?

I push the thought away as quickly as it comes into my mind, focusing back on Edmond.

"That is where the Guardian comes in. It is said that the land of Dawnlin is protected by a guardian, a being who is the only one who can bring people on and off the island. The Guardian is the gatekeeper, the one that gives the chance to obtain the elixir to those who truly need it. The Guardian's identity is unknown, and how he or she travels there is a complete mystery. No one knows how the island selects who is brought there, or why, but that doesn't stop the hope that one will be chosen.

"It has been many years now since such a miraculous recovery has occurred, making people wonder if Dawnlin actually exists, or if something has happened to the Guardian. Though much time has passed, hope is not lost, as those who are desperate for a cure still wait to see if such a grace will be bestowed upon them."

I wait for him to continue, but he just looks at me as if expecting a reaction.

He tilts his head to the side as he gazes at my face. "You seem disappointed."

Edmond can always tell my genuine emotions, no matter how much I try to hide them. He can always pick apart even the most stoic looks on my face.

This isn't one of those times.

I quickly loosen my lips and school my face back into a neutral position, not realizing my lips had been pressed together, my eyebrows drawn down. My feelings must be written all over my face.

"That wasn't what I was expecting when you said you were going to tell a story."

"Is the story of a mythical land that holds a magical cure for all illness and injury not a story enough?"

"I was just expecting...a plot."

"Not all stories need characters to learn from. Even the simplest of stories can teach us."

"Fair," I say. Edmond is like this often. He enjoys teaching in puzzles, pushing me to pull information from what he says instead of just talking at me and expecting me to regurgitate information. He likes to make me think.

"Are there any lessons you can garner from it?"

I think for a minute. I know this story is really special to him, but to me, that is all it is. A story. It sounds like one designed to give people hope, making them wish the Guardian would appear one day, and give them the ability to save someone they love. But that is where it ends.

Hope.

Hope for the families, hope for the ill. Maybe it gives a person peace, feeling they could be saved, but would that not make it more difficult to accept their fate when they aren't? Isn't it better to acknowledge it for what it is, a hope that will never be, and move forward with what you can control, processing the grief of loss and not believing in some sort of mythical magic?

The pain from last night floods my body as I relive all the dashed hopes of never meeting my mother. I clench my fists, taking a deep breath as my eyes flutter closed. I don't want to go through this again, especially since I worked so hard to distract myself and forget.

"I think the lesson is that hope can be dangerous." I open my eyes and meet his again, trying hard to keep the turmoil flowing through my body from showing.

He eyes me, face devoid of all emotion. "That is an interesting take. Care to elaborate?"

"It isn't logical to believe in something so wholeheartedly and hope so strongly that you lose your sense of reality."

"So, it is illogical to have hope?" Confusion flashes on his face, but he quickly hides it, forcing me to formulate an answer, not just respond the way he expects me to.

"Not exactly illogical. I think having hope is fine, but only to a certain point. Magic is not real. It's hopeless to believe only because of a story, and put all your hope and energy into waiting for it to save you. At that point, you have two choices. You can either save someone yourself, or accept the reality of their fate, and do what you can with the time you have left."

"Even at the expense of watching someone you love suffer?"

"I think hanging on to hope is the easiest way to guarantee you wait around and watch, rather than moving forward. Why not accept the grief and process it, so it doesn't hurt as much when the person is actually gone?"

My father has been holding on to hope for twenty-one years and look where it has gotten him. Hanging on to nothing, just to say goodbye anyway. It would have been better for him to just let her go a long time ago. It's not like my life would have been any different.

A single tear trails down my cheek and I swipe it away. I know Edmond saw it, but I also know he will not pry.

"Can amazing things happen?" I say. "Sure. But magic? Some magical element that can make someone whole again? It isn't realistic. There is too much suffering in the world to hope and believe something like this elixir exists. And who chose this Guardian? What makes him so special that he gets to choose who deserves to be saved and who doesn't? Why is he the one who gets to fulfill hopes of some but not others?"

I feel my emotions bubbling up again, fighting to spill over. More words pour from my mouth and I can't stop them.

"It's almost cruel to give people this hope and let them live their lives thinking magic will save them. Are they not suffering more knowing as every day passes that their suffering wasn't enough to be helped? How is it fair to choose one over another? My moth—"

I slam my mouth shut and tear my eyes away from Edmond. I try to blink away the tears, but instead cause more to fall. When I finally feel in control, I look back at Edmond, who is still watching me quietly. He knows what I almost said, but knows me well enough not to ask me to finish that sentence.

I don't want to.

I don't want to suffer more today.

Is this why he brought up this story? Why today? Why so suddenly?

I wonder if this has something to do with his son. Is today the anniversary of his son's death? Does Edmond believe in Dawnlin, and waited with hope to save his sick child, only to be disappointed he was never chosen? What lesson is he trying to teach me from his experience?

"Do you know?" I ask. I don't give him anything else. Silence stretches over the library as Edmond looks down, breaking our eye contact.

He knows.

"Is there anything else you learned?" He examines his hands, waiting to see if I respond with the proper lesson.

"Yes," I snap a little more forcefully than I intend. I am not upset with him for bringing this up. I'm more upset that I let my emotions break through the surface. If there is anything my father expects from me as the future queen of Blackwood, it is to always have a handle on my emotions, just as he does.

I shift in my seat and calm myself before speaking again.

"I think there is a lesson about humankind, or more so, a warning. There are always those who thirst for power, and it's easy to use hope against anyone in order to attain it."

He looks back up at me, holding eye contact again. "You sound very cynical this morning."

"If I'm going to be the queen of Blackwood, I need to be. I have to protect my people, and if someone is going to harm them or hold power over them, I need to be the logical one that isn't tricked and confused. I can't let emotions get in the way of that."

"So, it is the want for power that drives people to seek Dawnlin, not love that does so?"

I think for a minute before answering carefully.

"I think love influences decisions and pushes people to make bad ones.

Love makes people hope, and hope can be dangerous if you don't choose to act instead of just waiting around. But power? Power motivates people to act, and love blinds people from seeing it."

I swallow down all the things I don't want to say out loud. Things like love causes pain, and hope mixed with love causes even more pain.

Things like losing hope hurts almost as much as losing someone you love.

"Light always finds a way, even through the blackest woods."

I couldn't tell you how many times in my life I have heard Edmond utter that phrase, but this time, it doesn't comfort me like it usually does. I realize now that while I always thought it was encouraging, it was actually pushing me to feel hopeful, and I don't feel hopeful today. All of this talk makes me want to get as far away from hope and emotions as I can. I want to shut down and feel nothing, do nothing.

Maybe I need to find Brynne today after all and just work it out. I'm sure she would be delighted.

"Can we just move on, Edmond?" I say. I don't want to tell him I didn't enjoy his story, especially because the memory of telling it to his son seems important to him. I don't want to bring any more negativity into this conversation, or tarnish Edmond's memory about his son.

"Oh, we're done for the day," he says calmly.

I stare at him, skeptical. "We barely just started. What am I missing?"

"Not missing anything. I simply think we have discussed enough lessons for the morning. There is a lot to think about here."

"Alright..." I trail off, twiddling my fingers together uncomfortably.

"But I have something for you." He reaches into his coat and pulls out a small leather-bound book. It looks very used, the corners are not sharp, and the leather has divots and nicks.

"What is it?" I ask. Edmond leans over, placing the book in my outstretched hand.

"Something I felt you should have had a long time ago. But, nevertheless, you should at least have it now."

"I don't understand," I say, running my fingers over the binding. This book is a lot smaller than most we have used for lessons. I reach to pull open the cover, but Edmond stops me.

"I would recommend reading it when you are alone." He leans forward, pushing on the arms of his chair until he is standing in front of me. "But I would recommend reading it, Lennox, no matter how difficult it may be."

I stare after him, at a loss for words as he strides to the door. He gives me a brief nod before opening the door and slipping through it, leaving me in the silence of the empty library.

CHAPTER
FIVE

The click of the latch reverberates through the room as Edmond leaves me alone with only my thoughts and this book. What could possibly be inside that I need to be alone to read?

I scan the outside, looking for some kind of clue as nervousness overtakes me. I am slightly afraid to open it. Once I do, there is no coming back from whatever is inside. From the way Edmond acted, it seems really important.

I carefully peel back the cover and scan the first page.

Nothing.

Blank.

No clues to be seen. My fingers flutter over the corner of the first page, sliding behind it, ready to turn.

Curiosity overcomes my nerves and I flip it rapidly, eyes scanning to find the text. My eyes snag on the writing at the top of the page.

"My Dearest Daughter…"

The words begin to blur as I slam the book closed. The loud slap echoes off the walls and hits my ringing ears.

Daughter.

My dearest. Daughter.

Who wrote this?

What kind of joke is Edmond playing? No, Edmond would never play this kind of trick on me. This has to be real, and the thought sends my mind spiraling.

There is no way this could be from my father, so that leaves only one person…

My mother.

My hand shakes as I reach to open the book again, flipping to the first page. I scan over it quickly and let out a quiet sob as I take in the dainty script handwriting that fills the pages. I flip through the book, the pages filled with writing, almost to the end.

This was hers, and she wrote it all to me.

I fumble through the pages, making my way back to the first so I can start at the beginning. Edmond said I should have had this long ago, so who kept it from me? Was it him, or was it my father?

The pit deepening in my gut screams at me my father was the one who hid it. I can only imagine why.

I inhale a deep, shuddering breath before looking at the words again. I want to devour them, but I force myself to take them in slowly, and savor every ounce of her I can.

My Dearest Daughter,

Well, I am calling you that, because despite your father already planning to name his son after himself, I know deep in my heart that you are a girl. My Lennox. I've always dreamt of giving that name to my daughter, and I know that is exactly what will happen. The moment we found out you were coming, your father and I were overjoyed. We are counting the days until we get to hold you in our arms. We waited so very long for you, and we will wait ever so patiently now, knowing that you will soon be ours forever.

I wanted to write to you, my darling girl, every single day because there are so many things I just cannot wait to tell you. That is why I started this journal, to make sure that you did not miss a moment of the happiness your father and I are experiencing, waiting for our joy.

I love you, my sweet girl, more than you will ever know.

Love,
Your Mother Lyla

I cover my mouth to hide the sound of the sobs that are wreaking havoc over my body. Never once had I seen anything written by my mother, nor heard anyone talk about her feelings toward me. She has been a mystery, a ghost, but she is coming to life before my eyes.

I can't stop myself now. I read as quickly as I can, flipping the pages and soaking up this woman I never got to know.

By the time I reach the end, having read through every word a second time, the library is dark. My eyes are filled with a dull pain from both straining to read the words in the dimming light, too engrossed to stop, and from the constant tears being shed.

That's it. It's over. Those are the only words I will ever get from her.

Edmond was right. I needed to be alone when I read this. I am glad I listened, because I'm a mess. I curl up into a ball, sinking as deep into the chair as I can, clutching the journal to my chest and cry.

I let everything out, all the emotion that I tried to bottle in for the past twenty years. I let the sobs overtake me, my body heaving and my muscles clenching as I gasp for air. I can barely open my eyes, and my body feels as if it is made of stone.

I cry for gods know how long, alone in the library, hoping that no one will come looking for me.

I don't want anyone's comfort right now.

I only want hers.

I want to feel her arms wrap around me and hold me tight, petting my hair and telling me I will be alright. I want to know the sound of my mother's voice and hear her say the words she used to sign off every note.

I love you, my sweet girl, more than you will ever know.

A hole in my chest widens at the realization that I will never know her, never truly meet my mother, who wanted me so badly. I will never meet the woman who took so much time writing to me about her day, her life, telling me stories of her childhood and her hopes and dreams for mine.

How could Edmond be so cruel, giving this to me now, when he knew that her time is done? That I will never have a chance to meet her? That my hope for ever knowing her is lost?

Why would he give me this gift, only to have her loss be so much harder now that I got to see a glimpse of this amazing woman, this parent who actually wanted me? My childhood, my whole life to this point, would have been so different if only my mother were there, and I wasn't subject to a father who couldn't care less, who could barely even look at me.

I feel the loss drag me down, deep under the waves of tears and hurt and pain.

I lay there in the chair, in the dark until the sobs slow, my body so heavy and my energy so depleted that I can barely move. All I have now are my thoughts, and I can't get past the one repeatedly running through my mind.

Why would Edmond do this to me?

Why would he want to hurt me in this way?

What was he trying to teach me?

My mind strains as I try to think back to the events of the morning. Reading the journal had completely consumed me, and I try to focus on what came before it.

Edmond's story. The myth of Dawnlin.

Hope.

Was Edmond trying to give me the gift of my mother so that I wouldn't lose hope for her? It was a pretty fucked up and cruel way to go about it. I told him I didn't believe in the magic, but was there hope I could actually have?

Maybe that is all the magic was. What if it was a metaphor, something to help people understand they don't have to be hopeless?

Maybe I don't have to be.

Maybe it is time to consider letting her go.

No. I don't have to accept that. I can be the magic, and I can work to figure out how to help her. I told Edmond I didn't believe in sitting around and waiting for something magical. That would cause nothing but pain.

My mother has been lying in that bed for over twenty years, waiting for a miracle.

I don't have time to wait around for magic or myth.

The healers say that this is it, that it is time to give up hope.

I already said goodbye to a woman I didn't know, to the idea of having a mother, but I have her now. I have her in these words, in her book, and by some weird fate, she is still there, waiting.

Maybe she is waiting for me, not to give up hope, and to be the one to do something more, to find something that can help her, and not to just release all hope and let her go like they are trying to convince my father to.

This had to be why Edmond said I needed the journal now. He didn't want me to give up hope, to give up on her. He wanted me to see what I was losing and do something about it.

I suck in a breath and push myself up, wiping away the tears and trying to blink through the swelling.

I will do it. I won't give up on her, I won't give up hope.

But I don't have much time. All it would take is one word from my father, and they would stop providing her care and let her fade away. I need to act now. Clearly Edmond believes I can.

And maybe if I believe in myself and find something to bring her back to me, my father will finally see how worthy I am to rule this kingdom, and I won't be alone while I do it.

CHAPTER SIX

"If only Tila could see me now," I murmur as I scan my reflection in the mirror, looking over the staff outfit I had snagged from the laundry to make sure nothing about it would give me away.

I need to blend in, not only if anyone inside the castle saw me, but also so I didn't catch the attention of whoever I encountered outside of it.

I stayed in the library well into the night, pulling all the books I could find with any information that might be helpful for my mother. Edmond had taught me the basics of healing and the human body during my lessons growing up, so at least I understood what I was reading.

Despite being in the castle library and supposedly having the largest range of books and texts in our kingdom, I didn't find anything specific to a case like hers. I scoured the titles, poured over the table of contents, and spent hours reading anything that was even remotely related. I couldn't find any case like hers, or any sort of treatment for a body in a perpetual sleep.

It isn't until the windows brighten with the coming dawn that I made my decision. I needed to exhaust all possibilities and search elsewhere. Maybe written encounters of cases like hers never made it to the royal texts. Maybe they were out among the people.

I needed to check. So as my eyes were drooping and my mind was begging for sleep, I decided I was going to do something I had never done before.

I was going to sneak out of the castle.

That decision led me to this moment, staring in this mirror.

I pull my hair back and braid it sloppily, but my eyes catch on the color. Despite no one outside of these walls ever having set eyes on me, I feel that my long golden locks, so similar to my mother's, would be a dead giveaway.

I scan the surface of the vanity next to the mirror. Maybe I could use something to disguise it. I spot a powder Tila normally uses on my eyes.

Perfect.

I crush the powder, rubbing it between my hands and then wipe it over the surface of my braid. It isn't a drastic difference, but it is enough that I may get past anyone without a second glance.

I scan myself again in the mirror quickly.

It'll have to do.

I don't usually have training with Brynne scheduled for today, so it isn't abnormal for me to spend the afternoon in my quarters, reading or studying my lessons.

No one should miss me. This entire plan hangs on that, and I don't have time to waste.

I pull the dark cloak over my shoulders and clip the clasp across my chest, leaving the hood down so I don't draw attention or look like I'm hiding. I just need to keep my head down and walk with a purpose.

Ready or not.

I pull my door open slightly, stopping to listen for any footsteps or voices. When silence is all that greets me, I slide out of the door and pull it closed silently behind me. I glance down the hallway in both directions. Still no one to be seen.

I turn away from the main staircase, hoping the smaller one at the end of the hall will keep me from running into anyone. I push the doors at the bottom open and walk toward the kitchens, where a ruckus of pots, pans, and voices rise all around me.

Shit.

It's going to be impossible to slip past all these people without someone noticing me.

I pull up the hood, sucking in a deep breath and holding it as I drop my head and stride purposefully toward the delivery door in the back.

No one pays me any mind.

There is no halt in the conversation, no sign that anyone had even noticed me.

Has it really been this easy the entire time?

Have I really spent years of my life feeling like I could never leave this castle, simply because my father commanded it, but all it took was actually just walking out?

I will not test my luck.

I push open the door and step out into the frigid air. Shutting it quickly behind me, I pull the hood lower over my brow. I glance over my shoulder, eyeing the guards stationed at the gate in the castle wall. Since I never leave, I don't see the guards stationed here often. I say a quick prayer that they don't train at the same time as Brynne and I do before I turn to face them and start making my way toward the gate.

My heart pounds harder with every step I take, my palms sweating so much that I slyly rub them on the sides of my skirt under the cloak.

Please don't notice me.

"Evening, miss," the closest guard says as I stop in front of him. I drop into a quick curtsey, keeping my eyes on the floor in front of me.

"Good evening, sir," I say, trying hard to keep my voice low and steady. This is the closest I have ever been to the outside world. I can't fail now. I can only imagine my father's reaction if any of the guards recognize me and drag me back to face his punishment.

The lock clicks and the hinges squeal as one of the other guards swings the gate open.

"It'll be dark soon. Send word if you need one of us to accompany you on your return."

"Thank you, sir. I will be sure to do that."

I definitely won't be doing that, but as the future queen, it is nice to know the guards care for the well-being of all the staff. I give him another small curtsey before striding through the gate, acting as if I do this every day.

Not a big deal. This is normal.

It's not as though my insides are screaming at me, and my brain is trying to process every single detail to make sure I don't give myself away.

The moment I step through the gate, an immense weight is lifted off my shoulders.

I made it. I am outside of the castle walls. I have been dreaming about this moment since I was a little girl.

I take a step forward, feeling the unevenness of the cobblestones beneath my feet. The gate clangs closed behind me, and I start walking down the road when reality hits me.

No one knows where I am, or who I am.

I am essentially invisible.

Out here, I can be anyone I want to be. I can put aside the pressures of being the princess, the future queen, the one who makes decisions that affect every person in this city, in the kingdom.

I can just be…me.

I walk with a purpose, still trying to avoid the attention of the guards. I don't need to give them any reason to question me. Civilians pass by me, walking down the road, bundled up against the cold. I try hard not to make eye contact and focus on my goal.

I know the layout of the city well, despite never having stepped foot into it. Edmond ensured I had a good grasp on geography, not only of the principal city, but the entire kingdom of Blackwood and beyond. The businesses may have changed over the years, but I still know the roads well.

I turn down the next road and head toward the square. The closer I get, the more crowded it becomes. People carry loaves of bread or other items for tonight's meal as children run and chase each other. Horses are tied at watering troughs and chatter and laughter flowing through the air.

Town feels so…alive.

Blackwood has always been cold and gloomy. We rarely ever have sunlight, and if we do, it merely lightens the perpetual grey cloud cover and mist that rolls through our mountains and forests. It has always felt cold and dull to me. Lifeless.

Not now.

I slow my steps, raising my head slightly to get a better glimpse of the people, to see *my* kingdom. My lips curve into a small smile as I take everything in, but drops away quickly as a wave of anger comes over me.

My father has been keeping all of this from me. He isn't letting me experience our people or get to know our kingdom like he did for so many years. He walked the roads, made friends, met my mother. The kingdom knew him. He heard their concerns as their prince, and even more as their young king. He wasn't just a future king in name only, like I am.

Yet, he refuses to let them know me.

I hold my head a little higher, letting the hood fall back slightly, caring less if someone sees my face. He can't take this away from me. I'm already out of my cage. I won't let the feeling deep inside me that I'm breaking the rules or doing something wrong take away this experience. If he finds out and punishes me, so be it.

No one even glances my way, my disguise as castle staff helping me fit in perfectly among the people. I cross the square and head toward the library. The grey sky is still light over the tops of the black trees scattered throughout the city, but I know it will start darkening soon. I need to hurry so I don't have to walk back to the castle too late in the night, but I have a mission to accomplish. I will not quit before I find at least something that might help her.

CHAPTER SEVEN

The entry hall of the library dims once I shut the door behind me. The smell of old books with a hint of dust surrounds me, and immediately I feel relief, like I'm home, back in the castle in my favorite room.

An older woman sits at a dark wooden desk, writing in a large book on the desk in front of her. I hesitate. She is the first person I will ever have spoken to outside the castle. Despite knowing that my father kept any and all information about me secret, I still feel uneasy, like the moment I speak, my identity will be discovered, and they will send me straight back to the castle for the wrath of the king. I'm not ready to go back. Not yet.

I take a deep breath and school my face like I have done this a million times before, like I belong there.

"Excuse me," I say quietly, breaking the silence of the library.

The woman glances up at me. "Yes? How may I help you?"

"Could you please point me toward the healing or medicinal section?"

She nods and gestures to one side. "Yes, it is down this aisle, and to the left. There are a few shelves. Please let us know if you need any more assistance."

"Thank you," I say with a nod. "That should be fine." I almost let out a breath of relief as I turn toward the aisle, but I stop short at her next words.

"Is this for the king?"

There is no way she could have recognized me already. All the possibilities of how my father will react to me being escorted back to the castle start cycling through my mind. I won't let him deter me. I will hold my ground and defend my choices and reiterate how important this is.

"I did not get any word that the castle needed assistance, or I would have prepared for him," she says, glancing at the uniform I forgot I was wearing.

Relief floods my body, and my shoulders relax. The uniform. She must have known right away that I came from the castle. I wasn't expecting someone to call attention to it so quickly.

"No," I stammer as I try to think up a lie. I didn't realize that the library in the castle regularly sought the help of the librarians in the city, or that my father had, for that matter.

I mentally kick myself. Why didn't I prepare for this? Come up with some sort of plan or backstory before just waltzing out of the castle?

"This is for my own personal knowledge. I, um," I stumble through, trying to sound convincing. "I hope to become a healer one day. I finished my work at the castle early and thought I would come do some research."

She gives me a small smile and a nod. "Let me know if you need anything." She turns back to her work, and the library is cast back into silence.

Dodged that one.

I drop into a small curtsey and quickly head toward the aisle. I glance around the library, taking it all in. The single open room isn't very large, but it isn't small either. There are tables and chairs strewn about, and rows of bookshelves covering almost every surface, creating aisles in the open space. At first glance, it seems to be split into sections, reference books on the side the woman directed me to, and all other books for all ages on the other. That side definitely looks to be the more popular side of the library, with people of all ages strewn about, reading.

A group of girls who look just younger than me sit in the corner trying to stifle giggles as they pass a book back and forth, their voices low as they whisper to each other.

I bet it is similar to what lives on Tila's shelves. Maybe I've even read it before. I suppress the desire to walk over and see what they are reading.

A pang of jealousy hits deep in my chest as I spot mothers with small children sitting on the floor and looking at pictures drawn on the pages. My mind drifts back to one letter my mother wrote me, where she told me all the things she couldn't wait to do with me. Things I wouldn't ever get to experience. Sitting and reading to me, just as these mothers were to their children, was one of them.

Stop it, Lennox. Focus. You're here for a reason.

I shake my head, snapping myself out of the thought, and push on. Once I find the section on healing, I scan the shelves to see how many texts I have to browse through. There are quite a few, at least three full shelves of them. Less than we have at the castle library, but still more than I expected would be here.

I grab a couple at random off the first shelf and quickly flip through. Some look to be printed, while others are full of drawings and handwritten notes. Some aren't texts at all, but journals kept by healers over the years full of information on past patients, with different volumes carved into the spines.

No one has ever told me what is actually wrong with my mother. The only explanation ever offered to me was that this happened during childbirth…with me. I caused this. I ripped her from my life and didn't even know it.

It's one of the main reasons I am so determined to do something about it. Now that I feel the loss of her personally, saw the woman she was on the page, the mother that she was already and the one she wanted to be, I needed to right this wrong and fix what I had so innocently done simply by being born.

After scanning the shelves, I get to work. Intermittent coughs and footsteps break through the silence, but I ignore them, focused solely on my task. One by one, I pull the books off the shelf and flip through to see if it is relevant. Anything concerning childbirth, blood loss, unconscious sleeps, death. Something that might explain why she would have fallen asleep, never to wake.

I flip through the index if there is one, or skip the book if the title doesn't seem promising. Some of the printed books I have already seen in the castle's library, but many of the handwritten texts or journals are unique and we don't have copies. I take extra time on those, looking closely to make sure I am not missing something important at first glance.

By the time I reach the end of the first shelf, I have a large stack of books in my arms. I need to find a table to go through these before I continue on to the other shelves. I walk to the end of the row and glance to the right, but all the tables look full, or already claimed. I turn around to check the other side and smack straight into someone's hard chest.

CHAPTER EIGHT

The books fall from my arms and crash loudly to the ground, as firm hands wrap around my shoulders, steadying me as I lose my balance.

"I'm sorry. Are you alright?" The voice is deep, his words a low grumble, trying not to disturb the quiet more than the clatter of books already has.

My eyes slide up his body, taking in his broad frame until they land on his face. Blinking up at him, stunned, I hope he doesn't feel the shiver coursing through me as he holds me steady.

I hadn't noticed him when I walked in, because surely he would have stood out. I've never seen anyone like him before. He is young, maybe a few years older than me, and obviously tall as I crane my neck up to see his face.

I take in his hair, so different from the clean cut and shaven guards I am used to seeing around the castle. Dusty brown waves fall past his shoulders, the top pulled into a knot at the back of his head, as if he lazily tied it out of his way. Large amber eyes sit beneath full dark eyebrows, the same color as the bit of stubble along his sharp jaw and chin. As I scan his face, my eyes catch on a thick scar that cuts through his bottom lip.

I want to reach up and run my fingers over it.

"Are you alright?" He tilts his head and lowers his face to my level, trying to get my attention.

I quickly push the thoughts of touching this stranger's face away and clench my fists by my side. I can't help that I am completely distracted by him. He looks like a hero straight out of one of Tila's books.

"Yes, I'm sorry. I'm fine." I step back out of his hold and his arms drop to his sides.

"Let me get these for you." He crouches down and begins stacking the books scattered at our feet.

"Oh no, it's fine. I can get them." Now that I am out of his grasp, I can think clearly again. I crouch down as well, trying to beat him to it, hoping he doesn't notice the kinds of books I have gathered.

"I insist," he says as he rocks his weight back onto his heels, holding a neatly piled stack out in front of him. I hadn't been fast enough, too flustered from actually speaking to someone, let alone someone like him.

He smiles and I feel a flutter deep in my stomach.

Easy, Lennox. You don't even know this man.

"I'm Dane." He stands and extends his empty hand toward me. I reach out cautiously and shake it. That is what a normal person would do, right? Not be hesitant to touch someone who is being polite and offering their hand?

"Very nice to meet you, Dane." He pulls me up to stand in front of him, and I quickly withdraw my hand from his and take another step back. It's not a good idea to get too involved with anyone in the city, or someone may find out who I am. I can't take that risk, especially because I need to find an answer as soon as possible. I can't have any distractions. Maybe someday, after my mother is healed and I convince my father that I need to be involved with the people, I can find him again. Maybe then we can be friends.

But for now, he was kind after nearly plowing me over, so I can at least be cordial.

"And you are?"

I process his words. Again, something I didn't plan for. Why the fuck didn't I think I needed to come up with an identity? I shouldn't have rushed this. My emotions got the better of me, and just like Brynne always tells me, I can't strike with too much emotion. The same logic applies here.

"Oh, um," I stammer. I blurt out the first name that comes to mind, saying a small prayer that the one girl with this name who works in the castle isn't well known outside of it. "I'm Addy."

"Nice to meet you, Addy." Dane stares at me, waiting for a response, but my mind is blank. I don't know what to say. Silence hangs between us, neither of us moving, and I shift my weight back and forth on my feet uncomfortably. Is it obvious that I've never done this before? Never met someone new or even had to introduce myself?

Dane breaks the silence first. "Can I set these somewhere for you?" He lifts the books slightly, the motion drawing my attention to his arms. His tunic is tight over his chest and shoulders, and I can see the outline of muscle down his arms. I could tell he was strong from the way he held me steady, but now it was glaringly obvious.

And distracting.

Are you sure he's not a guard?

I don't recognize him at all, despite his body looking like he spends hours training in the rings like Brynne and the others. Maybe he works in the mills felling logs? Or maybe a blacksmith?

"Yes, thank you." I sneak a quick glance down at the hand that isn't occupied, still holding up my stack of books. There are definitely some calluses, but he seems too clean to be working outside all day. If he is a guard, he hasn't recognized me...yet.

"I think all the tables are full, but you are welcome to share mine." He gestures behind him with the stack, as if he read my mind.

"Oh, I don't want to take up your space—"

"It's no problem at all." He starts toward the table, and I follow closely behind him. The surface is already piled with a stack of books, and beside it, some parchment and vials of ink. After pushing some rogue papers out of the way, he sets my stack on the opposite end of the table and pulls the chair out for me.

"Thank you," I murmur as I sit. I scoot my chair closer to the table and feel it lighten underneath me. Glancing over my shoulder, I see Dane's large hands gripping the edges of my seat and helping me in.

I turn away quickly so he doesn't see the heat rise in my cheeks. Who is this man and why is he being so kind to me? Are all men outside the castle like this?

It's sad that my mind is immediately skeptical, believing he must have nefarious motivations, but I don't have a choice. It has been ingrained in me to assess the motivations of everyone I encounter. My position as future queen demands it. But is he just being kind?

I grab the book off the top of the stack, flipping to the table of contents and scanning the titles until I find one that I think might be useful. I hear Dane pull out his chair and sit on the other side of the table as I flip to the correct page.

It takes all of my willpower not to glance up at him. It's hard for me to believe that he can't see desire and curiosity all over my face. Dane is different from any man I've ever seen. His clothes look comfortable and warm, not like the cold royal outfits I am used to seeing guards wear. His face is rugged and intense, and he looks like he spends a lot of time working with his hands.

I push away the images that flash before my eyes of things he could do with his strong hands, things I'd only ever read about.

Gods Lennox, you just met this man. Control yourself.

I shift in my seat, crossing my legs, and try to focus back on the pages in front of me. There is no time to be thinking about a man I will probably never see again, especially when my mother's life is on the line. There are more important things than wondering what he does for a living, or why he is here in the library instead of home, with his family or wife.

Of course he has a wife. Look at him.

But more than the fact that he is extremely good looking, he is the only person outside of the castle that has spoken to me and was kind to me. I am not counting the helpful woman at the front desk. Such a simple act has shaken me so much that I am having trouble accomplishing what I came here for, focusing more on trying to avoid glancing across the table at him. While others would have brushed such a short and simple interaction off, it feels like a monumental shift in my life, like the axis of my world has tilted to the side and is shaking everything up.

I am outside of the castle for the first time in my life, talking to a man that I've never met, and no one knows.

I shouldn't be making friends. I should be focusing on finding something to help my mother.

I look toward the front of the library at the stained-glass windows on either side of the door. Still light, I haven't lost too much time to distraction.

I dip my head down closer to the text and read, scanning through a few sections, but find nothing different from the information in the castle library. The next few texts are the same, so I decide to switch to something handwritten, hoping maybe there would be different observations or ideas that might lead me in a different direction. I pick up the first journal and start flipping through, skimming the notes and descriptions.

Nothing.

A heavy sigh escapes me as I flip the book closed, a little more harshly than I expected.

Light always finds a way, even through the blackest woods.

I inhale deeply and reset my shoulders. I can find something. I will not get discouraged so quickly. I will not lose hope, even when I feel hopeless.

I shift the journal to the top of my finished pile and grab a new one. I lean in closer so I can focus and will myself to block out all the small noises and distractions around me. I don't know how much time has passed when a noise finally breaks my focus.

Dane clears his throat and shifts in the chair, which emits a small creak. I keep my eyes glued to the page, trying to find where I left off before his movement distracted me.

"Addy?"

It takes me a split second to remember that is my name before I look up and meet his gaze. "The library is closing. We should probably head out."

I glance around and sure enough, the entire room has emptied. More time had passed than I thought, and it was probably late.

Really late.

Shit.

I glance back at the front windows and can't see the design in the glass because of the darkness outside. I didn't intend to stay this late and risk someone checking in on me, only to find my rooms empty. It would most likely be Brynne, and if it was, I'd know the second I stepped out of the library. Guards would be everywhere, searching for me to drag me back behind locked doors.

But it is quiet. It doesn't sound like there are search parties scouring the streets.

"Okay," I say, my voice cracking with disuse, and probably because of the nerves coursing through my body. I stand quickly and stack the books into one pile. I need to put them away quickly, and my unfamiliarity with the shelves means it will take me a while.

"Are you going to keep all of those?" he says, as he fastens his cloak across his chest.

"I was just going to put them back." I incline my head back toward the healing shelves.

A look of confusion falls over his face. "Have you never been to this library before?"

Am I that obvious? I quickly try to think of reasons or explanations that might sound convincing, but the ones coming to me sound ridiculous. I decide to keep it simple and stick with the truth.

"I've actually only ever used the library in the castle. I didn't want to leave a mess on my first visit and cause a problem with the librarian." Or get noticed, but I'm not going to tell him that. I've already been noticed more than I wanted.

"It's alright. Agnes works at night once the library closes. Any texts that are left out, she sorts and puts away, so you can leave whatever you are done with on the table. The rest we can bring to her at the front, and she will hold them for you, for the next time you come back."

"Oh. That's convenient." It would save me a lot of time, not having to wander through the shelves again, trying to remember which texts I'd already looked through and which ones I hadn't.

He chuckles. "Yeah, it is, that is, if you plan to come back." I can't help but think that the look on his face is hopeful. Does he want me to come back? I feel a small flutter in my stomach at the thought.

"I do. Plan on it, that is." I planned on being here a lot, as much as I need to. I don't have time to waste, but that doesn't mean I can't enjoy his company if he is going to be here, too.

Dane's face breaks into a smile, and if I thought the quiet, serious man sitting across from me was beautiful, it pales in comparison to when he smiles.

I set the finished books back on the table and adjust the smaller stack in my arms. "I'm not finished with these, and there are still another couple of shelves I haven't gotten to."

"Here, let me carry those for you." He reaches out and takes the books out of my hands, his fingertips brushing mine as he lifts the stack. My first reaction is to snatch my hands away from his. Easy physical contact between people is foreign to me, as no one touches the princess. But I also don't need him carrying my things. I get enough of that in the castle. I don't need anyone fawning over me out here. I'm not Princess Lennox in this library.

"I can carry them," I huff as I awkwardly reach toward the stack, trying my best not to touch him again. I also don't want him seeing what I'm looking for.

"It's alright, I've got them." He takes a few steps toward the front desk and pauses, waiting for me to catch up. "You can let me help you. I won't bite." The ends of his lips curl up slightly, and I bite my lip, trying to hide my smile.

I am not used to someone helping me just because they want to. I've been surrounded by staff my whole life, and while I appreciate everything they do for me and for the kingdom, in the end, it's their job. They aren't acting out of the goodness of their hearts, like Dane seems to be.

Except for Tila and Edmond. I believe they stick around because they truly care, and it is more than just a job to them. Even Brynne's position is out of duty and honor, together with her desire to be the First Guard. I know she cares for me and would do anything to protect me, and I love her for it, but if she could protect my father instead, she would.

"I'm sorry. I'm not used to people helping me. I don't want you to think I can't do something on my own." I quickly catch up to him and we fall into stride, heading toward the front desk.

"Why would I ever think that? I have no doubt you could do whatever you set your mind to."

I shake my head in disbelief. "How would you know that? You don't even know me."

His face breaks out into a slow grin.

"Oh, don't worry. I know exactly who you are."

CHAPTER NINE

My body jerks to a halt and I stare after him in complete shock. How did this happen? What gave me away? Have I been putting on this charade, and he knew who I was from the moment I bumped into him?

"How did you know?" I say, trying my best to keep the panic out of my voice.

He stops and turns back to me, realizing that I am no longer alongside him.

"It wasn't that difficult. If you were trying to hide it, you did a terrible job."

Fuck.

I need to do damage control. I hadn't expected anyone to figure me out at all, let alone this quickly. Would it be better to just come clean, or to ask for his silence? I straighten my shoulders and lift my chin, trying to let my years of lessons take over and hide the fear coursing through my body.

"I ask that you keep this between us." My gaze meets his and I hold it, unblinking. I need him to know that I'm serious. My identity cannot get out, and news of this can't get back to my father. I'm not sure how he figured me out, but that doesn't matter now. He knows, and he needs to keep quiet.

"Why would I keep it between us?" He takes a few steps toward me, slowly closing the gap, his movements reminding me of the castle cats hunting their prey. "I think it is something you would want people to know."

"I don't," I say, my words harsh even to my own ears. He is inches away from me now, so close that my heaving chest can almost touch him. He towers over me, and I have to crane my neck to maintain our eye contact to show him I am serious.

"I think it is information that the people back at the castle would find valuable, don't you think?" There's a gleam in his eye that sets off unease in my stomach.

"That can't happen," I grind out. I am ready to bribe him if need be. Is a bribe what he was looking for the entire time? Was he being kind to lure me in, and then turning on me for his own profit? I open my mouth, ready to ask him what he wants when his face softens.

He dips his head down, bringing his face closer to mine, and his voice drops into a soft murmur. "Why wouldn't you want anyone at the castle knowing what an amazingly dedicated and hard worker they have?"

I snap my mouth shut.

Oh. *Oh.*

"Excuse me?" I need him to keep talking, to give me an explanation.

He gestures at my staff clothing with his free hand. "You're here after a full day's work at the castle, clearly doing some research in the healing section." He lifts the stack of books he is carrying for me, and his tone changes to almost playful. "Now, I've never worked at the castle, but I can assume your job doesn't start late in the day. I would think the kingdom would be happy to know what kind of person they have working for them. You're clearly someone who is trying to better themselves and move up in the ranks."

The panic in me starts to subside. I was wrong. He doesn't know who I am. I'm flooded with relief, but still need to back my way out of this. I know I came off defensive, and I don't want him to pick up on it and start questioning who I actually am.

I cross my arms over my chest and try my best to give him a coy smile. "I beg your pardon, *sir*, but if I didn't know better, I would think you were studying me more than your books."

"Maybe a little," he says with a smirk.

I look away to distract myself from the discomfort his words give me, but feel a flutter of thrill deep inside my stomach. Is this what flirting feels like? Is Dane flirting with me?

If he only knew *who* he was flirting with.

I glance around the library and realize we're alone, the only ones left in the large room except for a woman, I assume, is Agnes, standing at the front desk.

"I think we should probably go. We're the only ones here."

He glances around, taking in the same empty room. "I guess I got distracted. Let's go before Agnes gets upset with us."

At the desk, Dane sets the stack of books down and gives Agnes our names to hold them under. Once they are tucked away, she bids us a good night and we turn toward the front door. I pull my hood up over my head, although not as low over my face as it was when I first left the castle.

At the top of the steps, I stop and take in the city's calm. There's no sign of guards frantically searching for me. Brynne isn't wandering the streets, kicking in doors. Music and laughter echo through the mist covered streets, likely from the taverns and businesses still open this late. The liveliness brings a small smile to my face.

I want to see it. I want to see more of it than just the library and the fronts of the buildings in passing as I walk through the streets. I want to experience the people, the culture of our city and kingdom, not just read about it or hear stories from Edmond.

Maybe one day.

Dane stops alongside me. "It is late and dark already. I will escort you back to the castle."

"Thank you, but I will be alright."

"There's no way I am letting a beautiful girl walk home alone this late at night. Besides, I wasn't asking permission." He extends his arm toward me, waiting for me to take it.

I start at his words. I know objectively my looks are appealing, but beautiful? No one has ever muttered that word describing me except for Tila, and I always thought she used it to refer to her work and contributions toward my looks. Beauty was never important, only the skills required to be a successful queen. I wasn't sure the princes and nobles from other kingdoms coming to my birthday ball would even care about beauty when trying to seek an alliance and betrothal.

I don't know how to respond, so I blurt out the first thing that comes to my mind. "I'll be fine, really. I'm sure your wife will be worried if you get back too late."

He chuckles softly as he shakes his head. "No, she won't worry."

My head snaps to look at him. He actually has a wife?

What an asshole. Flirting with me all evening, while he has a family waiting for him at home.

He drops the arm that he's had extended and turns to face me. His eyebrow quirked and a small smile hints at his lips. "There would have to be a wife in order for her to worry. My sister might, though."

Sister. Not wife.

So, he's not an asshole. The amount of relief I feel at that revelation is…distracting. And I am not one to get distracted. I can debate war tactics with Edmond, recite poetry and quote literature. I can fight. But Dane distracts me. His beautiful eyes and sharp jaw should not be my focus at all. I need to focus on getting back to the castle unseen.

"Let's just go." I start down the stairs and hear a small chuckle followed by footsteps behind me.

I wrap my cloak tighter around me, the chill and moisture in the air so different from what I am used to in the castle. Dane catches up to me in a few strides, but I don't slow down.

The Blackwood trees tower over the structures, casting darkness and shadows everywhere. Fog seeps through the trees, billowing over the tops of the buildings. The only light that breaks through glows around the lanterns and the torches lit, marking the doors to the establishment.

It feels eerie, being out here this late. I know the city streets, but walking down them in the dark feels different. I suddenly am aware of how vulnerable I am, and a shudder works through my body.

"Too cold outside of the castle?" Dane says.

"That, among other things." Despite thinking he was an asshole looking to cheat on his wife a few minutes ago, I'm suddenly grateful that Dane is here.

Making a friend wasn't my goal for the evening, but maybe it wouldn't harm me to have one. I've wanted friends outside the castle walls my entire life, and Dane seems like he is interested in being friends with me, too. It would definitely make me feel more comfortable having someone to walk home with at night.

"I tend to run warm." He extends his arm toward me again and eyes me expectantly.

My gaze trails over his arm, remembering the lines of muscle that were visible through his shirt, now hidden by his thick cloak.

I wrap my arm around his, remembering my royal manners and keeping our arms linked exactly how I had been taught as a young girl. Despite the formal posture and extreme focus, every inch of my arm in contact with Dane is tingling with energy. I feel his warmth even through layers of fabric. No one inside the castle has ever touched me as easily as he does.

We continue walking, silence heavy between us, neither of us acknowledging our closeness or the last bits of our conversation.

Is this what it feels like to be normal? To be a woman escorted home by a man, where any physical contact didn't spur talks of alliances and betrothals? To just be free to do what I want, when I want?

"I haven't seen you around before," he says, finally breaking the silence. "Are you from Blackwood or from another kingdom?"

I need to keep this conversation general and stick to truths where I can. Too many lies might make him suspicious, especially if I get caught up in them.

"I've lived here my whole life, but I don't get out much."

"What made you come out tonight?"

I think back to the lie I told the librarian. I don't know how well Dane knows her, so I need to stay consistent. "I want to become a healer, so I've been working to build my knowledge. I've read mostly everything in the castle over my years working there, so I decided to see if there was anything more before I pursue it."

"Sounds like you'll make a great healer if you are willing to seek out more knowledge like that. A lot of them seem to be very stuck in their ways, at least the ones that I've interacted with."

"Thank you," I murmur. I don't disagree with him. After overhearing the conversation with the castle healer and my father, I couldn't help but feel that they weren't seeking out any new information. They gave up and told him it was time to let go.

I don't want to accept that, not after the gift Edmond gave me.

I try to turn the conversation away from me. "What about you? What brings you to the library?"

"I'm doing some healing research as well." I see him sneak a glance at me out of the corner of my eye, but keep my eyes trained on the road before us. "There aren't normally many people in that section of the library, so I wasn't expecting you to come around the corner. I apologize again for bumping into you. You seemed startled."

"I was startled," I chuckle, glancing over at him. "Look at you. You basically plowed me over."

His head falls back with a loud laugh, the sound infectious and bringing a smile to my face. "At least neither you nor the books were damaged in the process."

"We were not. Luckily for you." I smirk up at him and make eye contact briefly but turn away. What felt like a long walk to the library is flying by on the way home, probably from the distraction of his arm still wrapped in mine. I can already see the stone of the castle walls just ahead, and the guards in front of the gate I came through earlier.

I break my hold and pull away from Dane's arm, reaching up to pull the hood down farther over my face. I don't want to risk getting too close and having someone recognize me.

"Thank you for walking me home. I very much appreciate it," I say. "I don't want to keep you too long from your sister."

"Yes, I should be getting back to her. I hope to see you again Addy." He grins at me, and I feel something in my chest clench.

He wants to see me again. How has this night turned from the most intense and nerve-wracking to the most exciting night of my life?

"I will try to come in the evenings after work, but it depends. Hopefully I will see you again too." I give him a small curtsey and turn toward the castle, walking quickly with my head down so I don't catch anyone's eye.

"Evening miss. Glad to see you had someone escort you back," the guard says as he unlatches the lock on the gate.

"Yes, it was very kind of him," I reply.

"Have a good night, miss," he says with a nod. I curtsey before heading straight for the kitchen. The castle is quiet now, and I weave through the stairs and halls without running into another person before finally making it back to my rooms.

This almost feels too easy. Has leaving been this easy the entire time? Have I been so groomed to listen to what I was told and never try to do anything for myself that I sat locked in this castle when it was so easy to leave? Had all this suffering and isolation not actually been at the hands of my father, but my doing, because I was not strong enough to stand up and do something for myself?

That will not be me any longer. I am going to do what I want now. No one had noticed I was gone, so there would be no one to stop me. I will go out again, and I will find what I'm looking for.

Who knows, maybe I'll even find who I've been looking for, too.

CHAPTER TEN

I have left the castle and gone to the library almost every day this week, and not one person has noticed.

On the days I did not train with Brynne, I spent the evenings pouring through pages of texts. I paid extra attention to the time, ensuring I did not stay as late as the first night because I didn't have anyone to walk me home.

Dane hadn't shown up at all.

I was kidding myself if I said I hadn't expected he would. He said he hoped to see me, so why was he the one who didn't show?

Estelle, the woman who works at the front desk, grew to recognize and expect me in the evenings. Both she and Agnes became more and more friendly, suggesting different volumes to help me with my studies. They didn't know I was looking for something in particular and everything they suggested was nowhere near as specific as I needed, but I thanked them anyway.

Despite all of my effort, I am still coming up empty-handed.

And it is extremely frustrating.

There has to be *something*. Anything. Even just a sentence that hints at something new the healers can try. When I thought I finally found a set of documents from a healer that looked promising, it ended as expected. The patient never woke up, and no treatments were successful.

Any mention of unconscious patients always turned out the same, and it was always noted that nothing more could be tried. The only promising piece of information that gave me some hope was the length of sleep. Most patients hadn't lived more than a year or two after falling into the unconscious state.

My mother has been asleep for almost twenty-one years.

That has to mean something, that she was meant to come back to me. Whatever was going on in her mind that we could not see, she was fighting to stay here.

I need to find a way to bring her out of it, some type of plant or tincture that can wake her. There has to be another case where someone recovered from this. I just need to keep searching.

I'm not giving up.

I leave the castle earlier today so I can explore a bit more of the city. I don't want to waste the little researching time I have, but I also want to stretch my legs and observe, not just rush to the library. The guards barely even pay attention to my coming and going now, only politely greeting me each time I pass through the gate.

I try to take a new route every day to soak in as much of the surroundings as I can. The more I see of the city, the more I love it, and the more I resent my father for not letting me grow up in it. It is full of life and our unique Blackwood culture, and I don't feel like it is part of me, even though I am supposed to rule over it.

There is only so much I can learn about it by reading or from my lessons. I want to experience it, to really feel it. I want to talk to the people, see the art and the architecture. I want to go out into our forests, deep into the beautiful black woods that gave us our name. I want to see the villages and experience the mills that bring us our wealth.

Today I decide to pass through an older part of the city where the older structures still stand while newer ones were built around them. The buildings here are clearly different, the size and texture of the stones much smaller and smoother from years of the weathering and moisture in the air. Dark leaf covered vines grow up the sides of many walls, making the passages between the buildings even darker than others.

I wander through the alleys, nodding a hello to the occasional person passing through, but never stop to talk to anyone I come across. I finally decide to head back toward the library when I pass an opening to a small alley. A structure further in catches my eye and I stop, peering into the dim lighting.

The narrow alley widens around the structure, as if the buildings were built around it. I take a step closer, just inside the pathway, my curiosity making me forget my goal of getting back to the library.

It looks like a fountain, the light carved stone completely different from the buildings that surround it. I pause and listen, trying to pick up any sound of flowing water, but I hear nothing. My eyes snag on the chips and chunks taken out of the pool that surrounds it. Time has not been kind to it, with the damage and lack of water flow. It must have been here for ages.

I try to make out the carvings on the structure that stands tall from the center of the pool, but with the low lighting and mist filling the alley, I can't quite see. It won't take me too long to see what it is, at least while the sun hasn't set. I take another step into the alley when a low voice startles me to a stop.

"Fancy seeing you here."

I spin around quickly, clutching my chest and facing the entrance to the alley. A tall, broad figure completely blocks the entrance, trapping me inside the alley alone. Shadows cover his face, but the flutter in my stomach tells me I don't need to be afraid.

Despite only hearing it once before, I recognize his voice. It shouldn't be hard. He's the only person besides Agnes and Estelle outside of the castle that I know.

"Dane, hi." I smile at him as he steps out of the shadows and all thoughts of heading farther into the alley are gone. "You startled me. I didn't hear anyone come up behind me."

He crosses his arms over his chest and leans his shoulder into the stone wall. "I wasn't expecting to see you this far away from the library. What are you doing all the way out here?"

"Just exploring. I don't get a lot of time out of the castle, so I was making use of it."

He tilts his head and eyes me warily. "I thought you grew up here. Don't you know the city?"

"I did," I stammer. "I mean, I grew up in Blackwood, but not inside the city. I lived in Vorley. Have you heard of it? It's a small village close to the border we share with Portlin." I mentally thank Edmond for all the geography lessons and my father for insisting that I know all the cities and villages in the kingdom. "Once I moved into the castle, I didn't really have time to explore the city, so I'm trying to do that a little more now."

"Well then." He pushes himself off the wall and towers over me, a smile making his face light up. "It seems like you need an introduction to some of the fine establishments we have here."

"Maybe some time," I say. "Are you heading to the library as well? We could walk together. I haven't seen you there in the last few days." It feels so forward to say, but if he notices my discomfort, he doesn't seem to mind.

"I apologize. My responsibilities have called me away, but I spoke with Estelle. She said you have been doing more research."

"Yes, but I still have a lot of work to do. I should be on my way." I drop into a small curtsey and lower my face to hide the disappointment I am feeling. "It was nice seeing you again, Dane." I take a step toward his side, trying to squeeze past him and through the opening, but he slides in front of me and blocks my path.

"Wait." He reaches up and grasps my shoulders, holding me out in front of him. I feel a rush of excitement at his touch, the heat from his hands boring through my cloak. I raise my eyes to look into his and lift a brow, waiting for him to say something more.

"How about you take one night off? Just one. You've been working so hard, and I could help show you some of the town. I could show you my favorite tavern. They have great food if you ever need a place to eat in the future."

His rambling brings heat to my cheeks despite the increasing cold coming on with the setting of the sun.

He doesn't want me to leave.

I don't want to leave.

But I have more work to do and can't afford to lose a night of research and stall my progress. I'm pushing my luck taking so long. I bite my lip, thinking hard to come up with a way to say no, even though my body is screaming for me to agree.

"Please?" He leans down to my level and meeting my eye, a sort of shyness taking over his features. I feel his hands give my shoulders a slight squeeze, and feel my resolve disappear with the motion.

"Alright," I say. "But let's hurry, so I can still get some work done after."

His face breaks into a huge grin that I can't help but return.

"Deal."

CHAPTER
ELEVEN

oise and heat hit me like a wall as Dane opens the thick wooden door to the tavern a few blocks from the library. The boisterous voices of everyone enjoying their food and drinks ring throughout the large room.

Bodies are packed into the bar, and the tables are full two or three times over. Women are sitting on the laps of men, and there are card games with players sitting shoulder to shoulder. The servers behind the crowds of people call out for orders and chat with the customers. The occasional one weaves through the bodies to place food and drinks on tables.

I don't move from the entrance as I take in the whole scene. I've never seen this many people in one place, the closest being the training fields, and those are all soldiers. The commotion surrounds me, making it a little hard to breathe. Maybe it was a bad idea to say yes.

Dane looks around the room, searching for a free seat. He leans down, speaking directly into my ear so I don't have to strain to hear him over the sounds from the room. "There's an open table in the back."

The brush of his breath on my ear sends a shiver through me, and I bite my lip, trying to hide it. I force my face to stay neutral and nod as he straightens and points toward the table.

Dane takes my hand and starts toward the back of the room, weaving us through the tables and full chairs, dodging servers as they pass in front of us with plates and mugs balanced in their hands. We reach the back corner, which has a small table and two well-worn seats. It is amazing that he saw it. I gently pull my hand from his before I unclasp my cloak and slide into a seat.

"I'm going to order us some food," Dane says, gesturing toward the bar behind him. "Don't go anywhere or someone will take the table. I'll be right back." He smiles, and I return it before he turns and strides away, weaving through the tables toward the bar.

I glance around the room, observing the variety of people. Everyone seems so happy and well acquainted. The women serving food and drinks are laughing and smiling at the customers, talking with them like they know them personally. Maybe they do. I don't know anyone in this room other than Dane, but the more I sit and watch, the more I feel like I could strike up a conversation.

I won't. I can't risk it. But seeing more of the people makes me understand why my father had spent so much time outside of the castle.

I turn back to the table at the sound of Dane's chair scraping across the floor.

"Food will be here shortly," he says. "In the meantime, here's something to drink." He slides a large wooden mug in front of me, steam rising from the top.

"Thank you." I smile and raise it to my lips, taking a small sip. Spices and a touch of sweetness roll over my tongue, followed by the kick of hard alcohol. I clear my throat, nearly choking on the strength of the drink, but instantly feel myself relax. I have no idea what this is, but it is delicious. I need to be careful. Too much and I'll probably end up spilling all my secrets.

"So, a healer, huh?" Dane leans forward, crossing his arms on the table and gazes intently at my face. "Are you already an apprentice? Or do you do something else at the castle?"

"Not yet. I'm hoping to be soon though. I'm a maid currently," I lie. His face falls slightly. "Damn."

"What?" I'm unsure how being a maid could cause him disappointment. Was a maid not a good enough profession? The castle treated our maids very well, and most of them stayed on for years once they were employed.

"Honestly, I was hoping you might be able to help me with your access to the healers and medicine at the castle."

I look down into my mug and try to fight back a flinch at his words. Is he actually interested in being friends, or is he just looking to use me for my connections at the castle?

"Sorry to disappoint you," I say, my voice flat as I play with the handle of the mug.

"Hey." He reaches his hand across the table and stills the mug. "It's not a disappointment. I just thought I'd ask." He pulls his hands back and crosses his arms again.

Maybe he isn't taking advantage of my connections. My lie just aligns with something he needs. With as much as I have read on healing across the kingdoms, I know a lot more than the average person.

I probably could help him.

"Well, I have read a lot." I lean forward on the table, crossing my arms to match his. "Try me." I don't mean for that to come out sounding like a challenge, but it does anyway. I see a tiny glimmer in his eye like he thinks it too and accepts it.

"On second thought," he says as he reaches out to take a swig of his drink. "I'm not sure I can trust you. Something tells me you're not being completely honest with me."

I hold his gaze and fix my face into a look of indifference. "And what makes you say that?"

His lips shift into a pout, and I glance down at them before

looking back up again. He is trying to hold back a laugh. He seems…
competitive. No one besides Brynne has ever been competitive with me,
and I kind of like it. It feels normal.

Real.

"Call it intuition." His eyes twinkle as the corners of his mouth turn up.

"Or maybe it's because you don't even know me."

"Maybe." Now he fully smirks, and I'm back to feeling that he is
flirting with me.

"Well, I guess you aren't getting my help then." I pick up my drink,
leaning back in my seat and taking another swig. I swallow hard and the
burn forces me to let out a hot breath.

Dane chuckles, now the one to play with his mug, twirling it around
in a circle, balancing the edge on the table. I keep watching, waiting for
it to spill.

He keeps his eyes focused on his drink as he speaks. "I ran into you in
the healing section of the library because I'm doing research, too. Not to
become a healer, but for my sister. She's sick, and no one can figure out
why. She's already made it much longer than anyone thought, but nothing
is helping. I don't know how much longer she is going to live."

"I'm sorry," I say, my tone suddenly serious. I'm not trying to make
light of his situation, however easy it is to play games with him. It's clear
that his sister's illness is taking a toll on him, which is why he is working
to find an answer.

We have that in common.

I wish I could tell him.

"It's alright," he says, finally raising his eyes to meet mine. "There's
no way you could have known."

I lean forward and set the mug back down on the table. "Tell me what
she is suffering from. Maybe I've run across something in my studies that
might help." He doesn't need to know the extent of my knowledge from
Edmond. Maybe there's something simple he is missing. "How long ago
did it start?"

"Oh, I don't know." He blows a breath through his lips as he leans back in his chair. "I think it's been a few years now? Maybe longer since we started noticing things. She has good days and bad days, but she is younger than me, and looks so old and frail. She is weak and has trouble walking. No appetite most days, but she eats enough to stay alive. She is still as smart as ever, it's just as if her body is failing her."

"I'm so sorry," I say again, feeling the need to comfort him. Even with my knowledge, I can't pinpoint something specific based on his description, and can see why the healers are having difficulty treating her. It must be awful watching his sister deteriorate like that. "What have you tried?"

"It feels like everything. She never had a cough or any illness like that. We thought it may have been something she caught from a tradesperson coming to Blackwood from another kingdom, but it never went away and no one else ever got sick. I don't know what more to do. I don't want to lose my sister."

His lips tighten into a line and a muscle in his jaw flickers. I can tell he loves her very much, and it is hard for him to think about losing her. I know the feeling.

"When was the last time she saw a healer?"

"Last month. They stop in to check on her at least once a month, but she has been unchanged. They've tried everything and said nothing more can be done."

A knot forms in my throat, and I try to swallow it away. He really has no idea how similar our situations are, and it is taking everything I have not to tell him.

"There's got to be some herbs or tonics at the castle we can try." My voice cracks and I clear it quickly. While I know some of what he is feeling, I also wish I had someone who cares about me the way Dane cares about his sister. I never had siblings, and maybe I never would, even if my mother had lived. I can't help but feel after reading her diary that she would have wanted more children. My life would have been completely different.

"Please, don't worry." He reaches forward and places his hand over mine on the table. "I don't want you to jeopardize your chance to become a healer by trying to take something for me."

"It will be fine," I say, my fingers twitching under the pressure of his. No one would even question it.

"Sometimes I wish there was something that could just make her illness disappear."

I sit up a little straighter, my mind immediately racing to Edmond's story. Is he implying what I think he is? I nod quietly, waiting to see if I'm just imagining the reference.

Dane sits silently for a moment, his eyes glinting in the dim light. "Have you ever heard—"

He stops suddenly and sits up straight as a server walks up to the side of our table and sets plates of steaming food in front of us.

"Here you go Dane," she says, batting her eyelashes, her eyes never straying from his face.

"Thank you, Emilie." He smiles at her, an air of familiarity between them. I ignore the uncomfortable feeling deep in my gut. Is that jealousy? I've never had anything or anyone to be jealous of before, and I don't like it.

"You just come find me if you need *anything* else," she says with a small squeeze of his shoulder. She eyes me up and down, narrowing her gaze before turning on her heel and striding away.

Yep, definitely don't like her.

I scowl at the back of her head as she walks away. Dane's low chuckle brings my attention back to him.

"Thank you for the food. I, uh, don't have any money right now, but I can bring some next time I come into the city to pay you back."

He waves a hand at me, brushing off my words before leaning forward on his crossed arms again. "It's my pleasure."

We fall into silence as the scents of the roasted chicken and potatoes waft over us. I pick up the cutlery Emilie dropped off with our plates and start cutting off a piece of chicken. "So, what was it you were saying before?" I pop the bite into my mouth and almost groan. I can see why Dane says this is his favorite tavern, at least, hopefully it is for the food and not for the enthusiastic servers.

He pushes his plate to the side as he leans farther over the table and beckons me closer with a flick of his fingers. I lean over my plate, our faces mere inches apart.

His voice is low and secretive, and I can barely hear him over the roar of the tavern.

"Have you ever heard of a land called Dawnlin?" His eyes search my face, but I try not to react.

"I've heard of it." I tilt my head, showing my surprise at the question. "Don't tell me that is what you are searching for in the library."

He chuckles and leans back slightly. "No. I *am* actually reading the texts, hoping to find some way to help her. But the longer I go on without answers while my sister continues to suffer, I can't help but wish for something else. Something that would save her."

I shake my head, my voice lowered to match his. "It's not real, Dane. Magic isn't real. The story just gives people hope that something might help. It just makes it easier to watch them suffer, hoping that magic might fix it all in the end." I pause. "But it hurts that much worse when it doesn't happen."

"Spoken like a true healer."

"I'm just being logical!" I say with a laugh. "Don't you think that if it were real, we'd know more about it? How to get there? Wouldn't there be people lining up to get this magic potion to fix anything and everything?"

His face lights up with pure excitement, like he has been waiting to talk about this with someone. "What about all the stories of miraculous recoveries? No explanation, and no one in the family knew what happened. Not even the healers could explain it."

"That's what doesn't make sense! Why wouldn't the family know? Someone would have had to get this elixir for them. They can't just keep it a secret from the entire kingdom, or world for that matter."

"Maybe they're really good at keeping secrets."

"Or maybe it's just made up."

"Then what is your explanation for all the cases where people have recovered with no help from the healers?"

"I don't know, but it's not magic. It has to be something our healers just haven't discovered yet."

"Oh, come on." He scoffs and leans back in his seat. "Why don't you believe?"

"Because it isn't logical," I say, shifting to sit back as well. "It doesn't make sense that there is a magical land that has a magical drink that fixes any problem, no matter what. If this is true, why are there still sick people? Who determines who gets cured and who doesn't? There are too many questionable issues for it to be real. How do you get it? How do you get there? What—"

He interrupts me. "With the Guardian, of course."

I roll my eyes. "Okay, sure, 'the Guardian.'" He cracks a smile at my singsong voice. I know I voiced my doubt with Edmond, but talking to Dane about it feels different. It feels like a fun and playful conversation with a friend, not a lesson.

"Fine, fine. Don't believe." He throws his hands up in the air in mock exasperation. "I was just asking."

"Sorry, I'm not trying to make fun." It is easy to be myself with him, to really feel like the true Lennox instead of the princess act I have to put on in the castle. He's as easy to talk to as Brynne. I barely know him, but there's something about him that makes me feel so comfortable that I forget he doesn't really know me either.

I don't want him to think I am rude or laughing at him for what he believes, so I continue. "I just prefer to focus on real solutions. I don't want to sit around and just hope. I want to do something that will fix it."

He raises an eyebrow. "What if it's not just hope?"

I raise one back. "What if it is?"

"I thought you were just studying to be a healer?"

"I am."

His grin turns sly as he searches my face. "Then what is it you need to fix?"

Shit.

"It was a general it, not a specific it." I keep my face trained. I may have let that slip, but that's all he's getting. My heart races with the lie and I breathe in slowly through my nose, trying to slow it down.

He eyes me, like he is trying to read what I am hiding. "Alright, alright, keep your secrets." He glances across the room at the front windows of the tavern. "Looks like there's still some light out. We can still get some work done if we hurry. Are you finished?" He gestures to my plate.

"Yes, thank you." I take another sip of the drink and cough, and Dane's loud laugh echoes in the room, mixing with the rest of the noise. I run my sleeve across my mouth, wiping up any of the drink I may have choked out.

Not very ladylike, Lennox.

"Don't laugh. It's good, just very strong."

"I take it they don't serve drinks like that at the castle?"

"No, they most definitely do not." I stand and wrap my cloak around my shoulders, fastening it in front while Dane leaves a few coins on the table for the server, who has been watching us this entire time.

"After you," he says, gesturing toward the door. I lead the way, weaving through the tables and chairs, and past Emilie waving from behind the bar. I look around the room one more time and feel the longing in my chest to truly be part of this one day. In a few days, once I am old enough to rule, Father won't be able to stop me.

CHAPTER TWELVE

ane and I weave our way through a mostly empty library as we head toward what has quickly become my table. After setting our things up and settling ourselves in, we get back to work so as not to waste the little time we have.

I scan through pages, reading more in depth the ones I find promising, but just as before, it is another night of building frustration as I come up with nothing.

I slam the book closed with a huff and drop it on top of my discard pile.

Dane looks up at me from across the table and mouths, "Are you alright?"

I nod quickly and stand, silently groaning at the painful stretch after sitting hunched over and focused for so long. I gesture to the other side of the library and whisper, "Need a break."

He nods and looks back down at the page he was reading. I start toward the back of the room, hoping some movement will clear my head.

I take in all the murals painted on the walls and wonder how long they have been there. The colors get brighter and the images start to look less realistic the closer I get to the children's section. The details are beautiful and intricate, and I even recognize some stories Edmond read to me growing up. The memory brings a smile to my face. I walk through the shelves and let myself be swept away in the memory instead of focusing on the stress of my mother's time dwindling.

"Straying from your typical reading tonight?"

I startle, and turn to find Estelle standing behind me, holding a small stack of children's books.

"Oh, no, not really. I just needed a little break."

Her smile is kind. "Stories are a great way to clear the mind after lots of hard work. I could help you find something if you'd like." She gestures to the shelves with the stack in her hands.

I am about to tell her no when something stops me. I can't help but feel the story nagging at me, popping up in the back of my mind.

What if I am not actually doing the research I need to be doing? A lesson that Edmond always made sure I didn't forget was to be a good leader, you have to see everything from all sides, take in as much information that you can, and then make your decision. I needed to see the entire picture.

"Actually," I say, turning to face her. "Maybe you can help me."

I'd gone my entire life hearing nothing of this mythical place, but Dawnlin has now been brought up to me twice. Am I making a mistake ignoring it, not looking into it? If it is a story that actually represents a real place with better tonics and salves, or more advanced healers, then it could be worth finding. The only way to know is to get more information, and if it isn't true and this place doesn't exist, I will have more to prove that this is just a myth and settle it once and for all.

"Are there any story books that have the myth about Dawnlin? I was told the story recently and wanted to read it for myself."

"I believe we have one or two." She waves for me to follow her as she heads down the aisle of children's books. "That is a very old story, and there aren't many places where it is written down. I remember hearing it as a child." She crouches down and runs her fingers across the spines before pulling out a small, very brittle looking book. She hands it to me and moves farther down the aisle before selecting a larger book that looks just as old.

"These are the two I know at least mention the story. I can check with Agnes when she comes in and see if there are any others she knows of."

"Oh no, these are perfect. Thank you, Estelle."

"My pleasure," she smiles. "You know where to find me should you need help with something else." She hands me the books and walks back down the aisle, placing a book from her stack back on the shelf as she goes.

I'm not trying to hide these from Dane, but I also don't want him catching me reading them either, especially not after the conversation in the tavern. I need to read them. Maybe finally getting the full story will help put an end to this myth distraction. I need to focus on actual information, not hope from a children's book.

I find an empty window seat and plop down on the fluffy, colorful pillows. I wish my room had something like this because I would spend every spare minute in it. I curl my legs under me and pick up the larger book.

The brown leather cover is worn down at the edges, having had its fair share of readers over the years. I hope whatever is inside will give me what I need.

Opening it to the first page, my eyes dance over the swirled handwritten script. I flip through the pages, my focus catching on colorful sketches and pages of written words. There have to be at least thirty stories in here.

I would have loved this book as a child.

Turning back to the table of contents, I scan it quickly, hoping what I need jumps out at me. I start to question Estelle's memory until a title at the bottom of the list catches my eye.

Finally, someone who knows books as well as Edmond.

The Island Draught.

This has to be it. I flip to the right page and see that there is very little writing, and absolutely no sketches. I scan the words spanning only two pages, but it is almost the same as the story Edmond shared with me. If this is the only information I have to go on, I could feel confident killing the idea once and for all.

I close the book, setting it down on the seat beside me and open the next one.

I turn the pages more slowly, taking my time with the delicate paper. This book is so old, it feels like it is going to fall apart in my hands. There is no table of contents in this one, so instead I turn every page, reading the titles and hoping Estelle was right again.

This text is much more designed for children than the last, each page illustrated with faded color drawings. There's far less written in this one, and some have no words at all.

I turn another page and my breath catches in my throat.

Finding Dawnlin.

Yes. This is it. Maybe this has the answers I am looking for. Maybe this will point me in the right direction and tell me where to find this land of advanced healers. My eyes scan the spread, searching for the story, but am stunned to find that there are no words.

Instead, the story is told in the pictures. My eyes eat them up, trying to take in every detail. Hopefully there is a map, or some clue I can use to find Dawnlin on the maps in the castle.

The first picture is of a child kneeling next to the bed of what looks like a sick parent. The child has tears running down his face, but is looking up at a healer, hope written across his features. But the healer looks solemn.

My heart breaks for this poor fictional child. I know the feeling that comes with being told there is nothing left to do for a parent, and realizing you will lose them.

I blink rapidly and turn the page to find the child on one side, walking through the streets of his town, tears still streaming down his face. On the other, a hooded man is kneeling in front of him, speaking to the boy and reaching out to take the child's hand.

Is that The Guardian?

I turn the page again and the scene is completely different, lighter. The child is running and playing with his healthy father, while a hooded figure watches off in the distance.

I flip the next page, holding my breath and hoping for some text, but my eyes meet the title of the next story.

I quickly turn back and stare at the last page.

That's it? There's nothing else? No directions, or hints even? How the hell is this story about finding Dawnlin at all? I check the seams to see if any pages had been removed, but the binding is completely intact, and there is no evidence of any torn edges.

I stare at both the books in disbelief. This can't be the only evidence of Dawnlin in the entire kingdom. These few pages and faded sketches are the only pieces of information to lead anyone to the myth.

My disbelief morphs into anger.

What a terrible thing to do, to give hope that the story actually could be true enough to be written and saved for years, only to leave the reader expecting a magical hooded person will show up and whisk them away to the magical healing solution. But there's no evidence of how, or what actually happens, only a requirement to blindly trust?

No.

There has to be something I missed.

I can feel my tether of hope pulled tight and ready to snap at any moment.

Laying the books side by side, I flip both to the beginning of the stories. I scan the text of the first, looking for any hints or patterns in the writing, anything that can be turned into a code or cipher, but come up with nothing. I look more closely at the sketches, analyzing every detail, trying to find anything hidden or some elements that could point to directions or a map.

Nothing.

I flip through the pages almost a hundred times as I sit there analyzing every little detail, trying to find *something*.

That is it.

There is nothing here.

I fall back, my head hitting the wall behind me and let out a frustrated sigh. Pain shoots through my neck as I move, sore from hunching over for so long.

Wait a second.

An image flashes before my eyes, and I bolt upright. I grab the picture book and flip to the page with the crying boy. My heart pounds in my ears as I take in what I had missed before.

There.

Behind the crying boy walking through an old city is a tiny structure, a fountain, overflowing with water.

I draw the book closer, trying to make out more details.

It looks so familiar, almost like the one I had just stumbled upon earlier today. That one looked decrepit and broken, and this one looked beautiful and new. But the shape…

Could it be the same?

I looked at the rest of the sketch, but it looked nothing like Blackwood, mainly because of the lack of forest and fog. If this isn't Blackwood, could it still be the same fountain? The rest of the pictures were so focused on telling the story. Why would the artist put something in the picture if it wasn't important?

"If you didn't want to work with me anymore, you just could have been honest."

I slam the book shut and look up quickly. "Dane." His name comes out breathier than I intended, and I quickly clear my throat and breathe through my nose, trying to slow my beating heart.

He quirks an eyebrow. "Were you expecting someone else?"

"No, I'm sorry. I guess I took a longer break than I wanted."

For the first time since sitting down, I notice the window next to me is pitch black.

Fuck.

I need to get back to the castle.

"That's alright. Are you ready to leave?"

"Yes." I stand up quickly and leave the books on the seat. Dane's eye catches on the stack, but he says nothing as I step in front of them, blocking his view. We collect our unused books from the table and head back to the castle just like the first night.

I force him to stop again, about a block away from the gate, as I pull my hood up and low over my face.

"I'm sorry for keeping you away from your sister late into the evening again. Hopefully she isn't too upset with you."

"It's alright, she doesn't mind."

"So," I start, glancing down at my hands clasped in front of me. Why do I feel nervous saying goodbye to him? We're friends. Hopefully.

"Are you going to disappear again, or will I see you soon?" I wince at my forwardness, but his grin is reassuring.

"Why Addy? Did you miss me?" His eyes sparkle with the playfulness of his tone.

I almost correct him calling me the wrong name, forgetting for a second that I'm not Lennox, at least not to him. It has been so easy to just be myself this entire evening, and immediately the idea sours with the thought that he has been nothing but forthcoming and I have been lying to him.

He was right earlier. He can't trust me.

I pretend like I am thinking hard for a moment. "Yes. But I'd be careful if I were you. You said yourself you didn't know if I was being honest with you."

He clutches his chest and pretends to stumble backward. "You wound me. You can't blame me for being cautious."

I laugh. "No, I cannot. I would do the same." I definitely will not admit I already had.

"Then I will see you soon, Addy." He steps forward quickly, his hand finding mine, and raises it to his lips. He brushes them over my knuckles, his eyes never leaving mine. He releases me and I back away. I tug my hood down again and watch my feet as I walk.

I can't help the smile pulling at my lips and the feeling that despite heading back to my cage, I'm not ready to give up my coveted freedom yet again. Especially not when I finally have a friend.

"What the *fuck*, Lennox."

I gasp and turn toward the darkness that envelops my chambers, instinctively reaching toward my lower back, where my training dagger usually sits.

My hand comes up empty. I don't have a weapon of my own yet, not until my ceremony, but I instantly realize how quickly I've come to rely on it.

"Where the fuck have you been?" Brynne hisses at me as she stomps across my room, coming at me like she does in the ring. She snatches my arm out of the air, pulling it up to look at it.

"And you weren't armed? Have I taught you nothing?" Her voice is harsh, yelling but in a scary, hushed way, trying to keep from being heard. She looks at my clothes and I watch as fury takes over her face. "You better start speaking, and it better be a good answer."

"I'm pretty sure nothing I say will be a suitable answer for you, Brynne." I pull my arm out of her grasp and slip by, unclasping my cloak and throwing it down on the chair in front of the fire. The pillows are crumpled, and remnants of my dinner are scattered across the table. She has been waiting here for quite a while.

"Where. Were. You," she grinds out.

"In the city." I don't let my voice waver at all. I kick off my boots and walk to the closet, beginning to unbutton the dress I need to stow away in the laundry.

"You're joking."

I glance over my shoulder and meet her eyes. "No, Brynne, I'm not joking."

"What the hell could you possibly be doing in the city?"

"It doesn't matter what I was doing."

"Like hell it doesn't."

I pull a robe from the closet and drape it over my shoulders, cinching it at my waist. "All that matters is that I'm back, and I'm fine." I am not about to tell her my plan. No one can know. I don't need the sympathy or the help. This is something I need to do, and only I can do it.

She takes a few aggressive steps toward me, her voice raising slightly more than it was before. "Do you realize I almost had the entire guard out looking for you? If you had come back any later, I would have torn the city apart."

"I'm here, and I'm fine. You do realize that my father used to spend every day in the city, right? I don't know why you are so upset that I went out for one night."

"Because your father was guarded! He was never alone! You clearly don't have the same sense he did because you went by yourself!"

I roll my eyes at her and sit at the stool of my vanity. "No one knows who I am, Brynne. It's basically like being protected. I'm invisible." I pull my hair out of the braids, the golden strands peeking through the surface of the ones I still color dark.

Brynne eyes my hair with a scowl. "Was this the first time?"

I look at her in the mirror, still working my braids free. She tilts her head, waiting for me to answer.

I could refuse to say, and she would know it wasn't the first time, but I don't want to just cower to the crown and its rules and expectations. Not anymore. Not after I have discovered an entire world outside of these walls that I easily could have been experiencing. My blind following and fear of the rules and expectations my father placed on me has kept me from living, and I won't do it anymore. I am going to own my actions.

"No." I don't need to say any more. Technically, she answers to me. She can be as pissed as she wants to be, but there's nothing she can do.

"I need to report this to the king." She shifts into her more soldierly stance, squaring her feet and clasping her hands behind her back, her duty side taking over. I've seen it occasionally over the years, but usually never when we are behind closed doors.

I spin around to face her. "No, Brynne," I say, now almost yelling the way she was at me. "You are *my* guard. You are here to protect *me*. Part of protecting me is keeping this from my father. I promise you, I would not be doing this without good reason."

"It's my duty to the throne," she starts.

"Your duty is to me!" My anger catches her off guard and she clamps her mouth shut. My shoulders drop as I let out a long breath. "I'm sorry Brynne. I'm not mad at you. I understand I put you in a hard position, but please. I'm begging you, don't do this. I know you care about me just as much as you care about your duty." She shifts on her feet, and I see her face soften slightly.

"I need this, Brynne," I plead with her.

She glances down at the floor, her face staying stoic before she looks back up to meet my gaze.

"Has anyone seen you?"

"Obviously. I can't hide myself from everyone on the streets. But I haven't gotten so much as a second glance. I do my best to hide myself. I color my hair darker, and I go by a different name."

She nods.

"The guards at the gate haven't noticed."

She gapes at me before she recovers. Her mouth closes and her nostrils flare. "Fucking imbeciles. They are going to be replaced immediately."

"No, Brynne, don't. Don't do anything that will call attention to this. They've been kind and attentive to their position. They're just being tricked. It is on me, not on them."

"I'll need to accompany you if you go out again."

"You can't Brynne. It will be too obvious. You're the Second Guard. You aren't exactly inconspicuous."

She folds her arms over her chest and remains silent for a few moments. "I don't like this Lennox."

"You don't have to like it, but you have to follow my order."

Her jaw clenches. She knows she has to listen unless my safety is in immediate danger, which it isn't. I have proven that I am safe coming home, even late at night.

"You will be armed next time, just like we've practiced."

"Fine," I agree with a nod.

She visibly relaxes before spinning on her heel and walking toward the door. She places her hand on the handle, but before pushing it open, she turns and looks back at me.

"As your guard, I'm furious with you right now. But as your friend," she pauses and gives me a small smile. "I'm proud of you."

I smile back at her. "Thanks, Brynne." I hope she can see my relief at her words.

She pauses for a beat more.

"But I'll be standing guard in front of your door for the foreseeable future." She turns the handle and is out the door, closing it behind her before I can respond.

CHAPTER THIRTEEN

My skin slides against the soft satin fabric as I thread my fingers into the black elbow-length gloves that perfectly match my dress. I try to keep steady on my feet as Tila's assistants jostle me around, pulling the ribbons to tighten the bodice. My breath catches with one strong pull, but I ignore the slight discomfort.

The dress is magnificent.

It's the most beautiful dress Tila has ever made for me, a dress fitting for the importance of the occasion. Today is significant, not just for me, but for the future of Blackwood. She wants to make a statement, to ensure I look like the future queen I am to become.

I'd been fussed over all afternoon, hair pulled, and makeup applied, with Tila directing the ship and making sure the entire look went together flawlessly. I watched in the mirror as they transformed my hair into luscious smooth waves that cascade down my back, with sections twisted and wrapped sleekly around my head.

Kohl lines my eyes, and whatever it is she used to thicken my lashes makes me look completely different. Older and more powerful, and it gives me a feeling I've never felt before. The dust of gold glitter across my kohl blackened eyelids, completely ties in the dress, and brightens the green of my eyes.

The ties to the bodice pull tightly, and I suck in another breath. I try to focus on what I see in the floor-length mirror as they finish up the laces in the back.

I've never felt so stunning, or so much like a princess, before in my life.

Not a princess. A queen.

My eyes sweep over the dress and soak up every inch. Tila has outdone herself. The black satin bodice is sharp and clean, coming to a slight point on either side of my chest, and hugging my waist, the sleek satin accentuating all of my curves until the dress billows out into a huge, full skirt. The fabric ripples like liquid midnight, until it reaches the end, and the stunning design that encircles me.

Black trees, silhouetted by golden sparkles, rise from the hem up the sides of the skirt, mimicking the trees of Blackwood. With every movement, the gold glitters, as if the fabric was made of treasure that catches every speck of light.

My gloved wrists are adorned with gold bracelets, set with black stones that match the long dangling earrings and necklace that sparkle as I move, and are so heavy I don't know how I will keep from ripping them off by the end of the night.

My stomach tumbles with nerves as I stare at my reflection. The past few weeks have given me a distraction from worrying about tonight. I didn't have time to think about how I am to be paraded in front of and presented to representatives from all the kingdoms. I didn't have time to be nervous or remember that my father didn't want me to prepare to meet the other leaders. I'm only to be a trophy, to stand in front of everyone and secure requests for betrothals and alliances.

After these past few weeks, I know I want more from life than that.

I clench my hands at the thought, not only about seeing and meeting people from other kingdoms for the first time and having to deal with their first impression of me, but also of the loneliness I am about to endure. I wish I could have invited Dane to the ball, but that was impossible. He knows me as Addy, the maid, not Lennox the princess.

I smooth the fabric of my waist as I imagine dancing with him in this dress, surrounded by suitors who hope to catch my interest and secure their future as a king consort, as well as the security and prosperity that Blackwood has to offer.

Tears well in my eyes and I and quickly blink them away. Hopefully Tila and her assistants assume I am just overtaken by the beauty of the gown or nervous about the night and don't question me.

There is more behind the tears than the daydreams of a life I want surrounded by people I love.

I'd come up with nothing.

All of my hard work trying to find an answer for my mother was worthless. There was nothing in any of the city's or kingdom's records that could help her. There has never been a case of anyone staying alive while refusing to wake for as long as she has, and no knowledge of anything to wake her.

I'd failed.

And now that people will see me, will know who I am, there is no more sneaking out of the castle, pretending to be Addy. Someone in the city would surely recognize me and it would get back to my father. Despite my desire to change everything once I am, by Blackwood law, able to be queen, I still am not. There is little I can do if my father's will goes unchanged.

Not only had I failed, but I had probably seen Dane for the last time. Despite the great evening we had at the tavern, he hadn't shown up again, and now I was out of time. I couldn't have invited him to the ball if I wanted to.

My thoughts are interrupted when my eyes catch on Tila in the mirror, approaching me with a black wooden box. "Your father had this made for tonight," she says as she lifts the lid.

Nestled inside on a bed of black satin is a crown, glittering with diamonds and gold, accented with large teardrop black diamonds dangling from each of the spires. It is breathtaking and matches the dress perfectly. I bend slightly so Tila can place it on my head.

When I rise and my eyes find my own in the glass before me, the breath is sucked from my chest.

I don't see myself anymore.

I see a queen.

This feeling, this confidence, needs to get me through the night, and help me show all of these people who are inevitably judging me how competent and prepared I truly am. I will show all the other kingdoms that I am ready for this, ready to be one of them, but most importantly, I will show my father.

"Our work here is done," Tila says as she signals her assistants to gather their things. I reach out and grasp her hand. She looks over at me, a look of concern on her face.

"Thank you, Tila," I whisper, and give her hand a small squeeze.

"You are most welcome, Princess," she says with a smile and a deep curtsey. She squeezes my hand back before letting go and moving toward the door. "You have some time before you'll be called. We finished earlier than expected. Please take care. We don't want to be rushing to do touch-ups prior to your grand entrance."

"I'll do my best not to mess anything up." I smirk at her over my shoulder. "No promises."

She sighs, shaking her head, and leaves my room, closing the door behind her. I'd ruined enough of Tila's designs as a child that she knows anything can happen. This time, it was only a joke. There is no way I want to ruin this masterpiece. Not tonight.

The silence of my room envelops me, feeling thick and slightly ominous. Now the waiting begins until the ceremony and ball commence, but the emotions of the day are starting to overwhelm me. The anxiety and pressure to make the ceremony perfect weighs on me, and underneath it all is the constant gnawing reminder of my failure. This is no way to spend your birthday, especially such an important one.

I guess this is what it is like for future queens. Never a day of rest.

I glance around the room, looking for something to occupy my mind to keep my racing thoughts at bay, when my eyes snag on it. My mother's diary is sitting on my vanity, tucked into the corner behind the pots and brushes that were used to paint all of this on my face.

I finally stand, gathering my skirt in my hands and make my way out into the hallway. There is something I need to do before I go through with the rest of this.

CHAPTER FOURTEEN

I rest my hand on the doorknob, take a deep breath, trying to search deep inside myself for the courage to walk into this room. It would be too easy to turn back or wait elsewhere, to avoid the inevitable pain I am about to endure.

No. I need to face this. I've been avoiding this room for far too long, and now more than ever, I have things that need to be said.

I close my eyes and inhale a shaky breath before pushing open the door. I slip inside, pulling my gown clear of the doorway, and swiftly shut the black wooden door behind me with a soft click. I don't want anyone knowing I am in here, specifically my father. It will only stir up questions or conversations I am not willing to discuss.

I turn around slowly and face the room before my eyes drift toward her. I've avoided coming here for years, usually walking quickly by and averting my eyes if the door was ajar. The pain and shame I felt whenever I so much as walked past was too much.

Tonight is no different, and the pain and shame wash over me as my gaze travels to her serene face.

She is beautiful, as beautiful as the shrouded portrait I used to sneak glances at as a child when I started wondering who my mother was. She has grown older since the last time I saw her many years ago, the years of lying in this unrelenting sleep having done nothing to change the course of her aging, albeit slower than those of us who are moving through life normally.

What strikes me harder than I anticipated, is what I have avoided acknowledging despite many staff telling me over the years.

I finally see it.

The crown, gown, and makeup only add to the picture, helping me finally see the changes I've endured over the recent years that morphed me into a younger version of her.

The thought brings tears to my eyes, knowing that I am so much like her physically, but might never know if I am like her in any other way. A wave of sadness and hurt washes over me when a thought breaks through my mental comparison.

This must be why my father doesn't care to see me.

He can barely stand to look me in the face.

Because I remind him too much of her, and because it was I that took her from him.

I swallow down the pain and lean against the door, pressing my fingertips into the wood grain and grounding myself.

"Hi Mother," I whisper, my voice cracking at her name.

I know she won't respond to me, and I don't know if she can hear me, but if my father can talk to her, then I can, too.

"It's my birthday today. I don't know if you knew that."

As I say the words out loud, I realize the repercussions this day has had on my father. It is no wonder he never cared for my birthday. It was the day he lost her, the day he will always have to remember losing the love of his life.

It's also the day he gained me, but that wasn't enough.

I squeeze my eyes shut, my head shaking quickly as if of its own free will.

"What am I saying? Of course you don't know," I murmur to myself. "I'm sorry, I just…I don't really know what to say. I wish you were here today, more than just like this."

The lump in my throat grows thicker as I struggle to push my emotions down. I take a deep breath and try to form my feelings into words.

"I didn't know what I was missing, not until Edmond handed me that diary. It was hard, living my entire life not knowing everything that could have been, but now it is even harder. I needed you here. He needed you here, more than I needed him. More than he needed me."

A small sob escapes me and breaks the quiet of the room. I look up at the ceiling, willing the tears not to fall and ruin all the work Tila had done to my makeup, but no matter how hard I try, they still fall.

"I'm trying to fix it, Mother. I am. I've been working so hard trying to find a cure, but there's nothing. I've looked everywhere. I've scoured all the books on healing in our library at least twice. Nothing Edmond has taught me is anywhere near helpful. I even snuck out of the castle and have been going to the library in the city. I'm not sure if that would make you proud of me or furious with me. If you believe anything like Father does, you would probably be furious.

"I'm worried I'm out of time. I'm worried today will be the final straw for him to let you go. Today of all days, the day I ripped you away from us. I've heard stories of the man he was before me, before he lost you, and he's not the same man anymore, not the same king anymore. He's not the father you described."

I take in unmoving face, her sill hands and fingers, empty of the wedding ring my father placed on it years ago, lost the same day we lost her. Tears roll down my cheeks, as I wait for her to answer me. Wait for her to sit up magically from her sleep and tell me that everything is fine. I need her to take away at least some of the guilt I have been living with every day, watching my father hurt and long for a life that would never be.

Everything would be different if my birth hadn't cursed my mother into this purgatory, forcing her to stay in this state between life and death, and cursing the rest of us to watch her with no chance of recovery.

Bringing me into this world had taken her away from our kingdom, and from me. I am not convinced it was an equal exchange. I am trying to be the queen that our kingdom needs, but I've already failed in my very first assignment. Now, I am supposed to walk into the throne room and pretend that I am ready to rule over a kingdom that doesn't know me and doesn't love me, but is expected to respect me. I am to pretend, under the scrutiny of all the neighboring kingdoms who have traveled here for this day, that I am going to be a great leader.

Despite preparing for this day for years, I am not convinced I am the right one, so how am I going to convince all of them? Especially when the one person who is supposed to have been there for me, and believed in me, seems to doubt me and continue to shelter me?

I wipe under my eyes, not caring anymore about smudging the makeup.

"I'm not done trying," I tell her, standing up straighter and willing my body to feel like the queen I need to be. "I'll find a way. I don't know what the next steps are, but I'm not done trying. I just hope he doesn't give up on you before I can. Light always finds a way, even through the blackest woods."

I give Edmond a mental hug for this lesson he instilled in me many years ago. It is finally time for me to use it.

I drop my voice down to a whisper and hope she can still hear me.

"I love you, Mother. I hope someday I'll get to know you, and you'll get to know me."

I turn away, getting through the door as fast as I can and closing it solidly behind me. There is nothing left to do now except make my way down to the throne room.

So I do.

CHAPTER FIFTEEN

ila stands alone outside the doors to the throne room, waiting for me to arrive. She raises a cloth to my eyes as soon as I step in front of her and dabs the moisture away before reapplying the kohl lining.

She doesn't say a word but knows me well enough to expect that I would need those touch ups today.

Once finished with the makeup, she glances over at me one last time, shifting my hair over my shoulders and straightening my crown before her stern gaze meets mine.

"There's to be no more tears. I can't follow you around all night fixing your eyes." Her tone is sharp, but I know she is trying to comfort me in her own way.

There is a beat of silence before she speaks again.

"I knew your mother, and I promise you, Lennox, she would have wanted to be here tonight, and to see what a wonderful woman you have grown to be."

I've never seen Tila show any emotion, but her eyes grow misty as she speaks, causing mine to well up again. She blinks away her own tears, the hard look on her face trying to conceal the pain that she also must be feeling today. She snaps at me again, shoving the cloth back in my eyes to dab up the moisture. "I said no more tears."

"Sorry Tila," I murmur. I meet her eyes, trying to convey all the appreciation I have for her, getting me to this moment, and being the woman as close to a mother as I ever had. "Thank you."

Her face softens as she lowers the cloth, what I can only assume to be a look filled with love staring back at me. The throne room door behind her opens slightly and closes quickly as Brynne slips through.

"They're ready for you."

This is it. The moment I have been waiting for my entire life. I am about to be presented as the future queen, not only to my people, but to the rest of the kingdoms as well. Kings, queens, princes, princesses. Dukes, emissaries. They are all going to be in this room, and it is all to meet me, to see the mysterious princess of Blackwood, who has been hidden away for twenty-one years.

The weight of the moment overwhelms me, and I suddenly feel like I'm drowning. Brynne shifts into position behind me, forever the Second Guard protecting the now future queen. The familiarity of her presence is calming.

I can do this.

I've been waiting my whole life to be seen.

I was born for this.

I fix my face into a gaze that I hope conveys power and strength. They are seeing me for the first time, and I want that to be their first impression. Besides, after tonight, I am no longer the hidden away princess. My entire life is about to change.

Notes from the organ chorus through the room and echo through the closed doors. It is the song of Blackwood, and while I do not hear it often, I still know every note.

I take in one final calming breath and adjust my gloves that keep slipping from the moisture in my palms.

The doors open and I stare directly at the throne in front of me, and at the man waiting at the end of at the end of the aisle.

He is alone.

My eyes catch on the empty pews as I take my first step onto the black carpet runner. I break my gaze away from the throne and quickly look around, making sure my face stays trained forward.

I can count the number of people in the throne room on my fingers, and I know every single one of them. My breath catches at the realization.

No one came.

Not one person from the neighboring kingdoms is here. No emissaries, no dukes, no princes or princesses.

No one.

No one came to witness the queen of Blackwood's coming of age.

What will this mean for our relationships with the other kingdoms? What will this mean for my betrothal prospects? Am I that disrespected and uninteresting that no one cared to attend?

A thought strikes me.

Or was anyone even invited?

Has my father done it, yet again, hidden me away, sheltered from the entire world? Is he keeping me suppressed, not letting me grow into the role I am supposed to have? Has he thwarted all of my hopes and dreams, keeping me isolated and alone for the rest of my life?

I continue to take slow steps down the aisle, focusing my sight back on my father as I stare at him stone faced. I need to tamper down everything that is raging inside of me at the sight of him.

Fury.

I am furious with him.

This was the one night, the one time where this room should have been full of life, full of people from across the world that would at least give me a glimpse into the outside. He's kept me hidden for twenty-one years, kept me from seeing my people, from developing friendships and relationships. Kept me from becoming a leader in the eyes of my people and our world.

He hid me away, and on the day that I am supposed to be presented, just as he and every ruler of Blackwood were before him, he continues to hide me.

I am not going to be invisible anymore. I had a taste of freedom, and now that I am of age, I am not going to let him stop me from doing what I want to do, what I *need* to do, not only for myself but for the good of Blackwood.

King or no king, father or no father, I am going to prove to him, myself, and everyone else that despite being hidden away, I am valuable to this kingdom.

I just have to get through this ceremony first.

I reach the steps that lead to the throne and kneel on the black carpet, just as Edmond and I had practiced. Edmond is here, of course, seated in the front row, with a solemn look on his face, watching my every move, making sure the ceremony goes smoothly.

Despite my fury, I am focused and clear minded.

I recite everything perfectly and repeat after my father when I need to. I give the ceremonial oaths, pledging my life to the kingdom of Blackwood, and promising to follow through with the traditions and protections of the people.

I am flawless, and I hope everyone sees it, including my father.

Especially my father.

His expression hasn't changed since I walked through the doors, and I can see him staring at a point just next to my face instead of at me. He remains stone faced, no hint of emotion or pride, almost like he is annoyed at having to be here.

He turns toward a table next to his throne and retrieves a small item before coming to stand in front of me again.

"Princess Lennox Holt of Blackwood, rise."

I stand, straightening my spine and squaring my shoulders to make myself look as tall as my short frame will allow, even in the ungodly heels Tila put me in. My father slowly descends the steps and halts directly in front of me. I can see what he is holding now, the piece of the ceremony that signifies royalty.

"With this dagger, your position as future regent of this kingdom is solidified. You will be the queen of Blackwood, the beginning of your reign marked by my death. This dagger serves not only as a method of your own protection but also as a symbol for your protection of the kingdom and all of those in it. May you wield it, and your authority as queen, well."

He presents me with the dagger, and I'm shocked to find it is an exact match for the crown Tila said he had made for today. The filigree carved into the golden hilt sparkles in the reflected firelight of the room. The cross-guard is inlaid with black stones, and the pommel holds the largest of the stones, surrounded by gold and diamonds. The thin blade is made of steel so pure it is almost white, the edges gleaming and sharp, and culminating at a deadly point.

I love it. I am shocked my father could design something so beautiful, especially for me. As I stare at the dagger, it almost feels for a fleeting moment, like he actually cares.

But the empty silence in the room is all the reminder I need that he doesn't.

I reach out and take it from his hands. I hold it up in front of my face, blade pointed to the sky, just as Edmond and I had practiced.

"I promise to protect my kingdom, the kingdom of Blackwood, with my life. I promise to serve and do what is right for the betterment of the kingdom and its people until the day I die."

My eyes don't stray from his emotionless face as I say the words. I hope he can feel the anger exuding from my body on what is supposed to be one of the best days and celebrations of my life.

I slide the dagger into a small loop on my side that Tila had shown me acted as a holster for the ceremony. Having it at my side instantly makes me feel so strong and beautiful and *deadly*.

He gestures for me to turn to complete the presentation and his voice booms in the hollow room. "Princess Lennox Holt, first of her name, the future queen of Blackwood."

A chorus breaks out amongst the few people in attendance. "Long live the princess, long live the king!"

I finally turn and let myself look at everyone here as the underwhelming smattering of applause brings the ceremony to a close. Edmond is clapping alongside Tila who must have snuck in behind me. Brynne is standing at attention, along with a few other high-ranking guards she must have permitted to attend. Addy, as well as a few other staff I have known throughout the years, are also clapping with smiles on their faces.

That's it.

My heart swelled at the sight of them. Even though this is their job, I know each of them came tonight because somewhere deep down, they care for me. I don't know if they knew what my father had planned, but they showed up anyway. They were here for me when no one else was, but that couldn't overcome the overwhelming disappointment from the rest of this ceremony.

The clearing of a throat from behind me stops the applause. "As all in attendance this evening are from within our walls, a ball will no longer be necessary. All are welcome to the feast the kitchen has prepared—"

I don't stay to hear any more of what he has to say, not after all of this. I start down the aisle, without turning back, my abrupt exit causing his speech to halt.

I don't care. Footsteps and the clank of armor come up quickly behind me, and I swiftly lead Brynne out of the throne room and head straight to my chambers.

I am not staying for a feast. I won't be humiliated any further. It is a waste of my time. No wonder he had shrugged off any attempt at discussing talking points for me to prepare for the other kingdoms. He had no intention of having anyone here.

It is over. Done. The ceremony is complete. I am going to be queen, and there isn't anything he can do to stop me from doing what I need to.

I promised my mother I would not stop, and tonight's failure of a celebration is further reason that I need to find an answer. I need the parent that wanted me, the one who loved me before she knew me, not ignored me. Fury and hope and desperation mix in me as I stomp up the main staircase, trying not to trip over the once beautiful and now stifling gown.

I don't know what to do next. I don't know where anything is going to lead, but I know that it is time to take charge of my life.

CHAPTER SIXTEEN

I push the door closed behind me once I reach my chambers, but I don't hear it slam.

"Lennox." I knew Brynne was tailing me throughout the castle after I stormed off from the ceremony, but I had hoped she would give me at least a minute alone to collect myself.

"What Brynne?" I growl back at her. I rip the dagger from the loop holster, slicing right through it before I slam the blade onto the sitting table. Tila won't be happy that I sliced through her masterpiece, but at least it was only that and I didn't cut myself out of the bodice. Yet.

I reach behind me and start unknotting the ties, pulling and loosening the ribbons of the corset. My breaths are heaving, not only from my run through the castle, but from holding everything in through that piss poor excuse of a coming-of-age ceremony. I feel the bodice fall and rip it off as quickly as possible. I throw the dress on the chaise and walk over to my wardrobe, crouching down to dig out the new clothes I had stolen from the laundry and stowed in the back of the wardrobe.

"You must know that the king only wants to ensure that you are protected," Brynne says as she approaches me, her voice almost pleading.

I whirl on her, my feet snagging on the long silk slip I wore under the dress and causing me to stumble.

"You knew? You knew this whole thing was going to be a complete embarrassment? A farce? That he invited no one?"

Her gaze drops to her feet, and that is all the confirmation I need.

My rage echoes through the room as I yell at Brynne for the first time since she walked into the castle. "You let me go in there like that? Completely unprepared? Some fucking friend you are." I stomp over to the changing screen and start pulling on the new clothes. The pants and tunic are different than the normal servant uniform, but I don't care. I'm comfortable, like any old day in the sparring rings. I feel like me.

I want to feel like me tonight.

"If it matters, I didn't know until today. The king didn't make the final decision not to let anyone in until just before the ceremony."

I stick my head around the edge of the screen to look at her, trying to see if she is telling the truth or just trying to settle my anger.

"Other kingdoms were actually invited?"

"Yes, but they were not allowed through the gates at the last minute. It has been a bit of a situation, trying to settle down the tempers. You can imagine that there are some that feel lied to and tricked."

I huff and disappear behind the screen again. I don't give a shit if my father has to deal with some upset rulers. He did this to himself. Besides, they aren't the only ones feeling lied to and tricked.

"I know you're angry, but your safety is the priority."

"Safety from what?" I yell as I come out from behind the screen, tucking the oversized shirt into my pants. "The only time I've spoken to anyone outside of this castle was a few weeks ago, and none of them have any idea who I really am! What secret threat is my father scared of? Why is he depriving me of everything that every other king and queen of this kingdom has had? What is he so afraid of?"

"Where are you going?" She ignores my questions and eyes my outfit, puzzled.

"Out." I stomp over to the wardrobe and grab a pair of worn in boots. I drop to the floor in the most un-princess like manner I can muster, and start pulling them on, ignoring Brynne.

"You're not going anywhere."

"I am," I say firmly. I stand and pull a dark cloak from the rack and drape it over my shoulders.

"You are not," she grinds out, stomping toward me.

"I am. I can't be here right now, Brynne. I need to *do something*. I can't sit within these walls, being the perfect little obedient princess that he's still trying to force me to be."

"Not tonight, of all nights. It is far too dangerous, with too many unknowns in the city."

"And whose fault is that? If everything would have gone as it should have, I would have been under constant supervision. But I don't care. I'm going."

"No." She moves in front of the door, blocking my only exit.

I stare her down and drop my voice. I never want to speak to anyone like this, especially her. I hate pulling rank. She is my guard, yes, but she is also my friend, and a piece of my heart breaks knowing that I have to do this.

"As your future queen, I command you to stand guard of my rooms and inform anyone who comes looking for me I am not taking visitors."

A flicker of hurt flashes in her eyes. Her loyalty is to the crown, and after the past hour, I am now the crown. Any threats she made before to tell my father on the guise of me being in danger are now over. Sure, she could still tell him, but her duty wouldn't let her. I know she is trying to protect me, but it is her job to follow orders, my orders. She can't say no.

She nods, her jaw clenching before gritting out, "Yes, princess."

I turn to the mirror and pull up my hood. I don't bother darkening or braiding my hair, instead just shove it far back into the hood so it is hidden. My face is still covered in Tila's makeup, but I don't care. I'm not going to waste time taking it off. It is getting late, and the library will be closing soon, so I need to hurry.

"Will you at least tell me what you have been doing? What is so important that you're putting yourself at risk? If something happens, I need to know where to find you."

I weigh the consequences of telling her. If there is anyone in this castle I don't feel will judge me, it is Edmond, but I still hadn't told him. Brynne is a close second. I don't want her to pity me, or to think what I am doing is in vain. But I also don't want her to stop me.

I understand her need to ensure my safety, and I don't want anything to happen to her if I am successful and she has to explain. I need someone on my side.

I need to tell her.

"I've been trying to find a cure for my mother." The look of shock on her face startles me. She rarely lets her emotions show, but surprise cracks through. I keep going before she can interrupt me and take away the courage I had to muster.

"I read through everything in our library, so I tried looking in the city. I looked for weeks through anything that could help. Books, notes, case studies from healers. There was nothing. But Edmond...gave me something."

I hold back from telling her about the diary. It feels too personal to share with anyone. It is mine, the one connection I have to her, and my motivation for doing all of this. While I'm sure Edmond knows the contents, no one else needs to. I can hold that close to my heart.

"It made me see that I have wasted enough time ignoring what happened. I overheard the healer telling Father it was time to let her go, and now I can't fathom giving up on her.

"The problem is, I haven't found anything, and I have no idea when my father is going to decide he has held on for long enough. I had another idea, but it was something I never thought I would try. After tonight, though? After my father so clearly showed he doesn't care about what is best for me, I want my mother back. I need to do whatever I can to get her back, and maybe all of this," I gesture to the castle around me, "would change. Maybe I'd actually have a normal life, as normal as it can be for the future queen."

"So, what are you going to do?" she asks.

I pause, mentally pleading with her not to laugh at what I am about to say.

"I'm going to find Dawnlin."

I wait for the shock to show through like it did before, but it doesn't come. She stays collected, but she is clearly processing the information.

"Have you figured out how?"

"I'm working on it." I try not to sound too defeated. "I only just decided to start looking for it. I, uh, I made a friend…he seems to know a little more than I do. I was hoping to talk to him and keep researching."

She nods, and I wait in silence as she mulls over my words. "What am I to do, your highness? Stand here and pretend to guard your door and never know if you're going to actually be back?"

"Yes," I breathe.

"How am I supposed to know if you're harmed or just successful? What am I supposed to do when, I don't know, no one can find you?"

I haven't planned that far yet. I don't feel close to finding Dawnlin at all, so we have time to work out a plan.

"I don't know yet. We can figure that out. I'm sure Edmond would help you." The more I thought about it over the last few weeks, the more I felt Edmond had a motive in telling me his story. He'd told me stories for years, but never had brought up Dawnlin before. Why this one? Why now?

I want to ask him and see if he'd be honest with me or continue to hide his motives. I need more information, but part of me is scared to bring it up. What if I, like everyone I judged before, had simply latched on to hope that the story gave me and read more into it than there was?

I am not going to focus on that right now.

What I need to focus on is getting out of this castle and trying to find Dane. If I can't, maybe I can convince Agnes to let me into the library after hours.

"I'm not happy about this, Lennox," Brynne says tensely. I can see the anger on her face as she tries to accept that there is nothing she can do about my order.

"I know. I'm sorry. But I'm not staying here any longer." I move toward the door, and she slides in front of me again, blocking my path.

"Brynne—"

"Since you're forcing me to stay here and not letting me protect you, you have to keep your promise." She points to the table where I had thrown my dagger. "You promised that next time you'd be armed."

"Right." I turn back to the table and grab the dagger. It isn't exactly inconspicuous, so I need to conceal it, but I had nothing to protect it. I wasn't going to stay at the ceremony a moment longer to ask.

"Here." Brynne reaches her hand out to me, holding a sheath for the blade. "I was holding onto it for you. It should fit. You'll be able to keep the blade in your waistband like we'd practiced."

I give her a small, sorry smile. "Thanks Brynne." Even when I force her not to, she still does what she can to protect me.

She fixes the stoic face of a guard back on and steps away from the door. "You're lucky it's your birthday," she murmurs as I walk past her and place my hand on the handle.

I chuckle as I open it. "You can yell at me later. I'll be back soon."

"Be careful, Lennox. There are a lot of people out in the city tonight."

"I will," I say, tapping the hidden dagger at the back of my waistband. "I promise."

She assumes her guard stance in front of my closed chambers, and I make my way down the hall. A crack of light from my mother's room spills across the floor, and I slow myself as I approach her door. I step lightly in the boots, trying not to make a sound in case someone is close to the door. I strain to hear any sound as I inch closer, but a deep murmur makes my spine straighten.

The only person who talks in her room is my father.

I creep closer, staying flush against the wall to stay hidden. I want to hear what he is saying, tonight of all nights.

It is definitely my father. The low boom and timbre of his voice is unmistakable to my ears, especially when my body goes on high alert every time I hear it.

I listen harder, trying to pick out any words, but he is mumbling too much. He pauses, and I hold my breath, hoping he will not leave the room and catch me listening in.

"Lyla…she's not ready."

The words ring out clearly, and my blood turns cold.

Not ready? Is that what tonight was about? The fury that had been mildly tamed after my conversation with Brynne returns almost instantly and my blood that was cold only a moment ago begins to boil.

Not ready?

Of course I'm not ready. He has ensured that. Beyond my lessons with Edmond and Brynne, nothing has been done to ensure I will be a successful queen. This is his failure, and he's confessing to my mother, tonight of all nights, that it is my problem?

Is this the reason for the last minute change, revoking the invites he sent out and risking our relationships with all the other rulers? He decided at the last minute he didn't want to parade his inadequate daughter off in front of everyone who would clearly see me as a lesser royal.

What have I done to make me such an embarrassment?

Why doesn't he want me?

I don't care if he hears me at this point. I rush past the door and run down the steps, heading straight for the kitchens. I look back over my shoulder as I round the corner quickly, to make sure no one is following me when I slam into someone in the hallway.

CHAPTER SEVENTEEN

*O**h no.*

This is the first time I've ever been caught. My mind races, trying to come up with an explanation for why I am in a part of the castle I normally am not. The last thing I need is for my whereabouts getting back to my father.

I stumble back from the person I collided with and start stammering out an apology.

"My apologies, Lennox." I snap my mouth shut and feel my shoulders relax at the voice.

Edmond.

I release a sigh of relief. "No, no, Edmond, I apologize. I wasn't looking where I was going."

"There is no harm done. Is there a reason you are hustling through the hallways?" He looks me up and down, taking in my clothing, which is vastly different from what he last saw me in, not to mention something he's never seen me in before.

"I, uh," I stammer, searching for an excuse he would accept. "I am just…going to get some food."

"Ah. Well, I daresay there isn't much of a need for a hood and cloak in the kitchens. It might put you at risk of catching on fire." The edges of his lips turn up in a smirk. I'm not surprised that he has seen right through my lies, but it doesn't seem like he is going to call me out on it.

"Don't worry, I'll be careful."

"Yes." He moves to step around me, making his way down the hall. "Please do be careful, princess."

His words make me think he knows I am not going to the kitchen. But does he really know what I am up to? Has he known I have been sneaking out for weeks?

It is as if the gods are looking down on me, and I quickly decide this is my only chance to bring up what has been on my mind.

"Edmond, I have a question."

He pauses and looks back at me, clasping his hands across his stomach. "Yes?"

"You told me a story a few weeks ago."

"I did," he says with a nod.

"Why?"

"It's a popular story in our kingdom, and in kingdoms beyond."

"Yes, but why now? What made you bring it up after all these years?"

Is that a glimmer in his eye? The darkness of the hallway makes it difficult to tell, but from years of knowing him, it just seems like he is up to something.

"Sometimes we learn things at the right times in our lives. Maybe this was just the right time."

His answer isn't satisfying, but I don't think I am getting any more of an explanation than that, but I push anyway.

"I wanted to read the story, and I found a book that contained it, but it was short and mainly pictures. How is anyone supposed to know how to find the Guardian if there aren't directions?"

"I wasn't aware that we had any books in the castle that contained the story of Dawnlin." He stares at me pointedly, ignoring my question.

Fuck.

He caught me again. I should have remembered he knows everything about the books in the castle and chose my words better. Instead, I may have just confirmed any suspicion he had of my evening activities.

I roll my lips together and stay quiet. Even if he figures it out, I will not make it easy by admitting anything to him.

He tilts his head, and his eyebrows draw closer together. "For someone who did not like the story when she first heard it, you seem to have taken an interest. May I ask why?"

I shrug. "I don't know. I just thought maybe it was important."

He nods. "My understanding is, anyone who has heard the story, or seen the written version, has all the information needed to seek out Dawnlin and the Guardian. I believe if one truly wants to find it, trusts oneself, and has hope, it will be revealed to them."

"But what if I can't?" I ask, my voice barely a whisper.

Edmond's face softens, transporting me back to my childhood when he would teach me even the simplest of life lessons.

"I have worked with you since you were a child. I have seen you read through an entire library, decipher complex puzzles, understand political theories, process the knowledge of healing, and develop physical strength in addition to all of your many other qualities. I have no doubt someone of your skills and knowledge would be able to solve this puzzle if you only believe in yourself, and believe in the magic."

My chest tightens at his praise, and I feel a bolt of confidence shoot through me. Edmond is right. I keep wavering between fear of failure and determination to prove myself, and I need to stop. I have the skills. I have been trained. Despite what my father said only minutes ago, I am ready, and I am going to prove it by defying all of their beliefs and bringing back the queen of Blackwood.

"Thank you, Edmond," I say, fighting against the tightness in my throat.

"Now, do be careful. I hear the *kitchens* are quite busy tonight. It seems that most of the visitors to the kingdom are still celebrating your birthday, even if it wasn't within the castle walls." He winks and turns his back on me, making his way down the hallway.

Edmond knows.

I'm not sure how long, but he knows what I am doing. Has he been behind this all along, giving me her journal, dropping this story of Dawnlin, all to get me to think about it for weeks? Was he secretly encouraging me to pursue it?

"Oh, and Lennox?" He pauses, his hand on the corner of the stone wall. "One must not forget. Light always finds a way—"

"Even through the blackest woods," I finish his statement, for the first time really feeling the words sink in.

He smiles softly and disappears around the corner.

I doubted the story before, feeling like the idea of holding onto hope was unrealistic and eventually harmful. But hadn't Edmond been teaching me about hope for far longer than I'd known this story? Light will always find a way…having hope in dark times will get me through them. I was so quick to discount the story of Dawnlin, and the lesson of having hope, yet I had been taught to have hope for as long as I can remember.

I pull my hood farther over my head and drape it low over my eyes. I check one more time to ensure my hair is still pulled out of sight before stepping into the kitchen. I grabbed a bread roll and some cheese from the nearest counter and place them in my cloak pocket before heading out the door into the darkness of night.

CHAPTER EIGHTEEN

The guards at the gate barely pay me any mind as I stroll through. They are busy laughing and passing around a flask, acknowledging me only enough to unlatch the lock. The celebrating Edmond warned me about wasn't just outside in the city. I welcome the distraction, especially since I didn't disguise myself as much as I usually do.

Brynne was right. The streets are full of people and laughter. Singing and chatter spill onto the streets from tavern windows. Everyone seems so *alive*. This celebration and this day are important for me, but I didn't realize they are also important to all of them. The kingdom is still celebrating me, even though they don't know me.

Or maybe it is just an excuse to get drunk.

I keep my head down, weaving through bodies that crowd the roads and start down the most direct route to the library. I stay alert, scanning the faces for Dane while still trying to keep my face in the shadows of my hood.

I haven't seen him by the time I reach the library. I climb the stairs quickly, and as I reach the top, my hope falters. It looks completely deserted. I grab the handle and try the door, only to find it locked.

Agnes might have just locked herself in.

I knock using the big metal knocker and wait, but hear no movement inside. Pressing my ear to the crack in the door, I strain to hear Agnes coming to answer.

Nothing.

I try again, knocking harder this time, and wait.

Still nothing. Agnes must not be here. I can't blame her. From the look of the crowds and streets, I imagine she is out celebrating with her family and friends as well.

Trying to analyze the books is out of the picture for tonight, but I'm not ready to go back to the castle so soon. Not tonight. I don't want to be anywhere within those walls.

Dane. I need to find Dane.

Deep down, I have multiple motives. I can't do anything more at the library tonight, and Dane seemed to know much more about Dawnlin than I did. Maybe he knew more than the little he mentioned when he brought it up the other night.

Plus, I miss him.

I rack my brain trying to remember if he told me anything about where he lived or worked, anything that could help me find him, but besides talking about his sister, he hadn't given up many personal details.

Descending the steps back toward the square, I head back into the crowded roads toward the tavern Dane took me to for dinner. I'd check there first, and hopefully I'd get lucky and find him there or on the way.

When I arrive, the tavern is bursting with people. A group of men in the corner with instruments play lively music, with most of the crowd singing along. Patrons hold drinks in the air as they loudly, and very off key, sing songs in time to the music. Women sit in the laps of men, and couples are not hiding their affection, kissing out in public for everyone to see.

I feel my face heat. The night life and celebrations are a very different scene than when Dane and I ate dinner here. I quickly glance around the room, trying not to be distracted by the displays of affection, but it is difficult. No one in the castle is ever this physical, and it is abnormal to see it so open and informal.

What would it be like if I didn't have to behave like a princess? If I were just a normal person, celebrating the princess's birthday in the tavern, kissing someone passionately.

An image flashes before my eyes. Me, in a plain commoner's dress, smiling, laughing, with my arm draped around the broad shoulders of the man whose lap I am sitting in. I gaze up into his face, Dane's face as he grins at me. He leans in and kisses me, with no hesitation, despite the room around us full of other patrons. I don't hesitate either, leaning into the kiss and wrapping my arms around his neck.

The vision disappears as I am shoved from the side by a drunk man almost laid out on the floor.

"Sorry miss," he slurs, righting himself and stumbling to the bar.

I glance around the room one last time, but Dane is not here. My eye catches on several people who must be visiting nobles, their clothing different from the styles here, not to mention a much finer quality than anything else found in the tavern. They stand out like a sore thumb.

I reach up and adjust my hood again, knowing full well they wouldn't recognize me even if they saw me, before turning back out the door onto the road.

Knowing the layout of the city doesn't help at all when I don't know which way to go. Dane could be anywhere. Homes are sprinkled throughout the city, tucked in-between businesses and old buildings, but the farther away from the castle you go, the more the city roads resemble the makeup of outlying villages.

Trying to find where he lives would be almost impossible. There are too many taverns and establishments to check them all, and if Dane was to be at any, I would assume it would be his favorite. But he isn't. Besides, if all of them looked inside how this one did, then it is probably best I stay away.

Suddenly I remember.

There was one other place I'd seen Dane in the city. I start down the road in that direction, dodging groups of people as they stumble loudly on the cobblestones. The farther away I walk, the more the crowds thin, and the quieter the night becomes. Many people or groups walking the same direction as me trail off down alleyways or disappear into buildings.

I'd scanned the faces of everyone passing by, but with no luck. This entire night feels like a complete waste of time. Between the ceremony and the failed attempt to find more information about Dawnlin, I need to figure out when I am going to give up for the evening and regroup back at the castle with Brynne.

I keep walking and scanning, but fewer and fewer people are on the roads now. The darkness of the night is thick and the chill in the air makes me wrap my cloak a little tighter around my shoulders.

My mind wanders back to the pages of the story. Edmond believes anyone can figure out how to call the Guardian and gain passage to Dawnlin, especially if they know the story. His words run through my head, mixing with the pictures from the story, and suddenly an idea strikes me.

The fountain.

I think back to the image of the boy crying as he wanders through town, with the image of a fountain in the background.

It felt familiar when I looked at the page, like I'd seen it before. It was so small and lacking detail that I couldn't be sure it was the same.

But maybe it was.

There is only one way to find out.

Hope swells in my chest at the thought. Could this really be a clue? Was the story riddled with images of clues that I need to put together? I need to get back to the library and look at each of the drawings. Maybe there was some kind of code that gave directions?

That would be a task for tomorrow. In the meantime, I can at least try to find the fountain and see if I notice anything that might point to Dawnlin, or a cipher of some kind.

I don't remember where it is exactly in the city. None of our maps had any fountains on them, which also seems odd. Why would it not be depicted, especially when there are buildings surrounding it I know are on the maps? I walk faster, excitement fueling me, and look down every alley I pass.

Not a single person is around now, and the low burning torches lining the main roads are not giving off much light. A chill that has nothing to do with the cold mist in the air runs up my spine. I am alone, in the dark, far away from the castle and anyone who would help me.

I reach back and graze the dagger tucked into my waistband, feeling a small twinge of comfort that Brynne reminded me to bring it.

I round a corner and peer down the way, instantly recognizing where I am.

There.

This is the same place I had run into Dane before. I'd all but given up hope that I'd run into him tonight, especially since there is no one walking the roads this far out. My sole focus now is finding the fountain and figuring out if there really is a connection to the story.

I glance over my shoulder, making sure there is no one approaching, and creep into the alley. It is as empty as the first time I saw it, the surrounding buildings lifeless and dark. The cobblestones are broken and uneven, and not the same shape or quality as the rest of the roads in the city. It's as if this alley isn't connected to the rest of the city at all, or like it has been here for so long, the structures were built around it.

I glance around the alley as I enter, making sure there isn't anyone hiding in the shadows. The weight of my dagger in my waistband reminds me I am not vulnerable, alone in this dark alley in the middle of the night. I can protect myself.

As I slowly step closer, I get a clearer view of the structure in front of me. The fountain is old and worn down, very different from the one depicted in the story. There is no water flowing, as you would expect in a fountain. Not even a trickle. It just stands in the middle of the alley, stagnant and lifeless.

The carved white stone takes shape before my eyes. A pedestal rises out of the center and atop it sits what looks like a mountain. Empty holes are carved into the sides, which would most likely cascade into small pools below, creating waterfalls down the pedestal before falling into the large round base.

I lean in to examine it and see the design is far more intricate the closer you get. The small, empty pools are carved with animals and creatures, some that seem to be of other worlds. A beautiful woman has her hand dipped into the pool she is sitting above, which then pours into the base of the fountain. There are others like her, all with different carved designs but completely void of water.

I circle around the fountain, in awe at the beautiful carvings, when I stop short.

This is it. This has to be it.

There is a cup…no, not a cup. A chalice, positioned to catch water that falls from a hole in the mountain. Just above the lip of the chalice, as if it is rising out of the cup itself, is the sun.

Dawn.

Is this a sign? The symbol of dawn rising out of a cup of the elixir?

The fountain *has* to be connected to the story.

My heart pounds quickly in my ears, blocking out all other sounds. There has to be something to decipher, something that would lead me there. My eyes rapidly scan the carvings on the chalice. Families with babies, animals, flowers.

All things that are signs of life and growth.

Life that this magical elixir would bring back to anyone who drank it.

I'd found it.

I'd found the key to getting to Dawnlin.

Edmond was right. He said I had all the information I needed and had faith that I could figure it out. It was so subtle, the fountain in the back of the drawing in the story, but something about it stuck in my memory, pulling me back here to find it.

It must have known I needed it.

I want to tell Dane. He was looking for it too, to help his sister. Well, I assume he was, since he brought it up to me. I need to figure out how to call the Guardian, and then go find Dane tomorrow. We could go together and have twice the chance of being successful. I'd save my mother, and he, his sister.

I run my hands over the fountain, looking for anything and everything that might lead me to how to call the Guardian. A switch, or a button on the stone, even something that looks like the puzzle boxes Edmond gave me as a child. I search every square inch, but there is nothing obvious. I don't find any inscriptions or directions, no set of carved images that look like the story. There is nothing more indicating that this is the key to Dawnlin, other than the sun over the chalice.

Siting on the edge of the pool, I lean over to look into the water. The bottom is hidden under the layers of dirt and needles from the Blackwood trees, possibly hiding any inscriptions there. I scan the surface and hesitate. The water is less than inviting, and I cringe before I stick my hands into it and run them along the smooth stone, feeling for any hint, but my fingers find nothing.

All the hope drains from my body, and the helpless feeling of failure creeps back in. There must be something I am missing.

I wipe my hands on my cloak and glance over the water again. The fountain isn't flowing, and by the state of it, hasn't for some time.

Edmond mentioned in the story that no cases have been recorded for quite some time. Maybe that is it. Maybe the magic in the fountain has dried up with it.

In the picture, the fountain flowed freely, splashing into the pool that now sits in front of me. It is no longer that magical, beautiful fountain.

My head falls back as I feel the tears well in my eyes.

Despite telling Edmond that having hope was illogical, I did exactly that. I had hope. I hoped that after all of my hard work trying to find a cure for my mother, that this would be my answer. Deep down, I hoped I would find Dawnlin, find the potion, save my mother, and save me.

I fell for it.

I fell for exactly what I judged the other hopeful believers of the story for doing.

And now I would get to watch her go.

The hope made the pain so much worse.

Tears flow down my cheeks, and there is no use trying to stop them anymore. My body is wracked with sobs as I pull my knees up onto the ledge.

There are so many emotions behind these tears, I just let go. Everything from a lifetime of invisibility, and loneliness, made worse by the events of the last few weeks, bubbles to the surface as I sit here alone, this fountain reminding me of the death of my hopes.

I grab my shirt in a fist, trying to combat the tightness in my chest as the memories pop into my mind.

The pain of walking into the empty throne room.

My father saying I wasn't ready.

His face as he orders me never to leave the castle.

Edmond finally telling me my mother never woke after childbirth.

Fear, anger, hurt, disappointment, expectation.

Loss.

Years and years of emotions pent up behind these tears burst forth and I cannot stop them. My breaths are ragged, and I gasp for air between sobs. I slide off the side of the fountain and kneel next to it, folding my body over the edge and resting my hands on the cold stone, trying to suck in air.

It feels as if my entire world is crashing down around me.

All because I had hope.

More than the sadness, I am angry, and not just at my father or my situation. I am angry with myself. I am the one responsible for having hope, and now I have to deal with it.

I need to pull it together. I have no choice now but to head back to the castle, and I don't need to startle Brynne by looking like an absolute mess when I get there.

I climb back up on the bench and lean over, trying to glimpse my reflection in the water. I barely recognize myself. My eyes are swollen and red, and the makeup Tila's ladies had so expertly applied is streaked down my cheeks.

I inhale a shuddering breath as another wave of tears and sobs hit me quickly. They fall hard and fast, dropping into the water below me as I swipe a hand roughly across my nose.

Suddenly, something in the water catches my eye and I stop crying instantly.

I grasp the edges and peer down where my tears had broken the surface. Golden ripples grow from each drop, disturbing the dark surface of the water, and I suck in a gasp.

Tears.

That's it. How didn't I figure that out? My mind quickly goes back to the pictures of the story, where I had seen the fountain in the background. The focus of that picture was the little boy in the story, and he was *crying*.

It was so subtle, something you wouldn't think was important. I'd assumed he was just upset about his dying father, but was this the artist's way of telling others how to find Dawnlin?

It has to be.

Completely forgetting all the feelings from moments ago, I scan the water, looking for something more. The gold ripples fade before my eyes, and I wait, frantically looking for something else to happen, a next step that I need to follow in order to call the Guardian.

I lean over closer to the water, eyes searching for something, anything, when suddenly a hand clamps down on my shoulder.

I am not alone.

CHAPTER NINETEEN

A scream tears from my throat as spin around, reaching for my dagger and yanking it from the sheath. A large cloaked figure stands before me. The brown fabric hood hangs low over the person's face, casting shadows so I can't see any defining features.

"W-who are you?" I stammer, pointing my dagger toward the figure. I may feel terrified on the inside, but I refuse to show it. I can defend myself, and I won't be intimidated by this surprise attack.

"You called for me," a deep voice answers.

A man, then.

"I didn't call for you. Were you watching me? Are there others around?" I refuse to take my eyes off of him to check, which I know isn't smart. There could be a threat approaching from anywhere, especially since he snuck up on me so easily. Brynne will be pissed if something happens to me.

"You did." He gestures toward the fountain behind me. "Can you please lower your weapon?"

"No."

"Did you not seek the Guardian of Dawnlin?"

Holy shit.

"It is you," I say, my words barely a whisper.

The hood dips low in a nod, still concealing the person underneath.

A thrill courses through my body. I had done it. I found him.

Dawnlin is *real.*

After all of my doubt and failure, this is actually happening. Edmond and Dane were right.

And now my mother has a chance.

Oh gods. What about Dane?

I hadn't meant to actually call the Guardian tonight. I only wanted to find out how or get more information and find Dane tomorrow, so he could help his sister, too. Would he hate me if I did this without him? I don't know how much time she has, he never said.

If I turn the Guardian away tonight, he might not answer the call tomorrow. Am I willing to risk my chance to find Dawnlin?

I think of my mother's words to me, and the message from the healer.

This is my chance to save her. I won't sacrifice it.

I hope that Dane's sister will be alright for a little while longer, and I can find him and tell him once I return. Maybe he will have figured it out by then. He was here. He saw the same fountain days ago. If only he knew he was so close.

I slowly lower my dagger, sheathing it back in the waist of my trousers. My eyes flick around the alley, making sure there is no one else with us. When I see we are alone, I don't hesitate and decide to trust him.

"Thank you," I say quietly, "for answering my call."

"It is my duty as the Guardian to answer the call of those who seek to find Dawnlin and the magic that is held there. Is that your wish?"

I nod. "Yes, it is."

"Are you prepared to depart now?" His deep voice rolls over the words, the rumble sends a small shiver up my spine. It feels familiar, yet not. I wonder if that is part of the magic, that the Guardian helps ease any doubts or fears, so you follow him. Brynne would expect me to keep a healthy dose of skepticism, but my excitement overpowers it.

I nod again. "Yes. That's it? I just trust you and you'll take me to Dawnlin?"

"Hope and trust are two of the tenets of Dawnlin, so yes, Addy, you will need to trust me."

"Where do we go fr—"

I stop short, my gaze snapping up to the shadowed face. I narrow my eyes, trying to see past the darkness still hiding him. "How did you know that name?" I breathe.

"Remember what I said." He pauses. "Hope and trust. You need to *trust* me. Can you do that?"

I say nothing. I know I need to, but warnings are going off in my mind, and Brynne is yelling at me to retreat.

My body tenses as he reaches up, drawing back his hood and letting it fall behind him. My jaw falls open.

"*Dane?*"

"Hi Addy." His voice isn't the deep growl it was a moment ago, and instead is back to the familiar voice I have come to know over the past few weeks.

I slam my mouth shut, the reality of the situation washing over me. Dane is standing in front of me, claiming to be the Guardian of Dawnlin, and I feel like an idiot.

"Is this some kind of joke to you?" I spit at him, anger overtaking my initial shock. "How did you do it, huh? How did you make the water glow like that? Were you doing some potions research too during all that time in the library? Did you follow me here?"

"No, Addy, I swear I didn't—"

I cut him off. I don't want to hear excuses right now. "Did you have it planned all along to fuck with my head? To plant these stories and get my hopes up and then pull this? Who else knows? Who is watching and laughing?" I spin around, scanning the alley to see the people I missed hiding in the shadows, spying and laughing at Dane's little joke, but there is still no one.

"It's not a joke, Addy." He reaches forward to grab my shoulders, a pleading look on his face, but I push his arms away.

"Was there even a sister? Was anything you told me true, or was it all a lie?" My voice cracks on the last word, and I clear my throat, trying to rid myself of all the emotion.

I'd trusted him. I was so desperate to make a friend outside of the castle that I fell for his game. He showed me a little attention, laughed with me, touched my hand, and I believed everything he said.

I'm so stupid.

The bitter tears sting my already swollen eyes and I harshly wipe them away with the back of my hand, without breaking my glare at him.

"No, there isn't a sister, but—"

"Gah, I can't believe you!" I throw my hands in the air and spin away from him, setting my sights on the end of the alley. I need to get out of here. Brynne was right. I shouldn't have left.

Hell, my father was right. I had been alone for so long. I wasn't ready to be out in the real world. I need to get back to the castle and end this nightmare of a birthday.

He grabs my elbow, whipping me around to face him.

"Will you please listen to me?" he yells.

That shuts me up quickly. I snap my mouth shut and clench my teeth. No one has ever yelled at me before besides my father and Brynne, and I don't know how to respond.

He should be laughing at my gullibility, not yelling at me. If this was something he planned and plotted to make a lonely castle girl look stupid and hopeful, why was he begging me to listen to him?

I roll my lips together, preventing myself from saying anything more, but my eyes are still full of angry tears.

"Thank you," he says, releasing me and crossing his arms over his chest. His thick forearms flex as he clenches his fists, and I am slightly taken aback.

He's serious.

"Will you let me finish explaining before you cut me off again?"

"No guarantees," I say icily, not ready to jump in and trust him, only to humiliate me some more.

His jaw clenches as he continues to look at me, but not speak.

I wait silently. I want to hear what he has to say, what sort of excuse or explanation he is going to give me now that I am clearly upset at the ruse.

"You did call me tonight. I am truly the Guardian of Dawnlin, and my name is really Dane. No, there is no sister, but I lied for good reason."

I open my mouth to speak, but he holds a hand up, halting me. I close my mouth again and cross my arms, mimicking his stance and showing my impatience.

He laces his arm back in and continues. "I sometimes visit the areas near the fountains. It helps me notice if I'm going to be called soon. If I find someone who is looking, I try to speak to them, so they aren't frightened when I appear behind them."

He gestures to his body, causing me to trail my eyes over him. He is a very large man, and I admit if I hadn't met him before, I would have been scared to go with him, no matter how attractive he turned out to be. Hell, I pulled my dagger on him. Clearly, I was even surprised at first.

"I use the story that I have an ill sister so that there is reason for me to be around the information, around the healers. Near the fountain, getting to know the people who may need it. That is all. It wasn't a lie to trick you."

"Why did you bring it up to me? How did you know I was looking for it? I told you I was studying to be a healer."

He shoots me a pointed look.

"I warned you I probably was going to interrupt."

"I brought it up because I'd hoped that you would figure it out. You seemed very determined, and like someone who needed Dawnlin."

"But why would a healer need Dawnlin?"

"She wouldn't, but you aren't as convincing of a liar as you think you are."

Heat fills my cheeks. Hopefully, it was only Dane that saw through my lies and not everyone I lied to.

"Do you bring it up to everyone you meet?"

"No. I don't."

"Why me then?"

"I wasn't supposed to, but let's just say that I couldn't resist. I wanted you to need me." He breaks my gaze and looks down at his feet.

My fingertips start to tingle and my chest swells at his words. He wanted me to need him. No one has ever wanted me to do or be anything to them before. Maybe our time together had been real after all. At least, maybe it wasn't just to help me find Dawnlin.

"What else did you lie about." It is a statement more than a question. I need to know.

His eyes rise to meet mine. "Nothing, I swear. I just couldn't tell you who I was or the reason I was there. Everything else was real, Addy, I swear."

It was my turn to look down at my feet.

"What?" he chuckles nervously.

"Well…" I start. "In the spirit of honesty, I should probably tell you that Addy isn't my real name." I glance up to read his face. Maybe I wasn't as bad of a liar as he thought if he didn't figure out that wasn't my name.

The sides of his lips quirk slightly. "Oh really? And you were so quick to lecture me on being dishonest. Maybe I should be the one not trusting you."

I roll my eyes. I have every right to be mad. My name was a much smaller scale lie than being the gatekeeper to a mysterious magical land that no one knows how to find.

"My name isn't important, but you might as well know the truth. I'm Lennox."

His face breaks into a smile that reaches his eyes. "Nice to meet you, Lennox." He nods his head toward me but doesn't bow.

He still doesn't know I'm the princess.

That is a secret I am not willing to tell at this point.

"Nice to meet you too, *Guardian*."

His smile widens, and he becomes the carefree Dane that I had gotten to know over the past few weeks.

"This is real. This isn't a joke or a lie. You're taking me to Dawnlin."

"It is very real." He takes a step forward, closing the gap between us. "And yes, I'm taking you to Dawnlin, if you still wish to go."

"Yes." I can't utter the word fast enough as the hope of saving my mother swells back into my veins. "Yes, I still want to go. When do we leave? How do we get there?"

I look around, trying to spot any horses he may have tied up, but find nothing. I glance back at the fountain, but the golden ripples have disappeared, and it is once again stagnant and old.

"Right now, and with this." Dane reaches beneath his cloak and pulls out a large fabric pouch tied off with a golden rope.

He uses both hands to loosen the rope and open the pouch, and as he does, a golden glow similar to the ripples erupts from the contents and lights up his face.

I raise up on my toes, trying to peer inside, just as Dane lowers it so I can see. A flowery fragrance fills my nostrils, catching me off guard. The scent instantly calms my nerves and fills my body with happiness. Never in my life has something affected me this way.

Magic.

It is because I'd never seen magic before.

I peer farther into the bag toward the source of the glow and see a heap of fine sand-like granules that glow golden as the dawn.

"What is it?" I asked, inhaling the scent deeply into my chest again.

"That's another story for another time. Let's just get you to Dawnlin first."

I lower back down on flat feet as Dane turns to walk down the alley. He checks every shadowed area, finally peering down the main road in both directions, checking behind any crates that could serve as a hiding place before coming back and standing directly in front of me.

"Just making sure no one is watching."

"Has that happened before? Has someone seen something they weren't supposed to?"

"Yes," he says solemnly, "and I need to make sure it doesn't happen again."

He takes another step toward me, so our feet are almost touching. I look up at him, towering over me. He smirks as he reaches deep into the pouch, grabbing a small handful of glowing granules. He pulls the strings taut again before securing it back under his cloak.

"Are you ready?" His voice is low and gentle, like he was when I first met him.

"I still don't know if I should trust you."

"Well then, I guess we are going to have to work on that, aren't we?"

I nod. I know I've jumped into trusting him too quickly, but there is something about him I can't help but trust. If what Dane said was true and trust was a tenet of Dawnlin, if I didn't trust him right now, would I even get there?

"Now?"

"Yes."

His fingers lace through mine, and he gives my hand a quick squeeze. "Hang on."

I squeeze his hand back and shut my eyes as he sprinkles the granules over our heads. My skin tingles anywhere the dust touches, and it quickly spreads all over my body. Suddenly I'm weightless, like I am floating. I squeeze Dane's hand harder, reminding me he is still there, and before I can say anything to him, my feet hit solid ground again.

The tingling disappears almost instantly and is replaced by something new. Sticky, wet heat hits me like a wall. I keep my eyes clenched, afraid to open them and see what trusting this man has done. Instead, I take stock of anything I notice. The air feels different, the smells so opposite from the dusty dampness of Blackwood. It is fragrant and fresh, and tickles my nose as I breathe it in.

Next, I notice the sounds, so vastly different from home. Birds chatter and insects buzz. I feel a slight breeze and then hear it rustle through leaves, so different from the sound the wind makes through the needles of the trees in Blackwood. A crashing boom sounds in the distance, and I can't place what it is, never having heard anything like it before.

Bright oranges and yellows dance through my closed eyelids. It must not be night here. The light and warmth beg me to open my eyes.

Sunlight.

I've never truly seen it before, only the muted version that lightened the clouds and fog that covered our kingdom.

I want to see it.

I open my eyes slowly, blinking rapidly as they adjust to this unfamiliar sensation. What I finally see takes my breath away, and my jaw slackens as I take in this new world around me.

I am still holding Dane's hand as I stand there and gape at the beauty.

"Lennox," Dane says. "Welcome to Dawnlin."

CHAPTER TWENTY

I have never seen so much color in my entire life. Bright, vibrant shades of green and arrays of colorful flowers cover almost every surface. And the *light*. I've never seen anything like this. Blackwood's skies were never this bright and clear and *blue*. The dark shadows from the black trees and clouds are the opposite of the land in front of me.

It's so *alive*.

Dane and I landed on some kind of overlook. The worn grass underfoot is soft, with a path leading down the hill. I take a moment to look over the land in front of me, and it is stunning.

Dawnlin is an island, surrounded by crystal clear turquoise water. I squint against the light, trying to take in as much of the terrain as I can as my eyes trail over white sand beaches, bowl shaped coves, and cliffs that fall off into the crashing waves. Trees and plants cover so much of the land, but there are so many kinds it almost looks as if different worlds were mashed together into one impossible land. I do not know where in our world anything like this could exist.

Dense forests with trees like home cover some areas, and tropical flowers and palms are sprinkled into others. There's a mountain in the distance, with snow on its peaks. I wipe beads of sweat off my forehead as I try to make sense of this place. How is it this hot and there's *snow?*

But not just snow. Realization strikes as I gaze on the beauty in front of me. Coming off of the faces of the mountain are waterfalls.

Just like the fountain.

The fountain seems to be a replica of the largest piece of Dawnlin, the landscape that towers above it all, spewing water down into a river that slices the island in two. I'm left speechless.

I don't know how long I stand there just gazing at the island before I get distracted from the stifling feeling of my shirt sticking to my body.

"It's really hot here," I say, reaching up to undo my cloak and pull it off my shoulders.

Dane's eyes flick to my uncolored hair, then back to my face. If he noticed the difference, he doesn't mention it.

"It is, but you'll get used to it," he says.

"So, what now?" I ask, balling up my cloak so I can carry it. I didn't know what to expect in the mere moments I had to decide to travel to Dawnlin, and my choice of clothing would not be well suited for my time here. I don't know how I'll get them, but I need different clothes, or I will be ripping these up so they don't trap in as much heat.

If only Tila could see me in scandalous ripped clothes.

I chuckle at the thought.

Dane looks over at the sound, then up at the sky, squinting against the sunlight. "The suns will go down soon, so we better get to camp. We'll get you settled in, and then I will explain everything."

I glance up at his words and see what he means. There are two suns hovering at different heights above the water. That must be why it is so hot and so bright, but with two suns, I truly do not know where in the world we are.

Or if we are even in my world.

"This way," he says, turning away from the overlook and heading down a worn path into a densely overgrown area. I follow, taking a few quick steps to catch up with him. The last thing I need is to get separated in the lush foliage in a place I know nothing about.

We follow the path, weaving through the trees and leaves that hang in our way. The farther we walk, the more I notice that this isn't the only path in the area. Packed dirt trails veer off the one we follow or join in to it from other directions.

How many people have been here that there are so many trodden passages?

Eventually, the trees break before us and we walk along a natural stone bridge, the river I saw earlier crashing below us and draining into the sea. I shudder as I look down at it, doing my best to stay in the very middle of the bridge.

Blackwood is a landlocked country, and our mountainous lands do not have very many bodies of water. There is very little opportunity to swim for the average person, let alone someone who has never left the castle walls. I never learned how, and the idea of now being on an island surrounded by water with prominent rivers and waterfalls is unsettling.

I need to be careful. I can't ever get too close to the water, just to be safe.

Shadows elongate around us, and the darkness is making it difficult to see without a torch. I look up at the sky and take in the beautiful mixture of pinks and oranges. I didn't know the sky could be so many different colors other than grey. I want to see more of it, but I can't stop to look. I need to keep up with Dane.

I reach up and rip away at the collar of my shirt, trying to get any sort of air flow. If I thought I was sweating before, I am absolutely drenched now. For someone who trained as regularly as I did with Brynne, I am very out of breath, the moisture in the air making me feel like I'm drowning and forcing my body to work harder to keep me cool.

Brynne.

I don't know what is happening back in Blackwood, but I never came home like I'd promised her. Maybe she realized I had accomplished my goal, and was not kidnapped and taken away.

Well, hopefully that isn't what happened.

Edmond knew what I was doing, and I have the inkling that he knows more than he is letting on. I hope he will be there to help Brynne and prevent anything from happening to her position as my guard.

As much as I want to, I can't focus on Brynne or home right now. I came here for a reason. Secure the elixir and heal my mother.

"Are we almost to camp?" I ask, as I heave in breaths.

"Sorry, I'll slow down," Dane says, pausing for a second as I catch up the last few steps. "We don't usually walk around the island at night, especially with nothing to light the way. It can get pretty dangerous. I'll explain in a little bit. We're almost there."

We turn off the trail just as it narrows, and bushes and leaves scrape my thick pants. It doesn't seem like there is any path or guide we are following now. I lean to see past Dane but can't make out any markers. Glancing back the way we came, I only see the jungle we are pushing our way through, no longer defined trails like before.

I turn forward again before asking, "How do you know where we're going? I don't see a path anymore." I point over my shoulder, gesturing to the completely overgrown area we had just walked through.

"You'll get used to it, don't worry." He walks again and I trail after him. "It's that way on purpose, to help keep the location hidden and keep us safe."

"Safe from what?" I say warily.

"The Castaways."

"Who are the Castaways?"

"I promise I will explain everything you need to know. Let's get inside first." He reaches out and pushes through a wall of dense leaves, holding them to the side so I can step through. We trudge on for a few more minutes before we meet a dead end. A vine covered rock face rises in front of us, and there is nowhere to go from here.

I glance around for an escape route, the feeling of unease creeping up on me. Had I trusted Dane too quickly? Would anyone ever know if something happens to me?

The back of my neck tingles as I slowly reach up and set my hand on the hilt of my dagger. I'll be ready to pull it if this all turns sour. If Dane had lured me in to my death, preying on my desire to save my mother, he is going to have a fight on his hands. He may think that I am just a servant in the castle, but he does not know the years of training I have under my belt. It is the training now that tells me to stay alert and expect anything.

"I know it seems almost impossible to find your way here, but like I said, you'll get used to it. You'll start to recognize things after the first few days." He reaches toward the rock face, grabbing hold of a thick vine that is woven through many others. He pulls it back, lifting them all like a curtain and revealing a dark opening in the rock.

"After you," he says, gesturing toward the darkness.

"No, I think I'll follow you." I am still on alert. I won't let him overpower me from behind and block my exit as soon as he gets me alone in a cave. All the worst-case scenarios run through my mind, followed rapidly by ways to get out of them.

This was a mistake. I shouldn't have come here. I've done nothing but put myself at risk by being here, and if something happens to me, there is no future queen of Blackwood.

Keep it together, Lennox. Figure out how to stay alive.

He chuckles at my reluctance to lead the way. "I'm not going to hurt you, Lennox. Remember I said you needed to trust me?"

"I remember, but I don't think trust is blindly given. It's earned."

"I see your point." He holds the vine out toward me. "Grab here and lift. If it will make you feel more comfortable, I'll go first."

I take the vine from him, and he steps forward into the opening. The darkness engulfs him, and he completely disappears.

I think back to what Dane said in Blackwood, that the tenets of

Dawnlin are hope and trust. Hope got me here, so maybe I really do need to trust.

But just because I am going to trust, doesn't mean I will do so naively.

I take a deep breath and step into the darkness, letting the curtain of vines drop behind me. My ears perk, listening for any sound of an ambush, but I hear nothing. I say a quick prayer to the gods to get me through whatever dangers might lie before me and step forward.

CHAPTER TWENTY-ONE

can't see anything.

There is no light, no sound, nothing to indicate that Dane or anyone else is waiting for me inside this cave. I do not know where it opens to, or if it even opens at all. I just know I have to trust it will go somewhere, and I will not end up dead in a cave on a mythical island.

I take another small step forward, reaching my hands out in front of me to feel for any obstacles. Instantly, the darkness disappears, and I am standing in an open grassy clearing, the pinks and oranges of the sky peeking over the trees above me.

I whip around, looking back at where the cave had just been a moment ago, but there's no cave. The rock on this side isn't covered in vines, it is just darkness, as if there is actually nothing there. I look back and forth between the opening and the clearing I am standing in and can't believe it.

There is no tunnel. There is no cave. I just appeared.

It seems like…*magic*.

I was there, in the darkness, and then I wasn't.

I turn back toward the clearing where Dane stands, smirking. I know I probably look dumbfounded, because I am. I don't know how to explain what I just experienced, other than with magic.

If only Edmond could see me now.

"Come on," Dane says and heads toward the other side of the clearing. "Let me show you around."

The clearing is no bigger than the training courtyard back at the castle, and empty. What could he need to show me around? Is there something I'm missing? I glance around, expecting a camp, tent stakes, leftover burnt logs, even sleeping rolls. But there's nothing. Maybe everything is magically hidden, just like the entrance was.

"Where is everything?"

We reach the edge of the clearing, lined with thick trees and vines so dense I can barely see a few feet deep. Dane reaches around the back of a large lumpy trunk and pulls out a ladder made of rope and wooden rungs.

"Can you climb?" He ignored my question, but his was answer enough. I look up and can't believe my eyes. The tops of the trees surrounding the clearing are filled with structures and bridges, the entire camp built into the branches. Torches light spontaneously around the entire circle as the sky darkens above us. There even appears to be a lookout at the top of the tallest tree. A wooden sign with the word "Voyagers" carved into it hangs crookedly from a trunk. That must be what they call themselves.

"*This* is camp?" I ask, not even trying to hide the shock in my voice as I crane my neck trying to take it all in.

Dane plucks the cloak from my hands and throws it over his shoulder. "I'll take this for you. You're probably not going to need it here, but I'm sure you want to keep it."

"Thank you," I say as I place my hands on a rung just above my head. I grip tightly and lift my foot to the bottom rung, pushing as hard as I can to work my way up the ladder. Strong hands wrap around my waist and lift me slightly, and I almost lose my footing. He lifts me as if I weigh nothing, and I feel the heat of his hands sinking into my skin through my shirt.

The ease with which he touches me is still shocking, and something I am trying to get used to. Despite Dane knowing my real name, he still doesn't know who I am, and deep down, I want to keep it that way. I don't want to be treated as a princess here, by him, or anyone else I meet. I just want to be me, Lennox, who is here to find the cure for someone she loves.

Despite having strength in my arms from shooting my bow and fighting with the heavy training swords back at home, this climb is harder than I expected. With every rung, the ladder twists and turns, and it takes all of my strength to pull myself upward.

I feel the ropes pull taught and grip the wood a little tighter as I glance down between my feet. I am high enough that Dane has started climbing, and his weight makes it a little easier to keep going. By the time I reach the wooden platform at the top and pull myself through the square hole, I am out of breath and my arms feel heavy and boneless.

"Who are you?"

Two large bare feet step into my vision and I look up to see a man towering over me, arms crossed over his chest and a stern look on his face.

"She's alright, she's with me," Dane calls from behind as he pulls himself onto the platform. "Lennox, this is Storm."

"Nice to meet you." I stand and reach my hand out toward him.

Storm takes a step forward out of the shadows, and I can see him more clearly. He's young, probably close to Dane and my age. He extends his hand and clasps my forearm, a greeting I knew was common in a nearby kingdom.

It isn't just Blackwood that has a fountain, then.

"Lennox." His voice rumbles, reminding me of thunder, and I come to appreciate his name and wonder if it is real.

He releases me, taking a step back again.

"Anyone else back?" Dane asks.

"Not yet. Should be soon if they are coming at all." He glances up at the sky that is now turning a light shade of purple.

"Alright. I'm going to show Lennox around and get her a platform. I'll be back."

Dane steps off the platform onto a thin beam of boards above a net of ropes and starts making his way across it. I follow, more wary and slow than Dane's sure-footed gait and am grateful for the net below. Once across the beam and back onto more solid walkways, he gestures to the right, where a set of wooden steps wrap around the side of a tree and disappear behind it.

"This leads to the tavern, or so we call it. Food is prepared there, and if you follow the steps, there are some tables and chairs, enough for all of us."

I lean to the side, trying to see past the steps, but it must be too far back into the trees. My stomach gurgles slightly at the thought of food. I don't actually know how much time has passed since I last ate.

He continues on to the rope bridge on the other side of the tavern, his footfalls shaking the planks underneath me and causing me to stumble. I grab the ropes on either side quickly and stabilize myself as I try to keep up with him. I feel like I am walking on ice in the winter at the castle. Hopefully, I will get used to this for the time I am here.

He points to the right again at a smaller set of steps and a long, shrouded tunnel. "Back this way are the bathrooms and showers. Yes, there is running water, and no, I don't know how it works. It just does. Same with the food too. The island takes care of us, knows what we need, and it just happens. There aren't enough of us to have separate bathrooms, but there are separate sleeping quarters. Most people are shy when they first get here, so it's okay if you want to shower at odd times. Some of us don't at all and just go out in the water. It is up to you."

Bathe? With other people?

I hadn't ever had to share space with anyone before. Being the princess, I had everything of my own, and the idea of a bunch of strangers bathing at the same time me while I bathed was not something I was expecting to have to do.

Dane looks me up and down, his eyes trailing slowly over my entire body.

"We're going to need to get you some cooler clothes or this heat is going to get you."

I'm suddenly aware of how much my clothes must be clinging to me, and how much he may or may not see. Beads of sweat run down my back and my hair clings to the back of my neck. What was Tila's masterpiece hours ago is probably an absolute nightmare now.

The suns have now fully set, the only light coming from the fiery torches every few feet. Dane turns off the main walkway and starts climbing some steps up into a densely packed tree.

"Here are your bunks. Ours are on the other side over there." He points across the center of the clearing to the opposite end of the ring of trees. "Right over there is the armory, but you shouldn't have to worry about that yet. I'll show you tomorrow."

"Okay," I say, following his gestures and trying to see the areas he points out in the darkness.

"Doesn't look like Mara is back yet. She might not be tonight, so you'll have the place to yourself. She sleeps there." He points to a platform close to the bottom. "You can pick any one you'd like. They all should have what you need."

I nod and look around at the unclaimed platforms. They all have a thick sleeping pad, with a pillow and blanket stacked on top, ready for someone like me to show up. "Thank you, this is perfect."

"Are you hungry? Do you want to grab some new clothes?"

"Yes, but some new clothes and a bath would be great, actually." I need to wash off all this sticky sweat, although I have a feeling it will come right back. I hope I can get what I need and get back to Blackwood long before my body starts adjusting to this new climate.

"Let's go then."

Going back the way we came in, leaving the other half of the circle for another time. We still haven't seen anyone else yet, despite Dane saying they didn't stay out after dark. When we finally come to the so-called bathroom, I am shocked to see what is before me.

While I am used to bathing in a tub that Addy fills with warm water and oils, there is no tub here, only wooden walled stalls like the stables I rarely visited. A hollowed log grows out of the middle of the tree, branching into arms that drop one into each stall. Towels, soaps, creams, and oils are stacked on shelves carved directly into the thick trunk of the tree, and beneath it are piles of folded clothing, in different shades of earthy colors.

"You can take whatever you need. There are all different sizes and styles, whatever you feel comfortable in. There's a basin just back there. You can wash anything you want to keep. And the outhouse is just past it. Again, don't ask how it works, it just does," he adds with a smile. He sees the confused look on my face at trying to figure out how all of this is possible up in a tree.

"Thank you," I say timidly, walking over to look at the clothing options. "Um, do you think anyone else is going to be needing to bathe right now?"

He grins and leans against the tree, just inches away from me, and crosses his arms over his chest. "I'll guard the entrance for you. Make sure no one peeks." He gives me a wink and I can't hide the blush rising in my cheeks.

"Same goes for you," I say quickly, trying to hide how his words make images pop into my head of Dane peeking at me as I peeled myself out of these clothes.

Tila's books have really been a bad influence.

I turn on my heel, not giving him a chance to say anything more, and head over to the shelves. I quickly grab what I need as I hear Dane's footsteps fade down the tunnel toward the bathroom entrance.

I pick the farthest stall, just in case someone came back and needed the outhouse or something. I hang my towel and new set of clothes on the wooden pegs on the outside of the stall and step inside. I am not tall, so the walls of the stall give me a good amount of privacy, but I cannot imagine bathing like this with someone in the stall next to me. I stand on my toes to glance over the top, making sure Dane isn't *peeking*, as he said.

I slowly strip off my clothes and drop them into a pile just outside of the stall. I need to clean them and save them for when I return home. The light fabrics of the clothes here would not be warm enough to wear home. Once I am undressed, as if the island knows what I need, a steady stream of cool water flows out of the hollow branch above my stall, falling over my shoulders.

I groan as I lean my head back, running my hands through my hair and savoring the cool water on my overheated body.

I hear Dane clear his throat at the sound and I feel a flutter low in my stomach.

Maybe I can get used to shared bathing spaces.

I wash quickly, scrubbing off the entire day from my skin. Once I am dry and dressed, with my dagger tucked in the back of my waistband, I make my way back down to the main passage, only to find Dane standing at the bottom of the steps, holding a plate of food.

"I know it's been a long day, and the time doesn't exactly match up to Blackwood, so I figured you might be hungry."

"Thank you, that was really thoughtful." I take the plate from his hands and look it over. An assortment of fruits, nuts, and cheese is perfect for this heat.

"Of course." His lips turn up at the sides just as I let out a yawn.

I am exhausted. The excitement and newness of the day has finally calmed, and I can't help the wave of fatigue that comes over me.

"Since you probably want to get to sleep, what do you say we save the explanations for the morning? I can tell you everything when I show you the island." Dane reaches up and grabs a piece of dried fruit off the plate and pops it in his mouth.

"That's probably best if you want me to remember anything you say." I sigh deeply. "It's been a rough day."

"But I hope it got at least a little better, didn't it?" He holds my gaze and I nod.

"Yes," I say. "You're right, it did."

"Now let's see if you can remember your way back." He takes a step back so I can lead the way. It seems hard to get lost in a giant circle, but I manage to only make a wrong turn once. Eventually we get there, and Mara, whoever she is, still hasn't returned.

"Mara must be at one of the safe houses. Looks like it will just be you tonight."

Alone.

I know he and Storm are here, and anyone else who may have shown up while I was bathing, but they are all the way across the clearing. I'd never been alone before, without a handmaiden nearby or a guard standing just outside my door.

It feels…free.

I grin widely and feel as if a weight is lifted off my chest.

"Get settled. I'll come get you in the morning, alright?"

"Sounds great." I pause. I want to say more, but I also don't want to say too much. I am still new to real friendship, and with Dane it already feels like too much, too fast. I'm tired and emotionally drained from today, and I don't want that to influence my words. I stick with something simple.

"Thank you, Dane. I know I was pretty mad earlier about you lying to me, but you've been so kind and thoughtful. Just…thank you."

His lips turn up at the ends and he takes a step closer, enough that I have to tilt my head back to see his face. He reaches forward slightly, taking my hand in his. His thumb caresses my skin, each stroke tingling and sending a shiver up my arm.

"You're welcome. I'm glad you're here, Lennox. I'm glad I get to help you."

A smile breaks across my face, and I can't stop the thoughts creeping into the back of my mind. I want him to lean down and kiss me, but I can't. I shouldn't.

I have a task to focus on, and despite his actions tonight, and the trust I have placed in the island, Dane himself still has to earn it back. Kissing him would muddy those waters.

I step back, pushing the thoughts of his lips brushing mine out of my head.

"Goodnight, Dane."

"Goodnight."

At that, he turns and strides down the walkway and turns the way we hadn't yet gone. I watch the shadow of his body walk away, only illuminated every so often by the torches he passes. Once he is on the other side of the camp, I look up at the open platforms, spying the one I want.

I manage to climb up the wooden ladder, still holding his plate of food in my hand with my clothes hung over my shoulder, all the way to the platform at the top. There is an opening in the canopy of leaves, right in the center of the clearing, and from this platform I can see right into it. As I get to the top of the ladder and set my plate down on the bed, a small orb with a flame inside of it appears, casting a soft glow over the platform.

Dane was right, it has everything I need. A pillow and light blanket are stacked at the end of the thick sleeping pad. There are shelves above the end of the bed, and rails made of thick branches along all the sides, so there is no risk of me falling from the trees to my death.

I tug off my boots and set them off on the side of the platform and make myself comfortable. I devour the food quickly, and it is just enough to calm my growling stomach before making up the bed. Something else I've never really done for myself.

I lay down, staring up at the sky above me.

I'd never seen stars before, or the moon. It is huge in the sky, much larger than the scale of the drawings and sketches I'd seen back home. It cast light and shadows over the clearing, and I can't help but smile up at it, a single tear escaping.

I had made it.

I am in Dawnlin.

I am one step closer to finding the cure for my mother.

I am proving to everyone, my father especially, that I am ready, and that I can do difficult things that prepare me for my reign.

I think of Dane as my eyelids grew heavy. He is a distraction, but a necessary one. He is as much part of Dawnlin as the cure is, and I feel lucky that I met him when I did.

He seems like he truly wants to help me. I know that is his role as the Guardian, but it seems like more than that to me. It seems like he actually cares about me. My feelings for him have morphed into something over the last few weeks, but I don't know if anything could ever come of them. With his role and mine, I am not sure how that would work.

I don't need to worry about it right now. All I need to worry about is getting some sleep and being prepared to learn everything I need to know about the cure.

I close my eyes, happy for the first time in a long time. The clear skies and twinkling stars are the last thing I see before I drift to sleep.

CHAPTER TWENTY-TWO

Warmth from the sun caresses my face as I slowly drift out of a deep sleep.

The sun?

I sit straight up, a light blanket pooling around my waist as I quickly scan my surroundings.

Dawnlin.

It wasn't a dream. I am actually in Dawnlin, waking beneath the suns in the beautiful sky in a bed built into the trees. So much has changed in the past twenty-four hours, and the nervousness and despair I felt yesterday are replaced by pure excitement today. I am ready to explore this island with Dane and get the elixir.

I pull on my boots, run my fingers through my hair, and grab my dagger, securing it in the back of my waistband. I don't see or hear anyone in the camp and wonder how many people are here besides Storm and Mara. It strikes me as odd that they are here and didn't just go back home once they obtained the cure. I make a mental note to ask Dane about it later, but for now, I need to be ready when he wants to leave.

I make my way toward the tavern and just as I come around a corner, I run right into him. He isn't in his Guardian robes today, his trousers and thin linen shirt similar to mine. He must keep different clothing for all the kingdoms he visits, so he is prepared for anything because he definitely would have stood out in Blackwood dressed like that.

"I was just coming to get you. I knew you were probably tired, so I let you sleep."

"Is it really late?" I am not used to telling time based on the position of the sun because in Blackwood you never actually could. My entire internal clock is also very turned around with the change in time since being here.

"Not too late. Everyone is already gone. I grabbed us some food so we can head out there."

"I'm ready." I feel like bouncing on my toes, I am so antsy. "Is there a map or something I can have in case we get separated?

"No, we don't keep maps. The island has a mind of its own. Things can change, and it is out of our control. Maps would constantly need to be redrawn, so we don't keep one. Plus, if we did, it could easily fall into the wrong hands and lead Weston right to us. That would be a disaster for everyone."

"Who is Weston?"

We walk along the planks just past the rope ladder we climbed last night. Dane beckons me forward and we step onto a different platform before he flips a lever, and the platform slowly descends to the ground.

"He's the leader of the Castaways. He's dangerous. They all are, but he is especially."

We walk through the same dark entryway we came in through last night, and just as it did last night, I feel the same odd magical sensation thrum through my body as we step out the other side.

"Why is he dangerous? What has he done?"

Dane glances back at me. "This way," he says, pushing aside leaves and branches. "See these trees here? There are ten of them that line this path. This is the best way to find where you are going until you start to know the way." He points to a very tall, thin tree that has an intricate type of pattern in the bark. "This is the only place they grow on the entire island, so we think the island uses it as markers so we can find our way back to safety in camp."

I nod, mentally taking a picture of the patterns of the bark. If I wasn't allowed to have any sort of pictures or notes, I really need to pay attention.

"We all know it like the back of our hand now, but because the island can change, it is important to know details like that. You'll see."

The more he talks, the more questions I have. I want them all answered, but more importantly, I want him to tell me how to get the elixir. Knowing how to get back to camp is great, but I don't plan on being here long and don't mind staying with him the whole time.

"Wait. You never answered my question. Why is Weston dangerous?"

We push through the last bit of trees and come out onto the dirt path. I am already sweating, thankful for the light clothes from last night.

"I don't want to scare you, but you need to be aware," Dane answers, his tone serious. "The Castaways are a gang of bandits and kidnappers on the island led by Weston. They're vicious and ruthless. We don't know where they live or where they will show up, so we always have to be on alert. That's why we have the armory. Anyone who leaves camp can make sure they can defend themselves if need be."

This was not a development I was expecting. I expected to learn about the island, and about the magic that fills it, then to turn around and go get the cure. Now, I'm starting to feel like there is more to this world than I first thought.

"Have they killed anyone?"

Dane shakes his head. "As far as we know, no. They don't kill. But they've kidnapped many of us over the years, and brainwashed them, turning them against us and convincing them to follow orders."

"But why?" I plead. This island is a place of hope and magic that seems to know our exact needs. Why would it allow Weston and the Castaways to harm others?

"He wants the elixir for himself, and he will do whatever it takes to get it, including taking us and increasing his chances of finding it. No one has ever made it back to us once he's taken them and sunken in his claws."

The weight of my dagger on the small of my back reminds me I am armed and wouldn't be taken without a fight.

"Is there a bow in the armory?"

"Why?" Dane smirks. "Are you a good shot?"

"Some might say that."

"I didn't realize that they trained castle staff to shoot."

Shit. I'd gotten so caught up in simply being myself, I'd forgotten that this isn't a skill most royal maids would have. I need to lie, but still stay as close to the truth as possible.

"I've had a bow since I was a child. It's a skill I've kept up over the years. You never know when it will be useful."

"Well, I'm glad you did. We'll get you that bow tonight when we get back. Between that and your dagger, you'll be prepared."

He remembers I have the dagger. How could he forget? I basically threatened to kill him with it.

We approach a stone staircase carved into the side of the mountain and start climbing.

"What does he want with the elixir?"

Dane shrugs with a sigh. "I don't know. I don't even know how he got here, especially with his intentions. Besides," he reaches down and pats the bag of golden dust hanging from his belt. "Even if he got it, he wouldn't be able to leave with it. This is the only way anyone can get onto or off of the island. With permission from the Guardian."

"Do you think he wants to actually use it?"

"Use it, sell it, recreate it. Whatever his reasoning, we know it isn't good. If it was, he wouldn't be resorting to violence to get it. That is why we need to stay on our guard at all times, and gods forbid if he does ever take you, don't believe anything he says. Usually anyone who is new to the island stays with a partner until they know their way. Then they can venture out on their own."

"I'm confused. Why wouldn't we just go to where the elixir is, get it, and then I can leave? Isn't that the whole point of being here?"

Dane stops at the top of the stairs, waiting for me to catch up. With the humidity and heat, these stairs put the ones in the castle to shame. I am already tiring out and breathing deeply, and we've barely just left.

"That's the thing, Lennox. We don't know where it is."

My head starts to spin, and not just from the altitude of the climb. They don't know where it is. Is this why everyone is gone all day? Are they searching for it?

"What do you mean you don't know where it is? You're the Guardian of Dawnlin. Shouldn't you know?"

"I don't think any of the Guardians knew where it is. You know how difficult it was to figure out how to get here. The magic of the island will not make it easy to find the elixir, especially since there are people like Weston who would try to exploit it."

"You're not the only Guardian? There are others?"

"There *were* others," he trails off and gazes out over the island. "Only one person can be Guardian at a time, and that is me."

"How did you become it? It doesn't seem like something that anyone knows about becoming."

His face grows somber. "That's one reason I said you need to be careful and aware out here." His throat bobs, and he meets my eyes. "I became the Guardian because Weston killed the last one. I watched it happen, and before he could take it over, take over control of the island, I grabbed his things." He gestures to the bag again. "It just happened after that. I didn't know it would, didn't want it, but I couldn't let this fall into the hands of that monster."

I'm speechless. How could someone be so cruel and so evil, to take away any chance of hope of finding the cure? How could he kill an innocent person just to control everything?

Monster is the right word.

Dane takes a step down, closer to my level. "That's why I want to make sure you are careful. I don't know what I would do if he took you," he murmurs.

"I will be. I promise." I smile and he returns it, his grin lighting up his face and making his eyes dance.

"Come on, let me show you more."

We walk around the island for what feels like hours. Dane points out so many different things, I can see why people who are new need to travel with someone else until they get their bearings. I'd spent years learning maps and details of places I'd never been before, so I am not too worried about learning my way around.

In what seems like the early afternoon, we finally pick a spot in the shade to rest and eat some of what Dane brought with us.

"Do you like it so far?" He asks before biting into a piece of fruit.

"The food? Yes, it's great," I answer.

"No," he chuckles. "Not the food, the island."

"Of course I do. It's amazing. It's nothing like I expected, not that I actually expected anything, since I didn't know until yesterday that I was even going to try to find it. But I have a question."

His eyes meet mine, waiting for me to ask.

"Is this it? We just try to find the elixir every day?"

My heart pounds as I wait for his answer. I'd been so caught up in his warning about Weston that I hadn't really processed the reality of his words. No one knew the location of the elixir, which meant that this would not be a simple task. I would not return home today with a fond memory and a future with my mother ahead of me. I need to know the truth of what to expect for my time in Dawnlin.

"Unfortunately, yes." His eyes drop to the food in his hands. "Since Weston killed the last Guardian, there was no one to pass along any of the instructions or secrets of the island, if there even were any to begin with. We've all just been trying to figure it out as we go. None of us have found it yet though, and everyone has chosen to stay even after all this time."

"All this time? How long has it been?"

He looks up at me again, a tight smile on his lips. "For some it hasn't been as long as others, but for many it has been years. It's hard to really know how long unless I pay attention to time when I'm called off of the island."

"How long have you been the Guardian?" I hold my breath, waiting for his answer.

"Probably for your entire life," he breathes and then takes another bite of fruit.

My eyes trail over his features, his strong jaw, his smooth skin, and his young, muscular body. Something doesn't make sense.

"If it has been over twenty years, then why do you, you know, still look like you do?" I gesture to his face, his body. He only looks a few years older than me, but if he's been here my entire life, and who knows how much longer than that, he definitely shouldn't look my age.

"That's another thing about Dawnlin I haven't told you yet. Time… stops here. No one ages or changes as long as they are on the island. Dawnlin doesn't exist in the real world. It is a timeless world of its own. It's part of the magic."

"If so many people have been here for years searching for the cure, and still haven't found it, are their loved ones even still alive?"

Dane shrugs. "We don't know. Most people don't want me to check. It's too painful to think about. It's easier to focus on accomplishing what they came here for and enjoying each other's company in the meantime. They feel they got this far, and they need to see it through and not give up hope. It is likely that most of them are not there any longer, but how am I supposed to tell them to stop?"

I understand that. I only just got here, and I am itching to start looking, but this new information makes me uneasy. If so many of them have been searching, day in and day out for the elixir and still haven't found it, what makes me think I wouldn't spend years here as well?

Am I ready to spend years here? Am I ready to leave my kingdom behind?

I picture my mother laying in her bed, my father giving the nod to the healers to finally say goodbye. My eyes fill with tears, and I swipe them away roughly.

I am not going to leave anyone behind. I am determined to find the elixir and save my mother. I will not spend years here. I have come this far, and I am going to do it.

I don't have another choice. There's nowhere else I belong.

If I don't come back, or if I spend the next twenty years roaming the island, my kingdom will have no ruler. My father will have no chance to have another heir. The future of Blackwood depends on my return, and I won't return empty-handed.

I stand up, dusting off the back of my pants and pushing my hair out of my face. "Ready? I want to see more."

"Sure," Dane says, gathering our things and standing as well. He takes a step and then halts, as if he's hit a wall. His eyes widen, seeing something I cannot, and then his head shakes, snapping him out of the trance.

"I have to go." We'd traveled deep into the island, and while I had some bearings, I don't entirely know which way to go next.

"What do you mean you have to go?" I ask, hoping he doesn't notice the unease in my voice.

"I'm being called," he says. "I don't have a lot of time. I have to leave. Stay here. I'll come back for you. Just try to stay hidden, okay?"

"Okay," I nod, slightly nervous that he is just about to disappear on me after warning me about the Castaways.

He reaches down into the pouch at his side and grabs a pinch of the scented dust. "I'll be back soon. Just please, Lennox, stay put, alright?"

Before I can answer, he reaches up, drops the dust over his hair, and then vanishes before my eyes.

I'm still mildly in disbelief at witnessing magic so up close. I sit back down in our rest spot, I realize how open and exposed I am, and my mind wanders to the Castaways. Dane said to stay here and remain hidden, but I can't really do both in this spot.

Time drags on as I wait for him to return. I have nothing to keep myself occupied besides looking at the small slip of island around me, and trying to process all the information he told me.

I feel like I am wasting time. I came here to get the cure, and bring it home, not to sit around waiting. He warned me of the dangers, but the danger of losing my mother is also real.

I jump up, unable to contain my energy, and start pacing. He told me to wait, but I am armed. I am trained. I don't know my way around, but I can figure it out. I glance around and listen, making sure I don't see or hear anything moving before setting off the same way we came.

The immediate surroundings look fairly familiar as I retrace our steps, and the open parts of the path help me see where I am in relation to other big markers on the island. I follow along, keeping my bearings and moving quickly. I'm confident that I am going to make it back to camp, and remain on high alert, scanning my surroundings and listening for any abnormal noises. Dane would be proud, and maybe he won't force me to tag along with someone else for days.

The path narrows ahead of me, and walls of jungle rise on either side. I slow as I approach it and can't help but think that something feels…off. I strain to listen, trying to pick up on anything that would indicate why I suddenly feel the hair rising on the back of my neck, and that's when I notice it.

Nothing.

I hear nothing.

Where before there were sounds of leaves rustling in the wind and birds chirping and cawing, now there are none. The silence is deafening. It's as if this entire section of the jungle had gone still, warning me that something is not right.

I should have stayed where Dane left me.

I don't stop moving, trying not to give away that I noticed anything, in case someone is watching me. I pan the walls of trees, keeping my head still and straight forward. The inability to see anything through the dense vegetation makes me nervous for an ambush.

I need to get to more open ground, but I can't remember how long until the trees open up again. I have two choices, stand my ground and wait for an attack, or get the hell out of here.

I go with the latter.

I don't hesitate. I run with all my might, boots slamming into the packed dirt path and trees whooshing by. I keep my head straight and don't look back, focusing only on getting back to camp.

An arrow whizzes past my ear and strikes a tree in front of me.

Fuck, they are shooting at me.

At least I know the threat is a person and not some magical creature I wouldn't know how to defend myself against. I know I should weave, because a moving target would be harder to strike, but the path is too narrow.

My lungs burn and my legs still carry me as fast as I can. There are no breaks in the trees, but there hasn't been another arrow, so maybe I have to outrun whoever is following me.

I risk a glance back and don't see anyone, but I refuse to slow down. I'm not out of trouble yet.

I look forward again just as a thick rope of vines snaps into place right in front of me. I can't stop myself and slam into it, my momentum knocking me to the ground.

I can't breathe. I lay there gasping for breath, black dots flashing over my vision, when I hear multiple bodies step out of the trees around me

"Well, well, well. What have we here?"

CHAPTER TWENTY-THREE

I try to move, try to do anything to reach back and grab the hilt, but I have no breath. All I can focus on is sucking in air, trying to breathe again. Pain sears through my wrist as a boot crushes it, preventing even my small movements from going any further.

"Ah, ah, ah, not so fast." This is a new voice, different from the first. I mentally tally the number of people, so I know what I am dealing with.

The boot lifts, and hands wrap tightly around my wrists, squeezing and jerking me forward. "Give me that rope!"

A thick rope wraps around me, pulling tight and cutting into my skin. The dark spots are slowly disappearing, and my breath is returning. I can make out at least four people standing over me, all of varying heights.

This is bad.

I should have fucking listened to Dane and stayed put. Here I thought he was going to be proud of me for finding my way and getting back to camp safely, and instead I am here, hands bound, and at the mercy of these people.

Edmond's hostility training immediately comes to mind. I never thought I would need it, especially never having left the castle, but now I am glad I listened to him. When I can't fight, I have to be smart. I have to listen. I have to find out as much information about my attackers so that I can persuade them to free me, or at least get on their side and bide my time to escape.

"I've never seen her before."

"Neither have I, but that doesn't mean she isn't one of them. Scum that thinks they run the island." The speaker spits, not on me, thank gods.

"Bind her feet too. We'll carry her if we need to. She can't get away."

I'm pulled to a seated position, hands bound in front of me as someone kneels next to me and begins wrapping a rope around my feet. I could kick and scream and try to get away with my hands tied, but who would hear me? The only people I know here are Dane and Storm, and one isn't even on this island anymore.

I decide on a different tactic as soon as I notice who is binding my feet. A girl, slightly younger than me, at least by my world standards. She pulls tight on the knot, cutting it into my ankles just above my boots.

"Mara?" I ask.

Her eyes snap up to mine, a look of shock on her face.

"What did you say?" she sneers.

"Is your name Mara?" I try again. "Dane wanted me to meet you last night, but you didn't come back."

"Shut the fuck up, you filthy Castaway." It was the first voice again. He leans down and yells in my face, finally giving me a good look at my captors. They are not at all what I expected. The youngest looks barely ten years old, and no one looks older than Dane. Mara is the only girl among them, which verifies what Dane told me last night in the sleeping quarters.

I let out a sigh of relief.

These aren't the Castaways. They are with Dane. These are my people. I'm safe.

But they don't know me, and they clearly assume I am a Castaway.

"Dane is going to be beside himself when we bring her back. We finally got one!" The youngest jumps up and cheers.

Footsteps pound from behind me. Not one set, but two.

"What's going on?"

"We caught one! Now we can finally get answers to where they're hiding and smoke them out," the second voice says.

"But I'm not a Castaway! Dane brought me here last night. None of you were there. I didn't get to meet anyone."

"Liar!"

"That's exactly what a Castaway would say."

"I was there. I would have known if Dane brought someone new."

"I swear," I say, trying to keep the pleading out of my voice. I need to remember to stay calm. "How would I know Mara's name if I wasn't there?"

"Your brainwashing won't work on us, bitch."

"Where's your leader now? Is he going to come save you?"

"Maybe we can use her as bait and finally snag Weston!"

"Enough!"

The scrawniest of the boys is the one to speak, breaking the silence. He doesn't look to be the oldest, but definitely commands the most respect among them. Maybe he has been on Dawnlin longest.

"I'm being honest with you," I say, speaking low and slow. "I'm not a Cast—"

A foot slams into my stomach, knocking the breath from me yet again. I double over in pain, curling into myself, gasping again for air.

"Gag her," the boy says. "Blindfold her too. We're bringing her to Dane."

I hear the tear of fabric, then feel a thick gag being pulled between my teeth, followed by a blindfold over my eyes.

I have no way of convincing them I am who I say. It will have to be Dane who does that. But Dane isn't here, and I don't have any clue how long he will be gone. Once he sees me, he will know that they made a mistake. I just hope they stop injuring me at this point. Traipsing through the island and searching for the cure will not be easy with cracked ribs. I need to stay quiet and wait this out.

I'm just thankful they aren't the Castaways.

There is a lot of rustling and whispering before I am jostled around, and two bodies come along either side of me. They pick me up under my arms and drag me between them as they walk.

The journey back takes drags on as I hang between them. I don't know if it is because Dane and I were so far from camp, or if the blindfold just makes it difficult to get my bearings. Once we finally push through the trees and the light on my blindfold is cast into darkness, I know we've arrived at camp.

I stay quiet, letting them jostle me around at their disposal. They keep any communication to a whisper so I can barely hear, but now I'm not really trying to. I know this will all blow over once Dane returns. It just need to wait them out.

They don't bring me toward the rope ladder I climbed last night. Instead, they stay on the ground, heading to the other side of the clearing. I didn't realize there was anything else down here because Dane didn't show me any of it last night.

I hear a creak before I'm thrown onto the ground, dirt and dust kicking up into my face. The creak sounds again, followed by a clicking of a lock.

"Maybe we should wait until tomorrow before we tell Dane about her. A nice long night might help loosen her tongue a little bit."

My two captors laugh loudly as they walk away, and I'm left here alone.

Oh no.

Hopefully they will be too excited to have caught a 'Castaway' that they won't leave me in here overnight. If Dane goes back for me and I am not there, surely he will come looking for me. Though I doubt he would think to look in their own prison.

But what if he thinks the Castaways took me, after only just warning me about them?

Please please please tell him tonight.

I don't want to be locked up in here alone all night, all because of a misunderstanding and a bunch of children who won't listen.

My hands and feet are still tied, and every time I try to move them, the ropes bite harder into my skin. I listen for a minute, trying to hear if anyone has stayed behind to guard me. Voices in the distance confirm I am alone, and I reach up and push the blindfold away. The gag is harder, tied much tighter than the blindfold, and I can't reach the knot at the back to get it off.

Great.

I roll onto my back and rock until I am sitting upright so I can take in my surroundings. I am in a wooden cage, one I hadn't seen in the clearing last night, but it still must be within the confines of camp.

I guess this is it then. I just wait to be rescued.

I shake my head at my stupidity. I easily could have avoided meeting everyone like this if I had just listened. Now, I get to wait them out, because trying to escape before Dane returns would only convince them I am a Castaway, and who knows what they would do then?

I have nothing more to do to pass the time other than to think about all I learned from Dane this morning. I am so grateful it wasn't the Castaways that attacked and captured me, even though I know I will have a huge bruise from where the boy kicked me earlier. I'd take that rather than having my chances at finding the elixir ruined.

The elixir is hidden, and it doesn't seem like anyone has found it in years.

According to Edmond, there hadn't been any mysterious cures in a very long time. Could it be because of Weston? Because he is trying to keep the elixir to himself but can't get off the island? Dane mentioned that Weston and the Castaways had been slowly kidnapping people he had brought here. Was Weston so cruel that he would take away the hope of those by force, only to trap them on the island and let the loved ones die?

I shudder at the thought. If Dane hadn't already painted him as a monster, he definitely is in my mind now.

I need to find it and bring it home to my mother, Weston be damned.

As long as you don't stay tied up like this for days and can actually get started.

A small glimpse of the pink sky peeks out from the trees above the cage. The suns are setting, and soon it will be dark.

Those bastards are leaving me here.

I don't know how long it normally takes Dane to answer a summon. Mine took a while because I completely doubted who he was based on our prior friendship. He may be back already and is out searching for me, oblivious to the fact that I'm actually waiting for him to rescue me here.

The grumbling of my stomach distracts me. As a princess, I've never been without a meal unless it was of my own choosing. If those children wanted to play games and leave me here starving, I will not be so nice to them when I finally am released.

Children…can I even call them children? Some of them could be two or three times my age, despite looking exactly as they did the moment they left our world. If time doesn't move here, and no one has found the elixir in years, I could be the youngest and most inexperienced out of everyone. That doesn't justify them treating me like this.

The excitement turns out to be too much for them, and only moments later, I hear a barrage of voices, talking and shouting over each other.

"We got one! We finally got one!"

"Dane, you'll be so proud! We pulled the vine and SPLAT! She went down like a tree!"

"We finally have a lead on where they're hiding! If anyone can get it out of her, you can!"

The commotion gets louder as they get closer, but that means only one thing.

Dane is finally back, and I am about to be set free.

CHAPTER TWENTY-FOUR

"Everyone stay back. I'll handle this."

Dane's voice is low and authoritative as he makes his way toward the cage, toward me. I hope he isn't too angry with me, but I know he has every right to be. I didn't follow orders, and now, after witnessing everyone else and his authority over them, I know following his orders is not up for discussion. I know I'll eventually be out searching on my own, following my own orders, but I am not ready for that yet. I am not familiar enough with the island or the dangers it holds.

Clearly.

I wasn't expecting the dangers to come from people on my side.

Heavy footsteps echo through the trees as Dane approaches my cage. I can't help but feel a little uneasy as he gets closer, even knowing that there is no reason for me to fear him. My father never really scolded me. It was punishment enough to have his disappointed scowl directed at me, or just outright ignore me. If Dane were to truly be angry with me, I'm not sure how I'd take it.

I wait as he comes through the trees and into view, hoping that he is more concerned than angry.

"Lennox?"

He actually sounds surprised, thank the gods.

"This is where you've been?" Concern laces his voice as he quickly works the lock open and yanks on the door handle.

I grunt a response against the gag.

He drops to his knees in front of me and reaches behind my head to untie it.

"I'm going to kill them," he murmurs. His eyes are etched with concern, and I feel them drag over every inch of my face as he looks me over. "Are you alright?" His hand reaches up, thumb brushing across the top of my cheek and wrapping around to my hair.

Pain shoots through my jaw as I open and close it, and Dane's eyes catch my wince. "I'm fine. These are really hurting, though." I raise up my hands, showing him the ropes that are still confining me.

"Hang on, let me get them." He reaches into his boot and pulls out a small rustic looking knife with a serrated edge. He saws through the ropes until they break away, then drops the knife to grab my forearms. He turns my wrists over, inspecting every inch of them.

The trail of his fingertips over my skin causes tingles that directly combats the pain from the ropes.

"The skin is rubbed raw. We'll need to put some salve on them." He moves his attention to my ankles, where he does the same. They don't hurt as badly as my wrists, as my pants protected the skin from most of the rubbing, but they are still sore.

"Did they take your dagger?"

"No."

"But you didn't protect yourself?" he says, aghast.

"I didn't even have time. They were shooting at me when I tried to get away. I was running when I got knocked down. I could barely breathe, let alone reach for my dagger, before they were tying me up like a criminal."

"But they didn't take it?" He asks.

I shake my head. "They didn't even check me for a weapon."

"Fucking idiots." He stands, reaching down to grasp my hands and pull me to my feet. "You should have stayed where I told you. This never would have happened."

"I know. I'm sorry I didn't listen, and that was stupid. I'm just glad it was them and not the Castaways. As soon as I hit the ground, all I could think was 'I need air' and 'Dane's going to be so mad that I was captured after only a day.'"

That gets him to laugh, and the sound puts me a little more at ease. He wouldn't be laughing if he was too angry. "I'm glad it wasn't them, too." His gaze turns intense as he stands over me, overwhelming me.

I look away, trying to stop some of the discomfort from the intensity. He is still holding my hands and being so careful with me. It is a different careful than back in Blackwood. Everyone there treated me like glass or like I didn't exist, but Dane. Dane is treating me like I mean more than just another person seeking a cure.

"I need to take care of this. Please, just stay quiet until it's dealt with. Then I'll introduce you to everyone."

"Alright." He drops one hand and leads me out of the cage. I wince with pain as I walk, the skin on my legs stretching and pulling with each step. Just before we come out of the trees and back into the clearing, Dane releases my hand and steps directly in front of me.

Everyone is standing in the clearing, waiting, and there are more of them now than had originally captured me. News of having caught a Castaway must have spread, and they all rushed back to camp to see the prisoner.

"Why'd you let her out, Dane?"

"Don't tell me she tricked you!"

"Tie her back up!"

"Did she give them up that quickly already?"

The outburst is just as loud as it was before, everyone speaking over each other, and by the sounds of it, I'm sure this happens often.

"Enough," Dane says. He doesn't yell, but it is clear he is not joking. "Who is responsible for this?"

"I am." The boy from before, who was giving the orders, steps forward and clasps his hands behind his back. "Did she give you any information about the Castaways?"

Dane ignores the question. "Did you find out who she was?"

"I didn't need to. None of us know her, so I knew she wasn't one of us."

"You didn't ask her?" Dane crosses his arms over his chest, his muscles tensing as if he is holding himself back.

"She said you brought her here," Mara says from her spot in the group.

"Typical lie from one of those brainwashing spawn," the boy spits. "We couldn't trust anything she said."

Dane's jaw ticks. "Did you check her for weapons?"

"Ye—" He starts before cutting himself off. He snaps his mouth shut, and the realization hits his eyes.

"Did you?" Dane pushes again, taking an intimidating step closer to the boy.

"No. We didn't."

"So, you mean to tell me, you were so caught up in having caught someone you assumed was a Castaway that you didn't check her for any weapons, and then sent me in there alone? Without knowing whether or not she would attack me within the cage?"

"I— I—" He stammers, his eyes widening as he realizes his mistake.

"Stop." Dane raises a hand, then turns to face me. "Lennox, can you show them, please?"

I reach behind me, into my waistband, and pull out my dagger, holding it up so they can see the glint of the weapon that they didn't even attempt to take off of me.

Multiple faces drop. Some look angry, some surprised. Some even look like they want to take my dagger away and keep it for themselves.

"She's not a fucking Castaway," Dane says, his voice a loud growl. "I brought her here last night. She's only met Storm."

"That's why she knew my name," I hear Mara mumble.

Glad to see she finally figured out I wasn't lying or manipulating her.

"You were the leader in this?" Dane says as he directs his attention back to the boy.

"Yes."

"You're on watch duty for the next two weeks."

His face breaks as he responds with shock and dismay. "But Dane! That's not fair! How was I supposed to know who she was? I thought she was lying!"

The arrogance and authority he displayed earlier today is gone with Dane's command, and I'm glad. From the way he behaved with me earlier, he needed to learn a lesson.

"You took a captive without checking to see if she had a weapon. You let one of us go into a cage with an armed prisoner. You didn't question her yourself. And you harmed one of our own. We don't harm our own. We're better than they are!" Dane is almost yelling now, and I can feel his anger rippling through him. "I could keep going on with all the ways you endangered your family, but I think that's enough."

The boy's head hangs as he accepts Dane's wrath.

Would he have been this angry if it had happened to anyone else in the group, or was he more upset because it was me? I don't want special treatment, especially if it might set me apart from the group. I don't need to start relationships with these people in a negative light.

He nods and keeps his eyes downcast as he steps back to rejoin the group.

Dane doesn't speak as he glares at them.

My eyes travel over them too, taking in each of their faces. Some look guilty, some suspicious, some outright angry. Hopefully they will all move past their feelings quickly. I don't know how long this will take, and while the goal of being here isn't to make friends, I don't want to make enemies, either. Having some friends wouldn't be so bad.

Dane finally speaks, the rage gone from his voice.

"Everyone, this is Lennox. She arrived yesterday. She's from Blackwood." He proceeds to point out each person in the group and says their name. I've never met so many people at once, so I know it is going to take me some time to remember them all. I'd remember Mara, since she was the only other girl here at the moment.

"We have another new arrival back at camp. He's waiting in the tavern for us. He's young. I expect everyone to be kind and help him out."

A chorus of agreements sound off before Dane nods at the group and everyone disperses back to camp. The severity of the past few minutes seems gone as they race each other and fool around as they head up into the camp.

"Come on," Dane says to me, stepping aside so I can walk in front of him. "Let's go get some salve on those wrists."

CHAPTER TWENTY-FIVE

My wrists are now bandaged and treated with a magical salve, thanks to Dane. He had brought me straight to a small infirmary next to the armory and tended to my wounds with such gentle hands. The person in front of me was the complete opposite of the Guardian I saw back in the clearing.

It was like looking in the mirror. On the outside, I was a princess who had to behave a certain way and follow orders, to be the face of her kingdom. But on the inside, I didn't feel like that person. I am tired of being both, and just want to be me.

That's who I get to be here.

We head to the tavern, my stomach growling loudly after such an eventful day. I stand behind Dane, watching to see how the magic of the tavern works. A plate of food appears in the hollow of one tree, and Dane reaches in to grab it. Steam rises from the pile of roast meats, vegetables, alongside a chunk of crusty bread. Dane steps aside and waits for me to do the same. I peer inside the hollow and watch as a similar plate slides out of the back of the tree, appearing out of thin air.

I don't think I'll ever get used to magic.

"Right over there," Dane says, pointing to a table with a few boys already seated. One looks young and a little timid, and I wonder if this is the new arrival, like me.

Dane steps to the side so I can walk ahead. I almost jump when his hand grazes the small of my back, guiding me toward the table. I do my best not to react and give away the way his touch affects me.

He is so open about touching me, especially here in Dawnlin. He wasn't afraid back in Blackwood, but was more cautious about it. Proper. He probably wouldn't be this forward if he knew who I was, all the more reason for me to keep that little secret to myself.

I weave through the tables and benches, past the boys chattering happily and eating. I catch a glimpse of Mara out of the corner of my eye and see her noticing Dane's hand on my back. Her face turns stony, and I look away quickly.

What was that about?

Was she jealous of Dane being close to me? Or...

Were they together? Dane and I had never actually discussed anything here or in Blackwood. He was just always friendly. Very friendly. I assumed he may have had more than friendship feelings for me, but what if I was wrong?

What if he has had someone here waiting for him? They have probably had years of time together, and here I am just showing up and changing everything.

I already started off my time in Dawnlin on the wrong foot. I didn't need make it worse, and I wasn't going to interfere in someone else's relationship.

We make it to the table and sit, me on one side of the young boy, and Dane on the other. He looks up at us sheepishly, fighting with his fingers, his hands tucked deep into his lap.

I feel the strong desire to make him feel comfortable. I can't imagine what he must be going through being here this young.

"Hi, my name is Lennox. What's yours?" I ask him, leaning down with a smile.

"Fin," he says quietly.

"Hi Fin, it's nice to meet you."

He smiles shyly but doesn't speak.

"I'm new too. I just got here yesterday, right before you. We'll have to figure things out together. Sound good?"

He nods, his smile a little bigger now, and straightens his spine. He seems to be warming up but is still flicking his fingers under the table.

"Did you get enough to eat already?" He has a plate in front of him, but he's barely touched it.

He shakes his head, so I give him a little nudge. I pick up a wooden fork and spear a piece of potato. "Well, I'm starving, so I'll be sitting here for a little while if you want to eat some more."

He timidly picks up his fork and starts eating as he watches everyone around him.

I catch Dane on the other side of Fin, watching me. It occurs to me I don't have any experience talking to children this young. There are none that live in or visit the castle, none that I had ever encountered. I don't have any siblings. I hope to have children one day, but that hope feels out of reach because of how isolated I've been.

But talking to Fin feels natural. It makes me happy. I want to make him feel secure and comfortable, and to be a friend.

"How old are you?" One of the boys across the table, I think his name is Slade, asks.

"Six," Fin says, his voice slightly louder and more confident than before.

"Why'd you come here Fin?" A boy named Roley asks.

"I didn't mean to. My nana told stories, but I didn't know how. My sister is really sick. No one knows what's wrong with her. I was just sad. I ran away because I didn't want to watch her die. I was crying, and then Dane was there." Fin looks up into Dane's face as if he was his savior.

"I'm really sorry to hear about your sister," I tell him.

I am struggling with how to convey my emotions, besides telling him how sorry I am. He is clearly suffering with the struggles of his sister, and the magic led him here to give him a chance to help.

I realize as I look around at everyone else in the tavern, eating their meals, laughing, and chatting.

Every single one of us is in the same situation. Everyone has a person they love they want to help, to save. Many of them could have already lost someone, and didn't get to say goodbye, all because they can't find the elixir.

And then there's Weston and the Castaways, ripping hope away and endangering all of us.

I rub my hand across my chest as my emotions settle there. Everyone here is hurting. The only difference is how long they have had to cope with the pain. Tears well in my eyes and I blink them away. I am not the only one suffering. These people understand me, even if they don't really know me.

I clear my throat before I speak again. "We're going to do everything we can to save your sister, Fin."

He smiles then, and shifts on the bench, scooting a bit closer to me. It makes the pain I feel in my chest lessen slightly, knowing I have brought him some comfort.

My gaze meets Dane's again as he mouths, "You're a natural."

Dane has been dealing with people in his role as the Guardian for years. He's used to comforting and providing support, where this is completely new to me. I'm glad he thinks I'm doing something right.

"Did Dane explain everything to you already?" I ask him, taking another bite and watching as he mirrors my movements.

He nods. "Yes. But the Castaways scare me. Dane told me about them. Weston sounds mean."

"I know, he does," I agree, "but we are all here too, and we will help protect you. We can even teach you how to protect yourself, so you don't have to worry." I look at this sweet boy next to me and despite only just meeting him, I already feel protective of him. His small, almost frail body hints that he did not come from affluence back in our world. It would be nothing for Weston or one of the other Castaways to snatch him. "I could teach you how to shoot, if you want."

He nods quickly, a big smile lighting up his face. "I've never held a bow before! You know how? Where did you learn?"

"My friend Brynne taught me. She taught me lots of things." I see Dane's eyes cut over to me and then back again to the conversation he is having with the other boys.

"Maybe we can go check out the armory after we finish eating. Although, it might be hard for me to shoot for a couple of days." I hold my wrists up so he can see the bandages. "But that's alright. I can still show you."

"Lennox," Dane says, butting into our conversation. "Tomorrow you'll be with Mara. Fin, you'll be with Storm. They'll show you around, and then you'll switch to someone new, just until you get acquainted and comfortable."

I take another bite with a nod. I hope Mara won't make things difficult tomorrow, based on that stony look she gave me earlier. Maybe if it is just her and me, and Dane isn't around, it will be fine, but if there is a history between them, or if they are together, I do not have high hopes for how tomorrow will go.

These feelings I have toward Dane, whether they are friendship or something more, are completely new to me, and so is the idea of jealousy. I really need to clear things up with Mara, and hope that Dane really is a good guy, not leading either of us along.

We finish eating just as the suns finally set, casting the camp in darkness, the magic triggering all the torches to light around us. Everyone clears their places and scatters to different parts of camp. Exhaustion from all the events today hits me like a crashing wave, and I find myself unable to stifle yawns.

Dane gives me a small wave goodbye as he guides Fin toward their side of camp. I send up a quick prayer to the gods that his first night alone and away from his family goes smoothly. Being so young and away from your family has got to be tough, so I hope some of the other boys take him under their wing.

I shower quickly, successfully avoiding anyone else, then head back to our bunks, ready to finally climb into bed. When I come around the corner to climb the ladder, I almost let out a scream. Mara startles me, standing in the entry with a scowl on her face and her arms crossed over her chest.

"I'll advise you to get some sleep. You think you're tired today, just wait until tomorrow. You better be able to keep up."

She turns on her heel before I can respond and goes straight to her bunk.

Fine. If she doesn't want to be friends, we don't have to be, but she can at least be civil. I have done nothing to her besides come here with the same hope and goal she did and be wrongfully imprisoned.

"Goodnight Mara," I say directly as I walk by her bunk and start climbing toward mine. I'll be ready for tomorrow. She says I need to keep up, and that won't be a problem, as long as I keep down enough water in this humidity. I want to get out and search just as much as she doesn't want me with her. I am going to use these days to my advantage and soak up all the knowledge from the experienced Voyagers as I can.

Edmond always taught me I need to have a strategy, a plan of attack, and a goal in mind. I know what my goal is. The elixir. To get home to my mother. And now I need to use every piece of information and knowledge that everyone else has gained over years and years of searching to get me there.

I take my boots off and climb into bed, barely remembering moments after my head hits the pillow, but ready for whatever the morning brings.

CHAPTER TWENTY-SIX

I wake up to something hitting me in the face.

My eyes fly open, the sky above me still a deep blue of the early morning. Something from below comes flying at my head again, and I swat it away before feeling around my bunk to see what had hit me. I reach over and grab balled up socks, then stick my head over the side of my bed to find Mara standing with her arms crossed, a look of impatience on her face.

At least she used something soft.

"I'm leaving in one minute. You're either with me or you're on your own," she yells.

I fling my blanket off and hurry to pull on my boots. "I'll be right there!" I call down. I grab a string of leather that I had taken from the extra clothes and supplies in the bathroom and quickly braid my hair, tying it off at the ends. Having it off my neck will hopefully help with the heat. I slide my dagger into my waistband and start climbing down the ladder.

Mara is already striding down the walkway by the time I make it to the last rung and hop down.

Rolling my eyes at her back, I hurry after her.

So this is how today is going to go.

A bunch of boys are eating in the tavern when we arrive. I glance around but don't see Dane or Fin. He is probably letting him rest after the shock to his life from yesterday, just as he did with me.

I inhale breakfast, trying to keep up with Mara, who clearly doesn't care if I am left behind. We finish eating wordlessly and clear our plates, and she takes off toward the armory. She opens the doors, pulling out a sword and a dagger and strapping everything to her waist.

I take a moment to glance at the contents of the armory. An array of blades of all shapes and sizes hang along the wall. Bows and crossbows hang from pegs, and quivers filled with arrows stand on the floor. There are some weapons I've never seen before. I move past them, reaching for a bow and a quiver full of arrows. I sling them across my back to keep my hands free for anything we might encounter on the island.

"Do you even know how to shoot that thing?" Mara asks, a tone of annoyance coating her voice.

"Yes." I don't offer her anything more. I'd have plenty of practice being diplomatic and not letting my emotions show through my words. If this was how she wanted things to be between us, then I would treat her with respect and nothing more.

I've never realized how much the lessons Edmond had been drilling into me actually applied to life. They always seemed so tedious, and mostly unnecessary. But now, as I am out interacting with people and in different, potentially dangerous situations, the lessons flood back to me and help me think through every decision I make.

"Let's go then." She leaves the doors to the armory open, and we slide past another group coming to grab their weapons for the day.

Once we are out of camp and through the trees, Mara moves quickly, heading in the opposite direction Dane and I had explored yesterday. It's difficult to pay attention to my surroundings while trying to keep up with her, but I do my best. Clearly, she knows the island well, and is pushing me to keep up.

We cut off the main path and head down a hill, into a valley. I follow wordlessly, focusing on trying to keep up with her pace and mentally making a map. After a few more minutes of blindly following, I decide to try to break the ice.

"What are we doing today?"

She whirs around, stopping me in my tracks, and stomps toward me, shoving her face into mine.

"Are you sleeping with Dane?" she spits, the look of anger and jealousy written across her features.

"What? No!" I splutter. "Why would you think that? I just met him."

Her eyes bore into mine, like she's trying to figure out if I'm telling the truth. "He was gone. For a long time. Then suddenly, he comes back, and he comes back with you. Were you sleeping with him back home, and came here to steal him and the elixir from all of us? Is that how you got him to bring you?"

"No, Mara, no. I'm not here for Dane. I'm here for my mom." I didn't even think about the words before they left my mouth.

Mara is the first person I've told that the reason I came to Dawnlin is my mother. Dane doesn't even know, and he's never asked. Maybe the Guardian can't, or maybe he simply doesn't need to know.

Mara hasn't given me any reason to trust her. She hasn't even really given me a reason to like her. But I did. Maybe giving her a glimpse of me will convince her I'm not here for the wrong reasons.

She doesn't speak, she just stares at me, her eyes boring into me as she tries to decide if I am telling the truth.

"I'm not trying to steal anything from anyone. I just want to help my mother."

She takes a step back and looks down at her feet, and a single tear runs down her cheek. She wipes it away angrily, as if the tear betrayed her.

"I can tell he likes you."

I shrug. "Maybe. But that's not why I'm here. I didn't coerce him to bring me. I actually pulled a blade on him when he startled me at the fountain."

I don't want to talk about any feelings I may have toward Dane with her. Although, if this conversation is any indicator, she may have feelings for Dane, and I don't know how long those feelings have been growing.

The corners of her lips rise a little before her face drops again. "I'm here for my mom, too. She was all I had. Is all I have. It was always just me and her."

I stay quiet, watching another tear fall on her cheek. She doesn't wipe this one away.

"It's been…a long time. I keep looking every day, but deep down, I think she's already gone. I didn't want to give up, to give up on her. I thought that maybe if I found someone, I could just stay here. I don't know if I could handle being home without her. She'd want me to be happy, right? I have nothing to go back to if she's gone. I've been too afraid to have Dane take me back to check."

My heart breaks for her. Everyone I've encountered on the island so far has such a tough exterior. They are so determined and strong. I realize now it is just to hide the pain they feel every day that they return unsuccessfully. Every day they are afraid of going home empty-handed with time wasted, to find out it was too late.

I don't want that to be me. I want to succeed. I don't know how I can differ from everyone else trying, but I want to be. I will do everything I can, use all my skills, and do my best to trust the island and not lose hope.

"I know you have no reason to trust me, but thank you for telling me your story. I'm not trying to take anything from you. That's not my goal here." I pause, trying to decide if I really want to know the answer to the question. "Were you two ever together?"

"No, but I always hoped that one day he might finally see it." She crosses an arm over her body and grips her elbow tightly. "And now here you are. You're so beautiful. You couldn't have just left Dane alone and chosen any of the suitors that I'm sure you had falling all over you at home?" There is a hint of humor in her voice, but I can tell she is still disappointed and discouraged.

I blush at the compliment. I've never had anyone call me beautiful that wasn't preparing me for a ball, and it was usually Tila.

"Believe it or not, there aren't suitors lined up at home for me. I'm pretty alone back home, too."

She scoffs. "Yeah, sure. I believe that."

We need to move forward, for both our sakes, instead of dwelling on possibilities and feelings. I can hear Edmond murmuring in the back of my mind, "*Be diplomatic. Find a common goal.*"

"Let's not worry about that, or about Dane. I know we got off on the wrong foot, but maybe we can learn to work together? To trust each other? We both want to save our mothers. We have a better chance if we focus on that, not on how Dane feels."

She eyes me, cautiously. "Do you actually know how to shoot that thing, or were you just lying to me?"

My change in subject tactic worked.

I pull the bow off my back and grab an arrow, nocking it and turning to point it at her. Fear flickers over her face before she schools her features again, trying not to portray any sort of weakness. I aim and release. The arrow flies past her head and slams into the trunk of a tree about fifty feet behind her. Dead center.

She lets out a breath as she spins around to look at the arrow, then turns back toward me.

I hang the bow over my body again and shrug. "Have I given you something not to trust me about yet?"

"I guess not," she answers, looking back at the arrow. "Alright. But I promise you, as soon as you cross me, you're done."

I nod. "Agreed."

"Follow me. I was going to look down by the river today."

She turns and strides away quickly. I follow behind and can feel nerves rising throughout my body.

Now isn't really the best time to be honest with her and tell her I am deathly afraid of water.

CHAPTER TWENTY-SEVEN

"Have you been to the river yet?" Mara yells to me as we make our way toward the center of the island. I'd seen the river when I first arrived, flowing from the lush waterfalls coming off the mountain and splitting the island in two. From the quick look, I knew some parts seemed calmer than others, but either way, I want to stay far away from it.

"No," I yell back. "Dane and I started our tour on the other side of camp."

Noise from the canyon ahead gets louder as we approach. I don't know where along the course of the river we are approaching, but it must be somewhere near rapids. The closer we get, the more the roar of the water drowns out her voice, making it hard to hear her warnings.

"I know this part looks dangerous, but don't let the parts that look tame fool you. There's a nasty undercurrent, and all kinds of creatures that lurk beneath the surface."

"Stay out of the water. Got it."

"We're going to need to cross. I want to search the other side today." She points across the way, and I notice a difference in the trees. It is odd, as if this side of the river is tropical, and the other side is more like the forests back home. "There's a bridge a little farther down. Follow me."

She jogs closer to the edge, and I follow, paying attention to my feet and staying far from the cliff. At one point, I make the mistake of getting a little too close and slightly lean over the edge to peek, and my stomach drops. The canyon is deep, and the crashing water below could easily throw me against the rocks and pull me beneath the surface.

Nope. I need to stay away from there.

A few minutes pass and I am feeling breathless from the jogging when I see a crossing in the distance.

I gape at the structure I'm expected to cross. "*That's* the bridge?"

I was expecting something made of stone, something sturdy that didn't look like I was about to fall to my death.

No.

This bridge looks like it would snap with a strong wind. The plank steps that had definitely seen better days, are spaced out and held together by thick ropes, with thick rope sidings to hold on to. This bridge barely looks like it could hold the weight of one person, let alone two. The river below it is much calmer than the rapids farther upstream, but with Mara's warning of the undercurrent, it doesn't give me any more confidence.

"What, are you scared?"

"Actually, yes," I say matter-of-factly. "Now is probably a bad time to mention that I can't swim."

She chuckles at my admission. "Not being able to swim is the least of your worries. Even if you could, those guys wouldn't let you swim far."

I peer over the edge to see the stuff of nightmares. Huge, deep green reptiles fill the calm water below. Long, sharp yellow teeth stick out of their mouths at all angles, and red beady eyes follow any movement we make. Some are floating calmly, while others gnash their teeth, jaws snapping at another in a fight for some unknown prize.

I'd seen artist renditions of dragons and other non-existent creatures, but these…I can't believe what I am seeing. Nor can I believe that I'm supposed to calmly walk across a death trap of a bridge above these creatures, just to search the other side of the island. At least they are all the way down there, and we're up here.

"Just whatever you do, don't stop on the bridge, and don't look down," Mara says as she strides confidently over to the entrance.

I suck in a breath, and nod in agreement, mostly trying to psych myself up rather than acknowledging her, since she isn't even looking at me anymore. I push my fear of water far from my mind and try to focus only on getting to the other side.

Mara takes the lead, stepping onto the planks of the bridge and grasping the ropes with each step. Her directions to me were dripping with confidence, but I can see the whites of her knuckles from her tight grip.

"Should I wait until you get across to go?" I call after her.

She doesn't turn around but yells back at me. "Yes!"

In a few breathless minutes of watching her feet steadily step on each plank, she finally reaches the other side. She turns back and waves her hand at me, signaling my turn.

If I thought I was breathless watching her, it is nothing compared to the way I feel knowing it is now my turn.

I step up to the edge and try not to look down at the river below, but fail. The beasts are still laying across the surface, some on top of each other, and others swimming in small circles around the rest of the group. It's like they are waiting for me to make a misstep, to be their next meal.

I wonder if anyone ever has.

I tightly grasp the rope on each side, trying to mimic Mara's sure steps in the center of each plank. The first few steps I take slowly and carefully, doing my best not to jostle the bridge or do anything that will cause me to lose my balance. It takes a second to adjust. The planks are nothing like the stone hallways I walk across every day, and these are even more flimsy than the walkways back at camp. Plus, there's no net to catch anyone if they fall.

"Don't look down!" Mara yells.

I keep moving, one plank at a time, keeping my eyes trained on the patch of land on the other side. I've made it halfway. A rush of confidence fills me, and I keep going, keeping my pace and thinking of nothing else but the solid ground on the other side.

A loud creak breaks my focus.

I barely have time to register the sound before I am weightless, falling straight down into the hole where the plank had snapped beneath me.

A scream pierces my ears, and I barely even realize it is my own. I don't have time to do anything but react, throwing my arms out in front of me and trying to grasp anything that will keep me on this bridge. My fingers claw at the next plank before gaining purchase, and the weight of my body catches up with me as I jerk toward the river.

"Lennox!" I hear Mara scream, but I can't see her. All I can see are the planks before me and the wood I am so desperately trying to cling to.

I hear splashing below but refuse to look down. I clamp down hard on the splintered wood, begging the gods that this plank will hold. I try to swing my leg up toward the rope and let out a gasp as the pain in my side from being kicked and dragged prevents me from getting anywhere close.

Fuck.

I am totally fucked.

I make the mistake of looking down at the horror that is in the river.

The monsters below that have been waiting and watching are now clambering up, piling on top of each other, snarling and gnashing, trying to get to me. The pile they have created creeps closer and closer to my dangling feet, and I realize their sheer size makes the depth of the canyon a lot smaller than I thought before.

Then they start jumping.

Climbing closer and pushing off with their massive legs, snapping their jaws at my feet with their eyes focused on their prey.

I scream and turn away, focusing back on the bridge and trying to figure out how to get back up. My muscles burn and my fingers start to slip as I try to heave myself up. I fight with every ounce of my strength to get my chest up and over the edge of the plank.

The sound of jaws snapping is right below me, and I feel one of them hit the bottom of my boot. I pull my legs up toward my chest, my ribs screaming at me, my fingers begging me to let go.

No.

It is not supposed to happen this way. I am not supposed to die like this. If I fail, here and now, my kingdom wouldn't only be without a queen, but my mother's fate would surely be sealed.

I guess I never thought that someone could die in a magical land like Dawnlin, but I was wrong. Someone could, and that someone could be me. I wouldn't have a fighting chance if I fall into the rushing river without these monsters, let alone with them. But here I am, dangling by my fingertips above a river I don't know how to swim in, trying to escape the mouth of a beast that I never would have believed existed except in the depths of my nightmares.

I don't want to let Edmond or Brynne down. I don't want to let my mother down. No one in Blackwood would ever know what happened to me, because Dane doesn't know who I am. He can't go back and tell any of them, tell the king his daughter fell to her death trying to save the mother she never knew.

I need to try. Another of Edmond's lessons pops into my head, making me adjust my grip on the board and squeeze tighter.

If I am going to fail, I am going to fail trying.

I take a deep breath and pull with everything I have. I move forward, edging over the plank when I am stopped abruptly.

Fuck!

The end of the bow I have draped over my body caught on the rope, lodging itself between it and the plank and keeping me held down.

I can't pull myself up with it stuck, but if I let go, to try to get it off, it might be the last thing I do. I feel another small bump on my boot and a snapping that follows, so I kick my feet wildly, trying to ward off the next beast that gets close.

I'm out of time.

I let go with one hand and quickly reach up and pull the bow over my head, dropping it in the river below. My other hand slips even more, my entire body being held up by the strength of my fingers. I stretch forward, grasping for a knot in the rope, something I can grab and use as leverage. My fingertips brush it, stretch to close that tiny gap. I feel my strength starting to wane and panic washes over me.

This is it. It's the end.

I hope Edmond and Tila and Brynne know how much I love them.

I hope Dane finds the cure.

I hope they remember me.

Suddenly, fingers wrap around my free hand and hold them tightly.

"Lennox! Hang on!"

Mara.

She's come for me.

She didn't have to. Minutes ago, she hated me, and after we talked, for all I knew, she barely even liked me. It would be easy to let me fall and let the island claim my death. It would mean less competition for her, not only for the cure, but for Dane, too.

But she didn't.

Her fingers move to grasp my wrist and she commands me to do the same.

"I got you! You need to let go and grab my other hand."

"I can't let go!" I yell at her, panic lacing my screams.

"You don't have a choice!"

I look down at the monsters below me and know she's right. Her grip tightens as I release the board, turning my hand to clasp her arm. She jolts forward, all of my weight and my life in her hands. She pushes both feet against the knots in the rope before she leans backward, pulling me up and over the edge. I clamber up and away from the hole, my chest heaving and heart pounding furiously.

"We need to get off the bridge," Mara yells as she glances over the side, watching the monsters still jumping and snapping at us.

Scrambling to my feet, I take off behind her, neither of us taking our time like before. Our only goal is to get off this bridge as fast as possible. I am stumbling. My body is not fast enough to keep up with my mind, but I will my feet to keep moving and beg the bridge to hold.

The second my feet hit solid ground, I throw myself onto the floor and roll to my back, gasping for air.

"That was fucking terrifying," I pant. I can see Mara out of the corner of my eye, hands on her knees and head hanging, also sucking in her breaths.

"I saved your ass," she says between breaths. "Leave it to the newbie to get herself into trouble like that on her first day out."

I point back at the bridge. "That was not my fault. Why would you want to cross that death trap?"

"It's been fine for years. The planks have never broken before." She straightens and rests her hands on the top of her head. "Guess you're just lucky."

"If that's lucky, I don't want to find out what unlucky is." My breathing slows, and I stare up at the bright blue sky, trying to work up the courage to ask Mara a question.

"Why did you come back for me?"

"What do you mean?"

"I mean," I say as I push myself up, sitting with my legs still sprawled out in front of me. "You could have left me there. You could have let me fall. It would have been easy, and I wouldn't have been in your way anymore."

She sits quietly for a moment, thinking. "I almost did," she admits. "But I thought about my mom, and I know that isn't the person she raised me to be. I'm not cruel. You needed me, so I helped. Plus," she adds,

"Dane would have killed me if something happened to you on your first day and that definitely would have ruined my chances with him."

I burst out laughing and catch a smile spreading across her face.

"Way to lighten the mood," I say with a smile.

"It had to be done. Besides," she replies as she stands up, brushing the dirt off her pants. "We don't hurt our own."

She reaches a hand down to me and pulls me up. "We still have a lot of day ahead of us, so no use dwelling on all of this. That won't help us find the cure."

She is right. This whole event has completely shaken me to my core and opened up my eyes to the dangers that Dawnlin possesses. It makes sense though, that the island is full of peril, making anyone here have to earn what they sought. That's how getting here was. It was a challenge. It had to be put together and discovered. It wasn't just handed to you with easy directions. There is now nothing that made me think finding the elixir was going to be any different.

"What are we waiting for?"

CHAPTER TWENTY-EIGHT

"Where to now?" I ask Mara as I take in our new landscape. "Through here," she says, pointing to a pathway that cuts through the rock.

"Are you going to tell me what we're looking for now?" I ask.

She scans the rock walls as we move. "Dane already explained to you we are looking for the cure, right?"

"Yes, he told me that no one knows where it is or how to get it."

"Did he tell you anything else?"

"No. He was in the middle of showing me around the island to get acquainted when he was called away for Fin."

"Right. It's important to get to know the island like the back of your hand. That's why we go out searching every day."

"Maybe I'm not understanding something correctly. I'm assuming you've been here…a while…and you go out and search the island every day. You and all the other boys know every square inch of it. So, why is it you haven't found the elixir yet?"

She stops in the middle of the path, turning to face me.

"It's because the island changes. The land stays the same, but parts of the land, they're different. It's like a giant obstacle course with traps along the way, and every day you don't know what different place you'll find. Any of them could lead us to the right place, to the hiding place. We have to keep trying every day."

"How do you find them?" I ask, as I take in our surroundings. The rocks, the trees, the packed dirt from being trodden repeatedly every day for years. Nothing looks like it is fake or constructed. It all looks so real, so solid. But maybe that is all magic. It is all an illusion until you fall into the right place. "Everything looks so normal to me."

She turns and continues down the path, climbing up over a boulder that is blocking the way and hopping down to the other side.

"Me personally, I think Dawnlin is alive. I think it is watching us all. I feel like it *chooses* to show you things when it wants you to find them. Dane doesn't agree with me. He says if that was the case, then why have none of us found the hiding place yet?"

"He's got a point, though. Wouldn't the island want to help you find it?"

"Maybe it's protecting it. It was hard to get here, right? Maybe it is making us earn it."

I agree with Mara. So far, everything I have seen and learned about this place has been earned. The myth says nothing about how to find it or how to find the elixir. You have to figure that out on your own in order to get here. It almost feels as if the accomplishment is acknowledged by the magic that lives here. Maybe that magic *is* actually protecting the island and the cure, and making sure the person who finds it is deserving.

Like keeping it away from Weston.

But how does it know?

"What kinds of things do we look out for?"

"Some are obvious. An enormous hole in the ground, a trip vine. Some are less obvious, and you just stumble upon them. But whenever you think you want to look somewhere you discovered again, it might not be there. It will be something else or just gone."

"So that's why you can never stop looking. There's always somewhere new to look."

"More or less. Sometimes, they can be pretty dangerous. Sometimes, it's just a dead end. You always have to stay on your toes."

I eye the pathway with the boulders and sharp rocks differently now, realizing that at any moment, anything could change. "So, between the island basically trapping you every day, and keeping an eye out for the Castaways, how does anyone survive here?" I say.

She smirks. "That's what makes it fun. It's also what makes it seem like you haven't been doing the same thing every day for years and years." She glances down at her feet and kicks a rock off the path.

"If you don't mind me asking Mara, how long have you been here?"

"We don't really keep track. It's—"

Mara is cut off by a scream as the ground drops out from under us. Before I know what is happening, we are tumbling, head over foot, down a steep slope that is completely shrouded in darkness. My body slams into the hard ground as rubble and sharp rocks stab into me while we tumble. I clench my eyes, trying to block out the dirt and gravel kicking up into my face.

Mara cries out as my body slams into hers, coming to a halt against a wall.

"Fuck!" Mara groans as she rolls onto her back, untangling herself from me.

My entire body aches from the beating it just took. I open my eyes and try to look around, but wherever we fell is pitch black, and I can't see my hand in front of my face.

"You alright?" Mara says.

"Yeah, yeah I'm fine." I stand and reach my hands out, trying to feel anything around me. My fingertips find soft fabric and I grab onto Mara's arm. "But what do we do now?"

"We need to find a way out." She takes my hand and places it flat against the wall we crashed into. "Grab on to me with the other. We need to feel along the wall to see where this goes."

We make it a few steps forward, sliding our fingertips along the wall to guide us when a torch lights suddenly in front of Mara's face. The flames illuminate the tunnel in front of us, but only as far as a few steps. Packed dirt and hanging roots make up the roof, and a damp musty smell meets my nose.

"So we just blindly follow it?" I ask, squinting into the darkness to make out if there are any threats just past the ring of light.

Metal sings through the space as Mara draws her sword. She grabs the torch and extends it in front of her. "We just blindly follow it."

I unsheathe my dagger and hold it at my side. I'm regretting dropping my bow into the river right about now, thinking how much better it would be to have the ability to strike any opponent from a distance.

This will have to do.

We follow the tunnel in silence, but on high alert. I have no idea what direction it is leading, and there's no way to get my bearings.

"How far do you think this goes?" I ask, breaking the silence.

"I don't know," Mara says. "I haven't been in one of these in a while."

"So this isn't the first time this has happened?"

"First time I was dropped into the ground? No, but the first time it happened in that spot."

She said it so nonchalantly, yet my mind is still reeling from falling into the ground and how this tunnel which would have taken months to dig out back in Blackwood is just here today, and possibly gone tomorrow.

"Do you ever think you've gotten close?" I say after a few moments more.

"To the cure?"

"Yes."

Mara sighs. "Maybe? There's not really any way of knowing. There have been times where I thought I must have gotten there, only to be met with a dead end. It can be hard, especially after such a long time. It's easy to get discouraged and wonder what it is about you that can't figure it out, or isn't enough."

"What makes you keep going?" I ask. "Especially after all this time."

Mara stops and turns slightly to face me, the light from the torch illuminating the soft look on her face.

"Hope." She turns back and keeps walking.

That one word fills me with warmth. It isn't just me that feels it, that needs it to be here. Hope is driving all of us and keeping us going. Despite all of our previous lives, our backgrounds, our relationships, we all have something that binds us together and gives us a purpose.

I hurry to catch up. Just as I am about to reach Mara, my foot depresses into the ground and I freeze.

"Uh, Mara?" My voice wavers as I try to figure out what that step just did. She turns back to me and looks down at my foot, sunken into the ground. Her eyes widen and she quickly scans the tunnel around us, looking for whatever is coming.

A deep boom sounds, and the tunnel around us shudders. We stare at each other, unable to move. I watch as Mara's face changes from wary to terrified.

"Run!" she screams and bolts into the darkness.

I don't wait. I tear after her, trusting that whatever she saw was worth running from. Legs pumping and chest heaving, I sprint after her, and that's when I realize what is happening.

The rock wall to our right is moving.

The tunnel is closing in on us.

Terror clutches at my throat as I stare straight ahead, refusing to look at the wall creeping in. All I can focus on is the ground under my feet and begging for an exit ahead.

"I see something!" Mara screams. "Go, go, go! We can make it!"

The wall is inches away from my shoulder and I can feel the panic bubbling up. If Mara is wrong, we are moments away from being crushed.

I push harder, my toes almost touching Mara's heels as we sprint toward whatever she sees. Seconds later I see it too, an arch of rock that looks like a portal. I pump my legs, the rock now scraping my arms as they swipe by with each step.

"Argh!" I let out a cry and push Mara forward, just as we reach the archway. She tumbles into the portal, and I follow behind, losing my balance from the force of pushing her. We hit the portal and fall straight down, landing in a heap in a pile of leafy plants.

"Sweet mother," Mara pants. "That was so fucking close, Lennox."

I gasp in breaths, and take in the scrapes up my arm and the blood dripping down my skin.

"Yeah," I gasp. "What a great first day."

Mara giggles, and I can't help but laugh too. I don't know which death would have been worse, eaten by the river beasts, or crushed underground. Either way, I thank the island for scaring the shit out of me, but also for letting us survive.

Maybe Mara was right. Maybe Dawnlin is watching us.

Maybe it is fighting us, but what if it is also helping us?

I look around to see where it spit us out and realize that despite this being my first real day, I recognize where we are.

"Are you kidding me?" I push to stand and take in the lush plants and wall covered with vines just next to us. "We went through all that, just to end up literally back at camp?"

Mara stands and slides her sword back into its sheath and holds the torch away from the foliage. She chuckles and says, "Welcome to Dawnlin."

CHAPTER TWENTY-NINE

I stand at the edge of a cliff, looking out over the waves crashing into the rocks below. I don't dare step too close to the edge. There is no way down except for a free fall into the deep waters and deadly currents.

It is cold, which strikes me as odd from my time on the island. An icy wind rips over the cliff and cuts through the thin linen clothes I have worn since I arrived. I wish I had my cloak.

The swish of long grass startles me, and I turn quickly to see who approaches from behind. It's Dane, a bright smile lighting up his face. I wave and smile back, wondering why he found me today.

He draws closer, and I see that what I thought was a smile isn't one at all. He grimaces, his face full of anger and hatred. He reaches into his belt and pulls out a knife, stalking toward me as if I am his prey.

I gasp and reach into my waistband to pull my blade, but my hands came up empty. Shock and fear blazes through me as I look back at Dane. My mind races as I try to figure out where to go, what to do. Why is he doing this?

The glint of his knife catches my eye, and I realize it isn't his. It is mine.

He brings his hand to his lips and lets out a sharp whistle. Creatures emerge from the grass behind him, followed by everyone from camp. They stand firmly behind Dane and stare me down.

"You're a liar!" Dane snarls. "A traitor!"

I stammer, not knowing what to say or what he is talking about. "No, I'm not! What do you mean, Dane? It's me! Lennox!"

"I know exactly who you are. You were a liar this whole time."

"I'm not!" I urge, slowly backing away before halting. I feel the rock shift under my foot as it falls down the cliff and into the churning water. My mind swims and panic rises and settles in my throat.

I swallow the lump and beg, "Dane, stop this! Please!"

The others draw their weapons, the look in their eyes like death. Even Mara and Fin are poised to attack, the hatred so pure and clear in their eyes.

A beasts from the river stops next to Dane as if waiting for a command, its jaws snapping and saliva dripping from its mouth.

"Bring her to me," Dane grumbles, his voice low and malicious.

"Dane, no!" I scream before all of them charge forward, a war cry escaping their lips. I turn abruptly, trying to find a way out. I peer over the edge of the cliff, the dark rocks so harsh against the crashing white waves. I don't know what more to do. I have to try to save myself. I glance back over my shoulder only to see them gaining on me. I turn back, pushing off the edge of the cliff with all my strength and leap into the air, falling...

I scream as I fall toward the depths below, toward my death. I jolt, hitting the water, only to throw my eyes open and realize that I am not in the water. I'm in my bunk, gasping for breath. I frantically run my hands over the padding, grounding myself.

It was a dream. A nightmare.

Tears stream down my cheeks, my body shaking and covered in sweat. There is pounding in my ears, and I reach up to place a hand on my chest, trying to slow my beating heart. It takes me a moment to realize that it is not just my heart in my ears. Those are footsteps. Someone is running.

"Lennox?"

My platform shakes as someone clamors up the ladder. Dane's head pops above the edge and he pushes up until I can see him from the waist up. His eyes race over me, looking for any sort of threat. "Are you alright? What happened?"

My head spins, probably from the short shallow breaths I can't control. The hatred in his face keeps flashing in my mind, and my stomach still feels like it has fallen out of me from the leap off the cliff.

It's too much.

My hands shake and the sobs come again, despite trying to breathe through them.

"I...you were...I..." I try to tell him what happened but my body won't let me. This is beyond anything I have experienced before. I have had maybe a handful of bad dreams in my life, but none have ever been this vivid or had anything to do with water. I hardly remember them when I wake. This was not like that. It was real. Felt real. It was too hard to separate from this new reality.

"Shh." His hands cup my face, and I lean into him, needing the comfort and safety his touch brings me. "It was just a dream. It wasn't real."

"It was...terrible..." I choke out.

His thumbs stroke across my cheeks, wiping away the tears that had fallen.

"Try to take a deep breath," he murmurs, then inhales deeply, his eyes keeping contact with mine the entire time. I try to breathe in with him, but my breaths are staggered by sobs.

"That's it," he croons. He brushes a stray piece of hair off my forehead, his fingertips gently caressing my head in a way that no one ever has before.

We stay just like this, breathing together for a few moments until my breaths are less labored and my calm has returned. He hasn't moved, hasn't wavered. His soft amber eyes stay locked on mine the entire time, tearing down any memory of the harsh angry ones in the dream.

"Thank you," I mutter, feeling slightly embarrassed that I am so worked up over something that wasn't real.

"Of course." The pad of his thumb runs across my jaw as he slides his hand into my hair.

I ignore my heart rate picking back up for a different reason this time and ask, "Why were you awake?" I look around camp, but it is still dark, and no one else is wandering around or ready to leave for the day.

"Couldn't sleep. I was going to get something to eat when I heard you scream. I thought you were in trouble. I worried it was the Castaways."

I shake my head and sniffle. "Nope, just my dreams."

"I hate to say this, but I'm glad it was just that." He removes his hands from my face and grasps the top of the ladder. His head tilts in thought before he speaks. "Grab your stuff and follow me."

"Why?" I ask warily.

"Just trust me," he says with a smirk.

"I thought we already established that you had to earn that back?"

"Right. Well, let's start here. Come on."

His head disappears from the side of my platform as he descends the ladder. I quickly run my fingers through my hair and wipe the tears from under my eyes before grabbing my dagger and tucking it away.

If I am not careful, Dane will charm me into trusting him, and I am scared of what it would mean for me if I do.

CHAPTER THIRTY

Dane clutches my hand as we weave through the paths shrouded with trees. The island looks so different in the dark, especially on a moonless night like tonight. Dane doesn't seem to mind. He knows exactly where he is going and how to get there.

"Where are we going?" I say as he tugs me along.

"You'll see," he says. "But we have to hurry."

"Is this safe to be doing at night? I thought you said we don't go out at night because it's too dangerous!"

"Generally, yes, but the island won't harm me. I'm the Guardian. You're safe, trust me." He looks over his shoulder at me, his last words reverberating in the air between us. I told him I couldn't trust him, not after he lied to me so much back in Dawnlin. He needed to earn that trust back, and since I've been here, he hasn't given me any reason not to.

I grip his hand tighter, enjoying the feeling of his fingers woven through mine. "Okay," I mutter back, blindly following and trying not to trip over rocks jutting out of the ground.

The trees finally open and the path continues into a field full of taller grass, and my body tenses. I look around at this new place and my stomach starts to churn.

This feels too familiar. Too fresh.

I pull back slightly on Dane's hand, slowing us down.

"Are you okay?" Dane slows as well, looking back at me to see what was stopping me.

I clear my throat. "Yeah," I say. My eyes dart around the field until they land on the cliff.

I've never been here before, so how did I know exactly where it would be? How was I just here, leaping to escape the attack of everyone on the island only moments ago in my sleep?

"Dane…" I stop walking. I don't want to get any closer to that cliff, not after the dream. Not after the feelings from it.

He stops and comes toward me, his eyes scanning my face for some clue why I won't go any further. "What's wrong? Please tell me."

"It's just," I start. I don't want to admit what happened in the dream or relive the look on his face. I don't want him to think I have even more reason not to trust him after a dream wasn't real. But I can't help but feel uneasy coming to this place so soon after I had just been there.

"I can't swim," I settle on.

He quirks his eyebrow and tilts his head. "What does that have to do with being here?" He gestures to the surrounding field.

I lean around him and point toward the cliff. "Can we stay away from the cliff? I'm afraid of falling into the water."

He takes a step closer, closing both of his hands over mine. "I'd never let you fall, but we don't have to go any closer if you don't want to."

I let out a sigh of relief, my shoulders releasing the tension they had been holding.

He isn't about to push me off the side of a cliff to my death then.

"Thank you. What are we looking for?" I look around to see if someone is coming or if there is somewhere else we are going.

"Just wait. I think you'll like it." He steps behind me and grabs my shoulders, turning me to face the cliffs to look out over the sea. His hands fall away, but he stays close enough that I can feel his clothes brushing against mine.

The stars twinkle brightly above us as my eyes trace over the dark horizon.

I wait.

A few minutes pass while I try to focus on whatever it is I am supposed to be looking at instead of standing in the dark, alone, with Dane.

Suddenly, the sky bursts into color as a sun peeks above the horizon. Oranges and reds pierce the darkness as the first sun rises above the line of the sea. The second follows, off to the right, sending a brighter cascade of pinks, the light so bright I have to squint.

My face breaks into a grin as I watch my first ever sunrise. I lean back into Dane, my body moving of its own accord.

He leans down, his breath tickling my ear as he speaks. "I figured you never really got to see one of these in Blackwood before. I wanted to be there when you saw the sunrise for the first time."

My face heats and my stomach flutters. Dane brought me to see the sunrise, because he knew I had never seen one before, not living in Blackwood.

He cares about me, and not just cares in the sense that the Guardian cares about everyone on Dawnlin. No. He brought me here to make me happy, to make me feel better after a terrible nightmare, and he's tried to keep me safe.

It feels like more.

More is terrifying.

I can't have more. I am a princess. I have duties and responsibilities. My life isn't here, and it never can be.

But his life is.

He knows nothing about my life because I haven't been honest with him.

I spin to face him, craning my neck to meet his eyes. His arms wrap around my waist, both of his hands settling into the small of my back and pulling me closer. His movements feel so comfortable, as if he has known me for years, not just a couple of weeks.

"Dane, I…I need to be honest with you. I can't help but feel like there's something…more here."

"What makes you think that?" The corner of his lips turn up and his eyes shine playfully.

"This," I say, gesturing to his arms wrapped around my body.

"And what if there is?" He shifts on his feet, the distance between us closing. My breath hitches, but I lift my hands and firmly place them on his chest to keep him from getting any closer.

I need to make sure I choose my words carefully. The idea of being with someone is foreign to me. It has always been a dream, a distant one that I pictured late at night when I was awake and alone, with only books to keep me company. It was one whenever someone mentioned my parents' love story in passing, but never bothering to tell me the full thing. It was one that I hoped for whenever I was confronted with the idea of betrothals and alliances.

My relationships have never felt normal, and I had accepted long ago that they never would be.

But this one does, or is starting to.

I can't let it. It isn't going to last. I may have met Dane in Blackwood, but his life is here, and mine is not.

My entire reason for being in Dawnlin is to find the cure and leave. I now know the timeline isn't what I expected, and I could be here for a long time. A large part of me hopes I am not, but then part of me also hopes I am.

I tear my gaze away from his face and stare at my hands against his chest, trying to find the courage to push away the first thing that has ever felt like a normal life.

"There…can't be." I say. "You know why I'm here. You know I have to return to Blackwood, and you are needed here. I can't stay with you, and I worry that whatever this is will be a distraction and keep me here longer than I should be."

I feel a pang in my chest as the words settle between us. Distraction may not be the right word, because I hate to admit to myself that he feels like hope.

Hope for a more normal life, one where I have friendships with real people who care for *me*, not for Princess Lennox.

Dane gives me hope for more.

Hope for love.

While hope fills this magical world, I can't have hope when it comes to Dane.

"I don't want to distract you," he murmurs as his fingers brush my cheek. They trail along my face and under my chin. He lifts it, forcing my eyes to meet his again. "Trust me. I don't want to be a distraction. I want you to get what you came here for." His eyes dart over my face, and I know he is telling the truth.

"I already told you I can't trust you."

"You did. And I told you I was going to change that."

"Are you?"

"I'm working on it." He grins and his gaze drops to my lips. His hand wraps around the side of my neck, his thumb grazing over my pounding pulse.

"Do you trust me?" he grumbles softly.

I don't say a word. I can't move. I am frozen in his arms.

He leans down painfully slowly, daring me to pull away. His lips brush mine, barely even a touch. His eyes meet mine, as if asking permission.

I don't move. I know I just told him that this can't happen, but despite my words, I want it to. He knows I do.

He leans in again, lips firm and sure, and a fire ignites in my body. I sigh, and fist his shirt, leaning into him. His grip tightens on my waist and neck, the heat from his hands only fueling the fire as he draws me in.

I have never kissed anyone before. I'd never had the chance. There was no stark rule in Blackwood that the royal line could not have relationships, but my father's authoritarian hand ensured that even though it wasn't legally forbidden, it was for me.

That didn't mean I was clueless as to what went on between lovers. There were plenty of times I'd stumbled across guards and maids tucked away together in the dark corners of the castle. I'd seen Addy steal a few kisses with one of the stablemen and read plenty of Tila's not so innocent books.

Knowing and experiencing are not the same.

A whirlwind of emotions tears through me as I sink into him. Hope, longing, fear, desire. Where one starts and the next begins is inconceivable.

He tilts my head to the side, changing the angle to deepen the kiss. His lips part mine, and I respond, opening them and inviting him in. I almost gasp as his tongue brushes against mine and meet his long strokes.

I want him. I want to have a future with someone I chose, and it is clear he wants me too.

A small voice murmurs in the recesses of my mind.

I can't have him. Not really.

I break away and flatten my clenched fists on his chest to push him back to arm's length. His eyes are glassed over with desire, the look of them fueling that fire inside me that I had felt only moments ago.

"Dane—"

"Shh." He cuts me off with a thumb, stroking my lower lip. "I know you are worried about this, and I know you say you can't trust me. I know you want to get back home. All I ask is that you consider giving me a chance, even if it only lasts while you are here."

His hopeful eyes dart between mine, waiting for an answer. His request isn't unreasonable, but I still feel uncertain. Could I get involved with him, knowing that it will not last, that it has an end date? Would I subconsciously try to extend our time by not picking up on signs and clues to where the cure is hidden, only so I could stay longer? Could I let myself feel everything I had longed for but never thought I would have?

I don't want to get hurt, and leaving Dawnlin, leaving him, after having all of this, could break me.

His hands stroke my arms, sending reassuring tingles through my body. "I don't ever want to distract you. I know that is your biggest concern. I know you are worried about leaving. But let's live in the here and now. You're here, now. We can be whatever you want to be."

He slides his hands down and entwines his fingers with mine. "I have to be honest with you, Lennox," he continues, rubbing his thumb across the back of my hands. His eyes break contact, and he rolls his lip between his teeth. The strong, confident Dane I have been getting to know actually seems unsure of himself for once. "I feel very drawn to you. I knew it the second I saw you in Blackwood. If it wasn't for who I am, and you had nothing to return to, I would want this. Us. I hope you feel the same."

I don't answer. I don't know what to say. He isn't wrong. The moment I bumped into him, I felt a spark. I attributed it to being the first time I spoke to a man outside of the castle, but I feel like it might be more than that.

Neither of us has the freedoms others have. The Guardian isn't free to live a life he chooses, and I can see that pain hovering beneath his tough surface.

We have this in common, this duty and commitment to something bigger. Maybe because of that deep understanding, the here and now could be possible. Maybe Dane is right, and we can be together, knowing it will come to an end.

"Alright," I whisper.

His eyes snap to mine, and the look of joy on his face makes me want to lean in and kiss him again.

"Really?"

I nod with a small smile. "Promise me you won't interfere with my search. You know I have to leave, eventually. Please don't make it harder for me."

He nods firmly. "I understand, and I promise not to interfere with your searching time."

"Thank you."

His face lights up again, before wrapping his arm around my shoulders and turning us back the way we came. "Let's get back. I don't want to use up any of your time. Who are you with today?"

"I think Gauge told me he would show me around today."

"I like Gauge. He's a cool kid."

"Me too. He's been nice to me."

"Everyone else treating you well? Especially after the other day?"

"Pretty well. I'm still trying to get to know everyone. Mara and I had a little bit of a rocky start, but I think it's better now."

He pushes back some branches and I duck under them. "What do you mean by rocky?"

"Well," I start, unaware of how people normally have these conversations about jealousy and relationships. "You know she has feelings for you, right?"

"Mara? No she doesn't."

I giggle. I'd overheard some of the female staff at the castle talking about how clueless men could be to their advances, but I am now seeing it first hand. "She does, Dane. She was cold to me at first. She didn't like that you, um, you touch me."

"What, you mean like this?" He grasps my waist and pulls me flush to him. I giggle again and wriggle from his grasp.

"Yes, like that." I say.

Dane shakes his head. "Mara is a good kid, but I don't think of her that way."

"I kind of feel sad for her. We talked yesterday, and I like her. I don't want to hurt her by being close to you."

He reaches out and threads his fingers through mine. "You let me worry about that. Mara will be fine."

I believe him. I'd seen the way Dane speaks to everyone in camp, even when he was pissed at them. He treats everyone with respect, like he truly cares about every person here. I assume he cares about Mara too, even if it isn't in the romantic way she longed for.

"Now let's get you back. You have a busy day ahead of you."

We set off down the path, the suns rising high behind us, so I can get ready for another day of searching.

CHAPTER
THIRTY-ONE

It was true what Mara said. Keeping track of time on Dawnlin is difficult. The days and nights feel different than back home, and there is no way of knowing if the same time is passing here as was in our world. After days of searching with each of the Voyagers, I started to be very familiar with the island. The more comfortable I became, the more I was itching to go out on my own.

At first, I wasn't prepared for the physical challenge that was searching the island, but I feel my body changing. I was already strong from years of training, but this is different. Climbing, running, and scaling trees are all things I never could have done in Blackwood. The more time I spend on the island, the more confident I become in these new skills. I am not afraid of falling or getting lost anymore and trust myself to do what I need to keep searching for the cure.

No one new has joined us since Fin, which means Dane didn't have to leave. After the morning on the cliff, things were different, but still calm. I could tell Mara knew something had happened between us, but I avoided the topic with her completely. Dane agreed to keep any displays of affection between us, mostly for Mara's sake, but it doesn't stop him from a slight graze or pointed looks whenever he can.

The nightmares haven't stopped. I shouldn't be surprised after almost dying twice since I've been here, but I have barely slept. I know I need to, keeping up my strength requires it, but I can't help but wake up gasping for air or to a scream. Every night as I lie awake after one of the terrors, I can't help but worry about how much time is passing.

What is happening back at home? Does my father care that I am gone? Was Brynne punished? Or Edmond? None of this was either of their fault. It was my choice. When I come back with the cure, Father will understand that.

Tonight, I lay in bed after a particularly bad dream about the river monsters, contemplating how to go about searching when I am out on my own. I think about the years of study on war strategy and know that this could be considered the same thing. I need a plan of attack, and these plans always start with one crucial element.

A map.

The one thing that would help me accomplish my goal was the one thing Dane said I couldn't have.

As soon as the decision solidifies in my head, I hear a faint rustle on the shelves behind my bed. I crawl over to them and can't believe what I see. A small packet of parchment and a block of charcoal lays on the shelf, alongside a lit candle. I sit up and grab the packet, unfolding it to find it is blank. I look over my shoulders, around the camp and into the sky. It's as if someone has been watching me, reading my innermost thoughts.

How does it know?

It doesn't matter how it knew, the fact is, the island knew.

It knew what I needed when I decided I needed it, almost as if it granted me an advantage to help me discover the treasure it keeps hidden. Maybe the island does want me to find it? Maybe it is helping me. I shift on my bed, folding my legs under me so I can stretch the parchment out on the shelf. I pick up the charcoal in my hand and move the candle so the light illuminates the page.

Dane said maps weren't allowed, but clearly Dawnlin doesn't agree.

I will deal with him if he ever finds out, but I need the cure, and having this tool is the best way for me to do that.

What he doesn't know won't hurt him.

I need a plan of attack, not just a haphazard way of searching as it seems that the others have adopted. Edmond always taught me to be methodical and purposeful, and that is what I am going to do.

I close my eyes and picture everything I have seen over the recent days. Once I determine where I need to start, I open them, put the charcoal to the page, and start to draw.

"Are you ready?"

I pull my focus away from Fin and his story to look toward the owner of the deep, gravelly voice. Dane stands over the table where Fin and I are eating a quick breakfast, the dawn still barely over the canopy of trees.

"Yes," I say, brushing off my hands over my empty plate and swinging my leg over the bench. "Who am I with today?"

One corner of his smile turns up and I feel my eyes drawn to his lips. We haven't kissed again since that early morning sunrise. He has been keeping his promise and not distracting me from the search, but I can't help but miss the feeling of his arms around me, his tongue stroking mine.

"Lennox?"

My attention snaps back away from thoughts about his mouth. "Yes?"

He crosses his arms over his chest, smirking at me as if he knows exactly what I was thinking. "I thought it was time for you to do something different today."

"Okay," I breathe. "Am I going with you?" Searching the island alone with Dane wouldn't be a bad thing.

Focus Lennox. The cure is the goal.

"Nope. I think it is time for you to head out on your own. Are you up for it?"

"Yes! Absolutely. I'm ready." I try to squash down my excitement and seem more serious than I feel. I am ready. I am prepared. I am stronger than I ever have been. I know how things work, and I have gotten out of quite a few difficulties since being here. I want a chance to do things my way.

The map that I shoved into my shirt, hiding it in my undergarments, burns against my skin. I worked on it until morning, drawing in every detail I could remember, including all the large landmarks of the island. I need to keep it on me at all times to ensure no one else sees it, especially Dane.

He nods. "Good. Fin?" He leans to the side to look past me. "You'll be with Taril today."

Fin is learning a lot in the time he's been here, but he still needs some help before Dane decides the youngest of us all is ready to venture out on his own. Everyone is being so patient with him, including Dane, and helping him as much as we all can.

I reach over and ruffle Fin's hair. "Stay focused out there, bud." A few days ago, Fin told me I remind him of his sister, and since then I can't get it out of my head. He might return to find her gone, his last bit of time with her stolen away in an attempt to help her. My vision blurs at the thought, and I look up at the sky to blink the tears away.

I don't know what kingdom Fin is from, but I know it would hurt to not have him in my life anymore. I know he doesn't come from much, and I wonder how I can find him after leaving Dawnlin. I will do everything in my power to take care of him and his family. Send them money, offer them jobs, whatever they need, if I can find them.

I may never have siblings, and if Fin is the closest I get to it, I don't want to let him go.

"You too Lennox," he says through a bite of eggs.

I giggle, ruffling his hair again before turning and heading out to the armory. Dane stands off to the side of the tavern in a deep conversation with Storm. He glances up as I pass and offers me a small wave.

"Be careful," he grumbles, and turns back toward Storm.

My cheeks heat and I turn away, stepping out onto the walkway, quickly heading over to get my bow. It still feels odd having someone care about my well-being like Dane does.

I am going to be alone today, with no one else to rely on for help or protection. I've been traveling light, but now I feel the need to make sure I have a little bit more protection without weighing me down too much.

I pull on my bow and quiver and look at the selection of blades. I don't want to carry a sword like Mara. I'm not great with one, and it would just weigh me down. Same with the axes. They can be helpful for survival if I get stuck somewhere, but I'm not prepared to use one for self-defense.

I settle on a long blade with a serrated edge. Gauge carries one, and it was useful cutting through branches and make-shifting any traps or warnings that we needed.

I wrap a leather belt around my hips and cinch the buckle tight, then attach the sheath with a snap. Sliding the knife in I make sure everything feels secure. I keep my dagger in the back of my waistband. It is a comfortable reminder that I still have a piece of home, a reminder of who I am, and a deadly weapon to use against any of the Castaways that want to hurt me.

This will have to do.

I close the doors of the armory and head to the elevator to let myself down. The tavern hasn't fully cleared out yet, some of the boys pass me heading toward the armory as I go. I grab a pouch of water and a few pieces of fruit and sling the pouch over my shoulder before heading out again. I let myself down and make my way to the entrance of camp.

Today feels different than any other day. Today feels real, like I am no longer learning and am the one in control of my time here.

I take a deep breath, inhaling the sweet scent of the flowers and tropical trees on the other side of the portal.

I step through, feeling determination rushing through my veins.

This is it, Mom. I'm going to find it for you.

CHAPTER THIRTY-TWO

Thick, sticky mud covers every inch of my body.

Today feels like a complete waste.

I spent all day trying to extract myself from trap after trap, wasting hours of precious time. Spit out in another part of the island, caught in a net, spun around in the opposite direction. Finally, after spending the last hour slugging through a pit of mud, I decided it was time to head back to camp and regroup tomorrow.

It's like the island is laughing at me.

Just when I think I'm ready, having a plan and a strategy in place, the island humbles me.

I swipe at my face, pushing off as much of the mud as I can. I can't wait to get back to camp and rinse this all off. I reach inside my shirt and pull out my map. Despite having my ass absolutely handed to me today, the map is pristine. It must be protected by the magic.

I shove it back into my undergarments and straighten my shirt. It was the best hiding place I could come up with, because I couldn't risk it falling out of my pants pocket, or having someone see a corner sticking out after a tiring day of searching.

I can't figure out why Dane is so against having a map. He says it is because Weston could find us if he has one, but that doesn't make sense to me. If Weston has been capturing Voyagers for years, everyone that he took knows how to get back to camp. Yet he's never attacked it, never come after us.

A tiny seed of doubt settles in my mind. Is Dane being honest with me? Is there another reason he is against maps? Or are they truly unnecessary because of the island changing?

I kick as much mud as I can off of my boots before starting the walk back to camp.

I've learned so much from being paired with each of the Voyagers, arguably things I couldn't learn from books. Porter taught me how to climb trees for a higher vantage point, especially the ones with thick sturdy branches that tower high in the sky. Rylan had shown me which foods I can salvage if I am stuck outside of camp at night, and needed to stay until the morning. Many of them had shown me small overnight shacks constructed across the island that could provide shelter. Taril had shown me lots of different poisonous plants that tended to be in the jungle areas, which, despite having the day I had, I did a great job of avoiding.

I never went back to sleep after I started sketching the map last night. I worked until sunrise, documenting everything I could remember. I have a good amount of detail so far, even though it is nothing like the maps I am used to studying with Edmond. Those had taken years to construct, and I don't have that kind of time, let alone working on it in secret. I don't pride myself on artistry either. My father had assigned me a drawing tutor who advised the king after years of working with me, that drawing would never be my strong suit, and maybe I should try to master other arts to impress foreign princes.

My skills are enough for this map, though. I don't need to impress anyone, I just need to be able to get my bearings and take in any clues the landscape might provide.

It didn't seem like any other Voyagers had a specific strategy for searching, or if they did, they did not share it with me. I don't function that way. I need to be methodical and purposeful. I decided before heading out today that I was going to work each section, rotating around like a clock, starting with the area closest to camp. Even though I didn't stray far, so much of my time was taken up by the tricks and I barely even covered any area at all.

So tomorrow will be another day. I hope the island will take pity on me and leave me alone. I can't help but feel slightly discouraged. I can't imagine being beaten down like this every day for years on years.

I trudge down the main path back to camp and pull the water skein off of my belt. I wipe the mud off the top and chug some of the cool, fresh water. It doesn't hit me until now how exhausting this day was, and how much work my body had put into getting free. I pause to clip the skein back on my belt when I hear a rustle in the trees nearby.

Not again.

This is way too familiar, too close to my first day on the island. But I am not day one Lennox.

I keep walking, hoping that I'm wrong and it's just a scuttle of a small animal in the brush, but the rustling doesn't go away.

I stop abruptly and listen, trying to determine which direction it is coming from. When I stop, it stops. Goosebumps rise on my arms as I realize that it definitely isn't an animal. Whoever is out there is stalking me.

The Voyagers all know me, so there is no reason for them to creep in the shadows. The island has never outright attacked us on the main path, which can leave only one thing.

It has to be a Castaway.

I push my legs to carry me faster down the path, without running. I don't want whoever is following me to suspect I know they are there. Hopefully, it will just seem like I am eager to get back to camp.

Camp.

I can't go back to camp. I can't lead whoever this is there. Even if they already know where it is, I can't endanger everyone else by having someone follow me back, but being alone didn't help my chances of being captured either. I need a new plan. I need to lose them.

Screw it, I need to run.

I take off, fast as my body will let me in this exhausted state and hope it will be enough.

The rustling follows me, matching my speed, but still completely out of sight.

I look back, but don't see anyone. This can't be the island playing tricks on me, can it?

When I turn back, a large figure steps into the path directly in front of me, and I don't have time to slow myself down. I plow right into it full force and yell as we crash to the floor. Large arms wrap around my shoulders as I land on top of this person.

We hit the ground hard, and my face slams into the firm chest beneath me. I reach toward my dagger, ready for a fight, when the chest under me starts shaking, the arms squeezing me tighter.

Then I hear it.

Laughing.

"Dane?!"

"You really just plowed me over, didn't you?"

I push myself off of his chest so I can see his face, grinning and eyes sparkling.

"Why the fuck were you following me? You scared me! I thought you were a Castaway!"

"First off, I wasn't following you. I heard yelling and had been trying to figure out where it was coming from, then I heard someone on the path and stepped out to see who it was."

"I thought you were going to kidnap me," I say with a slap to his chest. He holds his hand over mine, flattening my palm against his chest.

I can feel his heart pounding, and his chest still shaking from the giggles he is trying to suppress.

"This isn't funny."

"I'm not laughing." His face turns serious, but his lips keep turning up as he tries to keep the smile off of them. "Why are you covered in mud?"

"Ugh," I say, dropping my forehead to his chest. "This day has been awful. I feel like I got nowhere." I roll off of him and push myself to stand, seeing that he is now almost as dirty as I am.

Dane stands and brushes the dirt off his back. "You aren't alone. It was your first day. Don't beat yourself up too badly. You know how long many of us have been here. It's good to accept that you made it through the day, didn't get hurt, and get to go back out tomorrow."

"Yeah, I guess," I say with a huff. "I just…never mind. I don't want to talk about it."

"How about we do something to celebrate your first day, and get your mind off of whatever it is you are feeling?" He wears a hopeful expression, and I can't help but wonder what he has planned.

I look down at myself, then back up at him. "But I'm covered in mud. And so are you."

"Where we're going, that won't matter."

I tilt my head, trying to figure out where on the island we could be going, but after the day I had, decide it doesn't really matter. I could use a little fun.

"What do you have in mind?"

CHAPTER THIRTY-THREE

The shadows around us elongate as the suns quickly set, shifting the sky into the nightly change of colors that I can never get enough of. Dane clutches my hand as he leads me down the pathways in the opposite direction of camp.

"Where are we going?" I ask.

"I am serious about making sure you trust me. It doesn't help me if I just tell you." He winks, then pulls me to his side and drapes his arm across my shoulders

"You are frustrating sometimes, do you know that?" I say with a glance up at him.

He lets out a low chuckle. "I've been told that once or twice."

Stars are starting to peek through the deep purple above as darkness falls over the island. While I normally look forward to their appearance every night, I'm filled with unease tonight.

"Shouldn't we go back? It's getting dark fast."

"We need the dark this time. We'll watch for the Castaways. Don't worry."

A cool wind picks up as we approach the edge of the island. The cliff in front of us drops off just ahead, and I start to pull out of Dane's embrace.

"No, Dane, I told you before, I—"

"Lennox," he says, stopping and stepping in front of me, blocking my view of the drop. He wraps his hands around my waist and pulls me in closer, his fingertips pushing slightly into my ribcage. It feels comforting, like he won't let me fall. "I'm not going to bring you anywhere that you are afraid of, but it's okay to let go a little bit. I know we haven't talked much about your past. I hope we can change that, but I think you had to rely a lot on yourself, and you didn't let many people in. I want to change that. I know I wasn't honest with you when we first met, but I'm here with you now, and I want you to trust me."

My eyes stay locked on his before I give him a small nod. He leans down and brushes a soft kiss across my lips, and a shiver that has nothing to do with the breeze runs down my spine.

"We're going to approach the cliff, but it isn't what you think. You can hang on to me the whole way if you need to."

"Alright," I say quietly and wrap my hands around his arm. The muscles beneath my fingers tense, then relax as I hang on to him. As we get closer, I see a divot cut into the ground. Dane positions himself on the side closest to the cliff, easing my nerves slightly.

Steps carved out of the dark stone wind down the side of the cliff toward a black sand beach below. The beach and cove are tucked away under a cliff, hidden until you stumble upon it, so I hadn't seen this place from the lookout when we arrived.

"We're going down there?" I ask.

Dane nods. "We are."

He starts down the stairs in front of me, and I keep a steady grip on his arm. It's not the cliff itself that makes me nervous now that I know there isn't a long fall into roaring waves below. It's the proximity to the water that sets me on edge. I know I'm safe as long as I stay on hard ground, but I haven't been to any of the other beaches yet. I do my best to avoid searching there, not wanting the island to spit me out into the sea to see if I can swim.

We stop when we reach the last step.

"You might want to take those off," Dane says, nodding toward my boots. He reaches down and pulls off his own, shoving his socks inside them. I do as he suggests and step forward to squish my bare toes into the dark, cool sand.

"It's beautiful," I say, taking in this new piece of Dawnlin. The moon shines off the water in the middle of a crescent cove made of jagged black stone. Calm waves slowly lapping at the black sand, the sound repetitive but soothing. The beach is small, not long and winding around the edges of the land like the others I had seen.

This one is quaint, quiet. Secluded.

I wish we had places like this in Blackwood.

"You're shivering," Dane says. He runs his hands up and down my arms, the movement bringing me some warmth. "Come this way." Just ahead, closer to the water, I see a blanket spread over the sand with a basket sitting on top. Next to it lies an unlit fire with wood stacked up into a peak.

"Didn't see the sense of wasting the wood before we got here." Dane crouches and starts striking a flint rock at the base of the woodpile. Some sparks light on a bit of kindling shoved underneath, and he crouches down to blow on it, igniting the flames which start engulfing the larger logs. "It'll be warm in a few minutes. In the meantime…"

He reaches down and picks up a coat off of the blanket and wraps it around my shoulders.

I push the coat away. "It'll get all muddy," I laugh. He ignores my refusal and wraps it around me anyway. His scent immediately engulfs me, and I draw the coat closer, breathing in as much of it as I can.

He pushes a piece of stray muddy hair behind my ear. "It doesn't bother me. Are you hungry?"

My stomach growls at the mention of food. I never had the chance to eat the food I brought with me today. I was too busy struggling my way through all the traps.

"Starving," I say. I glance over at the small basket of food sitting on the blanket and plop down next to it, with Dane following suit. He leans over and begins pulling out wooden containers and opening them up between us. Steam and smells rise into the air when he lifts the lids, and my eyes widen with surprise.

Blackwood is a landlocked kingdom, and despite being royalty, we can't try any foods that are commonplace in seaside kingdoms. I'd read descriptions and recipes for these exotic dishes, but had no idea what they would be like. I imagine now is my only chance to try anything like them, and Dane has brought them right to me.

He lays an array of dishes in front of us. The mixture of garnish and spices overpowers the scent from his coat, and my mouth waters. I lean forward, eyeing each dish, trying to decide where to start.

Dane chuckles next to me, glancing down at my growling stomach. "Sounds like we made it to dinner just in time."

"I haven't eaten since breakfast," I say sheepishly.

"There should be plenty," he says, opening the last of the containers. "Do you know what any of it is?"

"No, you're going to have to tell me. Unless you think it's best I don't know, otherwise I won't eat it."

He throws his head back and laughs. "No, not this time. Maybe next time you can be a little more adventurous. But if you don't like something, it's okay, that's why I brought extra."

He hands me a wooden plate with utensils, and pulls out serving spoons, then points out what is inside each of the containers.

"Over here we have some simple fish steaks. Those are what's called shrimp. These here will take some work to get the meat out. I can show you." He points to a bunch of long, hard looking things. "This is lobster tail. These are oysters, and then we have some pasta and bread, just in case you don't like any of the fish."

My eyes drag over the food. It is so different from anything I had ever eaten before, and I want to try it all. Dane spoons some of each item on my plate, and I eat. Flavor explodes over my tongue as I try every new dish. Dane shows me how to crack the crab legs and pull the tender meat from them, and how to pluck the meat from the oysters.

A moan escapes me as I try an oyster, the cheese and butter melting on my tongue. I slap my hand over my mouth and giggle uncontrollably as Dane smirks from behind his bite.

"Sorry," I say. "It's just all so good."

"I'm glad you like it. You didn't even question it, you just trusted me. I think that's a win for me."

I nudge his shoulder playfully with mine. "Okay fine, you're right, that was a win for you."

"Good, because we're not done."

I eye him warily. "What do you mean?"

He stands and reaches down for my hand, pulling me up with him. "Come with me." He laces his fingers through mine and leads me toward the edge of the water.

"Dane, no, please." I pull back against his hand.

"Don't worry, we aren't going in the water. But we're going to be close to it." He faces me and continues to walk backward toward the surf. "Will you trust me again tonight? I won't let anything happen to you. I promise."

My heart pounds harder in my chest the closer we get to the water. It isn't the water itself that scares me, it is the fear of losing control. I can't swim, and submerging myself in the ocean is vastly different from sitting in a bath back in the castle, which I'd done countless times.

If something goes wrong, if a current sucks me under, I won't be able to get myself out.

Dane stops next to me, facing out toward the cove. He points out into the bay. "See that set of rocks right there? We're going to go stand out there. We won't be in the water, but we are going to get wet. I don't want to push you, but know I'll keep you safe. If we're going to do it, we have to hurry."

"Why do we have to hurry?"

He smirks. "That's part of the surprise. *And* the trust."

I take a deep, settling breath. I've come this far. I've done so many things and had so many experiences that months ago I never would have expected I'd do. I trust in the magic and have hope for change. I can do this. It isn't like he is asking me to jump in without knowing how to swim.

"Alright. Let's go," I say firmly, clenching his hand a little harder in mine.

We cross the beach and step out onto the strip of rocks that forms the edge of the cove. Dane walks backwards, holding my hands for balance as I watch my feet to anticipate any slip or stumble. The darkness surrounds us as we slowly creep along, the light from the moon our only guide as I carefully place my feet on the rough surface of the rocks.

"This should be far enough. Any second now."

We wait in silence for a few moments, but nothing happens. The quiet sounds of the soft waves in the cove and the crisp smell of the salt of the water overwhelm my senses, especially in the darkness.

"Dane, what are we waiting for?"

"Shh. Just one more second."

Barely a second later, my eye catches on the sea beyond the cove. Waves are rolling toward us, but they aren't like the gentle waves near the shore. The waves are glowing. As they roll toward us, bright blue light glows from within and rolls in the sea right into the cove.

"That is amaz—" I call out, but am cut off by an enormous wave slamming into the rocks. I shriek, digging my fingers into Dane's shoulders, clutching onto him for security. He wraps his arms around my waist and pulls me in closer as the water comes crashing down around us and soaking me completely.

"Oh my gods!" I yell, reaching with one hand to push my now drenched hair out of my eyes. I can hear Dane's boisterous laugh above the crashing of more waves around us.

"Look down!" He yells and takes a partial step away from me. He keeps his hands on me so I don't fall, but there's enough room so I can see the rock below.

I gasp at the beauty unfolding underneath us.

Everywhere the waves crash, the rock lights up around us. Pinks, greens, blues, and yellows, glowing like nothing I have ever seen. I bend down slightly, steadying myself on him and see that it isn't the rock itself, but the world that lives in and on it. Plants and animals all glowing as soon as the water touches them, showing off their beauty underneath a clear twinkling sky.

I don't care at all about the surrounding water, or the waves crashing over me, or the rivulets of mud washing off my skin. I crouch down, careful of where I am moving my feet so I can get a better look.

"This is incredible. I've never seen anything like this!" I look up at Dane, my cheeks hurting from all the smiling. Between the thoughtful dinner and now this, I feel like I am floating.

He looks almost shy as he smiles back. "I hoped you would like it. It happens every time the tide comes in." He gestures to the cove, where the rolling glowing waves are still rolling in and crashing into the beach. "Was it worth taking the risk of coming out here?"

"Absolutely." I look around at the rest of the cove and see that every surface of rock is glowing, and the cove itself is bright and full of life. "It's gorgeous. Can you show me more?"

"Of course." He crouches down and points out different creatures along the rock. There are so many, even some that I don't know if they exist back in our world. Glowing blue crabs scuttle along the surface, and tiny bright pink fish swim through the caverns carved into the rock.

I am moved by the effort Dane went through to bring me here and show me this. He knows about my fear of the water, but for a few moments, I've completely forgotten about it. I even feel comfortable enough to walk along the rock face on my own and explore new areas.

Dawnlin is changing me, maybe more than I had realized.

I never had the opportunity to let anyone into my life. Brynne and Edmond were the only two I truly trusted. Living in isolation, with nothing to look forward to, nothing to hope for, made me pessimistic and resentful of everyone experiencing life outside of my walls. It made me angry for my father's decisions, layered on top of the guilt I felt, knowing I had been the ultimate cause for him to make them.

But Dane…Dane has given me someone new to trust. This place gave me a new hope, not only for something more for my life and relationships here, but for eventual change in what was waiting for me in Blackwood.

Edmond was right. Maybe hope was something that everyone needed. Dane was right too, and he had definitely earned my trust tonight.

CHAPTER THIRTY-FOUR

We stay out on the rocks for what feels like hours, looking at the wildlife and enjoying the night, not a care about the Castaways crossing my mind. As the night draws on and the stars and moon brighten, a stronger breeze comes in off the ocean. Gooseflesh covers my skin, and the wet hair and clothes plastered to my body to make me shiver.

Dane notices my shaking and scoops me up, cradling my body against his chest, and heads back to shore. Despite the chill of the wind hitting my soaked clothing, I revel in his warmth and rest my head in the crook of his neck.

He sets me down on the blanket and feeds the fire, building it up so the roaring flames throw off enough heat to be comfortable despite the wind.

"Why don't more of the Voyagers come down here?" I ask once he sits back down beside me.

He rests his forearms on his bent knees and scoots his body closer, his thigh brushing mine. "Everyone does at some point. Sometimes more often than others. Right now, I think everyone is really focused, not particularly paying attention to the joys of this place. That tends to happen when new people come."

"Why?"

He stares into the fire, the light of the flames dancing across his cheekbones, casting shadows on his face. "I think it reminds them of why they're here. It reminds them that there is still something they are searching for, and of the reason. Reliving the same day every day can feel monotonous. Every time someone new shows up, like you and Fin, it reminds them that the hope still exists."

I nod slowly. "I'm glad I could give them that." I hope I don't need that reminder, eventually, but if I do, I hope someone shows up who can give it to me.

We stay silent for a few moments, listening to the gentle crashing of waves, the heaviness of the sentiment filling the air. I look out over the cove at the water, still glowing brilliant blues.

"Do you think I can find it?"

"Hmm?" Dane tears his gaze away from the fire to meet my gaze.

"The cure. Do you think I can find it?"

"I think," he says as he shifts to face me. "I think, of anyone, you can definitely find it."

"What have I done to give you that much confidence in me?"

"Just a feeling. You give me a feeling."

My cheeks heat and am glad for the cover of darkness and shadows of the fire. I turn away from his stare and look into the flames. "You say that to all the girls that come onto the island, don't you?"

He chuckles. "Definitely not."

I chuckle. "Mara would be even more in love with you than she already is."

"She'll get over it." A smile plays on his lips. "So," he continues, "did I convince you to trust me?"

"Almost," I say playfully.

He groans and slams his fist over his heart, pretending to stagger backward. "Ugh, you wound me!"

A laugh bursts out of me, and I try to stifle my giggles as I look over at him, watching me. The grin on his face pulls more giggles out of me, and I feel completely under his control.

I clear my throat. "Maybe if I got to know you a little better."

I'm not sure how getting to know Dane better would make me like or trust him any less, but I do still have questions I want answered. There are things that still don't sit right with me and haven't since I found out he lied about everything when I first met him.

"Ask me anything. I'm an open book."

I make a face at his comment. "Are you going to be honest this time?"

"I was honest last time! I just couldn't be *really* honest."

"Alright, fine. Are you going to be *really* honest this time?"

"Of course I will be. What's your first question?"

"Are you going to ask me questions, too?"

"That's your first question?"

"No it's not. It's *a* question, but not one of my questions."

"Alright. No, I'm not."

"Really?"

"Really."

"Why not?"

"Because I already know everything I need."

The fluttering in my stomach is distracting. I can't focus out of pure delight that he feels he knows me and trusts me, but guilt quickly takes over. I have been hiding a huge part of myself from him, a part that explains a lot of who I am and why I am here.

Maybe it is better that he isn't asking me questions. I don't want to lie, but I just don't know if I am ready to be treated like a princess again.

"Are you ready?"

He sits quietly, waiting for me to ask my first question.

"Is Dane your real name?"

"Yes."

"Do you have a last name?"

"I'm sure I do, but if I do, I don't remember it."

"Where are you from?"

"I'm from here."

"No, I mean before Dawnlin. Where did you come from?"

"I grew up in Fonden a long time ago. But since being the Guardian, I've been to all the kingdoms, so it doesn't really feel like any one place is home anymore. Except here. Have you ever been to Fonden?"

"No, I haven't. I haven't ever left Blackwood before coming here."

"Really?" He looks confused, like something I said didn't add up. "You seem like you know a lot about other kingdoms."

"I do, but not because I've been there. I read a lot." I leave it at that. I don't want to give anything more away that might hint at my background.

"You should visit them someday."

"Maybe," I mutter. "Alright, next question." I think for a moment before asking something I really want to know. "Was any of what you said in Blackwood true? The stuff about your sister?"

"Yes, it just isn't true any longer. That all happened a really long time ago."

"Is that why you found Dawnlin?"

"Yes. I wanted to help her, but…" he pauses. His throat bobs and his jaw tightens. I can see it in his eyes. He is looking for the right words. "I'm still here, and that was a long time ago. I'm sure you probably put together that a lot of us are in the same boat, not knowing if who we were here to save in the first place is still there to be saved."

He looks down at his hands, emotion overcoming him. He probably has not had to deal with anyone asking about his past in quite some time. It touches me that he is willing to share it now, despite how painful it seems to be for him. I lift my hand and set it on his knee, squeezing it softly, and hope it is comforting. I didn't intend to cause him any pain, I just need to know what is real and what isn't. I don't want to keep upsetting him, so I move on to something that is hopefully easier to answer.

"Have you enjoyed being the Guardian?"

"I have, for the most part. I wish we would have at least one person who found the cure so that more of our families could be helped, but besides that, it has brought great people into my life." He looks at me pointedly.

"Did you want to do it?"

"Yes and no. I didn't think anyone else that was here was ready for it, and I didn't want it falling to Weston."

"He was here? You didn't bring him to the island?"

"Yes, he was here already."

"So you know him?"

"Well enough to know that he is poison for this island and everyone on it."

"Why hasn't he been captured? Why not throw him in the cage and lose the key if he is just trying to get the cure for himself?"

Dane huffs haughtily. "Don't you think I've tried? We all constantly are on the lookout for the Castaways. I've searched every inch of this island. It's like they have vanished into thin air. We know they are still here, but…" He shakes his head. "It's why I make sure that everyone is ready to be on their own before I send them out. No one can be unprepared. Not when it comes to Weston."

"As if the dangers of Dawnlin weren't enough, we have to worry about him too," I murmur.

He shifts his head so his eyes met mine again. "You should always be prepared, but your focus should be on the cure. That is what you are here for." His eyes are earnest, like he is imploring me to stay safe, but still accomplish my mission.

He has been so honest and answered everything so quickly, I don't know if there was any more reason for me not to trust him. I understand why he couldn't tell me who he was before, even if I didn't like it at the time. I see now how important it is keeping this place hidden from anyone whose intentions weren't pure.

I don't want to end this night talking about Weston, so I decide to ask something a little lighter. I lift my arm to reach across his face.

"Where did you get this?" My fingers lightly brush the scar that cuts through his lip.

He lets out a low grunt and reaches up to touch the scar, his fingertips grazing mine. I pull my hand back, but he catches it in his and holds it between us. "Sorry I keep underwhelming you with stories, but this one isn't exciting either. I was a little boy, chasing my sister through the house. I tripped and fell into the corner of the doorway. Mother yelled at us for a while. We didn't have the money to go see a healer, so instead, I got the scar."

"I like the scar," I say.

"You do?"

"Yes," I say. It comes out more breathless than I intend.

"Can I ask you a question now?"

I try to hide a smirk. "I thought you said you didn't need to ask me any questions."

"I don't need to, but this one I want to."

"Alright."

"Do you have anybody waiting for you back in Blackwood?"

Of course I have people waiting for me. I have an entire kingdom waiting for me, and I hate thinking about what is going on in the castle, especially with my father. I hate wondering if he's let her go, listening to the healer's advice, or wondering if Edmond told him where I am, trying to give him hope to hold on to her longer.

I start to speak. My first reaction is to be honest, especially after how open he has been with me all evening. But the thought of giving up my identity stops me. I pause and think for a moment, trying to come up with an answer and finally settle on a response. "What do you mean by anybody?"

"I mean, if this doesn't work out, if you are here for longer than you intended like most of us…are you going to stay?"

Oh.

So he isn't asking about who I am bringing the cure home to, or what responsibilities I have. He's asking about me, about my relationships, about me staying here with him.

"I," I stammer, "I don't think so." I feel a pain in my chest as soon as the words are out. This place has been everything I have ever dreamed of, and the thought of leaving it is devastating. I finally escaped the prison of the castle walls and found a place I feel I belong. This island is filled with the possibility of happiness, friendship, and love. I don't want to leave it.

But the future queen of Blackwood doesn't have that choice. My duty is back in my kingdom, whether or not I am successful.

A decision I have yet to make is how long I am willing to stay without finding the cure. But in the end, the answer will always be no, I will not stay.

He nods quietly, his face stoic.

"I'm sorry," I say, trying to do anything to save the moment, save this amazing night from ending so badly.

"I understand. It was unfair for me to ask. I just—" He straightens and spins toward me, extending his legs on either side of me and sliding in closer. "I just felt like I knew. I knew the moment I saw you, you were everything I had been waiting for."

His words tear through me. No one has ever said anything like that to me, and I don't know what to say.

I don't know what to feel.

How can I tell him that in such a short time, he has become important to me? That he isn't the only one with feelings, and that I wish I could change my future and stay here with him. How can I tell him it isn't only Dawnlin that gives me hope for a better life, but him as well?

Words escape me, so I do the only thing I think will help convey the emotions swirling inside of me.

I push up on my knees and lean over him, placing both my hands on either side of his hips before bringing my mouth to his. He sinks his hand into my hair and pulls me to him, and I crawl over his body until I'm straddling his lap.

Delicious heat licks through my body as he pulls me closer, the flames of the fire no longer necessary against the cold. His lips part mine and his tongue delves deep as I caress the stubble on his jaw.

I let out a gasp as he flips us over, his powerful body pressing me into the soft sand. He runs a hand down my side, tickling and teasing until he reaches my hip. His fingers wrap around it, squeezing for a moment before he slides it around to my backside, squeezing the soft flesh before continuing down the back of my thigh. He hitches my leg up over his hip, changing the angle so his hips press into mine.

I moan against his mouth, the sound fueling his movements and he leans into me harder, the feeling of his excitement pushing against me. His tongue continues to stroke mine relentlessly, and I drive my hands into his hair, clutching him tighter. Fingers graze the front of my thigh, working their way back up toward my waistband. He reaches the ties and slowly loosens them.

I don't want him to stop. This feeling, tonight, the heat pulsing between my thighs. It's all because of him, and I just want to feel him.

He breaks the kiss, his lips peppering my jaw with more, and slowly drifting down the column of my neck as his hand flattens against my abdomen. Slow strokes of his fingers on my skin send me reeling, anticipating his hand moving lower, where no one has ever touched me before. I push my hips into him, silently urging him on.

He pulls his head away and looks at the sky as a crack of lightning flashes above us. He groans loudly, dropping his forehead to my chest before cursing and looking up to meet my eyes. The warmth of his hand leaves my belly and moves to cup my face.

"We need to get off the beach. This is probably the most unsafe place for us to be."

"It's fine," I pant, still reeling from everything that just happened.

He groans again, this time filled with frustration. "Fucking storms." He pulls back and kneels in front of me, reaching down to clasp my hands and sit me up. Lightning cracks again, and the following thunder feels like it is swallowing the beach. "We need to go. Now."

I nod and scramble up, grabbing my boots and weapons while Dane covers the fire with wet sand. We scramble up the stairs and back to camp, my mind reeling from what almost happened between us. He is captivating and pushing me to be more of myself in ways I never thought possible. He is showing me what it is like to be cared for, and to live life the way I want to live it.

He's showing me more.

As I lay in bed that night, trying to calm myself from the volley of emotions, I try to stay in that moment, and not let it go. I want to live there, those emotions, those feelings, those thoughts about the future, because I know that even though we discussed it, and we expect it, I know that when the day comes, it will be too hard to say goodbye.

CHAPTER
THIRTY-FIVE

I swipe the sweat off my brow and reach behind my head to gather my hair into a knot. I've become accustomed to Dawnlin's heat since being here, but today the suns feel hotter than usual. I reach into my shirt and pull out the map I have been adding to over the past few weeks.

I'm proud of the progress. All the landscapes are filled in, and I marked places I had faced any challenges, like those monsters under the bridge. Despite keeping my distance from them and not having any life-threatening experiences since then, the nightmares hadn't subsided. Night after night, I wake gasping into the stifling night air, and it still takes orienting myself before I remember that I'm not in danger.

At least not at that moment.

I shield my eyes as I stare up into the clear sky, then back down at the base of the mountain in front of me. I've worked my way through the jungle, to the mountain, the large pillar that stands between the opposing sides of the island. It is so large, I don't even know where to start. I can hear the roar of a waterfall coming from the other side, but I'm not ready to go near it, especially alone. Staying on the back side is a fine place to start.

I glance down at the map once more before folding it up and shoving it back into my shirt. I have no idea how to scale a mountain, let alone any equipment to do so, but there is no way this entire area has gone unexplored. There has to be a path or hike of some kind that Voyagers have tried before.

I squint against the light and look up toward the peak. Something in my gut tells me that the mountain is essential. I can't figure out why, I just know in the depths of myself that I need to set my sights on it. I'd spent the last few weeks traipsing through the surrounding areas, fighting my way through all the traps that are thrown at me, all to find nothing, and trying to fight the disappointment and stay focused. But something about the mountain just reminds me of a fortress, like the castle back home. Large, grey looming stone, protecting what lies inside.

Protecting or hiding? Or both?

I walk along the base of the mountain, scanning the rising rock, looking for any sign of a path.

"Hey Lennox!"

I turn toward the voice I've become familiar with, a lightness filling my chest.

"Fin! How's it going, bud?"

He emerges from the trees and skips to me, wrapping my legs in a hug and squeezing tight. The bow he carries is too big for him, and drags along the floor as he walks, but ever since I taught him how to shoot, he has been carrying it everywhere.

"This thing bothering you?" I say, lifting it out of his hands.

"I trip on it sometimes, but I like it. I'm getting better! I've been practicing just like you showed me."

"I'm glad," I say and ruffle his hair. I kneel to his level. "Let me show you how to make it easier to carry." I drape the bow over his shoulder, the string taut across his body from his shoulder to the opposite hip. "This way, you can grab it if you need to, but it keeps your hands free."

"Thanks Lennox. Can we practice more later?"

"Of course. After dinner, sound good?"

He nods with a wide, toothy smile.

"Where are you headed off to today?" I ask.

"I dunno," he shrugs. "Where are you going?"

"Well, I was going to check out the mountain a little bit. See if there's anything up there."

"There's only one way on this side. I saw it before. Come on! Let me show you!" He reaches up and clasps my hand, dragging me toward the base.

"Right here!" He squeezes his body between two large chunks of rock and disappears.

"Fin?" I call, panic rising in my voice. The space is too small for me to squeeze through, and I can't see past it. It's as if he's vanished.

"C'mon Lennox!" I hear his small voice from behind the rocks.

I eye the small space warily. There's no way I will fit through, and I'm shocked he did. The surfaces are too slick to climb over, and there doesn't seem to be a way around.

"Just walk through!" he calls out.

I decide to trust him and step up toward the boulders. I turn my body sideways to squeeze through, hoping that the jagged rock won't tear my clothes or scrape my skin. I slide against the surface, and it is as if there aren't any boulders there at all. My body glides right through a hidden portal to the other side, just like at camp. I pop out on the other side to meet Fin smiling up at me.

"Let's go!" He yells, grabbing my hand again and pulling me forward up a steep rocky slope. We clamber over rocks and hug the side of the mountain to stay away from the edge.

"How did you find this before, Fin?" I peek over the edge and try not to get dizzy from how high we have climbed.

"It was on accident!" The excitement in his voice makes me crack a smile. "I wanted to climb on those big rocks, and I just went right through! Do you think it's important, Lennox?"

"It could be. We'll have to keep looking and see."

"Let's go, let's go!" He sprints across the rocks in front of us, hopping over some sharp points that stick out across the trail. The higher we go, the hotter it gets. Without the shade of the mountain, and the coolness of the soil and trees below, my body is dripping, and it is definitely slowing me down. My eyes sting from the sweat falling into them, and burn from squinting into the light.

I step over the sharp rocks Fin has just passed and come to a halt, pulling my water skein off my belt and taking a swing. Fin is just ahead, looking between two different paths. I hand him the water and he takes a quick drink.

"I went that way last time," he says, pointing to the right at a steep path that wraps up rather than around.

"You did that by yourself?"

"Yeah! It was fun. It didn't go anywhere, though. Just a dead end. So I came back down. We should try this one." He points to the other path.

"Let's do it. I'll lead. We don't know what we will run into."

"I'm not a baby Lennox," he pouts, crossing his arms over his chest.

"Oh, I know you aren't. You climbed that thing all by yourself. But I can still try to protect you. Would your big sister let you go first?"

"No..." he mumbles, a dejected look crossing his face.

"Alright then. Let's get going. We still have to get back down and back to camp before it gets dark."

Luckily, this path is more flat than the one Fin had already tried, but the height is making me nervous. I'm beginning to feel like we made a mistake as I take in the path and how much less trodden it is than the others. Thoughts of what the island could do to us flash before my eyes, many of which end with us dead at the base of the mountain. I glance back at Fin, but as always, he seems fearless.

That could change at any time.

I decide to keep him distracted from the potential danger ahead. "So tell me, how has your search been going? Where have you been looking?"

"Fine. I haven't found anything special. I can't make it too far, but it has been fun. It's almost like a game my father plays with us back at home, so I don't get too sad about not finding it. It's like I'm home again."

"Do you miss everyone back home?"

"Yes," he whispers.

My voice softens. "You know Fin, it would be alright if you went back home with your family. I know you came here by accident. I know Dane would help you if you really wanted to go back."

He doesn't respond, so I stop and turn back to him. His face has fallen, the excitement and pride previously there from finding and scaling this mountain by himself, gone.

I kneel in front of him and watch a single tear fall on his cheek.

"Hey, hey, hey," I say, reaching up to stroke my hands up and down his upper arms. "I didn't mean to upset you."

"I just want to help her," he pushes out, hands swiping at his face. I wrap my arms around him and he curls his body into me. He rests his head on my shoulder and his tears soak my shirt. I squeeze him tighter before quickly releasing him and holding him at arm's length.

"That is what we are going to do, alright Fin? We're going to find the cure. For you, for me, and for all the other Voyagers." I stand up and extended my hand to him. "Are you with me?"

He sniffles and nods, reaching out to clasp my hand tightly.

"Now, let's see where this goes. It could be important."

We keep hugging the side of the mountain and make our way up. I run my fingers along the side, searching for any false rocks or seams, anything that might lead to an opening. Fin trails me, but still grips my hand tightly, his sniffles getting less frequent as we trudge on.

Just ahead, the path catches my eye, and stops me dead in my tracks.

"Can you see that?" I ask him, crouching down and pointing up ahead. "Does it look like the path is missing to you?"

Fin steps beside me and squints his eyes. "I think so. Maybe we should go back."

"No, you just stay here. I'll go look and see if there is a way we can get across."

I slowly approach the gap, assessing whether or not it is safe to get too close. The ground disappears a few steps ahead, a chunk of the mountainside missing. I look across and notice that the path doesn't continue on the other side, whatever was here before, lost to the rest of us.

I take one step closer, my boot crunching in the gravel as a huge explosion thunders in my ears. I am thrown backward, my body slamming into the sharp rock behind me. Dust and rock rain down over me and I frantically try to cover my face.

Then I am slipping, the explosion causing the ground under me to crumble and slide down the side of the mountain.

My body follows, sharp rock scraping and cutting me as I fall. I dig my fingers into the rock, grasping for purchase. I can barely see through the debris as I feel myself falling down the side of the mountain.

The ringing in my ears blocks out everything except my thoughts.

Fin. Where is Fin?

"Fin!" I scream, at least I think I do. I can't hear myself, only a loud, high-pitched noise as I still try to grab onto anything around me.

This is it. This is how I am going to die. Falling from the side of the mountain, trying to save my mother, to save Fin's sister, Mara's family. Hopefully Fin cannot see me, so he doesn't have to watch another sister die.

My grip on the rock is weakening, my muscles straining to keep hold. But there is nowhere else to hold. Nothing around me to grab.

I hope my father will find an heir he is proud of.

Something hits my hands and I look up, squinting through the dust and dirt.

A dull sound surrounds me, but I still can't make anything out.

It hits my hands again, and I focus on it.

It is the end of a bow. Fin's bow.

I raise my gaze higher and see something take shape. Fin is above me, kneeling over the edge with the bow, and yelling at me. I eye the bow that is still resting on my hands.

I can't pull on it like I'm sure he's telling me to. He is too little, too light, and I would surely pull him over the side with me.

My voice sounds distant in my ears as I yell up to him.

"Hook the bow around a rock so I can pull on it!" The dust is settling now, and I see him nod in acknowledgement. He pulls it up and hooks the edge on a large rock jutting out of the top of the path.

I hope it holds.

His actions put it just out of reach. I kick my feet along the side of the mountain, trying to snag on something I can stand on, but the rock face below me is too smooth. My fingers start slipping, and the panic in me rises. If I do nothing, I will fall.

I will die.

I have to get to that bow.

I flatten my boots onto the face of the rock so I can pull up and scale the side of the mountain. My arms strain, pain flaring through them as I pull. A scream slips through my lips as I pull my body up with all my might, and hold myself suspended in the air. I let go quickly with one hand and reach up to snatch the end of the bow, hooking my hand between the wood and the string.

I suck air through my teeth as pain sears through my hand. I clamp down as hard as I can before reaching up and grabbing the bow with the other. It shifts on the rock as it supports all of my body weight, and I worry it might not hold.

I need to get up over that ledge before it gives way. I tighten my grip and walk my hands up the wooden shaft of the bow, my feet flat against the side of the mountain step by step.

Almost there. The edge is within reach.

Snap.

The bow splits from the string and falls, crashing down into the chasm below, but not before I pull myself up, throwing my body over the edge. My elbows and chest catch just enough so I can swing my leg up, my heel snagging on the sharp rock edge. I roll over twice, landing on my back, but far enough away from the edge not to worry.

I gasp for breath, hand clutching my chest as I suck in air. The ringing is slowly improving the longer I lay here.

Fin's knees hit the side of my chest as he drops next to me.

"Lennox! Are you okay?"

"I think so," I breathe. Now that my life isn't in imminent danger, the pain I ignored before explodes all over me. My hand is throbbing where I sliced it on the bowstring, and every inch of me feels like I've been beaten. I will be lucky if I didn't break anything. "I don't think it's safe to go that way." I tilt my head toward the gaping hole next to us.

"No. We should go back to camp. You're hurt."

"I know," I breathe, chest still heaving. "We should. I just need a minute." I lay there for another few moments before slowly sitting up. My hand is bleeding badly, and it feels like there might be more running down my face. I rip off a strip of fabric from the bottom of my shirt and hand it to Fin.

"Can you wrap this for me?"

"I, I don't know what to do," he stammers.

"It's alright, I'll walk you through it." I tell him what to do until he has it tied tightly around the slice in my skin. The fabric quickly soaks through with blood, and I wince as I clench my fist.

We hobble back down the path, taking extra precautions now that we know the mountain might explode. It is still early in the day. The suns have barely started their afternoon descent, but there is no way I can do any more searching today. I can barely move. I need to rest before heading back out tomorrow.

The idea is frustrating. I am going to lose half of a day of searching. Every day that goes on without success makes me more and more eager to find this cure, and watching Fin get upset today didn't help.

Families out there truly are suffering, and no one has found the cure for so many years. How long would the island continue to let people suffer? Why did it seem like it was giving everyone false hope?

As we trudge back to camp, I look down at Fin and feel a pang in my chest. I don't want to give up, just like he doesn't. At what point is it giving up versus being logical? At what point should I leave and return to my kingdom? At what point will Fin be satisfied with his efforts and decide to leave and see his sister before she dies?

This hope that the island gives every one of us is a beautiful gift, but also a curse. How do you move on from the hope that you had when reality isn't supporting it anymore? Tears prickle my eyes at the thought.

"Are you alright Lennox? Do we need to stop?" Fin's small and hopeful voice breaks through my thoughts.

"I'm alright. Just thinking."

He gives my hand a reassuring squeeze and keeps walking beside me.

"That was scary today. I thought I was going to lose you too," he mutters quietly.

I can't stop the tears now, at his words, at the events of the day. I sniffle, but pull my face together, trying to show him confidence that I am not exactly feeling.

"You didn't lose me. Not yet. It's going to take a little more than Dawnlin coming after us for me to go away." Another pang hits me. I will be gone once we are in the real world, back in my kingdom and he in his. No updates, no knowledge of his family's fate. He would just disappear from my life as if he was never there.

But he is here. This tiny person for whom I have grown so fond in so little time. "Promise me you won't go back to that mountain, especially not alone."

He nods. "I promise, Lennox."

"Good."

"My bow broke," he says suddenly, hanging his head a little lower.

I chuckle. With all the danger that happened today, if a broken bow worries him the most, I'll take it.

"Don't worry," I say, reaching up and lifting mine off of my torso to hand to him. "You can take mine."

CHAPTER THIRTY-SIX

he clearing is bright and empty as Fin and I come through the portal back into camp. I expect and welcome the quiet. Everyone will probably still be gone for hours, and my ears haven't stopped ringing slightly since the explosion. All I want is a nice cool shower, and to lie down for a while.

It takes me longer to make it up the ladder, my grip strength still recovering after hanging off the side of the mountain. After pulling myself onto the platform, I am immediately met with heavy footsteps getting closer and a deep voice calling out.

"What happened?"

Dane is in front of me in moments, his hands cupping my shoulders, his eyes assessing me, taking in all of my scrapes and bruises. "Are you hurt?"

"I'll be okay. The mountain exploded."

His face is etched with concern that doesn't ease at all with my statement.

I place my hand over his and give it a small squeeze. "I'll be fine. I just really want to wash all of this dust off."

"I'll get you some food, Lennox!" Fin yells before sprinting toward the tavern.

Dane moves to my side and wraps his arm around my waist for support as I hobble along the planks.

"Did you break anything? Anything serious?"

"I don't think so. I'm going to be really sore. I have a pretty nasty cut on my hand that I need to clean out and put some salve on. Otherwise, I just really want to lie down."

"Where were you? How did you make it out?"

I tell him everything, all about the paths and how the explosion left me hanging above the jagged rock. "Fin saved me. We broke his bow, though."

"Another one should appear for him, if not now, within the next few days."

"That's alright, he has mine."

Dane doesn't respond, and when I sneak a glance at him, he looks thoughtful.

"Which side of the mountain were you on?"

"The back side. I'm not ready to go near the falls yet."

He nods, lost in thought.

We walk up the stairs toward the showers and his arm slides away from my back.

"You aren't going anywhere, right? Can I talk to you after?"

"I don't have to go if you don't want me to." He smirks and closes the distance between us, his eyes glimmering with mischief.

I roll my eyes, but I can't hide the heat in my cheeks. I give him a playful shove that is met with a low chuckle.

"Alright, alright, I know what you mean. I'll meet you in the tavern?"

"Thank you."

He brushes a light kiss over my lips and winks before turning to stride back down the stairs. I shower quickly but thoroughly, letting the cool water soothe the aches and pains and wash away the mixture of dust and sweat plastered to my skin. While I'd become more accustomed to being around so many people, it is nice to have a little space to myself to just think.

I'd been so close to death today…*again*, and it didn't get any easier to deal with.

The highs of surviving are starting to wear off, and I can feel the sinking realization of how this place is not just the wonderful and magnificent, magical island it appears to be.

It is dangerous. It is unkind and possibly unforgiving.

It makes me wonder, has anyone died here? I want to ask Dane. I still haven't decided how long I will go without finding the cure. Maybe knowing what I am risking will help me better decide the point of surrender.

I dress and pull my hair up into a high knot, letting the wet strands continue to cool me down, then make my way to the tavern. Dane is sitting at a table alongside Fin and Mara, who look over at me when I enter.

"Gods, that looks like a nasty gash."

I reach up to touch my forehead where Mara is staring. It had been burning during the shower, so I knew I had something else that needed treating. I must have gotten cut by some of the falling debris.

"It's not so bad," I say as I slide onto the bench next to her.

Fin filled the table with plates of food, so I grab something and started nibbling.

"Good thing you have such a hard head," Mara says with a laugh before turning back to Dane. "Anyway, I swear I saw someone. It was really quick, but it couldn't have been one of us."

"Where did you see them?" He looks serious, and I wonder if he is worried.

"Down by the cliffs. It was a quick flash, and then they were gone. I ran over to look. Obviously, I was armed, but there was nothing."

"Male? Female?"

She shakes her head. "Couldn't tell. It was too quick. There were boot prints, but I lost them in the rocks."

"Damn." He leans back in his chair with a sigh.

"One of the Castaways?" I chime in, looking between Dane and Mara.

"I think so," she answers. "This could be a lead. Maybe their camp is close by."

"Maybe. I will have to go take a look."

Mara swings her leg over the bench and stands up behind it. "I'm heading back right now while it is still light out. Maybe they are getting lazy."

"Alright. I'll be down there in a little bit." He nods at me. "I'm going to make sure everything is good with Lennox first."

She nods at him. "Want to come Fin?"

"Yeah!" He bolts up out of his seat. "Let's find some Castaways!"

"Be careful!" I call after him as he sprints out of the tavern. Mara gives us a wave and strides after him, disappearing around the corner.

"So," Dane starts as I turned back toward him. "What did you want to talk about?"

"I almost died today." His face drops at my words, but I continue. "It just got me thinking. Everyone that is here, have they been here the whole time? Has anyone gone back without it?"

He shakes his head. "No, no one has gone back. Everyone has stayed here on the island, at least since I've been Guardian."

No one has been compelled enough to give up, to return to their loved ones without a cure. Is it because too much time has passed? Is it because they have been here so long, they'd forgotten about their home? Is it because this place and this way of living just gradually became their new home?

"Has anyone...not made it?"

He looks solemn, his jaw ticking slightly before he speaks. "I don't know about everyone. Some have become Castaways, and I don't know what happened to them. But no, some have not made it." He stands and rounds the table, reaching for my hand. "Come with me. I'll show you."

We make our way down to the clearing and wind through the path that leads towards the cage I was kept in on my first day here. It seems like so long ago now. So much has changed.

We turn off down a less trodden path and weave through the trees. A small clearing opens up ahead, and as I look past Dane at the space before me, I let out a small gasp.

It is beautiful.

Wildflowers of all different colors, shapes, and sizes bloom from the trees and weave into a colorful canopy. Below it lie a handful of graves, each marked uniquely, some with flat stones, some with piles or structures made of tree branches lashed together.

"The island makes sure this place stays beautiful for them, and for anyone else who may follow them," Dane says quietly.

"I'm glad," I mutter weakly. I feel overcome with emotion. This could have been me. I could have been brought here after what happened today. Dane could have been burying me here instead of showing it to me.

Dane shifts behind me. "That's why I asked where you were. Most of them have died on or near the mountain."

"You warned me. You said this place was dangerous."

"I did. For more than one reason."

I turn toward him. "Do you think you'll find anything at the cliffs?"

"I'm not sure. It's not like we haven't looked there before. We look everywhere. But if Mara saw someone, it's a start. I'd say come with me, but you need some rest and to fix up that hand."

"Yes, I do." I tug on the bandage Fin had tied on, still wet from the shower. Dane starts back down the path and I follow, but pause for a moment and look back over my shoulder toward the graves. I say a silent prayer to the gods for the souls of those who gave everything to help someone they loved. After a moment of silence, I turn and make my way back toward camp.

Dane helps me apply the magical salve to my face and hand and changes the bandage on my wound before heading out to meet with Mara and Fin. I hope the salve works quickly on my hand. I need it functional enough so I don't have to skip a day of searching.

I head to my bunk, tediously climbing the ladder all the way to the top, my muscles and joints screaming as I pull myself higher. All I want to do is put the shade up and lay my head on the pillow, but first I have to update the map. I pull it out of my shirt and open it, flattening the creases and spreading it across the shelf. I trace out the mountain path and draw in the gap with a large 'X'. Maybe, if this map ever falls into the hands of someone who needs it, knowing that path is dangerous might save their life.

I try to relax, but something Dane said keeps popping into my head. Most of the deaths occurred on or around the mountain. If that is true, why is it more dangerous than other places? Could it be simply because of the treacherous terrain? Or is there more to it? Was the island more dangerous the closer you got to the cure? Is there a reason it is trying to keep us away, and how can we beat it?

Am I right in thinking that the mountain is the key to finding the cure?

I look over everything I have sketched so far. All the other traps and diversions I ran into in other areas of the island haven't been that bad. I've been able to get out of them on my own, or if I was with other people, it was usually a misdirection. But today was more than that.

The area surrounding the mountain needs to be my new focus, no matter how dangerous it is. That's the point, isn't it? To do what needs to be done to find the cure?

I take in the details of the sketch and my chest tightens as the realization kicks in. There is no avoiding it. If my theory is true, and the island is hiding the cure in or around the mountain, I have no choice.

I need to explore the sides surrounded by water.

I need to get over my fear, and fast.

CHAPTER THIRTY-SEVEN

My palms are damp and my heart pounds wildly as I stand at the base of the mountain, right where Fin and I had climbed yesterday. I haven't even taken a step toward the other side yet, but the fear and anxiety of being so close to the water is already gripping me.

The salve had worked wonders. The slice on my forehead looks like nothing but a scratch, and my hand has healed quickly, leaving only an angry, dark red scar. The aches and pains from being tossed into the jagged granite surface will take longer, and I am lucky I don't have a head injury. I am sore, but I can move, albeit with a little less range of motion than normal. Brynne would scoff at me and tell me to work through the pain, but she wasn't here to throw jabs at me today.

Today it's just me and the water.

I take a deep breath and start the walk to the front of the mountain. There's a clear path, but I move quickly. The path is unprotected, and just to the right, the trees come to an end, leaving me vulnerable in the open.

Dane and Mara had found no hint of the Castaways last night, no clues to their mysterious hideout. Dane has a theory they don't settle in one place, and move only under the protection of darkness, which makes them so difficult to find.

His theory makes me feel a little better about searching the island during the day, but if Brynne taught me anything it is that I should still expect the unexpected and be prepared for an attack, especially since Mara's sighting was in the middle of the day.

Today is just as hot as yesterday, which does not help my anxiety going into this search. I am already uncomfortable with my plan, and the discomfort from my clothes sticking to me and sweat dripping down every surface of my skin just makes it worse. My intention for today is to take in as much as I can. I haven't spent a lot of time on this part of the island, so I want to get to know it while still staying away from the water.

I'm about to round a bend when I hear a snap in the trees. I reach for my bow to nock an arrow, but my hand comes up empty.

Shit. I gave it to Fin.

I stand still, squinting into the light and trying to see through the dense vegetation and shadows, but can't make anything out. I continue on, and don't make it another twenty steps before I hear a sound again, this time movement through the leaves.

"Dane?" I call out loudly, stopping to assess my surroundings. There's no response. "Dane, this isn't funny."

I break my eyes away from the forest edge to glance at the tops of the trees.

No breeze. The rustling had to be caused by something.

"Is someone there?" I call out again. If it is a Voyager, they should answer me, unless it is Dane trying to be funny and sneaking on me like before.

After a few more moments, I keep walking but remain alert. If Dane is right and the Castaways are only out at night, then whatever is responsible for the noise is doing nothing but using up my daylight hours.

I weave through the rocks and boulders in the path until I hear it. A dull roar fills the air, and I know the waterfall is just on the other side of the last bend. I round it and my senses are overwhelmed. A mist much thicker than the one in Blackwood fills the air, soaking every surface. But the mist has nothing against the deafening roar of the water falling into the pools below.

If I wasn't so terrified of it, I would think it is beautiful.

Water crashes off the side of the mountain, cascading down under a natural bridge of slick rock that crosses over to the other side. Under the bridge, the water flows quickly, then drops into a handful of waterfalls that feed into a blue green lagoon.

I take a step closer, mist soaking my hair and clothes, and crane my neck to see more without getting too close. The lagoon down below is breathtaking. Gushing waterfalls fall over dark rocks covered with lush green moss and plants, and into an elegant pool below. I've never seen such vibrant blues and greens, even in art or books back home.

My foot slips on the smooth bridge with my next step, and I throw my arms out for balance before I hit the ground, or worse, slip over the side into the water.

I squint through the mist, trying to make out what is on the other side of the bridge. From here it looks similar, a path continuing around the other side of the mountain, but also one that follows the curve of the sunken lagoon.

I don't know which way to go. Now that I've seen it, I can fill in details on my map, but I am not satisfied that this is enough for today. I need to take a closer look, see if there are any hidden passageways or caves in the rock, but the thought of getting closer to the edge makes my stomach roll and sweat break out on my already misted skin.

I can see the opposite side of the lagoon fairly clearly, and from this vantage point, notice nothing out of the ordinary. But I can't see the side I am standing on from here without dangling over the edge. I need to get to the other side, to ensure I have at least done a quick observation of both. Maybe once I have seen it all, I can come up with a plan of attack.

I keep my arms extended as I step out farther onto the bridge, my gaze trained on my feet and the slick ground underneath me. I stay in the middle, trying to give myself the best chance not to fall into the water below if I slip.

I heave out a sigh once I make it across and my feet hit solid ground again. Glancing between the two paths, I decide to scout out the other side of the lagoon instead of heading back toward the mountain. I don't need explosions two days in a row.

I will have to talk to the others at dinner tonight and ask if any of them have tried to explore the lagoon before. The water is clear, but the color darkens toward the middle. I assume it is deep, but I don't want to be the one to figure that out. There could be underwater caverns, but I won't be the one to find them. Maybe someone will want to team up and test my theory.

The shrubs and foliage increase the farther I walk along the path of the lagoon. The waterfalls below still roar, but it isn't as overwhelming as being directly under the mountain. I find a good vantage point for the rock wall on the other side of the lagoon where I had just been standing, and scan it for any clues.

I catch movement out of the corner of my eye and look toward the water. Something flicked the surface, causing ripples in the otherwise calm area of the lagoon. I haven't heard any of the Voyagers talking about fishing on the island, but wouldn't surprise me if there were fish in the lagoon. I'd have to keep it in mind if I ever stayed in one of the safe houses and needed to catch some food for the night.

I follow the curve of the lagoon a little more, just to make sure I don't miss anything when I see it again. It is bigger this time and looks like an actual fin.

Those must be some pretty big fish.

Suddenly all of my nerves and fears about this side of the mountain vanish, and all I feel is peace.

There is no reason to be afraid. It is just water. It's harmless.

I should go closer and look.

My limbs move as if of their own volition, taking me closer to the edge above the lagoon. I need to see over the edge, see what is hiding behind the beautiful water.

I will be fine. The island won't harm me.

I step out onto a large point that juts out over a dark part of the lagoon, and I feel like I am on top of the world. Overwhelming happiness and joy washes over me, and I wonder why I ever had any fears of being here in the first place.

I look down into the lagoon and see a flicker in the water again, but this time, it looks different.

Is that a person?

I crouch down on all fours, gripping the edge of the rock and leaning as far over as I can to peer into the water, but there is nothing there. It's as if she disappeared.

I need to know. I need to see who that is in the water. I know I will be safe. She will keep me safe. I just need to step off of the rock.

I scramble back onto my feet and position myself so I am perched right on the edge, the toes of my boots hanging just over the water. All I need to do is step off and I will be with her, will find her. She will keep me safe in the water. She won't let me drown.

Warmth spreads over my body, and I smile. I take in one last look at the lagoon and gorgeous water flowing into it from the falls.

I will be fine.

I step off the edge, only air surrounding me. My body is weightless. My feet break the surface of the water, but I am not afraid. She will find me. I am surrounded by beauty, and a soothing melody infiltrates my ears. It calms me further, reminding me of when I was young and the staff used to sing to me.

A slow stream of bubbles escapes my mouth as I relax into the feeling. Something touches my calf.

Is that her? She will bring me to safety, I know it. I am safe with her.

My eyes drift closed as I listen to the beautiful melody, and darkness overtakes me.

Everything will be fine.

CHAPTER THIRTY-EIGHT

arkness envelops me, and I am in a complete void.

No noise, no light, no feeling.

I am floating in an abyss.

There is nothing. No roaring of waterfalls, heat from the sun, or mist on my face.

Nothing.

Then suddenly, there is burning.

I cough and splutter, water bursting from my mouth. Light and pain flood my senses as fire burns through my chest. I feel the hard ground under my body as I cough repeatedly, head pounding and mouth gasping for air.

I am afraid to open my eyes. I don't know where I am, or what has happened. My last memory is crossing the stone bridge in front of the waterfall.

My chest feels like it has caved in as I continue coughing and gasping, spitting out the water that had infiltrated it.

Air. I need air.

"Breathe, just breathe," a low voice grumbles over me.

My spine stiffens at the sound.

I am not alone.

I throw my eyes open and immediately flinch, the light such a stark contrast to the immersive darkness filling my eyes just moments ago. My vision is blurry, but I can make out a shape in front of me.

A person. A face, hovering mere inches above mine.

My heart continues racing and my limbs start to shake. I blink rapidly, the person's features slowly coming into focus. I'm met immediately with a pair of bright teal eyes, framed by long dark lashes and thick brows, slanted in concern. Droplets of water fall off his face and hair onto mine, as he too takes deep heaving breaths.

The eyes roam my face, assessing, then soften slightly. I'm taken off guard at the relief I see reflected in them, as if the world is back in order now that I am breathing.

"You're alive," he breathes, his breath mingling with mine.

I'm alive.

Wait.

The panic that his eyes had soothed moments ago comes slamming back into me in full force. Who is this man? He isn't a Voyager.

That can mean only one thing.

A Castaway.

I scramble to put my hands underneath me, pushing myself backward and away from him. I stand and almost immediately my knees give out underneath me, and black spots mar my vision. My head spins as I gasp for more air. Strong arms catch me before I hit the ground, and I fall into a wall of solid muscle.

I try to push away, my limbs weak and difficult to control as I look around for anything that can help me. We are in a cave of some kind, with a stream of water flowing over the only visible exit.

I'd have to push through that strong wall of water to get out of here.

And him.

He is standing between me and my only way of escape.

"It's alri—"

He stops speaking and his head snaps away from me at a commotion coming from above.

"Did she surface?"

"Can you see her?"

"She can't swim!"

I can barely hear the shouts over the roar of the water echoing through the cave.

Suddenly I am moving. No, not moving. He is lifting me. It happens so fast, I barely have time to process it before my back is pressed against the stone, hips pinned to the wall by his. He grasps both of my wrists and holds them over my head, then clamps his other hand over my mouth.

I suck in a breath, ready to scream, trying to alert the Voyagers above searching for me.

He lifts one finger off my face and puts it to his lips, his face coming so close to mine.

Heat pools low in my abdomen at the press of his body flush against mine, followed by absolute horror as I push the feelings away.

What am I thinking?

This man is the *enemy.*

"Shhh," he hushes, eyes imploring me to listen.

I can finally see him clearly. His eyes are striking, but they are not the only striking feature. His strong square jaw is covered by the beginnings of a beard, shaved close enough that I can still see a muscle tick in his jaw as he urges me with his gaze to stay quiet. Short dark tendrils fall loosely over his forehead, still dripping wet, and his dark clothes cling to his drenched body, leaving little to the imagination. Every curve of muscle in his shoulders, arms, and abdomen stands out. A thick belt sits low on his hips, with a sword at his side.

He leans in closer, his body still trapping mine, cocooning it, protecting it from the commotion that is breaking the silence of this small, isolated cave.

"Please?" The deep rumble and earnestness of his voice makes my insides melt, and I blame the lack of air. My knees buckle, but the pressure from his body keeps me from sliding down the wall. Everywhere his body presses against me feels like it is on fire, my nerves sparking and igniting to consume me.

I barely muster a small nod, but the relieved smile lights his lips when I do makes me breathless again.

"I'm heading down! Keep the arrows nocked and cover me!"

He glances toward the water again before releasing me. The loss of the pressure feels like a weight has been lifted, not one I want to be rid of, but one that I *should* want to be rid of. He turns away from me and darts to the back of the cave, along the wall, and disappears around a bend.

"W-wait," I croak, my throat still burning from coughing up buckets of water. I scramble after him and round the corner, only to see him place his hand on the stone wall in front of him. It opens under his hand, a doorway forming in the stone large enough for him to slide into it.

I am moving then, stumbling across the stone, trying to make it to the doorway, but by the time I reach it, it is solid again. I place my hand on it just as he had, but nothing happens. I push, slightly at first, then again using all of my weight.

"Wait!" I scream, banging on it with my fists, but nothing budges.

I spin around and look back at the cave.

I am alone.

Trapped.

I need to get out of here.

I stagger to the front of the cave, just behind the falls. I try to look past it, but can see nothing except for the wall of water.

"I'm here," I croak, my voice barely audible. No one is going to hear me. I need to be louder. I cough, hard, trying to wake up my voice so I can get help.

"I'm here! Hey! Help! I'm here!"

I have nothing else to make any noise, so I just keep yelling as loud as I can.

"Lennox? She's here guys! I found her!"

Mara.

She slides behind the wall of water into the cave and wraps me in an enormous hug.

"I thought you were a goner. How did you get out of there?"

"I-I don't know," I stammer. Warnings sound in the back of my head, telling me not to say anything to anyone about the man who helped me.

Logic says I should. If this was one of the Castaways, which it most likely was, everyone needs to know. Dane needs to know.

I can't help but listen to the small voice that says to keep it a secret.

He'd helped me, saved me even. He pulled me from the water as I was drowning and somehow brought me back to life.

He looked so relieved when he saw I was alright, and he pleaded with me to keep him a secret. Could I give him that? *Should* I give him that?

This is the one favor I would allow him. One for one. We are even after this. Next time I come across one of them, I won't hesitate to fight or to bring down the wrath of everyone else on the right side of this island.

"You're one lucky bitch," Mara laughs as she slings her arm across my shoulders. "Come on, let's get out of here." She slides behind the waterfall again, and I follow, mimicking her exact moves and trying to keep away from the water as much as possible. The opening lets out to a pile of slick rocks between two falls with enough grip holds to climb up to the bridge.

Mara is already halfway up as I place my hands on the closest holds, hauling myself up the slippery rock behind her.

I focus on the rock, making sure I don't lose my footing and slip back into the deadly pool below. When I reach the top, she sticks an arm down to help pull me up, back onto the rock bridge where I had started this whole excursion.

Storm stands beside her, crossbow at the ready and pointed at the water below.

"What is in there?" I ask, winded from making the climb and still recovering from almost drowning.

"Sirens," Storm says gruffly.

"What are those?" I look between him and Mara, both their faces stoic.

"They are half fish, half people. They live in the lagoon," Mara answers.

"Why are both of you okay, but I wasn't?"

Or the man who saved me?

"Clearly you have fears," Storm grunts.

Mara rolls her eyes just as Roley jogs up to join us.

"Everyone has fears, Storm." He grunts in response, but Mara continues. "The sirens prey on your fears and make you feel happy. Am I correct to assume you were afraid of searching out here by the water?"

"Yes. I'd been dreading coming here all day."

"You can't swim Lennox?" Roley asks.

"Nope. The kingdom I'm from doesn't have any water."

"Not even lakes or rivers?" He asks, surprised at my clear lack of life experience.

I shake my head. "We have them, but I've never been to one."

"The bigger question," Mara says, interrupting us, "is how the hell did you get out of there?"

"I don't know," I shrug.

Storm glares at me, his eyes narrowing. "You sure?"

Mara throws an elbow into his side. "Seriously Storm? Has she given us reason not to trust her?"

I stare blankly, trying to look honest, even though my insides feel like a whirlwind of lies, with that voice still tugging at the back of my mind, telling me to stay quiet.

"The island does all kinds of weird things. Maybe almost dying two days in a row was too much for it and it gave her another chance," Mara says.

Storm grunts, then strides away.

He doesn't seem convinced, but I wondered if that was just Storm, or if he didn't really care for me. I need to tread lightly around him. If it gets back to Dane that I lied, potentially exposing the Voyagers to the threats of a Castaway, it would drive a wedge between us. Not only between Dane and me, but also between me and the other friends I have made.

If something happens again, I will deal with how to tell them then, but for now, I am staying silent and granting him a courtesy for saving my life.

"So you really can't swim, Lennox?" Roley cuts in again.

I chuckle as we head back across the bridge and toward camp.

It feels wrong lying to them, but I can't shake the look in the man's eyes when he saw I was breathing.

Please.

It makes me shudder just thinking about the quiet plea for me to stay quiet and hide him, as if what he was doing was just as wrong as what I was.

I ignore the fluttering low in my stomach, and instead focus on the guilt I feel for the lie I am about to tell Dane, and for the feeling I got when another man touched me.

I need to feel something more than guilt. Anxiety rolls through me as we get closer, my fingertips tingling and stomach in knots. I need a distraction to clear my mind, and I know a great way.

CHAPTER THIRTY-NINE

Dane isn't at camp when we return.

It is still early, but the suns are starting their descent and the sky is turning pink over the trees. I shower quickly, scrubbing myself raw with all the scented soaps and oils, trying to wash away the lagoon water and guilt from my body. My skin is bright pink once I decide I've abused it enough.

I dress and braid my hair, one long plait down the back of my head, my skills in caring for my hair having drastically improved since being here. The suns have lightened it with brighter bits peeking through the deep, golden waves. The glow from my skin is also new. I didn't know it was possible, never having been out in the light before.

I like it.

The thought of losing this reminder of my time in the warm sunshine once I return to my cold, dark throne upsets me.

I push it away and head to the tavern for dinner, sliding onto the bench next to Fin and Roley, who are having a competition to see who can finish their plate the fastest. The torches begin to light around us halfway through our meal. I look around, but there is still no sign of Dane.

Is he in trouble? How would we know if something happened to him and he needed help? Or is he even on the island?

It's easy to forget that he actually has a purpose here, more than searching for the cure and the Castaways every day.

I bounce my foot on the bench underneath me, trying to hold in my impatience. I need to do something to expend this energy.

"Wanna go shoot?" I say, looking over at Fin.

"Yeah! Let's go!"

I clear the table and drop my barely picked at dinner and Roley and Fin's empty plates into the tree on our way out. "I need to grab a bow. Meet you down there."

Fin is still using my bow and I've been waiting for the armory to give me a new one. I make my way over and pull the doors open. Sure enough, there is one hanging on a rack, as if the island knew I was coming.

Roley has joined us, and it makes me happy to see that Fin has made a friend. He is older than Fin by a few years, but still a child and total goofball. I don't have it in me to ask how long Roley has been here, but I can imagine that it has been quite some time, and he may not have any family left to return to.

Some of the older Voyagers have made their way down to the practice grounds and are throwing axes or spears into the wall of targets. The regular thunks are familiar and soothe my nerves, giving me something to focus on other than waiting for Dane.

After a few rounds of my own, I turn to focus on Fin and Roley. Fin has taken to the bow quickly and is getting much stronger, but I still make sure the pressure on the bowstring is low enough for him.

"Make sure your fingers are right by your mouth. There you go. Now breathe in and out."

He follows my directions and lets the arrow fly, striking the target on the second ring.

"Yeah!" He yells jumping up and down, giving Roley a high five.

"You did great. Now do it again!"

I sound like Brynne.

I watch him and Roley shoot the next few rounds, offering pointers and encouragement when needed, and even jumping in to show him myself.

The sky is dark and everyone has started winding down for the evening, but Dane still isn't back. Someone starts a bonfire in the clearing and we head out to join them. I sit in one of the wooden chairs close to the fire facing the portal, and stop myself from looking up at it every minute.

I listen half-heartedly to the scary stories the boys are telling. Fin and Roley are on the edge of their seats, soaking up every word. Gauge brought down a pile of treats and is popping corn over the flames. Smells and laughter waft into the air, the cheerful mood warring with the sinking feeling inside me.

Movement catches my eye past the fire, and I quickly sit upright.

Dane appears through the portal, but he isn't alone. A young girl follows him, looking scared as she takes in the surroundings.

I push up out of my chair and stride over to him. His face breaks into a grin as I approach.

"Lennox—"

I throw my arms around his neck and press my lips to his, cutting off his words. I don't know what has come over me. Maybe it's the guilt, maybe it's the worry something had happened to him. We agreed to keep this between us, not in front of the other Voyagers, so hopefully he isn't upset that I broke that agreement.

His hands splay over my sides, fingers flexing into my ribcage to grip me tighter.

Not upset then.

Whistles and whoops sound from the group behind us as Dane pulls away. A slight flush creeps across his cheeks, but he presses another short, chaste kiss to my lips before gesturing to the girl next to him.

"This is Lilly. I'm going to give her the tour and have Mara get her settled." He bends down, his lips hovering over my ear, his breath tickling my skin and sending shivers down my spine. "I'll find you after."

I nod and turn to Lilly to introduce myself. I reach my hand out to shake hers, remembering my manners. "Hi Lilly, my name is Lennox. I'm fairly new here as well."

She gives a shy wave, her eyes flitting back and forth between Dane and me.

"Come on, Lilly, let me show you around," Dane says.

They head to the rope ladder and I return to my spot at the fire.

"Ew, gross," Fin sing-songs as soon as I sit down.

I giggle. "Someday, Fin, you will take that back."

"Never," he says.

"That's right," Roley chimes in. "We're gonna be Voyagers forever!" He thrusts his small fist into the air like he is stabbing it with a sword.

Sadness falls over me as I look at Fin.

"Is that true? You don't want to go back to your family now?"

He shrugs and digs a stick in the grass in front of him. "I don't know. What if I never find it?"

"We'll find it. I know we will." I look him in the eye when I say it, with as much reassurance as I can muster. I realize it's not only for him but also for myself.

"And if we don't, VOYAGERS FOREVER!" Roley roars, beating his fists on his chest.

"Aahhhhh!" Fin yells, jumping up and chasing him around. I giggle as they play. It feels amazing being around children like this. Looking around at everyone here makes me feel like I missed out on a huge part of life. I'll never get that experience back in my childhood, but hopefully one day I would be blessed with children with whoever my father deemed appropriate to sit on the throne beside me.

I choke that thought down as my thoughts return to Dane.

It will never be him.

I clear my throat and focus back on the boys.

"You two need to head up to bed soon." I stand from the chair and dust off my pants.

"But they're all staying awake," Fin whines, gesturing to the older boys who are still laughing and joking around the fire.

"Yeah, Lennox, you aren't my mom!" Roley sticks his tongue out at me.

"No, I'm not, but I care about you boys. You need to be rested to stay safe searching tomorrow."

They both groan loudly, throwing themselves on the floor.

"Fine," Roley whines. "We'll go in a couple of minutes."

They jump up and fake a sword fight and I laugh, shaking my head. "I'll see you two tomorrow." I stride back over to the training area and pick up my bow again. Now that it is quiet and my mind isn't running away with thoughts about where Dane could be or if he was safe, I can focus on the target and pass the time.

I go through almost a dozen arrows, hitting the bullseye nearly half of the shots when I feel someone behind me.

"Don't miss," Dane rumbles in my ear.

I loose the arrow, striking the center of the target and spin around in his arms.

He regards the arrow impressed, then looks back toward me. "Sorry I took so long," he says, his voice low and husky. His body curves around mine as he wraps his arms tighter. He walks me backwards, holding me tight as my feet try to keep up with him. I drop the bow to the ground at my side and wrap my arms around his neck.

"It's alright," I murmur before reaching up and brushing a kiss across his lips.

In one swift motion, he scoops me up, wraps my legs around his waist, and leaves the training area. His hand cups the back of my head and pulls my face to his. The kiss is heated, and I meet his every move, my lips pressing hungrily against his. The light fades as we get farther away until all I can see are shadows from the glow of the moon.

"I have a feeling you missed me," he says against my lips, his breaths becoming short and shallow.

"I did," I breathe as my back hits something solid. My mind flashes to being pinned against a wall today. To when *he* pinned me to the wall. I push the thought from my head and try to focus on this moment.

We are tucked away in a cove of trees, completely hidden from everyone left in the clearing, but I can still hear soft snippets of conversation.

"I thought something happened to you." I pant, diving back in for another kiss. "I was worried."

Dane's grip tightens around the curve of my backside as he holds me against the tree. His right hand slides down, stroking the backside of my thigh.

No one has ever touched me like this, only him. No one was ever allowed to get close, unless I was training with Brynne looking on.

His lips move across my jaw, tracing a trail that starts down my neck. I throw my head back into the tree, giving him more access. His lips caress a spot at the base of my neck, just above my collarbone. His tongue flicks out and strokes my skin, sending shivers down my spine.

I close my eyes, and instantly a pair of teal eyes flash before mine.

Please.

I squeeze them tighter, willing them away. I can't think about how he made me feel, the way he made my stomach heat and my knees buckle. The way every inch of my skin that he touched made me burn. Not right now.

Not ever.

I pull Dane's face back to mine. He opens my mouth with his lips, his tongue slowly sliding against mine. He angles his head and leans over me, hiking my body higher and firmer against his.

I kiss him harder, trying to push everything that happened today out of my mind, but they won't stop. Flashes of those eyes. His eyelashes. The strong jaw. The perfect lips.

I wish these were his lips.

I break away from Dane's kiss in shock at the uncontrolled thought that flashed through my mind. What am I thinking?

"Are you alright?" Dane pants, his eyes searching my face.

"Yes," I lie, trying to break through the intrusive thoughts. I grab his face and bring it back to mine again. He meets my kisses strongly, his tongue working against mine and leaving me breathless.

Dane's hand trails back up my thigh and to my shirt, pulling it from my waistband. He slides his hand up under it, causing me to gasp into his mouth, which only encourages him. His warm fingertips caress my skin, leaving goosebumps in their wake.

He chuckles into my mouth before he flattens his hand across my stomach, dragging it across to run his fingers up and down the curve in my side. He leans into me more, his hips lining up with mine so I can feel his excitement against my core.

I suck in a breath and groan into his kiss.

I want this.

Right?

Teal eyes flash across my vision again, the memory of his hips pinning me to the wall.

No. No, that was wrong. This is right.

Dane lets go with his other hand, using only the pressure from his hips and the strength of the tree to keep me aloft. His kisses are still strong and sensual, but I can't get lost in them like I had on the beach. There is too much on my mind.

I try to only feel, to focus on the feel of his hands and breath on my skin.

His other hand slips under the edge of my shirt, both of them now slowly caressing my skin. His fingertips tease me, slowly making their way up. I feel my nipples harden as I wait for his touch. His knuckles brush the underside of my breasts, caressing the lace undergarment.

My breath hitches as his head lowers. He takes my nipple in his mouth, sucking through the fabric. I whimper and arch my back, pushing my chest closer to him, my mind finally clearing.

His fingers shift under my shirt, grasping my breast and bringing it farther into his mouth. All that's left between his skin and mine is just a little lace and a bit of parchment…

FUCK.

My mind snaps into focus instantly.

The map.

The map is tucked into my undergarments.

Just a little higher, and he will find it. I can't explain it. I just need to stop it.

"Wait, wait, wait," I say. I reach down and grasp both of his wrists, pushing his hands down to rest on my stomach, where it was safe. "Stop, Dane, please. I need to stop."

He releases my nipple and lets out a long breath.

"I'm sorry," I breathe.

"Don't apologize," he says, meeting my gaze. He lifts a hand to stroke the side of my face. "I got carried away."

"It wasn't just you," I smirk.

He lets out a breathy chuckle. "No it wasn't. But I can't help how much I want you."

He moves his hands back down to hold me, cupping the curve of my backside. "You make me crazy, Lennox."

My stomach flutters at his admission. It feels good to make a man feel crazy, to have someone as invested in me as Dane is. It is something I'd only ever read about, something I never thought I would have.

He leans in and places a soft sweet kiss on my lips, then looks me in the eye.

"I want you to stay." His eye contact breaks on the last word, as if the vulnerability of admitting this is too much for him.

A tear runs down my cheek.

Emotions battle inside me. Sadness, loss, regret, guilt, frustration. So many reasons for that tear.

"I wish I could."

He nods and slowly lowers me to the ground. I steady myself on his shoulders before he wraps me in a tight hug.

"I know what it would mean if you stayed," he says into my hair. "It would mean you never found what you came here for, and that is the last thing I want to happen."

I nod and take a deep inhale. His scent overwhelms me as I feel another tear drop onto my cheek.

We turn to make our way back to the bunks, and I try to break the tension after what just happened between us.

"Is everything alright with Lilly?" I ask.

"Yeah, she's a sweet kid. She seems nervous. I hope Mara didn't scare her too badly."

I laugh. "She definitely didn't welcome me sweetly, but now that she isn't fighting for your attention, I think she's lightened up. Hopefully, Lilly isn't too intimidated."

"I think she'll be fine. We'll pair her with some easy-goers in the beginning."

We climb the ladder and head toward my bunk, but before we get far, Dane stops me.

"I need to tell you something," he says, his voice low as he looks around to make sure no one is near.

"What's going on?" I ask.

We stopped in the middle of the walkway, between the light of the torches so we are hidden in shadows just enough. He reaches down to the sack that never leaves his side and lifts it, opening it between us. The glow of the dust lights my face, the same way it did back in Blackwood when Dane and I stood by the fountain, and he offered me a chance at the solution I'd been looking for.

Dane had brought two people back to the island after me, Fin and now Lilly, and the already very empty pouch looks even more so.

"The dust is running out. I don't know how many more trips I have left."

"What do you mean it's running out? Can't you just get more?"

"That's the thing," he says urgently. "This has never happened before. I've never had to refill it. When I took over as Guardian, this pouch was full, almost to the brim. The last Guardian didn't leave me with the knowledge of how to get more."

Of course he didn't, because Weston killed the last Guardian.

I wonder how much knowledge about the island was lost because of that act. Did the Guardian actually know where the cure was, but now no one does?

I stay silent, trying to process what he is telling me.

His voice drops even lower. "I'm worried that there may be a day where I go but can't come back."

"No," I say furiously. "There has to be a way. Maybe the island just refills it once it gets down? This place is magic. What is stopping it from replenishing on its own?"

"Do we want to take that chance?"

I release a frustrated sigh. "No, of course not."

It is impossible that the island would just cease helping people from the kingdoms because the dust had run out. That would mean that no one else could ever visit Dawnlin and everyone already here would be…

"Trapped," I breathe, my eyes glazing over and unable to focus.

"What?" Dane asks. He places a finger under my chin and lifts slightly so I am looking into his face.

I clear my throat and try again. "If there is no more dust, all of us here, we'll be trapped. It won't matter if we find the cure or not. There will be no way to get home without it."

"That would put an end to Dawnlin. We can't let that happen."

I gaze into the pouch at the small amount of dust at the bottom. "How much do you think is left? How many trips will that get you?"

"There and back, maybe three? Or four? It's just an estimate. I can't be exact. It takes more dust if there are more people."

I nod. "Okay, then we need to keep searching for the cure, but also try to find out if there is any information on how to replenish it. Maybe the previous Guardian kept notes or journals? Have you found anything like that?"

He shakes his head. "I haven't looked, but we could try."

"We have to try. We can't strand everyone here. It was a choice before, choosing to stay, but if we run out, then that choice is taken from everyone."

He cracks a smirk. "Just like old times, trying to find answers hidden away in old books." I roll my eyes, not wanting to recall his deception early in our relationship.

Now I'm the one being deceptive.

He pulls the strings, closing the pouch. The glow disappears, and he hooks it back to his belt. "We need to keep this between us. I don't want to spread panic among the Voyagers."

"Absolutely," I reassure him. I don't want to deal with the potential fallout of everyone being trapped on the island, either. I don't even want to think about it myself.

"Good."

Despite our plan, I know I am going to be worried all night, reeling with the thought of being here forever.

As if enough hadn't already happened today.

Dane gives me a sweet but heated goodnight kiss before heading back to his side. I don't see Lilly on the climb up to my bunk and assume she took one farther down. I sit down on my bed and reach in my shirt to pull out the map. This small thing could have made tonight end much differently. I toss it onto the shelf and lay on my side.

Today was a nightmare. I hadn't even told Dane everything that had happened. I doubt Storm would keep it from him, but that was the least of my worries. My mind is elsewhere.

Had I been trying to force things with Dane tonight, doing anything to erase the guilt? Did the touch of the man in the cave really affect me that much?

I huff angrily and roll onto my back, staring at the stars blinking in the sky.

I don't want to admit to myself that maybe the map stopping anything from happening tonight was for the best. I care for him, and he for me, but I don't want to be with him in that way if it is tinged with guilt and other emotions.

That isn't what I want.

I fall asleep trying to put the thoughts out of my mind, willing my body not to feel the desire that had been coursing through me today, and ignoring the voice in the back of my head that keeps reminding me it wasn't for Dane.

CHAPTER FORTY

he next few days pass in a haze. I spend most of them alone, trying to work past my emotions and clear my head, using searching as a distraction. I know Dane isn't leaving the island any time soon unless he is called and has no choice, but it feels like I am avoiding him.

My guilt hasn't subsided, and I am keeping it to myself. I don't want anyone knowing that I had any of these feelings. I just need time to work them out. Besides, I feel somewhat embarrassed that I stopped him the other night, and I don't want to hurt him again. I know it was to protect my map, which is crucial to my time here. I don't know what would hurt us more, me stopping his advances the way I did, him finding the map, or him finding out I let a Castaway go.

I need to get my head on straight.

I spend the entire morning on the far side of the island, near the coast. I've come up empty-handed, not even a diversion from the island to keep me on my toes.

Hour after frustrating hour passes with nothing when I hear a low grumble in the distance. I peer out over the sea and sure enough, off in the distance are thick black storm clouds, moving quickly and heading directly for Dawnlin.

Might as well call it a day.

A tropical breeze blows on my back as I head back toward camp. We don't have warm storms back in Blackwood. They are usually frigid and icy, sometimes with a bit of snow. Another new experience in Dawnlin.

I run into Taril on the main path, who is also trying to beat the storm back to camp.

"Those look like dark clouds," he says. "I have a feeling this is going to be a rough one."

"Hopefully, everyone makes it back in time," I say with a glance at the sky.

"Make sure to bring all your stuff to the cabin."

"The cabin?"

"Yeah. During big storms like this, we can't sleep in our bunks. There's no protection, so we all go to the cabin."

"I've never seen it," I say as we walk through the portal.

"Go grab your stuff and meet me at the tavern. I'll take you there."

We go our separate ways once we get up into camp and I head to my bunk. I hadn't accumulated anything of value to me here, besides the charcoal and candle, but I can't risk Dane discovering those and decide to leave them here tucked under the center of my sleeping pad. At least they won't fall if the bunks rattle in the wind.

I arrive at the tavern with only my pillow and blanket and Taril is waiting for me, a sack slung over his shoulder.

"This way," he says, directing me back toward the boys' bunks. I follow closely, not having spent much time on this side of camp before. Just before we get to the bunks, he turns toward an enormous tree trunk with a door carved into it. He turns the handle, pushing the door open and steps inside. I follow, and once I cross the threshold, I realize he wasn't kidding about calling it a cabin.

Magic opens the inside of the trunk into a large wooden walled room. Lit sconces hang from the walls, casting a calming glow over the room. The floor is covered with cots, sleeping pads, and large fluffy cushions tossed haphazardly around with hammocks hanging from the roof. A mini tavern is to the right, already filled with snacks and an opening to grab hot meals. Some Voyagers have already set up inside, but it seems like most haven't returned yet.

"There's no point in splitting up in here. Just pick a spot before they're all taken." Taril takes off to the back of the room, and throws his sack down inside a hammock.

I weave through the cushions on the floor and make my way over to a larger fluffy pad up against the wall. I put my pillow down and spread my blanket across it, smoothing it over the edges. More Voyagers wander into the cabin, and soon Mara and Lily step inside.

"Hey," Mara calls out, stepping over some cushions and making her way toward me, Lilly following closely behind. "Just grab a bed, anywhere you want."

I sit down on my bed and cross my legs. "How was your first day, Lilly?"

"It was good," she says quietly. "Just still trying to wrap my head around all of this."

"It's a lot all at once," I agree. She sets her pillow and blanket on a cot next to the pad Mara chose. Mara has a sack of belongings, just like Taril. I guess that is an easy way to determine who has been on the island the longest.

"I'm hungry," Mara says once her bed is set up. "Anyone want food?"

Lilly and I nod and follow Mara across the room to the small tavern. A couple of boys in front of us grab their food, and we fall in line behind. I turn when I hear the door open, followed by a crash of thunder and the sound of pounding rain.

"Go in, get inside."

Several Voyagers hop in through the door, followed by Dane's large frame. He is soaked through and shakes his long hair away from his face as he too steps inside, closing the door behind him.

"You found it," he says as he wraps an arm around my shoulder and squeezes me to him.

"I did thanks to Taril, otherwise I would have been out there in the rain wondering where everyone went."

"Nah, I would have gone to find you." He winks, followed by a light brush of his lips over mine. "Get some food. I'm going to go get some dry clothes and make sure everything is in order."

I nod as he releases me, and move forward to grab my plate and make room for the line that is now forming behind us.

I follow Mara and Lilly back to our space and we eat, chatting easily between us. The more we talk, the more Lilly relaxes, offering tidbits of herself and her life back home. No one asks who she is here for. We try to keep the conversation light.

Boys run around the room, yelling, laughing, and tackling each other. Some lounge around in their beds, talking animatedly to the others around them. I can't help the smile that tugs at my lips as I take in the chaos around me. Something about everyone being together like this just feels different. We often eat dinner at the same time, but this feels like more.

It feels like a family.

I smile, turning my attention back to the story Mara is telling when I feel the cushion beside me shift.

"Any breakthroughs today?" Dane asks as he settles down beside me.

I shake my head. "No, unfortunately. I came back pretty early once I saw the clouds rolling in."

"Good choice. It is really wet out there. Things can get pretty unstable when it rains like this."

Lightning flashes across the window, lighting the room for a split second. Thunder rolls a few minutes later as the storm picks up.

I turn to him. "How long do they usually last?"

"Could be a couple days, but usually not more than that." He reaches over and picks some food off my plate and pops it into his mouth.

"Hey! Get your own!" I say with a small shove.

He chuckles and chews the bite. "Aw, come on, you'll share with me."

"The only—" I am cut off by a quiet voice standing in front of us.

"Excuse me, Lennox?"

I roll my eyes at Dane. "You're not getting off this easy." He smiles and snatches another bite as I turn toward the boy standing in front of me. "Hey Roley. What's up?"

"Um, I just, um, wondered if you had seen Fin? He isn't back yet, and um, I didn't know what to do."

Fear and dread trickle down my spine as I sit bolt upright.

No.

"What do you mean, he's not back? Were you with him today?" I ask.

Roley wiggles, shifting his weight on his feet as tears pool in his eyes. I have to remember, despite being on this island for years, he still is just a child, and is scared that something happened to his friend.

"Hey, hey, it's okay." I reach up and grasp his hands, squeezing them tight. "I'm not mad. I'm just trying to find out more information."

He sniffles slightly. "We always meet at the tavern for dinner, but he hasn't come back yet."

"Maybe," Dane chimes in, "he's out there wondering where we all are. He's new, remember? He may not know where to go."

I jump to my feet and Dane pushes himself off the floor behind me.

"We'll go check, alright? You stay here with Mara and Lilly." I run my hand over the top of his head and nudge him toward Mara. She throws open her arms, and he snuggles up to her, still wearing the worried look on his face.

"It'll be alright," I hear her whisper to him. "We'll find him." He nods slightly and sniffles again.

Dane takes my hand and pulls me to follow as he weaves through everyone lounging on the floor.

"Dane, I'm worried," I say.

"There's probably a simple explanation. Don't be worried until we have something to worry about."

He pulls the door open and large raindrops blow inside. He ducks out of the frame and I follow, shutting the door behind me. The wind and the rain are strong, making it difficult to see, and I am drenched in seconds.

"I'll go check the bunks, you check the tavern," Dane calls over the wind.

"I'll go to the training grounds after. Maybe he's staying under the trees."

Dane nods before squeezing my hand. "We'll find him."

He jogs toward the bunks, and I speed in the opposite direction.

"Fin!" I scream as loud as I can, hoping he can hear me over the storm. "Fin!" I barrel down the walkway toward the cavern. I can hear Dane calling out for him as well, which means he isn't at the bunks. "Fin!" I scream again as I round the corner and looked into the tavern.

Empty.

He isn't here. I run quickly, calling his name repeatedly and check every area I can think of. The showers, the girls' bunks, the armory. Nothing.

He isn't here.

I need to get down in the clearing. Maybe he took shelter under the trees.

The storm clouds make the evening darker than normal, and I know night is rapidly approaching. I slide myself down the sides of the ladder, not bothering to wait for the platform to lower.

"Fin!"

I run across the clearing, rain pelting my face as I squint, trying to see clearly. I run to the training area, scanning it and the surrounding trees, but it is empty.

Dane's calls get closer. He must be in the clearing now, too.

My breaths are becoming shallow and my fingertips are tingling.

Where is he? Why isn't he answering?

"Have you found him?" I yell toward Dane as I run back onto the path, checking the cages I was locked in on the first day. They had a roof. Maybe he sought them out for shelter.

"He's not over here," Dane yells back.

I try to choke back a sob.

No. There is no way he is gone. He always makes it back, every night.

I run back to the clearing, straight to Dane. "I need to go look for him."

"We can go just outside the portal, but we can't go far. It's too dangerous."

"It's dangerous for him too!" I yell at him, fury rising in my veins. I am not angry at Dane, and he doesn't deserve that. I take a deep breath and let it out slowly. "I'm sorry. I just need to make sure he's okay."

Dane's arms wrap around me and he pulls me in close. We stand in the middle of the clearing, rain pouring down on top of us, and I let the tension in my shoulders drop. Another sob wracks my body, causing Dane to hold me tighter before I push him away.

"I'm going to go look for him."

I climb the ladder faster than ever before and barrel through the walkways to the armory. I sling weapons across my body, making sure I am heavily armed going out at night in this storm. Dane comes up beside me and pushes the door wider, pulling out his own weapons and stowing them on his body.

"We can't be out long. The rain isn't letting up, and it's not safe."

I whip my body toward him. "It's even more unsafe for Fin." I slam the door to the armory and run back to the platform. I need to get out there.

These emotions are foreign to me. I've never cared this much about anyone in my life. I had no one I needed to look after or make sure they made it home. If something happens to Fin, I will be devastated. I won't even know how to break the news to his family, how to find them. I might not even be able to try if we can't figure out how to replenish the dust.

When my feet hit the ground, I run toward the portal. I can hear Dane behind me as I step into the darkness. I emerge on the other side with him beside me, holding out a torch for me to grab. I hadn't thought about how dark it is going to be. The light might make us easy targets for any Castaways out in the storm, but it is the only hope we have to see anything.

"Fin!" I call out, pushing away leaves and tromping through the wet trees to the main path.

The torch stays lit despite the downpour, and I am thankful for the magic that is helping me try to find him.

"I don't even know where to start," I say as I glance back and forth in both directions.

"We need to stay together," Dane says. "Do you have any idea where he was today?"

"No. Roley didn't say either. I don't think he knew."

"Alright. Lennox, I need you to listen to me. We might not find him tonight. I need you to understand that. But he's a smart kid. He's learned a lot."

I don't want to say it, but I need to. I need to prepare myself for the worst. "What if they took him?"

His face turns grim. "We won't know right away. Try not to think that way."

I swallow down the lump in my throat. If it isn't safe to be out long, we need to get going so we can cover as much area as possible.

We search the section closest to camp, scouring the paths and offshoots, checking everywhere he could have stopped for shelter. There is no sign of anything amiss, no footsteps in the mud or broken branches that might indicate a scuffle.

Despite being soaked to the bone, I am not cold. The storm is hot and muggy, and the air is filled with buzzing and rain. The warmth makes me push to keep looking, but the longer we are out, the more my fear rises that we will not find him tonight.

"We need to call it."

"No, just a little more. Maybe he's down at the beach?"

Dane shakes his head. "I doubt it. There's nowhere there to hide from the storm. It's time, Lennox. We need to head back."

I let out a scream of frustration. I don't want to give up. I can't. Not on Fin. But if we don't head back now, we would put ourselves in more danger. If something happens to us, we won't be able to help Fin at all.

I finally concede, and Dane leads us back to camp. I feel numb, and the gaping hole in my chest widens with each step back to the portal. He will be alright. He has to be. I promised he wouldn't lose me, but now I'd lost him.

Tears streak down my face, unnoticeable in the rain. Dane takes the torch from me as we arrive and places them back in the sconces he took them from. We slowly walk back to the cabin. I don't know how long we'd been gone, but almost everyone is asleep when we step inside.

Mara perks her head up, moving only slightly so as not to disturb a sleeping Roley tucked into her side. She meets my eyes, silently asking for news. I shake my head and look away, trying to hide the defeat and worry that is eating me alive.

Dane places his hand on the small of my back and guides me past the tavern to a small washroom. I go first, toweling off and wringing out my soaking wet hair. I change into new clothes and gather up all the weapons I had to take off before I walk outside. Dane slips into the room after, while I make my way over to my bed and set all the weapons down on top of it.

I probably should get something to eat, but the thought of food makes my stomach churn. I had barely taken a bite when Roley asked about Fin. There is no way I will be able to eat, or sleep for that matter.

In a trance of my thoughts, I don't see Dane approach. He extends his hand down to me and I take it. He pulls me up and we walk a few spaces over to an empty large fluffy sphere. He plops down in a sitting position and extends his arm, making room for me to plop down beside him. I sink into the cushion as it molds around me and turn to lean into his chest.

"I'm not going to sleep tonight," I murmur. His fingertips stroke my shoulder gently, soothingly.

"I know, but you should try. You need to have energy if you're going to search tomorrow."

I nod silently, knowing that between the nightmares and worry for Fin, it is going to be a rough night ahead.

CHAPTER FORTY-ONE

I sleep fitfully despite being curved into Dane's side, but manage not to disturb him. After waking from the last gasping nightmare with Weston holding a sword across Fin's neck and me unarmed and helpless, I can't try to sleep any longer.

I lie awake next to Dane, staring at the one magical window in the cabin to see outside. The rain has eased to a drizzle for now, but the sky is still too dark to be morning. So I wait.

I can't stop thinking about Fin, how scared he must be, how helpless. How evil Weston is if he took a *child* captive.

Terrible thoughts keep circling through my mind. I don't know what methods Weston uses to turn any captive against us, but from what I know of torture and mind manipulations, I fear for him.

It's telling that I don't consider death the worst outcome for Fin's disappearance. Being held against your will, lied to, and manipulated all for someone else's gain is far worse.

Time passes slowly. I continue to stare at the window until it finally lightens enough to justify leaving camp. The storm isn't ideal, and I wonder how many of the Voyagers would stay in and wait it out.

That isn't an option for me. I need to find Fin.

I carefully lift myself from the cushion, trying my best not to wake Dane. He stirs slightly and rolls to his side once I am no longer there. I reach back and graze my dagger, making sure it is still in place before I quietly make my way over to the weapons I had stashed on my bed last night.

It's too risky to grab everything. The noise will wake everyone in the room, so I settle on what is easy and quiet. I slide a serrated knife into my boot and drape the bow over my shoulder. I hold the ends of the arrows so they don't rattle in the quiver, creep toward the door, and slip outside.

Dane and I had searched the area closest to camp last night, so I don't want to waste time there again. Surely if Fin was that close to camp, he would have made his way back as soon as it was light.

I decide to start at the mountain. He had been searching there often, and even though I told him to stay away from it, that doesn't mean he did. Plus, it seems to have so many dangers surrounding it, it would be best to make sure he didn't get caught there first. I hustle through the paths that have become second nature, annoyed that I am already close to drenched from the constant drizzle.

When the trees open up revealing the base of the mountain, I look up at the ominous structure, the top hidden by the dense storm clouds hanging low over the island.

I doubt he took the hike we had before, especially after the explosion. I run toward the waterfall, zigzagging back and forth across the open area, calling out his name. As I near the lagoon, I focus on successfully finding him. There are no Voyagers out to help me this time, so all the fears I have about Fin being abducted can't enter my mind.

Come on, Fin. Where are you?

I look down the paths on the other side of the bridge, trying to decide which direction I should go. The sheets of rain make it difficult to see very far, but I know I need to check the lagoon to make sure he didn't fall prey to the sirens hiding below the surface. I focus on successfully finding him safe as I near the edge. I lean forward and peer past the rock to the water below.

I scan the surface, looking for any sign of floating items, or worse, a body. Everything is calm and empty except for the ripples from the rain. The storm made the water murky and difficult to see into, but my gut tells me he isn't here, and I need to keep looking.

I turn around, heading back toward the base of the mountain, hoping to make the full circle as fast as I can. Running the paths and shouting Fin's name with worry is leaving me breathless, more than any amount of training and physical endurance could have prepared me for. The clouds unleash heavy rain again as I follow the other path around the mountain. There is no sign of him anywhere, not even footprints in the mud paths I am slogging through.

Fuck.

I should have waited for the others. There is no way I can cover this island alone. There are too many places to look, too many hazards in this storm.

If there were more of us, we could have spread out, assigned areas for each of us to search. This is basic military strategy, and I let my emotions guide me instead of logic and my years of training in leadership and strategy.

Maybe my father is right. I am not ready for this. I am not ready to hold the lives of others in my hands. If my emotions can so easily overshadow my judgment and affect my actions and cause me to make rash decisions, maybe I am not ready to run our kingdom.

That doesn't matter right now. Blackwood and my throne are far away, and worrying about it doesn't help me find Fin.

I search for hours. Hours of running through the rain, drizzle, mud, and floods all to come up empty-handed. There is nothing, no sign of him anywhere. I've stuck to the main areas, traipsing through the paths on the far side of Dawnlin, constantly checking my map to make sure I am not missing something.

I can't tell because of the cloud cover, but I assume it will be late by the time I reach the beach. Dane said it wasn't likely he was anywhere on a beach because of the lack of shelter, but I can't leave any stone unturned. I find a break in the rocks similar to the stairs Dane and I took. A trail winds down to the beach and I follow it. This sand is different from the black beach and sand of the cove, its light color darkened with all the rain from the storm.

"Fin!" I call out. Waves crashing are the only responses I hear. "Hello? Is anyone out there?"

Nothing but the shriek of the winds and rustle of palm fronds.

There is a break in the rain, thank the gods, but I don't know how long it is going to last. The storm seems to be picking up again, and the day is coming to an end, so I need to keep moving.

I scan the beach as I walk, staying away from the surf as much as possible. I need something, anything, some kind of sign that either he had been here, or one of the Voyagers had searched here already.

There are no footprints in the sand, the water and the surf having smoothed it all. My heart sinks, but I push on.

As I scan the sand and the rocks ahead, something catches my eye. Something is sticking out of the sand. I break out into a run and drop to my knees in front of it. I start to dig, grit sticking under my nails and the sand heavy with water as I toss it to the side. Clawing at the object in front of me, I finally pry it loose and my stomach bottoms out.

"No," I breathe as I realize what it is.

It is his bow. *My* bow.

Snapped in half, the two pieces held together by only the string. My eyes scan the surrounding ground, and I see them. The ends or tips of arrows poking through the sand, everything clearly signs of a struggle.

"No!" I scream. "FIN!"

My throat burns and my voice breaks as I let out a scream, my worst fears crashing down over me.

They have him.

The Castaways took him.

Gods only knew what they were doing to him or how they were treating him. Did Weston's brainwashing start right away? Would Fin even want to come back with me if I tried to rescue him? How would I find him when we have no idea where the Castaways are hiding?

My Castaway. I need to find him.

Not my *Castaway.*

If he had any decency like he did when he saved me, he would tell me where Fin was, or let me help him. I need to try.

I pull myself to my feet, throwing the broken bow back down into the sand. My feet move with a mind of their own, carrying me off the beach and back up to the paths.

I run as fast as my legs will take me, jumping past obstacles, stumbling over the storm roughed ground. Nothing is going to stop me. Not the scrapes and mud, not the torrents of water pouring from the sky. I run and run until I reach the mountain.

I have no fear as I approach the bridge. There is nothing for the sirens to prey on this time. Instead, I let my anger consume me and fuel my plan. Emotions be damned. I am going to let them guide me this time.

There is no reasoning with the Castaways, no strategy to be played. Emotion is all I have, and I am going to use it.

I climb down the rock between the falls as fast as I can without slipping until I hit the solid ground. I slip between the falls and the rock wall, not caring if I touch the water this time. I am still drenched, soaked from the storm, and too focused on my goal to care about its proximity.

I step into the dim cave and look around.

I am alone. He isn't here.

Somehow he found me before, so there is nothing to say he won't again. I round the corner where he had disappeared before and try the door, but the solid stone wall doesn't budge.

I walk back out toward the falls, and pull off my bow and quiver, so I'm ready to use it at a short distance if I need to. I lean against the wall not far from the opening and wait. No one can sneak up on me. I won't be taken off guard.

I stand watching the entrance, letting my anger stew.

I don't care how long it takes.

I will wait.

And then I will get Fin back.

CHAPTER
FORTY-TWO

"I assume you're waiting for me?"

I whip around at the deep voice behind me. He must have come in through the wall in the stone. He leans against the back of the cave, arms folded across his chest. I can actually see him now that I am not gasping for air after almost drowning.

He is tall, much taller than me, wearing clothes similar to ours, but in darker tones. He still wears the belt and sword, but today he has a leather vest strapped around his chest holding a variety of blades. His dark brown hair is tousled on the top, as if he has just woken up, but he isn't soaked to the bone like I am.

How did he get through the storm?

It doesn't matter. What matters is that he is here. He found me. I don't know how he knew, but he did.

I ignore my questions and focus on what is important.

Fin.

I push off the wall and square my body to him, crossing my arms to mimic his stance. The space between us is a chasm, thick with tension.

"How did you know?" I snap at him.

"Lucky guess. What do you want?"

"I want to talk to Weston. I want Fin back."

He glares at me, his body still as the stone behind him. "Fin is safe," he says finally.

"Sorry if I don't take your word for it. He's just a little boy. He is safe with us."

"What makes you think that, princess?"

A lightning bolt strikes me at the last word. "What did you just call me?"

"You heard me," he says, pushing off the wall and taking a measured step toward me.

It has to be a scheme, something to throw me. A stupid pet name he thinks will shake me and make me forget about my fury toward the Castaways. There is no way he has any idea that I am actually a princess.

"I'm not your princess," I spit back.

He shoots me a pointed look and takes another step forward, slowly closing the gap between us. "You never thanked me for saving your life."

If he thinks I am going to be deterred by his not so subtle subject change, he is wrong. "Your thank you was my silence and not telling Dane about you." His eyes harden, but he stays on course, continuing to step closer toward me. I don't budge. I won't let him intimidate me, no matter how much stronger than me he looks.

"You didn't tell him?"

I seal my lips shut. The conversation should not be going there. He is distracting me, changing the subject. I need to get back on course.

"If you will not take me to Weston, you can at least arrange for me to meet him somewhere."

He smirks. "What are you going to offer him? He's going to need to know before he decides to meet with you." Another step closer.

"I have nothing valuable."

"I disagree." Another.

I scowl at him. He is close enough now that I can reach out and touch him, but I am not backing down. I refuse to back away.

"How about a trade?" he says, taking that last step so we are almost touching.

"A trade? Fine. Name it. You know him better than me. What would Weston trade Fin for?" I pin him with my stare, and his teal eyes don't look away.

"You, princess. I'd trade for you." I feel the rumble of his voice deep in my abdomen, my heart beating wildly in response.

Me. I could trade for Fin. I *would* trade for Fin. I'm much more capable of handling the Castaways than he is, and I wouldn't rest until I escaped.

I open my mouth, ready to agree.

Then it clicks, what he said.

I'd *trade for you.*

Weston.

This man is Weston.

Not just one of the Castaways that saved me. The leader, the man responsible for kidnapping Voyagers. The man that wants the cure for his own gain.

This evil, dangerous man who had…saved me? Who had looked relieved when I was alive?

No.

It's all part of his mind games. He's already been using them on me since the moment we met.

Maybe he doesn't want me dead, but that doesn't negate everything else he is responsible for.

I fling out my arms, pushing him square in the chest. He staggers back a few steps, but holds my gaze. I pull my dagger from its sheath and hold it in front of me, just as Brynne taught me.

His eyes flick down to it, then back to me. "Please don't," he says. Then he winces, a movement so small, if I wasn't looking at him so intently, I wouldn't have seen it. In less than a second, his expression is serious again.

"You. It's you. You lied to me!" I scream at him, holding my dagger a little higher. He eyes it briefly again, his head tilting slightly as he assesses it.

"I never lied to you, princess."

"You did. You—"

He shakes his head. "I never said who I was. You assumed."

"Why? Why are you doing all of this?" I growl.

"That's a conversation for another time."

"There's not going to fucking *be* another time! Bring Fin back to me!"

"That's not going to happen, princess."

"Stop fucking calling me that!" My anger boils over at his denial and his nickname. I take a step and slash at him with my blade. He leans back, dodging it easily.

"I don't want to fight you." He holds his palms up to me in a mock surrender. "I asked you once. Please don't."

"I don't care what you want! I want Fin back!" I charge forward, swiping at him as I go, but each strike misses as he moves swiftly out of my reach. Just when I think I have him backed against the wall, he takes quick steps toward me, catching me off guard. I scramble backwards, my balance thrown off by his sudden movements. He grabs my wrist and twists, pointing the dagger down at the ground.

I cry out as a sharp pain shoots through my arm, causing me to loosen my grip. He snatches the dagger from my hand, then releases me. I stagger backward, clutching my wrist.

He stares down at it, shaking his head and clucking his tongue before cursing under his breath. I only catch a few words. "...piss-poor job."

"What did you say?" I snarl.

"I said whoever trained you did a piss-poor job," he yells back at me. He reaches up and sheathes my dagger in a slot in his leathers and I feel panic rising in me.

"Fuck you!" I spit at him. I reach out and try to snatch it back. He deflects my arm easily and steps away as I crouch down, reaching for my only other weapon. I pull the knife out of my boot and run at him. He ducks my strike, his arm reaching out to circle mine as he pushes forward, forcing me back.

My back slams into the wall, my head following. He grabs both my wrists and holds them above my head, pinning me with his hips just as he had the last time we were in this cave.

"Shall I disarm you again, princess?" he grumbles so quietly, I almost can't hear him over the roar of the waterfall. He stares down at me, our breaths mingling. I feel heat course through my body and my stomach bottoms out at the sound of his voice. I focus on my anger instead, letting the rage fuel me against this enemy. I refuse to let him distract me and disrupt my time here like he has since the moment I opened my eyes to his.

"I hate you," I grind out through gritted teeth and use all my strength to try to push him off of me. He doesn't budge, his size and strength too much for my slight frame pinned underneath him. His hand slides over mine and he pries the knife from my fingers.

"I'm sorry to hear that." He wrenches the knife out of my grasp and pulls away from me, causing me to fall forward. I hit the ground on my hands and knees, my palms scraping against the coarse cave floor. He saunters over to the cave opening and tosses my knife through the wall of the water.

"Hey!" I scream as I scramble to my feet. He picks up my bow and quiver and does the same, sending them slicing through the water and crashing down into the lagoon below.

"You don't need them," he says matter-of-factly as he brushes past me toward the back of the cave.

"I need them to protect myself!"

"From what?"

"From you!"

He scoffs, and fire blazes inside me at the dismissal.

Fine.

If I don't have any weapons, I'd have to use my hands. Brynne and I had sparred without weapons plenty of times for occasions just like these.

I run at him, my arm pulling back, ready to throw an upper cut. I land it on his back, and a grunt escapes him. He spins around and wraps his thick arms around my torso, pinning mine to my sides and moving so his front is to my back.

"Stop!" He yells. I ignore him, leaning back into him and kicking my feet into the air, trying anything I can to get free.

"Haven't you noticed," his voice strains, and he grunts as he works to keep my thrashing body contained, "that I've done nothing to hurt you? Nothing to strike out at you, despite you deliberately attacking me this entire time? I wonder why that is."

My feet still as his words sink in. He still holds me tight, not risking loosening his grasp just because I stopped moving for a moment. My chest heaves, my limbs tired from all the exertion while he seems completely unaffected.

"It's not me you need to protect yourself against." He pauses, the roar of the cave deafening. "I'm going to let you go now. Please don't hit me again, princess."

I hold still as his arms loosen and he releases me. Goosebumps rise on my flesh from his missing touch.

He takes quick steps toward the back wall and I stay where I am, glued to the spot, watching him.

He places a hand on the wall and stands, looking back at me.

"Why are you doing this?" I ask, my voice breathless.

He ignores me. "You aren't getting Fin back. I hope with time you'll understand." He pushes on the wall and it opens under his hand.

"No!" I scream and sprint toward him, but I am not fast enough. The stone closes in front of me, as it had last time. I pound my hands on it and let out a scream.

Everything I have been feeling, all of my pent up rage comes out as I scream and pound on the wall. My anger toward my father, the loss of my mother, my childhood. The loneliness I felt my entire life, finally mended during my time on Dawnlin, only to have it ripped away by this man. Weston. This man who, when we are alone, seems to differ from everything I have been told.

He is right. He hadn't ever tried to hurt me, despite everyone telling me he is the one I need to protect myself against.

He had saved me. He made sure I was breathing. He only defended himself against *me*.

Why do I feel like this night turned everything I know about this place upside down? What is right? What is wrong?

Who is telling the truth?

My face burns.

No. How can I be so stupid?

Weston is the king of mind tricks, and I fell for them, his sly words causing me to doubt everything I know.

He brainwashes any Voyager he captures, turning them against the rest of us. Within a few minutes I let him turn me as well, questioning who is telling the truth when I know it isn't him.

I hate him, and I don't know what to do now.

His final words lead me to believe that he isn't planning on meeting me again, that I won't be seeing him. If I don't see him, and have no clue where to look for him, I have no way of forming a plan to get Fin back.

I have nothing, except for an answer where he has gone, and a million more questions swirling about Weston and things he said.

I know Fin is with the Castaways, and I need to call off our search.

I make my way to the top of the rock bridge, drifting along the paths in the dead of night. It isn't raining anymore, but my boots still stick in the mud. I remain on edge, still glancing over my shoulders, waiting for a Castaway to jump out and attack me. The emptiness at the small of my back makes me feel vulnerable and unsafe.

It's not me you need to protect yourself against.

If he was telling the truth, and he wasn't dangerous, then what was he talking about? Is there another Castaway that is more dangerous, that is responsible for the abductions?

I shake my head and squeeze my eyes shut.

No.

He was lying. Again. He was wrong.

I need to tell Dane what happened, and I need to do what I came here to do. It is the only way that Weston doesn't get what he wants.

He won't get the cure, because I will have it. And once I do, his offer for a trade won't matter because I will be gone.

CHAPTER FORTY-THREE

’m met with the sound of arguing as I step through the portal back into camp. It’s late. The sky is still darkened by storm clouds, with no light from the moon or stars peeking through.

A few of the older Voyagers are gathered in the clearing, watching what looks like an argument between Dane and Mara.

“We have to go look for her! She’s always back before dark!”

“Give her a little more time. I trust her. She’ll make it back.”

“But what if she doesn’t, Dane? What if we lose two of us in two days?”

I step out of the darkness and both of their heads snap toward me.

“She’s here,” Mara says. She pushes through the crowd and runs toward me, hitting my body at full speed and wrapping me in a hug. “You’re alright,” she murmurs next to my ear as she squeezes me.

I wrap my arms loosely around her. “Yeah, I’m alright,” I say quietly. “But Fin is gone.”

Mara gasps, pulling away to look at me, trying to read the emotions that I’m sure are all over my face.

"Dead?" she asks.

Dane is beside me then, a concerned look across his face. He reaches up and cups my elbow, grounding me and giving me some comfort without overwhelming me.

I shake my head. "No, but the Castaways have him."

A strained silence falls, broken by a gasp from one Voyager, followed by a pained cry.

I look past Mara and see Roley, hugging Lilly around the waist, fear across his face.

"No. They can't take him!" Roley cries out. Lilly wraps her arm around his shoulders and squeezes him closer to her.

"How do you know?" Mara says, turning her attention back to me.

"I found his bow, my bow, broken in the sand on a beach. The arrows were everywhere. It was obvious there had been a scuffle."

"But you didn't find him?" she asks.

"No. There was no blood, no body. I didn't see him, but I just know that's where he is."

"I'm glad you're safe," Dane grumbles. He leans over and plants a kiss on the top of my head.

"How do we get him back?" Roley cries between sniffs, tears streaming down his face.

Dane breaks away from me and crouches down in front of him. He speaks softly, like a father comforting a scared child.

"We can't get him back right now. We have been trying to find them for a long time. Hopefully, we will soon."

"But he'll be one of them by then," Roley says with a hiccup.

"Maybe, maybe not. The best thing we can do to help Fin is to stay alert, stay safe, and keep looking. We can't help him if they get one of us, too."

Roley nods, his gaze dropping to the floor.

"Come on," Mara says, taking a few steps back toward the ladder. "Let's get back inside."

"Be there in a minute," I call after her. Everyone heads back to the ladder and the lowered platform and walks back toward the cabin.

Roley's sadness hits me deep in my chest. It feels like I have known Fin for years, even though it has only been weeks or months. I am not really sure.

It feels like I have known *all* the Voyagers for years. That one of us is missing feels like an enormous gaping hole has formed in this unsuspecting family.

"Are you alright?" Dane asks.

"Not really."

"I'm sorry," he says. He closes the distance between us and wraps his arms around my waist.

"You weren't going to come look for me?" I ask, confused. His and Mara's argument finally registers. It sounded like he was trying to talk her out of searching for me.

"I was, but Mara wanted to send out search parties since there were two of you gone. I have to remain the strong one here. I needed to talk her down to make sure everyone stayed safe. If you had come back just a few minutes later, just like you did, we'd have no way of calling back everyone who had left."

I nod. "That makes sense."

He lifts my chin, forcing me to look up at him. "What she couldn't see is that I was going crazy inside, wanting to run out and find you myself. I was going to give it a little more time before I allowed only Mara and myself to go search, just like you and I did for Fin."

"You were worried?"

"Of course I was worried. I can't let anything happen to you. You're too important."

My chest squeezes. Has anyone ever told me I am important before, when they weren't referring to me ruling a kingdom?

I tilt my head up toward him, silently asking for a kiss. He obliges, meeting my lips tenderly, like he knows that what I need right now is comfort.

I break away and plant my face into his chest, just before I feel myself break. He wraps his arms around my shoulders, pulling me close, and I let go.

I cry.

One advantage to being alone your entire life is that you never have to experience loss. I don't count my mother as a loss, because I never had her. Even grieving the loss of what could have been after reading her diary feels so different from this.

Fin is *gone*.

This little boy, a little brother I never had, has been erased from my life, and simultaneously erased from the lives of those back home waiting for him.

My tears soak Dane's shirt as he clutches me. He says nothing, just lets me grieve. This loss isn't new to him. It might not be new for any of the Voyagers except Lilly and me. But I feel like my heart has cracked, and will never truly heal.

Once my sobs have slowed and my breaths start to deepen, Dane leans back and pushes my hair off of my face.

"Let's go get some rest. It has been a long two days."

I nod silently, not meeting his eye.

My mind is blank as I go through the motions, following Dane back to our cushion. I don't want to talk to anyone, I just want to fall into a deep sleep.

Dane is right, we need rest. I don't want to deal with all the emotions swimming in my head, but every time I close my eyes and start to fade away into the relief of sleep, my mind finds its way back to that cave.

Haven't you noticed that I've done nothing to hurt you?

It's not me you need to protect yourself against.

Mind tricks. That's all they are. Slowly trying to eat away at me and get me to doubt everything I know.

I am not going to let him win.

The lack of pressure from my dagger at my back gives me a sinking and lonely feeling. While that dagger has come with a lot of heartache, it also is my reminder of home.

Now it is gone.

He took it.

I close my eyes and focus on the noises and feelings that surround me; the rhythmic breathing of the sleeping Voyagers and the heat coming off of Dane as he holds me to his chest. I am not going to let the Castaways turn me against these people, people who are trying to save someone they love.

I won't let this all distract me from my true goal, finding the cure. I am worried about Fin, but I don't know what I can do at this point. Weston said he was safe, but can I believe him? Whether or not Weston is lying about Fin's safety, I have no clue where to find him. Voyagers had been searching this island for years, maybe even decades, and couldn't find where the Castaways hid themselves away.

What makes me think I can? I need to keep hope that the island knows Fin is worth protecting, and make sure that he doesn't fall into worse danger.

I close my eyes and let the darkness consume me, hoping I won't be plagued by nightmares tonight. Just as I am drifting off to sleep, one last thought crosses my mind.

I hadn't told Dane about Weston.

Again.

CHAPTER
FORTY-FOUR

The storm blew over during the night, so we all brought our things back to our bunks the next morning. There doesn't seem to be much damage to the island or to camp, other than a little more mud and some large puddles.

I volunteer to be the lookout at camp today. I know the best way to get through this is to distract myself with searching, but I feel the need to take a step back and refocus. If I don't, I easily could find myself in danger or worse, because I didn't pick up on my surroundings or wasn't paying attention.

The empty quiet of the camp is calming. It is nice to have some solitude today to just sit with the heaviness. It's funny to think that this is solitude after I spent every day on the island searching alone, but it is different. Many days I run into another Voyager searching in the same area, but sitting here at camp in the middle of the day, I know no one will be back until late evening.

Dane told me he is going to follow up on some leads for Castaway sightings. He agrees it is as important as ever to find where they live, now that they have Fin.

I check the latch on the platform, making sure it is secure, before I sit and dangle my legs over the side. I gaze over the clearing and the surrounding trees in camp and let out a sigh.

How different my life has become.

I never would have expected to be in this position as I was nearing my birthday and ceremony. That feels like a lifetime away now. So much has happened since then. So much has changed.

This place is becoming part of me, more than Blackwood has ever felt despite my role in the kingdom. These people feel like family. The thought of saying goodbye to all of it and returning to my cold and lonely life in Blackwood, never able to live up to my father's expectations, makes me want to consider staying.

But I made a promise. I promised my mother I would try for her, and I am. Despite never having known her, it feels like she is with me somehow. Her words settled in my heart and made me believe in hope, and a life that could be. I want the chance to know her, to talk to her. I want the chance to hopefully have a parent who cares about me and who I am, who is proud of me and believes in me and what I could be for our kingdom.

I am not going to give up on her, and I am not going to give up on that dream for myself, either.

I just wish that I could bring all of them home with me.

There isn't enough dust for that.

Everything is moot if there isn't enough dust to get home. With all the chaos of the past few days, Dane and I hadn't talked about the dust problem. He was going to search through camp for anything from the previous Guardian that might hold an answer. He hasn't brought it up, so I assume he hasn't found anything worth mentioning.

I sigh and fold my arms over the rail.

Even if I find the cure, I may not be able to take it home. If I do, everyone else is closer to being stranded on Dawnlin, and there is nothing I can do to help from Blackwood.

I look around camp to make sure there are no stragglers, or no one came back through the portal. Everything is quiet. I am still alone.

I reach inside my shirt and pull out the map, smoothing it across my lap. I'd marked everything I could, every barrier or trap I had run into. I marked all our landmarks and tried to fill in the paths.

I stare, willing clues to jump out at me.

There has to be something I am missing.

I analyze the landmarks, trying to find patterns or something that would point me in a direction from the bird's-eye view.

Nothing stands out.

Think, Lennox.

I pull my gaze away from the map and look out over the horizon. What did I know about the island? Not just about the geography, but the place itself.

I think back to what Edmond had told me before I left. The myth of Dawnlin is about hope. The island gives hope to those who want to help others and gives them an opportunity to do that. I had to believe and have hope to find the fountain that led me here, so maybe that is what I am missing.

I'd become so singularly focused on searching that I forgot the crucial element. Hope. I'd become almost hopeless, searching day in and day out, coming up empty-handed every time. I couldn't help but feel discouraged.

With every setback or unsuccessful search, I went back to camp upset that another day had passed without the cure. I remained determined, but determination and hope are entirely different.

I am determined to continue, but my hope has become hardened, and the possibility of the dust running out, leaving us stranded with or without the cure, makes me feel even more hopeless.

I was hopeful when I found the fountain, and when I discovered it was the link to Dawnlin I had been searching for. My eyes flutter closed as I remember that moment, the excitement when I noticed the symbols. The chalice and the dawn, flowers, people.

Life.

I feel the rush of hope I had that night wash over me again and try to hold on to it. It feels good to remember why I am here, and not just continually fall back into the disappointment and darkness of life before, especially when bad things happen.

The island provides what you need.

My eyes snap open. Yes. The island gives us what we need. Clothes, food, weapons, shelter. Doesn't it know that what we need is to find the cure? Dawnlin isn't making the cure available, otherwise we wouldn't be searching for it. But that was the other purpose of the island, wasn't it? The magic was here to hide it, to protect it. Was the island designed to do the same?

I spin around on my knees and lay the map on the boards in front of me. My eyes fly over the landmarks and it feels like something clicks in my mind.

The mountain.

Everything surrounding it is extremely dangerous, compared to everywhere else on the island. The closer you get to it, the more risk there is of death. The reptile monsters, the sirens, the exploding rock, the sheer cliffs that fall into the churning ocean below. Dane even said that almost every Voyager that died on Dawnlin had met their fate near the mountain.

The real question is, why would the island be so dangerous that it became deadly, if the entire reason for us being here was to find the cure it was protecting?

It doesn't make sense.

There has to be more, and the only way to find out would be to find the cure. Which means only one thing.

I am going back to the mountain.

CHAPTER FORTY-FIVE

I quickly fold the map and shove it back into my shirt before barreling down the walkway to the armory. I pull the doors open and grab a new dagger and sheath, sliding it in the back of my pants to replace the one he stole from me. I pull a smaller knife and stick it in my boot. It's probably best to travel light, because I don't really know what searching the mountain will entail.

I close the doors and look around the clearing again. There's always supposed to be one of us at camp, in case the Castaways decide to attack, so I know I am not supposed to leave, but no one would know as long as I make it back in time. It is still early morning so I have time.

Plus, Weston had assured me I didn't need protection. While I don't believe him, if he doesn't intend to hurt me, then maybe they have no intention of coming into our camp like we fear.

It's worth the risk if I can find the cure today. I sprint to the platform, flinging the switch to drop to the ground as quickly as possible, and sprint straight through the portal.

I fly down the pathways, not bothering to pause and worry about any dangers the island might throw at me. I hold on to that swell of hope in my chest, hope and excitement at the possibility of being right.

Each time I searched near the mountain, I always approached from the same side. I don't want to do that this time. I need a different angle, a new perspective. I turn off the main path and head toward the bridge from my first day of searching. My gut tells me to start from there.

My heart pounds in my ears as I approach the bridge. Mara isn't here to rescue me if the bridge fails again, but I can't let that stop me. I stop at the entrance, focusing only on the land on the other side.

Movement from below catches the corner of my eye.

Don't look.

The monsters pile themselves up below, like they sensed me coming, but I am not going to give them anything today. I grip the rope rails and steadily walk across. No pausing, no wavering, nothing but focus until my boot lands on the other side. I don't even look back to see if the monsters had followed me, I just take off running toward the mountain.

I can't help but feel like I know where I am going. I feel this pull, deep in my body, from where I feel all of my hope. I can't explain it, but I just know it will guide me.

I burst through the edge of trees, the lagoon just ahead. The roar of the falls magnifies as I approach, mingling with the pounding of my heart and heaving breaths. It isn't fear causing them this time, though. It is excitement. Hope. Determination.

My eyes scan the lagoon, knowing there is a reason I need to be here, and it isn't to see Weston again. I walk along the edge, eyes searching the surface and scanning the walls, trying to find some abnormality or clue.

Then I see it.

I'd never seen the mountain from this distance before, always having come around from the other side. The last time I was here, I didn't even make it halfway around the lagoon before the sirens called me into it.

The rainbow.

We see them rarely in Blackwood, but I've never seen one like this before. Now that I see it, I feel foolish for missing it before. Maybe I was just too close, or not paying attention.

Or maybe Dawnlin hadn't shown it to me.

The hope swells in my chest again as I gaze at it. Then it hits me.

I'd seen this before, not this exactly, but something like it.

The rainbow, shining in a half circle on top of the rock bridge, formed the perfect dawn over the chalice of rock, just like on the fountain that brought me here. That image was how I knew I found the right place, and it is how I know the cure is hidden inside. It is in the mountain, and this, somehow, is the gate.

I sprint down the side of the lagoon, my sole focus getting as close to the mountain as possible. This time, instead of crossing the rock bridge, I stop just beyond it and peer into the pool where the waterfall crashes.

I crouch down on my knees, the rock biting into them, and look down into the pool. The water from the fall is flowing too rapidly, way too fast for someone who doesn't know how to swim to try to make it through. I can't tell how deep it is, and it is too strong to walk through. I will not risk being flung into the depths of the lagoon again.

I need to climb around.

I double back over the bridge and swing my legs over the side, dropping down onto the large boulders next to the water. They are slick, and soon I am soaked with mist and spray from the falls. I climb across on all fours, doing my best not to slip and fall into the rushing water.

I'm exhausted by the time I make it to the wall of the mountain, and I cling to it for a moment, sucking in deep breaths and resting my limbs. The falls crash next to me, but for once, I am not afraid of the ruthless water. I know I am in the right place.

I notice a small ledge and plant my boots onto it, my chest flat against the mountainside and my arms spread out, clutching the rock for my life. I slowly inch along the ledge, moving behind the deadly wall of water.

I can't think of a better place to hide the cure than that.

Inch by inch, I cling to the side of the mountain, and as I reach the edge of the waterfall, magic overwhelms me. It feels like I am entering a portal. My body tingles and the noise around me dulls. I push my body forward, trusting in the island's magic, and fall through the portal onto a smooth stone platform that juts out of the side of the mountain.

That wasn't there before.

I kneel on the platform and rest my hands on my thighs, using a few precious moments to catch my breath after that heart stopping climb.

This is it, I can feel it.

There is no way this is a trick. I stand up and take in my surroundings.

The back side of the waterfall is completely white, the water barreling down in front of me, but the sound muted by the magic. I am completely enclosed. No spray reaches me, and I can see nothing past the platform, which means it can't be seen from out there either.

The perfect hiding spot.

I turn and face the wall, knowing there has to be more than just this.

The rock face is smooth as glass, and I know it isn't just the years of being beaten with water that made it that way. My gaze trails over the wall, looking for any sort of seam or knob, something that indicates there is a door. I place my hands on it and push, trying to detect if it is another portal, but I don't move.

There is nothing, the dark slab smooth and glistening and seamless.

There.

Something at the bottom of the stone catches my eye. A small mark in the far corner. I crouch down to get a better look.

Hope swells in my chest again and I feel my already too fast heart beat out of my chest.

Carved into the stone is the symbol from the fountain and the lagoon, the chalice with the rising dawn.

I drop to my knees to get closer. There has to be an inscription or something more, some way to open the door.

I reach out and brush my fingers across the symbol.

Is it really that easy?

When Weston wanted a door of stone to open, he just placed his hand on the wall, and the island knew what he wanted.

It is worth a try.

I flatten my palm over the symbol, and the stone under my hand glows. I rip my hand away and see the golden symbol, lit against the darkness of the stone, glowing like dawn. I scramble to my feet and watch, waiting.

A cracking sound pierces the quiet and the smooth stone splits down the middle. Doors swing in toward the mountain, revealing the entrance of a dark tunnel and my chest swells.

I've done it.

I found the entrance.

I am going to get the cure.

I rush through the doors before they close. There is no turning back now, no thoughts of any dangers that might be ahead. My mind scrambles as I step into the darkness beyond the door, but there is one thought that stands out above all the rest.

I found it, Mom, and I'm going to bring it home to you.

CHAPTER
FORTY-SIX

The stone doors slam behind me, and I am left in complete darkness. I may have found where the cure is hidden, but I don't have any idea what lies ahead. Dawnlin set so many traps to keep the cure protected, so I can only imagine what is in store for me inside the mountain.

I blindly step forward into the darkness, and torches light along the walls, casting a glow only a few steps in front of me. I start to walk, using all of my senses to take in every detail and anticipate any attack that might come.

The tunnel winds out of sight, more torches lighting along the walls as I move. I walk for what seems like hours, winding deep into the mountain with nothing to guide me farther than a few paces at a time.

Is this it? Am I in an endless loop of tunnel, deep inside the mountain, with no way out? I stop abruptly and glance between where the tunnel is going, and where I came from, feeling panic start to rise.

The torches extinguish behind me. I take a step toward them, back toward the entrance, but unlike the ones in front of me, they don't relight. The island is telling me I can't go back. This must be right, and I'm not trapped.

I spin back around and press forward, still holding on to that hope. Step after step, the tunnel keeps winding, with no end in sight.

"I've got to be almost there," I say out loud to no one, or maybe to the island.

Can Dawnlin hear me?

Soon I pause. The next set of torches isn't lighting the way. I look around the narrow tunnel, but there is nowhere else to go. I step forward, toeing the line of the darkness before me and take in a deep breath. Even though it isn't showing me the way, I need to trust it and move forward.

"Here goes," I mumble.

I step into the darkness, and a large circular room opens up in front of me, carved from the stone of the mountain. Fiery torches light the walls, the room completely devoid of anything except some sort of decoration carved into the walls.

I look around, trying to figure out where to go next, what I need to do. There is nothing, not even an exit. As I slowly spin to take in all the detail, I realize the tunnel I'd come through is sealed behind me.

Trapped.

I am trapped in here. There is no way out, no obvious path to get the cure.

But it *has* to be in here.

I turn back toward the center of the room and look at the far side. Two stone stairs carved into the floor lead up to a platform. It reminds me of the throne room back in Blackwood, but there is no throne, only a small alcove carved into the far wall. I climb the stairs quickly and sprint to the alcove.

The stone is smooth inside the oval, and a small basin makes up the bottom. Just above the basin is a hole, smaller than my fist, with a stone spout beneath it.

This is it. This is where you get it.

I glance around, looking for something, anything, to hold the cure in. How could I have been so unprepared and come with no vessel to carry it in?

A booming voice startles me, stopping my frantic search. I whip my head around, searching the room for whoever is speaking.

I am alone.

It's the island.

I shake my head, focusing on the voice, to process what it is saying. The voice is commanding, but calming, and I find myself overcome with a feeling of happiness and safety as I take in its words.

The healing waters of Dawnlin you seek,
To help a loved one sick and weak.
The waters better than any cure,
Leaving the sick or injured pure.

With hope you came unto this land,
To leave with the waters in your hand.
Searched high and low with all your might,
Battling darkness to step into light.

A few more tasks must be complete
Or else your time here obsolete.
Carve the name of the one you must save
In order to keep them from the grave.

The voice stops, the chamber falling silent again.

Carve the name of the one you must save.

Carve the name where?

I look at the alcove in front of me, but it is as smooth as the door behind the waterfall. I turn and that is when I realize what I didn't see before.

The walls aren't covered in an intricate design or pattern. They are carved with *names*. Names cover every square inch of the walls. Big, small, legible or not, the entire chamber is filled with the names of those Dawnlin has saved. They are forever part of this island, part of the magic of the place that healed them.

It brings tears to my eyes, knowing I am not alone. So many people before me had made this journey, had found this island and held hope in their hearts, in order to save someone they loved.

And they had.

This room is proof of that.

I run my fingers across the names, some of them in languages from neighboring kingdoms. Tears well in my eyes as I see that no matter who we are, or where we come from, hope has brought us together with a unified goal.

I find a small break in the names and run my fingertips over it. Here. This is where my mother's name needs to be. I reach back and loosen the dagger from its sheath, a pang hitting my chest, knowing that I am not using my dagger from my kingdom to carve a piece of her into the island. Another moment Weston stole from me.

I carve, driving the sharp point into the stone until I am satisfied. I blow on the surface, pushing away any dust and bits of stone left inside the letters.

Lyla Holt.

I don't write Queen, because to me she isn't. She is my mother, and I am her daughter, longing for time with her.

I slide the dagger back into its sheath just as the voice speaks again, my task seemingly complete. I am ready for the next.

For eternity, the name remains
While hope and trust over this island reigns,
The second of which you must give
If you desire the person live.

A deal between you must strike
The terms once heard, you may dislike.
But trust of you is Dawnlin's need,
Before the offer can proceed.

Upon the use of Dawnlin's water
It matters not for son or daughter,
All memory of Dawnlin will cease to exist
For spreading its secrets, you might resist.

If on your return you are too late
The one you love one has met their fate,
Try as you might, your voice grows weak.
The secrets of Dawnlin you will not speak

A drop of blood means you agree
Your memory of magic will be free.
This price an easy one to pay
To confer the waters without delay.

My jaw drops as the meaning hits me. If I agree to this, I will lose all memory of Dawnlin and the magic that helped save my mother.

Dane.

I would lose Dane. Fin and Mara, and the rest of the Voyagers that had become family to me. I'd waited my entire life to have friendships like these, and they are about to be ripped away.

Tears stream down my face, a gaping hole forming in my chest. How can I give up the love that I have for these people?

This is how the island protects itself. This is how it prevents anyone from knowing too much of the magic. The myth exists back in the kingdoms, but not actually where or how to get there. It is because as soon as someone finds it and uses it, all knowledge of it ceases to exist. And if they don't, if they somehow choose to leave or don't make it back in time, they are bound by the magic to keep it a secret.

Now I have a choice to make.

My kingdom, my mother, and my duty over the love and friendships I have found here. Am I willing to give up on a chance of having a loving mother to have loving friends?

If I don't agree to this, is everything I have done worthless? Would I return to Blackwood empty handed, still having to fulfill my duties as queen only to live in misery, remembering all the love I left behind? Would it be better if I forget?

Would I even return to Blackwood?

I feel like I am being ripped apart.

I don't know how I am going to tell Dane. It will be bittersweet. We knew this would come to an end, that Dawnlin's never progressing time would not apply to us. But now that I found the cure, the others can as well. I can bring them to it, and we can go back and help our families, if they are still there to help.

The goodbye will not be easy. I won't get to say goodbye to Fin, and now he won't have the chance to help his sister because I can't find him.

I wish I wasn't alone. I wish Dane was here with me, helping me make this decision, telling me it is alright to let him, and everyone else go, because I know I only really have one choice.

I choke out a sob of acceptance.

I reach a shaky hand behind me and pulled out the dagger. Tears blur my vision as I look at the blade flickering in the light of the torches. I step up to the alcove that is now glowing brightly. I hold my hands in the alcove, over the basin, and press the sharp blade to the palm of my hand. A line of blood forms and I watch as the blood pools in my palm. My tears fall to the bottom of the basin as I clench my fist over the blood and turn my hand over.

The drops fall into the bowl, soaking directly into the stone and disappear with a small flash of light, just like my tears in the fountain back in Blackwood.

The voice booms around me again, and I have to concentrate to process the next words.

A selfless choice you did make
But more must be done for you to take
The healing waters for your use
In order to prevent outright abuse.

Deep inside the isle must look
Your heart will be read like an open book.
The magic of Dawnlin decides who is worthy
Your quest for the waters at its mercy.

Granted or not, the choice is not yours,
And this is how the isle ensures
The protection of Dawnlin and of the magic
So the story ends not in something tragic.

If deemed worthy, the water will flow,
The clear crystal liquid will pool below.
If empty handed you leave by dust,
In the magic of Dawnlin, you must trust.

I stand there stunned as the echo of the words fades. There is a chance that I won't be granted the healing waters to bring home to my mother.

That *can't* happen.

All of this would really have been for nothing. Doubt creeps over me, dimming the hope I had been grasping tightly onto.

A small glass vial appears from thin air and balances on the edge of the bowl. I pick it up and run my fingers over it. It amazes me that such a small amount of water would cure anything.

I drag my eyes to the spout and wait.

This is it, the moment of truth.

I hold my breath, waiting for the water to flow.

Please. Please.

I beg. I urge. I focus all of my energy on willing that water to flow. I stare at the spout, for I don't know how long.

It doesn't.

I clutch my chest as it implodes and fall forward, bracing myself on the edge of the bowl. My fingers grip it tightly, and sobs wrench through my body.

No. This can't be happening.

I'm not worthy.

I look up through blurry tears at the spout, reaching out to touch it. It is bone dry, not a speck of water flowed.

Dawnlin thinks I am not worthy.

This was it. My last hope shattered.

Why wasn't I worthy? What more could I have done? I want to save my mother, to bring her back to my father, and give myself a chance at a happy life with a loving parent. Did the island think my intentions are selfish? Isn't everyone here for a somewhat selfish reason, so they don't lose someone they love?

Why was it not enough?

If empty handed you leave by dust, in the magic of Dawnlin you must trust.

The last sentence echoes through my mind.

Trust? How can I trust it? I am angry and hurt. How is it fair for the island to determine whether my mother deserves to live or die?

I swipe angrily at my tears and push myself away from the bowl, and stumble back into the center of the room.

I'd done everything I could. I'd searched for answers from our world, I sought out texts and knowledge from healers all over. I even had hope for magic. It was all in vain.

The life that I knew back in Blackwood would not change.

I would return empty-handed, with no good explanation for why I disappeared from my duty for months.

I don't have to return.

What is truly waiting for me back in my kingdom? A father who doesn't care about me, who doesn't believe I am capable of becoming queen? A lonely castle, an empty life, a loveless arranged marriage?

I don't have to go back.

If no one thinks I am worthy, I don't have to live the life that has been chosen for me. My father, Dawnlin, the kingdom, they can all think what they want.

I am going to choose a new path.

I am going to tell Dane I made up my mind.

I am staying.

My mother's fate is sealed. The healing waters were the last hope.

I wasn't going to use the little dust we had left to go home empty-handed, and seal my own miserable fate.

No.

I am staying. I found happiness and love here. I can help others as they come to the island, *if* they can come to the island. I can help Dane figure out how to replenish the dust, and I can show the rest of the Voyagers where the healing waters are so they can have a chance to be worthy. I can find the Castaways and save Fin.

I can have a purpose here.

I look around the chamber, my mind made up and eager to return to camp. A dark archway appears to the left of the alcove. I assume this was Dawnlin's way of excusing me and asking me to leave. I don't ask any questions. I want to get out of here.

I want to go home.

CHAPTER
FORTY-SEVEN

$\mathcal{I}$ step through the archway into a tunnel similar to the way I came in, the torches lighting as I move through. This time, I don't walk.

I run. I need to get back to Dane.

Beneath all the anger and the hurt, another emotion threatens to burst through the surface, one I had been avoiding since before I arrived here. I don't want to think about it, don't want to feel it.

Failure.

I failed at what I set out to do, but Edmond always said even if I fail, I can change my perspective and see things in a new light. I may have failed at saving my mother, but in the process, I found a whole new life I never thought possible, and wouldn't be possible without this island.

Yes, it has deemed me unworthy for whatever its reasons, but I can still help other people. Maybe if I do, Dawnlin could change its mind. My mother has survived in this barely alive state for twenty-one years, surely she could make it a little longer. As long as my father didn't give up on her.

I weave through the tunnel, my breaths heaving as I run as fast as I can. A bit of light appears ahead, and I hope it is the end. I slow my steps as I approach, so I don't go barreling off a cliff and fall to my death.

You never know what the island has planned for those it deems unworthy.

The archway at the end of the tunnel is dark, lit only by moonlight.

I've been gone all day.

Dane and the others must be worried, especially since I was supposed to stay at camp all day. After everything that happened in the past few days, I'm sure they are out looking for me.

I cross under the arch and feel the magic of the portal surrounding me as I walk through.

My boots squish into sand as I step out onto a moonlit beach. I look back toward the portal so I know where to find it again. How has it been missed all these years?

There is nothing but rock, the cliff face of a beach. I reach out and touch it, expecting my hand to go through like the one back at camp, but my fingers only meet the smooth stone carved away by years of rain and wind.

The portal doesn't go both ways. There is no way anyone would have ever found it. It truly is hidden.

I turn back toward the beach, trying to get my bearings in the dim light of the moon. The sky is clear, the stars shining brightly in the crisp air, as if the island hadn't just been ravaged by a storm for the last two days. I take a few steps away from the wall, following the path in the sand that weaves between large boulders toward the open beach. I need to see which side of the island the portal spit me out on.

I pass the last boulder and stop short.

Wait.

This is the beach where I found Fin's things broken in the sand.

This is the beach where he fought the Castaways, where he was taken.

Was he here by chance? Was he this close to the healing waters and didn't know it?

Or…or had he…found them?

Was he leaving the tunnel just like me when they snatched him? Had he been given the cure or denied it?

Did he walk right into the enemy's hands, holding the one thing Weston had been seeking all this time?

I stride across the beach, heading toward the path that leads back to the top of the cliff, the same one that brought me down here a few days ago.

It feels like a lifetime ago.

I'm halfway there before I'm stopped by something cold across my neck, and something pressing into my back.

No…not something. Someone.

"Hello, princess."

The voice rumbles in my ear, sending tingles down my spine, tingles that are quickly replaced by ice cold fear.

It isn't Dane standing behind me, holding me close to him. I lower my chin slightly until the cold metal presses more firmly into my neck.

Shadows appear around us, coming as if out of nowhere. People, hidden by the darkness except for the moonlight glinting off of their weapons.

"Don't move," he grumbles, as someone steps in front of me, a scarf hiding their face except for piercing blue eyes. The person reaches out and grasps my wrists, holding them together as they tie a rope around them.

The rope bites into my skin, and I am brought back instantly to my first day on the island, when the Voyagers captured me and threw me in a cage.

But these people aren't Voyagers.

They are the Castaways.

Weston's hand glides down my back until it reaches the hilt of the dagger I have hidden in my waistband. He pulls it out and steps in front of me. He lowers the blade at my throat, and the glittering catches my eye.

My dagger.

He is taking me captive with *my* dagger.

Rage pools inside of me as he slides it back into the notch on his leathers.

He nods toward me, his eyes on the person who had tied my hands. They step between us and reach up, patting my shoulders and moving down my torso. I catch the light blue eyes with my gaze as their hands graze down and pat under my arms, shaking out my clothing as Weston watches.

The eyes soften, as if apologizing for invading my space, and that's when I see it. She is a woman. She is searching me, instead of him. He might be a monster, but at least he has the decency and respect to have her search me instead of groping me himself.

She crouches in front of me, patting down my legs until she finds the knife in my boot and shoves it in her belt. "That's all Cap."

He looks back at me and tilts his head to the side. "I'm glad you decided not to take the trade deal, because this is even better."

I glare hard at him, hoping he can feel the hatred seeping from me, but keep my mouth shut. He steps closer, closing the distance between us. His face lowers to mine as the corners of his mouth turn up in a smug smirk.

"Princess, you're coming with me."

ACKNOWLEDGEMENTS

Writing an acknowledgements page feels very surreal, because if I'm being honest, there were so many days where I never thought I would get to this point. My husband deserves all the thanks for making this book happen. I wouldn't have written it without him pushing me to believe in myself and accomplish something I always thought was an unreachable dream. Thank you for supporting me through it, and listening to every single rambling session to get ideas and work out plot holes. Thank you for working alongside me until 2 AM almost every night, after you worked a full day and commuted, to make sure I had a cover and a map and formatting and a physical book I am proud of. I love you.

Thank you to my sister, my alpha reader, who got the absolute roughest version of this book because I needed someone to tell me if I had anything worthwhile. Thank you for encouraging me and rereading when I needed you to.

Thank you so much to my beta readers Michelle, Alex, and JJ! Your feedback and reactions kept me going and I am so grateful for your support of this new chapter of my life!

Mary Reagan, thank you for being my bestie writing partner in crime, and loving on my fantasy romance even though you are not usually a fantasy girlie.

And to my hype girl and editor, Kay, I am so glad I found you and cannot wait to work on more projects with you!

But most of all, thank you to you, whoever you are, reading this book and hopefully loving my very vivid hallucinations as much as I do. Thank you, reader, for making my author dreams come true.

ABOUT THE AUTHOR

Amanda Briar has been an avid reader of romance, both fantasy and contemporary, since middle school, and loves to watch a good rom-com or fantasy series. After starting a family and deciding her career wasn't for her anymore, she took a chance to fulfill a lifelong dream to write books. As a self-proclaimed Disney Adult who grew up craving a happy ending, she now writes them herself. She currently lives in California with her family, and still loves reading, baking, movies, and going to Disneyland.

@ authoramandabriar

@ authoramandabriar

www.amandabriar.com

www.ingramcontent.com/pod-product-compliance
Lightning Source LLC
Chambersburg PA
CBHW022306310726
48973CB00001B/240